In the heart of the English cou
undergoing a transformation

Colin Furness struggles to comprehend the injustices that animals are forced to suffer, in their trillions, in order for humans to have a slightly better lifestyle and executes his plans to educate society and change what we put into our shopping basket.

On his farm, instead of the customary crop of hens, pigs and cattle the cages are slowly being populated with people. But this livestock is not destined for the butcher's hook; these wares will soon become bargaining chips in a game with macabre consequences.

Pitted against an insane and dangerous protagonist Detective Inspector Neil Dyson and his small team must unpick the clues to save lives, Dyson's relationship and ultimately his soul.

Join Dyson and team in a race against time on a journey that every thinking person should make.

Warning: The Soul Cages might well change your life......

For C
even though she will hate it…

The Soul Cages

Geoffrey Stanger
2014

Acknowledgements:

The Soul Cages is a true story, in spirit.
But the tale had to be altered to make it believable.

Let's keep this simple:
Huge thanks to all those who helped me make sense of what I was trying to say. I shall resort to the time-honoured and clichéd phrase, "…there are too many to name…."

Particular thanks though must go to:

Sally – editor, sounding-post and critic-in-chief.

To Nils-Hennes for his insight

To Patricia Colina for showing me that Colin really does exist in many guises and places

To Millie and Ping for being so tolerant (and crap at Catan)

To the amazing people at Combat Stress (staff and 'visitors'!)

www.combatstress.org.uk

Finally, a very, very special thank you to my great friend Mr Alan Walker who kindly granted permission to use his astonishing photograph.
I urge anyone who appreciates camera art to check out his other creations, most notably Spitfires…

The Soul Cages

The greatest griefs shall find themselves inside the smallest cage.
It's only then that we can hope to tame their rage....

D J Enright
On the Death of a Child

Prologue

December 1992 - somewhere in West Sussex

It was a foul winter's night on the South Downs.
The brutal wind was stripping the last clinging leaves from skeletal
birches and lacerating the thorny hedgerows with icy, horizontal
rain. In the dark the saturated ground was sinking beneath creeping,
coagulating puddles.

Howling an insane duet with the gale were the squeals of fifty or so
terrified swine as they were roughly herded from a filthy old
Serbian-built Fiat truck onto the glossy red Scania animal transporter
belonging to Graham Furness.

Furness owned one of the largest chicken farms in southern England
and occasionally handled other livestock, when he had a use for it
and the supply chain was favourable. "Favourable" meant cheap and
avoiding the officialdom which usually accompanied international
animal movements; he liked to keep as much of his hard-earned cash
as possible in his own pocket; any bureaucracy usually involved the
tax man getting his greedy snout into the trough.

Despite the cold, Bojan Babić, the short and paunchy Serbian
dispensing the animals was sweating, trying to encourage a filthy

and emaciated sow from where she cowered in the rear of his old truck by grabbing her ears and pulling with all his limited strength. The terrified creature was highly distressed and refusing to budge.

Graham Furness, peering through the driving rain into the back of the decrepit lorry shouted to be heard over the cacophony.
'Get a shift on Babić; I don't want to hang around any longer than I have to.'

Even on a night like this he was nervous of the operation being discovered by some chance observer. Extremely unlikely, he knew, but the fear remained. There existed no paperwork for this transaction; no legal process had been followed and nobody would learn about the origin of the meat when it finally got into the supply chain. In Furness' view nobody had any business knowing these things either.
'I can't get animal out.' cried Babić.
Furness suddenly appeared beside him and Babić caught the momentary glimpse of a dull metal sheen. He heard a mechanical click, like the cocking of a gun.
'What the hell that?' asked the Serb.
'Out of my way Babić!' growled the tall, wiry Englishman.
There was a sudden sharp crack, and the pig's legs collapsed beneath it.
'Now get the bloody thing off loaded.' he grunted.
'What that was?' asked the Serb.
'Bolt gun, used in slaughter houses in the humane world – explains why you've never seen one! How do you stun your livestock before you slit them open?'
'We use electrical bath, they are dragged through and shocked – when we remember to turn power on.' He grinned, showing teeth resembling a higgledy-piggledy row of headstones
'And electric not good where I come from, and expensive....sometimes we forget!'
He shrugged theatrically and his sickly grin was like a slowly-revealed oral graveyard.

Graham Furness was no stranger to animal deaths; anyone who worked with them as he did soon became immune to the pleading eyes and terrified cries. Chickens were his thing, easily handled, and if one became stubborn a simple twist of the wrist was all it took. Yes, he thought, give me chickens over these brutes any day. But there was surprisingly good money in pigs, and after a little fattening, with the aid of a few hormones, he had a ready market. Times for many were hard, after all, and as long as people put meat on the table they tended not to ask difficult questions. "Get it anyway you can" was the motto of the kind of people he dealt with; social conscience and animal welfare came way down the priority list.

In the cab of the English-registered truck a young boy heard most of this. Even the howling wind couldn't mask the horror of the bolt gun and the insults screamed at the poor creatures.
Colin Furness huddled deeper into the seat and hated his father more than ever for his insensitivity, the work he did and the people he did it with. Don't worry little pigs, he thought; Colin will make it better someday; somehow.

October, 2013 - Southampton

Colin Furness was sitting in the consultation room with Doctor Lars Erikssen. Doctor Erikssen was a diminutive, sixty-something, thin and hoary consultant psychiatrist at a clinic near Southampton where Colin was currently housed as an in-patient. The doctor was dressed in his usual style (Colin thought he looked like a stereotypical English history professor) of tweed jacket and waistcoat with a red and white poker-dot bow-tie, often accompanied by non- matching cravats, pocket handkerchiefs or similar accoutrements. His mousy face peeked out through a hedgerow of wispy grey hair and amalgam of beards and what little was visible of his shoulders was usually flecked in dandruff. He had something of an uncared-for and permanently dusty museum piece about him, and Colin wanted to strip him naked, shave him from head to toe and pressure wash him.

Quid pro quo, the doctor had an opinion on Colin's appearance which was slightly less than complimentary. Colin suffered from an extremely rare condition known as 1q21.1 duplication syndrome, a chromosome defect which caused physical and mental abnormalities. In Colin's case the physical manifestation was hypertelorism, a condition which causes the eyes to be sited further apart than is usual. The mental abnormalities had never, yet, been defined in absolute terms; Doctor Erikssen's diagnosis today might help to resolve that.

Colin didn't think he belonged here, well, not entirely. He was largely acting out a role; an integral part in his elaborate plan. Indeed he was barely paying attention whenever the doctor spoke, his eyes drawn instead through the old sash window to where the dappled grey mare cantered in the field bordering the hospital grounds. He thought now of Chestnut, his childhood friend and near constant companion who became seriously ill one Sunday. She had become lethargic and developed a high fever which caused the vet much head scratching. When the following morning Colin found her trembling on the floor of her stable his father had been quick to reach for his bolt gun to *"put the old girl out of her misery"*. No amount of pleading would alter his course and Colin had clung to her weak neck, his tears trickling to mingle with her sweat as she lie on the cold concrete ground and accepted murder as if it were the most natural consequence of being a servant to mankind.

The mare in the field reared and seemed to stare directly at the window. Colin resisted the temptation to wave an acknowledgement, but despite the distance he sensed she was making eye contact. He wondered briefly about reincarnation.

The doctor was writing on a form and Colin was brought back to the room by the scratching of the fountain pen nib on the expensive paper.
He had been a self-admission here, following the death of his father in an industrial accident on the chicken farm he had owned and managed. Indeed, it had been Colin who had found his father trapped inside the automated feed system which the old man had entered in order to undertake repairs. Since making the gruesome discovery Colin had complained of deep depression, anxiety and severe mood swings. Dr Erikssen had put Mr Furness through a detailed mental health evaluation and his concluding report diagnosed Colin with a

bi-polar condition which manifested itself as mood swings, typically ranging from anger and depression to euphoria. In his depressed state the patient would be morose and silent but could also become highly animated from minimal stimulus and incandescent with rage at the slightest provocation. His euphoric state presented with subtle prancing from foot to foot and hand-clapping whilst laughing or grinning vacuously. Not all of these symptoms were part of the act, Colin certainly had issues. The Doctor reflected privately that, had he lived a couple of centuries earlier, such behaviour in the euphoric state would have had his patient labelled as the village idiot.

Colin also bore some signs of paranoia, typified by voices instructing him to carry out aggressive actions against specific people. These were invariably wrong-doers in the eyes of Colin Furness and he seemed to take it upon himself to mete out a suitable level of retribution. As far as Dr Erikssen knew, this vigilante mind-set had so far existed purely inside Colin's head, i.e. no physical actions had been taken in reality. Dr Erikssen noted that this situation might be prone to escalation. There was no way the good doctor could possibly know that Colin had manufactured his father's demise. The young man really did have anger management problems.

Following an eight week treatment regime Colin was deemed fit to return to his daily life outside the clinic and was discharged with a follow-up care programme of weekly outpatient appointments and one to one therapy sessions. The risk assessment, which the clinic was obliged to carry out prior to discharge, could hardly be described as comprehensive. However, it ticked necessary duty of care boxes and allowed a bed to be freed up for the next inpatient; there was always one waiting in the wings these days. The bottom line bonus for the clinic was of course that Colin was now "in the system" as the hospital manager liked to phrase it. In other words, they'd made their profit from having him in, and income could now continue through his outpatient appointments. The accountant had likened this to having a royal mint in the cellar, because those who decided which potential patients needed expensive mental health care were the very experts who administered that care – they were integral to the system and stood to gain financially by referring patients to themselves. Any auditors or authorities could hardly question their competence or ethics and so in this way the hospital was poacher and gamekeeper. With the population growing and ageing and life becoming ever paceier there was no shortage of potential clients. For a privately run mental health clinic these were happy days.

The doctor's diagnosis and subsequent arrangements suited Mr Colin Furness perfectly.
His first task upon discharge was to contact his dead father's solicitors. There was a need for redistribution of the late chicken farmer's considerable wealth and a new regime at the farm. He allowed himself a small, almost unnoticeable prance, but resisted any clapping of hands or inane grinnery, at least in public.

March 2014- somewhere in West Sussex

The video was starting again on each of the huge screens which adorned the four metal-clad walls of the vast structure. There was little escape from the grainy grey pictures or the scratchy audio. Jenny had lost count of the number of times this one had been run over the last days. She'd tried to keep track of time at first, but being stuck in this artificial day/night cycle meant that she was reliant on trusting the lights on & off rhythm that was imposed upon her.

She worried about losing her mind. More and more she found herself sheltering in some secret safe place inside her head without knowing how she had got there but glad that she had. There it was softly lit, with some unknown yet strangely familiar instrumental music that seemed to infuse peacefulness into her strained body. She tried to drift again to that sanctuary but found the neuro-pathways blocked by the constant pain of the thick, rusting wire beneath her, biting through her clothes. She shifted her weight to find an area of her body that she could lay or squat upon that hadn't been bruised or lacerated by the mesh cage. During the first days it had been possible to find such respite, but lately relief was restricted to small degrees of less pain.

She thought again of the others around, below and above her. They had all been here longer than she had; at least she had seen nobody arrive since. At first she had gagged at the offensive stench - the place had reeked like animal enclosures she had seen at a wildlife park – wolves she thought, or wild dogs. An aggressive ammonia odour, tinged with something akin to bad drains. It took a couple of hours to realise why; Many of the "Disciples" as the freak liked to call them in his regular rants over the sound system, had been here long enough to have lost their grip on reality and had sunk into some sub-human state where they would go about their business with little regard to those around them. And those around them would act the same. At first she'd maintained a modicum of dignity, only relieving herself when she was sure she would otherwise burst, and even then she would shuffle tight into the corner of her cramped enclosure, as far away from the woman beneath her as it was possible to get. She would also, in the beginning at least, warn the woman below of her need but over time she realised that her downstairs neighbour had become almost impossible to communicate with. If she did ever reply, it was invariably deeply insulting. The guy upstairs, the Eastern European, had developed a stomach disorder which had spread within a day to all of them. She'd also submitted to its demands and had had to tolerate more wild ravings from the beast-woman below.

The whole place became some kind of disgusting human zoo – except here there were no keepers; nobody mucked out the stalls, no one fed them a diet fit for humans or checked on their welfare. Instead there was just the once-a-day (if the light cycle was to be believed) dose of dry pellets which came down the chute. If you were too slow, as she had seen with some of the others, then the pellets cascaded down to the human creatures below you, where they were scrabbled into hungry mouths or spilled wastefully out onto the concrete floor around the cages. Those pellets which ended up there would be consumed by the resident rat population. Funny how rats seemed so much more acceptable to her now than they ever had.

Jenny ate nothing in any case.

She wished that there was someone with whom she could plea bargain, someone who she could make understand that she was not supposed to be here and that there had been a terrible mistake, but no; all there was, was that freaky guy. The one who grinned insanely and bellowed at them about their cruelty and how their behaviour was being corrected now prior to their release back into a more caring society of the future, a society which they would help to shape...

He would rant as he washed them down with the fire hose, spraying the cages where they squatted, trying desperately to simultaneously evade the freezing and painful torrent of water, wash some of the filth from their skins and hair, and capture a few drops of precious liquid to slake their thirst. Usually by the time the water reached her it was contaminated with some kind of human detritus and completely undrinkable; but occasionally she was so desperate that she had to overcome the revulsion that retched up inside her throat and swallow a few mouthfuls.

She clung to one glimmer of hope – the fact that he mentioned releasing them back into society "cured".

...and the horse gazed deep into my caged soul
and saw the terrible beast that we call mankind....

Chapter 1

Diary entry 1
February 26th 2014

Deer father
You no how dislexick I am and if you could reed this you would larf
and call me simple, as you always did. I am far from that, but got
used to you discribing me so. I rose above it although it hert me
more than you coulb ever imagine. I can't reed or rite well because
of a misfiring link in my brain not because of stupidity.
My sychiertrist Doctor Erikssen, says I should keep a mood record
so that I can map my anger insidents and see if there are patterns. he
suggested I rite it as a diary and address it to a fictional person. That
person is going to be you. It works. It fits. You were never really
"real", never there as a father and never able to see that the life you
chose for yourself and for us was not the pathway I wanted to take or
even could have taken. We were the proverbial chalk and cheese.
More different than we were it's not within my imagination to forsee.

Perhaps it's ironic that I should choose you as the resipiant, the one
to share my deepest, most intimate thoughts. You who cared least for
my thoughts and conserns and who could never grasp the world as it
appeared to me. You were without a shadow of dowt the root cause
of my anger issues, and yet, conversly through your hatred of life
and inability to emperthise, tought me to be the gentle soul that I can
be.

Maybe it is because of the burden of my short temper that I have to take the path that is mapped out for me; the one of retribution, education and vengeants.

It is only fitting then, that I dedicate my work over the coming months in this pitiful place to you.

Today I am going to stay in an anonimus hotel to make my final preperations for my quest. I shall keep you updated, dear father, on my progress.

Your son
Colin

Ps; today I bort a horse; a brilliant black stallion. I have renamed him, Vengeance. He is not a replacement for my beloved Chestnut, nothing could replace her. He is a statement, an emblum, a sign of the changes at the farm. I will ride him every day and there will be no risk to him from Dedly Nightshade, I will personally see to that.

2

The day started to go wrong the moment Colin Furness realised there was no floor mat or towel or whatever the damn thing was called. It wasn't there, and in his intolerant state his short fuse moved a notch towards the point of ignition. He kicked the bathroom door and muttered to himself about room maids no longer having any idea ... He lamented the fall in standards of customer service. It just didn't seem to matter to people and was yet another sign of the decline of the human animal. The Swan Hotel with its elegant façade and pretty portico was supposed to be rated with four stars and had a reputation of excellent service.

What was probably a mild annoyance to most people was, for Colin, a big deal, because it showed a systems failure; a flaw in procedure.

Fuming, he sat at the uncomfortable desk in the hotel room where he'd just written his first "Mood diary" entry, and went through his complex plans once more. He had come here, not because he needed a bed for the night, but because he needed somewhere neutral, away from the distractions of his daily life and the memories that lurked everywhere. He needed a place of neutrality to think and to plan and to check. The Swan hotel was perfect for that; old, quiet and anonymous. He went through his check-list, ensuring yet again that all points were covered. Despite his occasional compulsive behaviour he was a careful planner, and these plans were as important as any he had made before. Colin nodded to himself. Plans and lists were the essentials which ensured success.

Checking his bag he verified that documents, licences, tools, heavy-duty adhesive tape were all there, all in the right place. He went to the heavy old oak wardrobe and checked the clothes hanging there; again, all was as it should be. His phones were fully charged and his computer too. The Land-rover keys in the zip-up pocket. He opened the zip just to check that they were still safely there, rubbing his thumb over the worn key metal thoughtfully. The Land-rover had been a constant in his life and gave him an anchor point. He'd relied on it for solitude, an escape channel when he needed to think or get away from his oppressive father, driving off into the downs via the barely-travelled tracks where most other vehicles could not venture; the beautiful old powder-blue truck had been a surrogate horse and had served him well. Colin was prone to fancy, something he'd inherited from his mother apparently. According to his brute of a father, she had spent half her life with her head in the clouds, wasting her time on poetry and whimsy, when there was real work to do on the farm. His mind drifted now and he thought of her, wondering for the thousandth time where she might be; whether she was even still alive. Turning the Land-Rover keys idly in his hand he wondered dreamily whether trucks had an after-life. He thought it would be a form of justice if they did. Maybe their spirits would return as plants and undo all the pollution they had caused in this life.

Well, when it finally gave up the ghost he would give the truck a decent send off, a fitting end to its laborious working life of service. But tomorrow he'd have a bigger truck to dispose of, all being well, and because he had planned so thoroughly that would be easily accomplished.

The little red light on his internet connection device winked comfortingly and his watch showed he was well within his defined time frame – early, in fact.
Good; he liked early.

Colin withdrew the maps from his holdall and traced the routes that he would use in the coming weeks with his finger, silently acknowledging the risk points he'd encounter during the various stages of his project and going through the contingencies for the hundredth time. No Sat-Nav for him; he knew they stored information, and information meant risk. Risk must be avoided wherever possible. A good old-fashioned map could be destroyed; burned; eaten…he chuckled at the irony, eaten, that was good.

He checked the other items, the three cheap pay-as-you-go phones, paid for in cash at different stores which had limited camera surveillance; hard to find these days.

He set his watch alarm to 18.00, telling himself that the time would go quicker if he slept. It always seemed to do that and he had never understood why, despite his mother's patient explanations during years of his childish questions. The second hand crawled around the dial at the same pace, regardless of whether he was awake, asleep, watching the clock or watching a film, even though it sometimes *seemed* to move faster or slower. He thought about that stupid philosophical question about a tree falling in a forest and whether it really made any noise unless someone witnessed it. He never really understood their point. Idiots-of course it happened. But the time thing; if he slept did it somehow sprint forwards until he nearly caught it out by waking? If only he could catch time out just once; wake unexpectedly and grab the watch and see the second hand desperately trying to slow down and convince him of its innocence. Cheating thing, he thought.

He laid the watch on the side table and himself on the bed, closing his eyes. He counted to 60, knowing, as he did, that he had measured exactly 60 seconds. He was well-versed in counting time and had an astonishing ability to predict fairly accurately what time of day it was without the advantage of a time-piece. He suddenly grabbed the watch and looked at it. It showed that exactly a minute had passed; it had not cheated him. He shook his head; was it even important? Did other people ponder the issue? Punctuality had been drilled into him by his ex-military father. 'Always arrive at least five minutes before agreed, that way you will never be late and you will earn the respect of everyone; everyone admires a punctual man, and it's a sign of his intelligence, dedication and determination. Never forget that.'

Without realising he must have drifted off because the next thing he was conscious of was the bleeping watch alarm. He sprang upright and grabbed the watch, simultaneously silencing the alarm and checking the velocity of the sweeping second hand. But there was no desperately-decelerating scrabble, just the smooth constant progress around the old-fashioned dial; regular as clockwork. He chuckled at that thought.

He felt a dull ache in his outer foot where he had earlier kicked the bathroom door and massaged the area. Checking the door he was relieved to see that he hadn't damaged the old wood. Thank goodness for solid quality; in a modern hotel his foot would have broken straight through the skin of the cheap materials they use nowadays. He really couldn't afford to give anyone reason to remember him, not even the useless chambermaid or housekeeping or whatever title they went by these days. Who were they trying to kid? They were cleaners and nothing better and they had failed in such a simple task. No floor towel, mat or whatever they called it. It annoyed him that he didn't know the correct term; he needed to be in control and ignorance was risk.

He picked up the room phone and called the reception desk.
'Reception.'
What? No "*how can I help*" or "*good afternoon*" or any kind of greeting? Definitely one of those thoughtless fools who strutted around as if they were the important ones and the guests just a tiresome irritation.
'Good afternoon. I have no floor mat; the maid clearly forgot it and is obviously not working to a list.'
'I'm sorry sir, is it the bathroom floor towel you need?'
'Yes, it's missing. What is the correct term for it?'
'Er…not sure really sir, floor towel is probably right.'
'Damn! That's no help, I need to know the right word.'
'Sorry sir, I'll see if I can find out.'
'No! Don't bother. Just get the maid to have a list in future, some guest in the next few days might have the same inconvenience and slip on your floor and hurt themselves.'
'Er…ok sir, I will see what I can do. I will ask housekeeping to bring one to your room now.'
'No, now is no good, I am going out and I don't need one. Forget it, it's too fucking late now.'

Colin slammed down the 'phone, realising instantly that he'd allowed his irritation to surface. That was not good. That would bring attention to him; maybe they would pay a little more attention to him. Silly and unnecessary; he absolutely must not make any more errors like that.

Time was ticking and he hadn't yet eaten. He needed to eat and often simply forgot; maybe he should add it to his to-do list. He'd get something English for his dinner, something hearty and healthy. It annoyed him the way foreigners slated English Cuisine. Try being a vegetarian anywhere else in the world and see how long you last! He had been on a trip to Germany where they seemed hell-bent on putting bacon in everything. His diet during the 2 weeks consisted mostly of salad or potato soup, everything else seemed to be either dead animal in a pool of brown liquid or sausage shaped. He had stayed in the same hotel and yet astonishingly the dumb arse waiter had, on three consecutive dinner orders, managed to serve salad twice and potato soup once with the seemingly obligatory bacon pieces. Moron! And when challenged had expressed surprise that this odd English guest should consider bacon as meat. Twat!
Colin punched the wall in frustration at the ignorance of that country.
People needed to learn, and learn they fucking well would.

The French were no better, with their annoyingly nasal speech and affected mannerisms. They also had zero respect for animals and murdered snails and tortured geese in order to play pretentious dicks in snooty restaurants. He needed to send a powerful message to all these European cunts. He'd do that by ensuring the presence of at least one of each key European country at his correction facility. Maybe he would call it his "Facilitie de correctione" he giggled in an imitation French accent. Yes; maybe he would.
Chuckling still to himself he took the old-fashioned lift to the hotel reception. He knew he'd struggle to get all those nationalities, and he hadn't planned it that way so would need to be realistic, but it was fun to think about.
Right now though he had enough on his mind; a lot to do, and people to catch...

3

Donna Southgate liked shopping. Not for groceries and mundane necessities; she had little tolerance for that stuff, but niceties; fashion accessories; shoes – after all, she always told herself, she was a girl! Except she wasn't entirely typical; she may have looked fairly "standard". Long blonde wavy hair, stunning clear eyes and a facial profile that movie stars might kill for. She had a size ten figure and was well balanced up top as her mum used to say – this was reference to her boobs rather than her brain, which was pretty fucked up.

Yes she was typical in some ways, but she was quite different to many of her girl friends in others, for example, Donna liked furs. She liked the feeling of them against her skin; liked to wrap herself and snuggle in their decadent luxury. Even watching her soaps and reality TV shows at home she was at her most contented with a cup of hot chocolate and a gorgeous fur wrap (none of your fair trade chocolate crap either - she *adored* the frisson that someone might have suffered to get the dark rich powder onto her tongue). You could keep your blankets and onesies; she'd choose a real animal skin any day of the week.

Her fascination extended beyond the furry and fleecy, to include rarer creatures. Alligators, snakes, the more ferocious they had been in life the more delicious they were to own and wear. She had read some psychologist article in one of her mags claiming that a girl's desire for fierce animal pelts was the symptom of a deep seated and primeval form of power exchange. And she agreed; she had an enormous feeling of dominance when she was engulfed in her trophies, and yet at the same time found a kind of protection in the way they enveloped her and it was a burning desire of hers to one day make a kill of her own; a big cat, a tiger probably. They were fierce, powerful and really quite rare - she'd heard that there were only 3000 Bengal tigers left in the wild; how fabulous to remove one from that total, knowing that "her" kill was important when they were down to such tangible numbers. Maybe a white tiger or snow leopard; they looked gorgeous and would make her feel sexy as hell when she indulged in her other favourite pastime.

She thought of this now as she browsed the shop windows. Walking all over pathetic men and subjecting them to the feel of her 4" heels or vicious whip came a close second to snuffing out the lives of dangerous animals and draping herself in their conquered skins. Combine the two, and well….no drug on earth could match that for adrenalin, eroticism and sheer "hit".

This was indeed where she differed most of all from many women; she was a professional Dominatrix, or Domme. Of her acquaintances, only her closest friend Abby knew about this secret life; and neither approved nor otherwise. In truth, Abby didn't understand the dynamic of a man subjugating to a woman; she was far too old-fashioned in the way she saw male/female relationships. The man went to work and earned the money; the woman stayed at home or had a cleaning job and spent the money either on the household needs or, occasionally small treats for herself. Poor married, delusional Abby!

Donna had been sent along this path serendipitously by her ex husband. He had been a manipulative, arrogant bastard who had been unable to maintain a state of physical arousal unless she was tied and helpless. In the early days he'd get his kicks from spanking her and forcing her to perform sexual acts which he knew she found degrading. In time the thrill seemed to diminish and he sought ever more extreme methods to get to where he needed to be. Towards the end of their relationship he'd progressed to brutal beatings and rape, and the final straw came one Friday evening when he brought a work colleague around to their house and she had spent the weekend being abused by the pair of them in turn or together. Something during those hours of deep horror had shifted inside her, and when her sick husband had hinted that he and his colleague might, for a change enjoy being tied to the headboard of their six foot bed by her, well a

21

new world opened. She'd exacted a devastating and relentless revenge. Once secured she had gagged them so tight that their screams were less than whispers as she ripped into the bare skin of their backs and buttocks with the selection of whips, crops and paddles, the stings of which she was only too familiar with.

Her husband had hit at least one orgasm during her searing onslaught, a fact that she had found astonishing at that time, although with the development of her current business she realised he was but one in a significant sector of the male population whose minds were able to convert excruciating pain and humiliation into a sexual trigger. In all the years of abuse she had suffered, she'd never once been aroused by the act of receiving such shocking abuse, but during the course of those few hours of utter authority she learned that being in control was the most erotic feeling she'd known. Her husband's work colleague had had a different reaction, and when Donna packed her bags and left the pair of them, still tightly immobilised back to back on her bed, she had seen tears streaming down his face and his body shaking with fear.

Donna had wanted to leave her brute of a husband a thousand times but somehow never had the strength of conviction or the confidence; what would she do without him? Where would she go? But now, as she walked to his car, with his keys and his credit cards, she knew exactly what she would do. And she had done it; she had set herself up in a rented bedsit dispensing a service to those men who were willing to pay for anything from errant naughty boy spanks, to mind and body control and, on occasion, hard core vicious beatings. Her friend Abby would never be able to "get" it. She'd never experienced the things Donna had been through; her cosy little world of marital bliss was too far removed from the harsh reality that had been Donna's life.

By sheer coincidence, her friend Abby was at exactly that moment thinking about her own marital status. She and Kevin were blissfully happy; or at least, she thought they were; one never could be absolutely certain. He said very little, never had really, but she knew him so well; gauging his contentedness from the way he moved and behaved, ate and slept. Abby found their relationship a balanced way to live; they were happy this way. Although lately something seemed to have crept between them; he didn't hold her hand quite as often as he once had; and there had been no little surprises for a few weeks. She was used to him coming home from work each Friday with a spray of roses, or some deliciously calorific chocolates, or, more rarely some naughty and far too expensive lingerie…she always knew what that meant, and would take extra care in her bedtime preparation. They'd been married for 12 years and she was proud that she had managed to hold his physical interest in her for that long; many of her friends hadn't achieved that in their relationships, and all of her siblings were divorced.

She knew that Kevin loved to buy these gifts; especially the naughty kind and she would often daydream on a Friday about what the gift might be. In reality she didn't mind, lilies or lingerie, it was the thought that was important, although she always secretly hoped for the undies. They had a straightforward sexual relationship; vanilla was how Kevin liked to refer to it, a little plain, very safe - you always knew what you were going to get - and nice enough to be a treat anyway. He sometimes joked that he'd like her to tie him up and do some kinky things, but she knew he was only kidding. Of course he was.

What Abby didn't know was that for ten months her best friend Donna, the Dominatrix, and her precious hubby had been seeing somewhat more of each other than might be deemed proper. Every Thursday evening to be precise, it being the night that Kevin supposedly went to his yoga class. He kept ahead of the game by ensuring he knew all the key yoga terms and would often tell Abby what a great class it had been – especially on those evenings when Donna had taken him beyond his known limits with her wicked and innovative mind. The 2 hours they had together were never really enough and he waited impatiently for the once a month all-nighter they enjoyed when Abby went to stay with her ailing mum some four hours away in Leeds. This necessitated her leaving before Kevin went to work and returning 30 or more hours later, exhausted and usually tearful after the physical and emotional journey.

Donna would tell Kevin how arousing it was to be dominating the husband of her best friend, behind her back. For his part, Kevin was just happy to be able to experiment and realise all those fantasies he'd spent recent years dreaming up. He loved it when Donna told him what a pathetic little tool he had, and reminded him of how plain his little wife was. He liked to think of his ordinary wife having raging affairs behind his back and would beg Donna to build fantasies based on such stories. This Donna did only too happily.

No money would change hands; Donna indulged herself in this relationship purely for the wickedness of screwing her best friend's man, and making him worship her every action. Usually Donna could be free for these trysts, but just occasionally would receive an offer from a client that she couldn't refuse. She earned fantastic money doing that which she liked best and as a consequence had ample funds for her precious furs and rare skins.

Donna worked around one night in three and on average once a week she'd have an all night gig. These were hard work as the client would want his (or her!) money's worth and sleep would be snatched naps whilst the paying customer recovered enough for another round. On these occasions she would sleep most of the following day in an effort to be fresh enough for any client she may have the following night. She enjoyed her work and was becoming slowly rich from the fees and the tips she received. What more could a girl want, she would say to Abby; sex as often as she wanted, and nearly always with someone new, loads of money for doing it and the pleasure of bending men to her will. She was especially pleased when the customer was a big-built guy; the pleasure of watching him whimper was magnified by the breadth of his shoulders and the size of his manhood.

On this particular Saturday Donna cruised her favourite West End stores searching for something arousing, something which was rare, exotic and gave her that power rush. She loved the synthetic enchantment of the dazzling shop fronts, the hoax welcomes of the kiss-arse marionettes in clone outfits grinning their gluttonous greetings, their eyes all the while betraying true colours as clearly as if a flag were run up a mast.

Donna largely ignored these annoyances, preferring to browse unmolested until something caught her eye or, more often these days, she'd leave empty handed. Today, aside from a few bagfuls of extortionate underwear and pretty hold-ups she'd failed in her quest to find anything much to wear. The shops here were becoming less and less interesting with all these bloody PC people warbling about sustainability and ethics. She'd have to take a trip to the Far East or Africa, maybe South America, they knew what the customer wanted there and money could still buy any amount of pleasure, regardless of its form. She finally spotted a sweet little snakeskin handbag which she knew would match some boots she had at home.

Had Donna been a little more attentive to her surroundings she might have spotted the tall man tracking her throughout the afternoon from shop to shop.

The almost fruitless search had taken longer than she'd planned and it was dark by the time she reached her car in the station car park at Horsham where she had parked to avoid too much London traffic. Horsham was an hour from her village on the South Coast and parking there made the day far less stressful. She cursed as she fumbled for the car keys in her lambskin gloves, trying to juggle several shopping bags.

'Let me help you.'
She was startled by the voice behind her and dropped the keys in a puddle beside the car.
'Oops, careful now, don't want to get those wonderful dead animals dirty now do we.'
'I can manage fine thanks.' She made a grab for the keys but felt a powerful grip on her elbow.
'Get off; what do you think you are doing?'
'Now now, let's not make a scene, otherwise you will get blood on your precious furs - not that they are entirely free of it as things stand.'

Donna immediately realised that she was in serious danger and her instincts took over. She dropped her precious packages and delivered a vicious kick to the guy's groin, then raked her sharp heel down his shin. At the same time she screamed for help at the top of her voice. Almost before the sound had formed in her throat it was cut off by a heavy chop to her windpipe and she fell to her knees into the puddle beside her keys, gasping for air. Before she could react the assailant had pinned her down and was forcing her to inhale some chemical through a cloth. Her final thought, before consciousness deserted her was that it might be nail polish remover.

4

The following morning at the Swan Hotel the receptionist was looking forward to finishing her shift in twenty minutes. She was loading some paper into the troublesome printer and cursing the damned thing under her breath when she sensed, rather than heard a presence and gave a start when she looked up to see a big man leaning above her over the desk. He was completely bald and clean-shaven and his eyes seemed to be too far apart. He looked like one of those sharks with the hammer shaped heads and eyes right at the extremities. The combination of his size, baldness and the eyes gave him an intimidating appearance.

'I'd like to check out please.' Said Colin.

His voice was in contrast to his appearance; soft and almost lyrical and surprisingly high pitched

'Which room sir?' She asked, standing and smoothing her skirt.

'306'

'One moment.' She looked up the details on her computer.

'Ah! I have it. You stayed just the one night and didn't use the restaurant – is that correct?'

'That's right.'

'Anything from the minibar sir?'

'Nothing, no.'

'And did you use the car park?'

'What's that got to do with it?' He asked looking genuinely puzzled 'Don't tell me that's chargeable!'

'Car parking is at a premium in this area as I'm sure you'll appreciate sir; it's £15 a night.'

'Fifteen quid? There's nothing about that on your website.'

'I'm sure it's there somewhere sir.' Said the young receptionist with an apologetic smile.

'It's fucking well NOT there, I know, I would have seen it. I want to see the manager; I'm not going to be ripped off like this!'

The girl flinched at the unexpected expletive and shifted back a step.

'I'm afraid there's no manager here until seven sir; There's just me and my colleague Amanda. Why don't we pretend you never used the car park.' She stuck a wary smile back on her face.

Colin's voice became louder and rose several tones. There was now an edge to it that was menacing.

'We don't need to pretend anything at all. It's not mentioned anywhere, no one told me at check-in and I refuse to pay it. Now give me the ticket to drive out please.'

Alerted by Colin's raised voice a second receptionist appeared through the office door behind the desk.

'Is there a problem Lucy?' She asked. 'Does the gentleman have a query?'

'I do *not* have a query.' Colin interjected, 'your hotel is trying to hoodwink the guests into paying for extras that are not mentioned anywhere.'

'If it's the car parking fee sir, that's mentioned under "Hotel facilities" on the website. I'm more than happy to show you.'

A flicker of doubt crossed Colin's face. Had he missed it? Really? That was surely impossible; he had checked everything as he always did. He would not have missed such an obvious point. He now worried that his plans may be flawed; if he had missed that simple point, what other errors might he have made. He calmed himself and told himself that his mind had clearly been distracted by the complex arrangements he'd been putting together. He realised too that he was attracting unwanted attention to himself. He needed to diffuse the situation quickly.

'Ah – must be my mistake! Fifteen pounds isn't so bad for this area I guess.' He smiled and handed over the additional cash.

Amanda had also noticed the broad spread of his eyes, which seemed to elongate further when he smiled, Creepy guy she thought!

'How was your room then sir?' Asked the first receptionist.

'Fine, fine thank you, nice and quiet.' Colin was shaking with the effort of remaining calm.

'That's good then sir.' She was relieved that he seemed to have calmed down, but it was bizarre how quickly he swung from one temperament to another.

'Which room were you in?' asked Amanda

'306'

'Ah – you had the missing bath mat – sorry you had that minor problem; I'll speak with housekeeping when they arrive.'

She seemed to be smirking; mocking him.

'Bath mat – that's it; bath mat – of course! But my dear girl, a missing bath mat is no "minor" matter. It's dangerous and worse still, a sign that the cleaners are not working to a list. Everyone needs to work to a list.'

'Well, we'll make sure it gets onto the check list then sir!' Amanda was somewhat annoyed at being called "girl" but she realised this guy was a little short of some social skills and let it ride.

'As you say, lists are always useful.'

She was definitely mocking him. Smug bitch! The first girl had turned her face to the side and Colin sensed she was stifling a giggle. Well he'd not tolerate being made a joke of, just because he wanted standards maintained. The world was slipping into an abyss of apathy and piss-poor service. He might not be able to single-handedly stop the rot, but he'd damn well not support it. But now he needed to get moving, time wouldn't wait for him. He took his receipt and with a final stern glance at each of the hotel employees he grabbed his baggage and left.

As the automatic doors slid apart he thought he heard an explosive laugh from one of the girls. It was almost certainly that cocky Amanda. He added her to his list. He'd need to check her out a little first though he realised. He'd have time for that tomorrow.

Colin was angry that he'd allowed his frustration to get through his defences yet again. He left the building and realised that he should have accessed the car park directly from internal stairs or lift. He was now faced with the prospect of clambering over a small wall and walking down a short vehicle ramp and ducking under the barrier, or going back through the lobby and past the giggling girls. He took the outside route and realised he'd be in full view of the receptionists anyway. Red faced and cursing his own stupidity, he stumbled over the wall, dropping one of his bags. He felt belittled by the whole experience and his temper boiled like a cauldron. With watering eyes he spat through grinding teeth.

'Fucking shit bitch Amanda, just you fucking wait you cunt!'

He had chosen his driving route carefully due to its low traffic, few people and lack of CCTV cameras. The bloody things were almost everywhere these days. Never mind, it gave an edge to his evasive manoeuvres. He enjoyed the challenge of evading his enemies, for that's what they were. Heavily resourced adversaries who were to be defeated through cunning and guile. He knew he would win through; he was fuelled by a sense of higher moral purpose.

He drove through a series of quiet residential streets but had no choice eventually other than to revert to the main A3 towards his farm or "Correction Facility" as he was now going to call it. He'd bin the stupid French name he'd thought of earlier though and stick to simple English – not, he thought, that there was anything simple about the language that is really just a bastardisation of multiple other tongues.

After 40 minutes of mostly sensible driving he arrived, relieved that the drive had passed with just one incident. He was prone to incidents when he drove, due to the stupidity of other idiots who didn't obey the rules of the road. The only minor event today had been some prick who had failed to indicate that he was going to overtake him. That was illegal and shouldn't be tolerated. Colin had subsequently raced up behind him, flashed his lights, hit his horn and shouted obscenities; spittle erupting around his lips and spattering the inside of his windscreen. After maybe ten seconds of this he had snapped out of it, realising the risk he had just exposed himself to. He pulled sedately into the slow lane and drifted back down to fifty miles an hour, allowing even the largest lorries to pass him. He was shaking a little for some miles but the soothing voice of his relaxation CD helped him to calm down at last. Still, it had been a warning and he had to manage these things as Doctor Erikssen had told him.

Dr Erikssen was such a calm, placid and hugely intelligent man who helped him with his angry tendencies and gave him tips and tricks to overcome the urges. The Doctor had helped him sort his thoughts out after a few situations, and had recommended this CD as a relaxation aid. It was a recording of water splashes and waves, pan-pipes and some other instruments which he couldn't identify. The sleeve notes said Oude and Ocarina, but he had no idea what they were, he made a mental note to find out; ignorance was risk.

Arriving at the farm, Colin drove past the old house and buildings, through a gate and down a small track to the lower, newer area; "The Facility", slowing and smiling warmly as he passed the beautiful new stallion in the lower paddock.

He felt the familiar feeling of pride in doing something so powerful, right and dangerous, but pushed the thoughts from his mind; he needed to concentrate now, he could dwell on the pleasure later when he was watching his first guests. Parking the old Land-rover under a lean-to beside the main barn, Colin strode back to where the great horse stood eying him impassively. They had yet to bond; yet to build that special relationship that comes only through riding and caring for a beast, yet Colin had no doubt at all that theirs would become a strong friendship and he stroked the solid muzzle before turning back towards the barn.

The barn was an enormous structure which his father had quite recently had built to house the millions of chickens which were the backbone of his poultry empire. Hens for eggs, hens for roasting and hens for soups and fast food. Well, "hens" was stretching it somewhat; the poor beasts had been skeletal bundles of misery. Colin had detested his father and had enjoyed the plotting and planning that he had been through before finally executing him. It had been fool-proof and clean, which in some respects was a shame. He would have preferred to see his father's blood spilled all over the concrete, as he had seen the blood of an impossible number of chickens at the hands of the wicked man and his equally sick employees. The sadistic monster had certainly writhed in pain and died slowly, but it had all been, sadly, largely invisible.

The accident had been perfect in every detail, even down to the genuine fault in the rotating drum of the feed distributor…how could his poor father have known that the thing would automatically restart once he had kicked away the piece of stubborn wooden pallet which was jamming the rotation. Colin had filmed it for his own gratification; filmed his father's frustration at the jammed machine and watched as the idiot waved his arms around in temper and entered the danger zone-exactly as Colin had known he would. He was impulsive, impatient and risk-tolerant. Colin had inherited some of these traits, but he could control them, most of the time.

He had watched as the old man kicked the pallet three times before it shifted, and then the horror on his face as the sudden freeing of that obstruction caused the hopper he'd had to stand in to tip. He would have seen the huge drum turning, and the realisation that he was going in there, the shiny stainless steel slippery as an ice rink and nothing to grab hold of. Interesting how the noise from his stubby, filthy fingernails desperately scratching over the brilliantly smooth steel had competed with his screams for help. A fanfare of fear. Although out of sight, Colin knew the old fool was trapped as the two-foot long tines inside the slowly rotating drum will have grabbed his overalls and in seemingly slow-motion would be pulling him up and over into the stored grain distribution mechanism. That's when the screeching of fingernails ceased and his priceless screams erupted in earnest. Here was the sound of a terrified man; these noises were the death throes of a murderous executioner; his final words from the depths of his evil belly, a last treacherous confession perhaps, a final deceitful reconciliation whilst trying desperately to free himself as the mechanical beast dragged him around so slowly, oblivious to his cries. Then the quieter time, the low frequency grumble of the rotating drum punctuated only by the regular thud, thud, thud as the old man was slowly tumbled and tossed around inside, falling to the bottom then being slowly dragged up again. The unhurried relentlessness of the machine belying the desperate panic in the human voice was delicious. It had taken an age for the long prongs inside the drum to tear his body apart so that the thuds became softer sounds and then almost inaudible as the old monster became a smear of liquids and pierced organs inside the new master, the bones being separated and largely wedged between the tines, or, as with the skull, hideously impaled through an eye socket, as if the machine were holding aloft a trophy of the one-sided battle.

The latter part of the video showed an excited and skipping Colin in front of the machine with a delirious smile; cackling and crowing like a demented being. It showed him clapping his hands as he pranced, and banged on the outer casing of the still-turning drum shouting;

'Father, father – are you in there? Are you in pain?'

More cackles and prancing, wringing of gleeful hands.

'Father you bastard – does it hurt very very much? Shall I call an ambulance? I'll have to dismantle my recording gear and watch the film first, just to make sure I made no silly mistakes. Oh father – well done! Well done!'

He knew he hadn't made a single error but the delicious sensation of mocking his father this way made him physically aroused and he wanted to watch the film for his own enjoyment, He could call the police later and report the old man missing. Tomorrow he might discover the body of the unfortunate man and be lost in his grief for the benefit of the emergency services. He'd need counselling and support; such a dreadful accident. Maybe even a convincing spell in the mental health institution he'd researched. In any case, he'd give it a few days before he contacted the insurance people. Meanwhile he'd lay back and enjoy the memory of the nasty old man and the uncaring, unhearing machine. He alone had heard the screams. He alone had witnessed the death. He alone would know the truth. This made him feel incredibly powerful. He told himself that he simply *must not forget* to get a good look at the stainless steel hopper surfaces; those fingernail marks would tell such a tale. Colin's erection was almost intolerably huge.

Occasionally, in the coming months and after a long and tiring day Colin would reward himself by viewing the footage on a huge flat screen TV and drinking red wine. Always red wine; the taste of pure nature, the colour of blood.

Back in the present, Colin offloaded his overnight baggage from the Land-rover into the facility, leaving his large, black holdall on the passenger's seat. He checked for the umpteenth time that everything in the huge barn was where it should be. Satisfied, he shouted a hearty "cheerio" to Donna. She was the first of his visitors and had made a huge row when she'd awoken to find herself in a metal cage. She cursed him noisily and he chuckled as he closed the huge doors.

Colin mounted the cab of the Land-rover. He had a very busy twelve hours or so ahead; he had to collect some things from North London and then in the early hours had to come back down south to see man about a pig. His travel arrangements were a little laborious so he'd need to get a move on and concentrate. He sat in the cab and wrote his mood diary entry for the day before firing up the old diesel engine and driving slowly out of the muddy yard onto the pothole and puddle strewn chalk track leading past the older house and up to the paved road that would take him towards his rendezvous with probably the stupidest and most offensive man he'd never yet properly met.

5

Hans-Werner Fromm finished the call to his mother in Germany. She seemed to be on the mend after her recent bout of 'flu and he was less worried now. Good news; now he could focus on his new and already successful IT business which he ran from offices in Brighton. More importantly, right now, it meant that he could give his full attention to the game. His team, Borussia Dortmund, needed to get at least a draw at Arsenal tonight in order to progress to the knock-out stage of the Champions League, and he fancied their chances, given the recent form of the London hosts.

He was being pulled along with the crowd which was in buoyant mood with sporadic outbursts of football songs and that rhythmic clapping which is an integral part of football ceremony universally. Hans-Werner thought about that and about how it must be some primeval tribal thing, reflecting that mankind hadn't, perhaps, evolved quite as far as we might sometimes think. He smiled to himself *"homo homini lupus est"*. But at least the violence that used to plague the English game seemed to have all but disappeared. It was a rarity now to hear of beatings, stabbings and mob rampages and this had made him feel much safer travelling to the away games as he liked to do. The safety improvements had been achieved in part by police intelligence gathering and the identification and isolation of ringleaders of the gangs which had been so damaging. He looked up at the CCTV cameras mounted high on the lampposts and took further comfort from their presence.

Hans-Werner caught the aroma of one of the many burger vans that dotted the route to the stadium. That smell reminded him of the *Bratwurst Buden* – the sausage stands – of his native Germany, always seeming to pull him like a magnet and he realised it he hadn't eaten since breakfast. He joined a small queue, self-conscious in his yellow and black scarf amongst so much red and white, but there was no real animosity between rivals, more of a friendly ribbing. Within minutes he had a long steaming Frankfurter-style sausage in a roll covered with a heart-attack inducing combination of fried onions, ketchup and mustard.

"Just vot ze doctor ordered" he thought.

In the act of turning to join the stream of Arsenal supporters snaking its way towards the turnstiles he clashed with a tall man hurrying against the flow and some of his precious hotdog sauce splattered onto the guys black coat.

'You fucking moron.' Shouted the guy.

'Woah – sorry, but I heffent seen you.' Responded Hans-Werner, genuinely embarrassed but himself a little miffed to have lost some of the tastiest portion of his snack.

'Why don't you look where you are going instead of sticking your face into the poor animal you are mutilating.'

The guy was clearly angrier than was probably reasonable, and Hans-Werner's self-protection instincts kicked in.

'Like I said, I am wery sorry, I vill giff you my number and if you get your coat cleaned I vill happily pay ze bill.'

'Will that wipe the guilt from your stupid brain too?' Ranted the big guy and Hans-Werner noticed spittle forming around the edges of his mouth. He also saw how far apart his eyes seemed to be, giving him a lunatic appearance.

'Not sure vy I should feel guilty actually' replied the German, himself starting to feel his own temper rising. 'And in any case, you bumped into me.'

'You fucking shit brains, you span around without looking.' raved the lanky, bald guy; a small crowd had now been drawn to the exchange, some of them smiling at the prospect of a spectacle.

'Pay ze stupid cleaning bill yourself zen, and I hope it's expensiff.' Hans-Werner sneered, turning away.

He felt a hand on his shoulder and was about to spin round and push the rest of his hotdog into the guys face when he saw the man smiling apologetically.

'Hey I'm sorry.' The man said. 'I over-reacted, and you must think me crazy, but it was an expensive coat and will cost a lot to get the animal fats and grease out. How about we split the costs between us?'

Hans-Werner became immediately calm and relieved that the incident was over.

'Of course; let me giff you my number and you can call me ven it's done and I vill send you a cheque.'

He fished around in his coat pocket and pulled out a slightly crumpled business card.

'Sorry, it's my last one; my mobile number is on ze back so just call whenever you heff news.'

They shook hands and parted; Hans-Werner towards the stadium gates and the tall man in the opposite direction.

'He was a bit of a nutter mate; thought you were gonna smack him at one point there.'

Hans-Werner looked at the smiling man bedecked in red and white and smiled back.

'He did heff me vorried for a bit.' Replied the German 'But he voss in ze end OK I sink.'

The game was a tight affair that ended in a 1:1 draw. That was fine for Hans-Werner's German side, but meant that the Londoners would have to sit out the rest of the competition, having failed to qualify for the nest stage. Hans-Werner made his way home via the tube and train and was eagerly anticipating seeing the other group scores on the late news. It was late when he finally arrived home and he was looking forward to a nice brandy to celebrate. As he opened the squeaking front door to his flat he caught the faint scent of something unexpected. He couldn't place the smell but knew he should recognise it. He often had that; he'd taste or smell something and although he had smelled it a thousand times couldn't put his finger on what it was. Once he knew the answer it would seem obvious and he would kick himself that he hadn't been able to name it.

As he turned and hung his coat on the hook behind his door the answer hit him – fried onions! He hadn't fried onions here for ages, how odd. It must be wafting up from the takeaway across the street although he couldn't recall having smelled anything from there before.

For an instant he was aware of a noise behind him, and as he span around he caught a glimpse of a tall character wielding a heavy object of some kind. He realised it was a hammer an instant before it struck him a stunning blow to the side of the head and the world went black.

6

Diary entry 2
1st March 2014

Dear father
A mixed day.
I had anger issues and must lay the gilt which comes with them at yoor door. How could you have neglected my needs so badly and for so long? Why did my mother not stay insted of you? She and I would have lived a peaceful and useful life together. Although her face sometimes eludes me now I remember her for her gentle kindness. She was everything a parent should be and you were the worst kind. You were the perfect monster. Why did she leave? I no you argued that day, but what happened?

But the hatred I hold in my hart for you is my driver. Through your evil I shall make the world a better place. You will tern in your grave when you see the way farmers will run their affares in the very near future.

But good news! My flock grows and I now have a German sausage muncher.
It was a coinsidental meeting in London, he munching dead animals, me breaking his skull. He was determined not to come but I persuaded him and he can spred the word throughout our European neybers. He will be a great asset.

I have to run now, or rather drive. I am having a trip into the country to meet an old frienb of yours. Remember that disgusting creecher Babitch? I shall meet him in two hours to relieve him of his delivery and persuade him to join me at the farm. He should see from a relatively close distance the damage he has done and how the world will change. In so many ways he was the catalist for that change, so I shall treat him as a disciple, a profit. A not for profit profit ha ha. It's called humor farther; something you never had an abundants of. Luckily I inherited mother's wit!

Your son
Colin

PS with a teeny bit of the inshurance repayments from yoor death I am buying a boat. A lovely big sailing yott I will call her "Salty Pig Runs Free". I will check the spelling of corse, I wouldent want to spell it wrong, after all she will be a memorial to you!

7

Bojan Babić was a Serbian pig farmer who would be deemed in his
own country to be of modest wealth. He had earned much of his
money via dodgy deals in English or Dutch country fields with
unscrupulous traders. As usual the load he brought tonight did not
meet the stringent demands of the two principal EU regulations for
transporting live animals across international borders. The
paperwork was all seemingly in place and the animals' provenance
appeared genuine, but the reality was that these creatures had been
transported illegally, with only enough welfare provision to keep
most of them alive and with no guarantees that the meat quality met
the modern standards regarding additives such as growth
enhancement hormones.

In this particular load three of the pigs had already died in the
cramped and cold conditions en-route from Vranje, Serbia. During
the forty two hour journey without rest, food or water the remainder
had become dangerously dehydrated, underweight and distressed.
Many were sick and few would have been passed fit for human
consumption by the UK Department of Food and Rural Affairs.
Bojan Babić didn't care a jot about that; it was easy money and he'd
never eat the meat. By the time this load was slaughtered he'd be
back on his little farm fattening the next brood of piglets courtesy of
the local waste collections he made. Life was good!

He'd been waiting at the dank and darkly wooded rendezvous point
for over an hour and was starting to feel a little nervous. He'd never
done business with the son before, although his father, Graham
Furness had been a regular client. Babić hoped all was as it seemed
and that it wasn't some kind of trap; he could do without being
arrested. He shifted his soggy, cold backside on the fallen tree trunk
to improve the circulation in his legs and poured the black dregs
from his metal thermos flask into the stained metal cup. The coffee

he'd topped up in France was long since cold and he wished he'd added more sugar; at least that would have made the nasty brew digestible. He swore as yet another cold drip from the leaf canopy above hit the back of his collar and trickled down his neck. He was cold and wet and wanted to get back on his way.

What Babić couldn't have known was that long before his arrival in the rain sodden wood, his contact had been in position, preparing things for what was to come. Piggy farmer Babić was going to get a very different kind of exchange from the one he was expecting.

Babić; Colin had researched it and it meant something like "old woman" or "hag" in Serbian. He grinned in the darkness where he lay in the cover of the undergrowth and scrub, and where he had hidden quietly since making his way by bus and on foot two hours ago. He was warm and dry, thanks to his meticulous preparation and he observed the pig man's obvious discomfort. As a boy Colin had studied the great generals of history - at his father's insistence - learned of their tactics, the way they fought and thought, the best times for attack and defence, and how to exploit situations and to weaken the mind of your enemy. He'd give piggy a little longer to sweat, or rather, to chill, and then when he was good and cold and would be relieved to see his contact, the Serb would relax. Then he'd be at his most vulnerable – not that Colin was in any doubt about his ability to take the little fat man, but why take risks when he didn't need to? The immediate future held enough of those already. And in any case, he enjoyed watching the fat little man's discomfort.

Finally Colin made his stealthy way to the pathway that lead to piggy's truck and, emerging from out of the darkness with a strong black holdall over his shoulder and his hands spread and slightly raised in front of him adopting an apologetic manner, approached piggy.
'I am so sorry Mr Babić.' He said. 'I thought I was being followed and took precautions – I am not used to this kind of clandestine operation as you well know, every minute that goes by makes me more nervous; can we please do the deal and get out of here?'
'By every means Mr Furness.' Laughed the squat little Serb, relieved and in full agreement with the proposal.

'I am happy to kick swine into your truck and make my way home; 4000 of your wonderful English Pounds better off!'
Babić thought for a moment;
'Where your truck is?'
'Oh it's hidden behind the trees'.

Babić was either too careless or too stupid to realise that, if his contact really had only just this minute arrived as he claimed, he should have heard his noisy truck. His attention was too focussed on the money to think of anything else. The cash from the animals which Babić brought across only made up a small part of his profit. In fact it barely covered his financial overheads, the Serb made most of his money on the return trip, carrying illicit tobacco products across international borders to places where cigarettes were still treated as hard currency.

'I'll just get your cash.' Said Colin, stooping to put his hand into the bag. But what came out was a 3lb club hammer, so recently used on another European's skull, which he swung in a wide arc at the back of the pig man's head. The impact of the heavy hammer upon the Serb's skull was loud in the stillness of the woods, and he thrilled at the way Babić collapsed like a sack of pig shit. He was a little worried that he'd struck too hard, but a low moan told him it was OK. Quickly he pulled strong adhesive tape, rope and some lengths of wire and linen from the bag and set to work immobilising the Serbian. The moaning became louder and distressed and Babić vomited where he lay.
'That's right fatty; get the puke out before the gag goes on, Uncle Colin would hate you to drown in undigested animal fats and cheap Serbian beer.'

Within two minutes Babić was gagged and trussed like a Christmas turkey and being dragged by his feet towards the Serb's own truck. Colin lowered the ramp and released the pigs to freedom. It had rained a lot recently so they'd find plenty to drink. Food was never a problem for pigs – they would eat pretty much anything if they were hungry enough; and these poor beasts were clearly on the verge of starvation. Colin knew that they liked truffles, and in this area they were plentiful, if a little hard to find. He was distressed to find the corpses of the three dead animals and sadly removed them from the truck. He guessed the other pigs might eat them eventually, but he wasn't really sure.

Colin strapped the Serb down to a set of fixed transport rings on the truck bed and made sure he was good and tight. He checked for breathing and then raised the loading ramp and climbed into the cab. Finding himself on the wrong side of the left hand drive vehicle, he slid across the bench seat. To his dismay there were no keys in the ignition. He leapt from the cab and once again lowered the ramp. He sprang into the back of the truck, agile for a man of his size, and went roughly through the guy's pockets but found no keys.
'Shit! Where are they you arsehole?'
He kicked Babić twice in the side.
'You know what your name means in Serbian? Eh? Babić; it means Old Woman! It must have been created especially for you, now where are the fucking keys you slimy turd?'

Babić could only make muffled noises through the gag, so it had to be temporarily removed. As soon as it was off the fool shouted for help. Colin pulled back his arm and punched the little man powerfully in the face and the Serb became silent. He was re-gagged and Colin was left with no keys and a feeling of rising panic.

'Shit, shit, shit, shit shit!' He muttered under his breath. He did a little dance of despair. His plans were already in disarray.
'Where would the slob have put them…?'

Out of the corner of his eye he caught the glint of something shiny laying half covered by the wet grass. It was a steel thermos flask lying on the ground by the rear wheels. Next to the flask were the keys on a pig's head-shaped key ring. Relieved, Colin closed the back of the truck and jumped back into the cab, realising that he was again on the passenger side he quickly slid across the bench seat. The old engine fired first time and he was off, struggling at first with the unfamiliar layout and failing to locate the windscreen wipers whilst being careful to avoid the dozens of pigs now snorting around in the shrubbery. Before long he was back on the road and heading towards the facility. He soon became familiar with the lorry's controls and quietly sang an improvised song about a Serbian pig farmer named Babić to the tune of Baa Baa Black Sheep.

"Pig man Babić
Didn't get his dosh
But he lost his pigs and got a
Head-busting cosh"

He smiled to himself and relaxed into the worn old driver's seat on the way to his barn. He would get his third guest settled in. Babić was going to find it an interesting experience at the correction facility. Colin Furness cackled quietly to himself. He wanted to get this job completed; he had places to go and other people to catch. Oh yes, and a boat to buy!

8

A few hours later Detective Inspector Neil Dyson drained his coffee in the busy little café off East Street. He liked the place; liked the atmosphere and the clientèle. It helped too, that the coffee was the best to be found anywhere in the city. It had also been the place where he had met his fiancée, Jenny; he especially liked it for that. They had both been in Chichester for a police training course; she with the Royal Military Police in the town and Neil as a raw recruit with the Sussex Constabulary. Jenny had been one of the last of the RMP trainees to be based in the city before that unit had moved their training base to Wiltshire. It hadn't taken her long to realise that military life was not for her, and she'd stayed in the city to study the history of the English language, which was where her passion had lain since primary school but out of some false sense of respect she'd allowed herself to be talked out of it by her persuasive ex-army father. Neil liked to think that she also stayed in order to be close to him!

Dyson enjoyed a flirty but otherwise completely innocent relationship with a waitress named Maria, who always made him feel special somehow with her attentive service and engaging smile. Neil knew enough people who managed to make a smile look like a veiled threat, as if to say "My smile is my way of disarming you". It was all in the eyes and Maria's look of true warmth always felt genuine.

Today Maria seemed preoccupied with a colleague who had clearly been crying.
'Is she OK?' Dyson asked as he settled the bill.
'Not really; her partner seems to have disappeared and she has no idea why or where he could have gone.'
'When did she last see him?'

'Yesterday morning at around 7.30 when he left for work. She knew he was heading straight from work to watch a football game; his favourite team from Germany was playing in London last night and he was really looking forward to going.'

The inherent policeman inside took over, and Neil asked whether the partner had friends or family locally, but Maria explained that he was German and had not long lived in England.
'Has she tried contacting his German family? Maybe he had an emergency message and had to leave in a hurry?'
'She said his mother wasn't well, but he had no plans to visit her, or at least he didn't mention any and it seems he is very reliable. She is sure he would have called her, or at least left a note.'
'She'll probably find that that's what's happened; he'll have had an urgent message and dropped everything to get to his mother's bedside.'
'You're probably right.' She smiled, but the little shoulder shrug told Neil that she disagreed.
Dyson had to get moving so he wished her friend luck, grabbed his sports bag and left.
He was headed for a rare mid-week Tae Kwon-do tournament in Birmingham and had decided to take the train. (A similar contest two years previously had resulted in a fractured wrist and, unable to drive, he'd had to abandon the car 200 miles from home).

Neil Dyson was 38 years old, 5'10", dark blond, lean and muscular and an accomplished martial arts exponent. He'd be fighting a similarly experienced opponent from potentially anywhere in Europe. He enjoyed the adrenalin rush that comes with the uncertainty of a physical encounter. As a kid he had sought trouble wherever it was to be found; at school, on the train, at parties. He had been through countless therapies as a teenager but became only worse once he discovered the thrill of alcohol and how it made others more willing to square up at the slightest provocation.

He'd been hurt, badly hurt on plenty of occasions, but that just seemed to make him more determined to come out on top the next time; and there had always been a next time. He had been a regular Saturday night visitor to the local A&E department, sporting anything from broken noses, arms ribs or, on one occasion skull. Almost without exception he'd been strongly under the influence of his favourite tipple, vodka. If he fought sober he invariably won. He never touched other substances, and took a bit of a righteous stance whenever an offer might be made. In any case, he'd been a police officer now for almost fifteen years and drugs were simply not an option.

Maturity (he claimed) and the responsibilities that came with his job had calmed his previously volatile temper, but he could still be a little hot headed and he was pretty sure that once he got into the right place mentally he would destroy any opponent today. Losing in these organised events was for him the absolute exception to the rule. He was respected in many European clubs and thrived on the buzz this gave him.

Owing to delayed trains (ice on the track!) and the ensuing chaos at Birmingham New Street where the swelling hoard of several thousand irate and selfish commuters barged, jostled and elbowed their way to get in front of at least one more fellow delayee, Neil arrived in the nick of time to prepare for the tournament. Prepare is over-stating it; he rushed to the changing rooms, swapped jeans for Dobok and protective gear and ran into the Dojang – the hall where the contest was taking place.

His opponent, a tall, gaunt guy from Ukraine, had finished his warm up routine and was eyeing Neil with a disdainful look, the kind that said "Ah, so you made it; well done! Shall we get on with it then?" Neil, on the other hand had just enough time for a few tentative stretches and quick bends and twists which were woefully inadequate. In hindsight he should have requested a delay at this point, but in his usual blasé manner he dismissed that thought on the basis that he'd get through the first of the three rounds in as good shape as he could, he'd then be nicely warm and psyched up too.

He entered the fray.

The two fighters bowed, touched gloves and became adversaries. A rapid counter-evolutionary process, peculiar to Eastern Martial Arts then took place; gentleman to sportsman to cave man in a matter of seconds.

As Dyson manoeuvred around a little on his toes to try to gain some extra warm-up time the first kick came; unexpected and seen too late. A kick to the head was three points to the opponent. It was lightening fast although thankfully not too powerful and he stayed upright easily enough. A little dazed and distracted momentarily by the loss of 3 points, Neil failed to anticipate the combination of punches to the head and chest that came next, and which both stunned and took away his ability to breathe. The jumping scissor kick put his chin where his forehead should have been and a fierce turning kick somehow came round his inadequate guard and struck his eye socket below the rim of his protective head guard. His eye felt like it exploded and he went down, instinctively from his brawling days curling into a foetal position trying to protect his vital functions from any further onslaught. He remained on the mat until he regained his senses.

Blinking rapidly to clear his vision he realised there was blood mingled with the fluid from his weeping eye and he feared the worst. Struggling to focus his damaged eye he was staring into the face of the squatting official and the look he saw reflected there filled him with dismay; the contest had been stopped and he saw his opponent dancing around with both arms raised celebrating his victory.
The lanky streak of shit is prancing around like a bloody ballerina he thought. He was defeated, humiliated and pissed off. The whole thing had lasted perhaps 15 seconds….all that bloody way for a quarter of a minute of shame.

Grudgingly Dyson regained enough decorum to go through the whole bowing-out thing and then slunk back to the changing room to lick his wounds and grab his stuff. He couldn't be bothered to change and, still wearing his fighting gear he traipsed dejectedly to the railway station.
Joy of joys, there was still ice on the lines (same lines, same ice he guessed-well it can be hard to predict if there'll be a winter every year) and he sat for a pointless and depressing 90 minutes reflecting on what had just happened and drawing plenty of sideways glances

from other travellers. He wasn't sure if they were staring at his Korean fighting dobok or at his rapidly worsening eye.

Dyson realised it had been a silly decision not to change, so went to find somewhere to swap clothes. The toilets were all over-subscribed and less than charming due to the swarms of stranded commuters so he left the station complex and walked maybe half a mile until he found a wine bar. Ignoring the odd looks cast his way upon entrance he ordered a large and extortionately priced House Red and whilst it was being sorted slipped into the gents to change. The grotesque monster staring back at him in the mirror had an almost comical look, and Neil knew he'd need to get the eye looked at by a medical professional sooner rather than later.

He still had ages before any trains would be leaving so he called Jenny to tell her the woeful tale of farcical defeat, at the same time lazily watching the people; mostly business blokes and girls, smart, loud, pretentious and a little over lubricated. One guy in particular caught his attention as Neil spoke to Jenny's voicemail (*why* did she never answer!). This guy was dressed in the widest, loudest pin-stripe suit Neil had ever seen and was clearly playing the role of entertainer-cum-impresario.

As Dyson watched, two new guys came in, they were dressed very much in the same style as the majority of the clientèle, but something looked out of place. He couldn't put his finger on it; maybe it was the out of proportion face of one of them. He had a huge permanently smiling mouth and it looked almost as if he had a coat hanger behind his lips and gave the impression that he found everything funny - and so many teeth! Dyson's eyes seemed to gravitate towards the newcomers. He watched them separate; laughing boy came near to Dyson at the bar whilst the other went directly to the loos. When this one came back from the Gents he didn't go back to his wide-mouthed pal, but headed towards the middle of the room and sat down alone. This struck Neil as a little odd, so he looked on with more interest as a little drama unfolded.

He saw Laughing Boy take his own wallet out of his pocket and start waving it at the centre of attention, Mr Stripy Suit.

'Is this your wallet mate?' he asked.

Stripy Suit put his hand to his back pocket and clearly felt his wallet there.

'Nope, not mine, but I'll have it if it's going begging.'

At that moment Laughing Boy's mate joined them.

'Oh, it's mine.' he said 'Thanks!' and he took the wallet from his friend.

Neil was intrigued; why the hell were they pretending not to know each other, when they were clearly pals when they entered the bar? He was really interested in what was going on now and all his senses were on high alert.

'Pleasure!' Said Laughing Boy. 'Get me a drink and we're quits!' Some of the yuppies laughed at this then turned their attention back to Stripy Suit, who had reverted to his stand-up comic role.

Dyson wondered what the hell that had all been about and almost missed it; if he hadn't spent most of his life looking for minute details at crime scenes and studying people and locations so intently it may well have slipped his attention. Laughing Boy moved away and his mate drifted into the slot where he had been standing and with an almost imperceptible flick of his hand, lifted Stripy's wallet from the back pocket which had been so clearly signposted by Stripy himself to the two obvious pickpockets. The whole thing had taken only moments and within a minute Laughing Boy and pal were sauntering through the door onto the street and were lost in the crowd.

The detective's immediate reaction was one of highest admiration for the slickness of the operation and the ease with which they'd pulled it off. Laughing Boy, through his little wallet act, had got Stripy to show the thief exactly where the money was! Dyson admired true pros – regardless of their field of expertise, it was always good to see a job well done.

Then he glanced at Stripy, blissfully ignorant in his world of buffoonery, yet probably several dozen quid and a bunch of credit cards poorer than he had been minutes earlier. Served the pretentious twat right. Dyson knew he had to take action whenever he saw a criminal act, but for the first time he found he had absolutely no motivation. Maybe it was the disappointment of the farcical fight he'd lost or the frustration of the journey's delays, he couldn't say. In the end he compromised and approached Laughing Boy, who was still performing to his avid audience.

Quietly Neil took him by the elbow to one side and told him to get the manager to check the CCTV footage because he'd been robbed of his wallet.

At first annoyed at being interrupted, the guy in the stripes soon become concerned when a pat down of his pockets showed his wallet to be indeed missing. He swore loudly, muttered his thanks quietly, apologised to his fans and explained that he needed to report a crime. With that he headed off towards the rear of the bar to track down a manager.

The incident had actually served to calm Neil and relieve some of the frustration that the day had dumped on his shoulders and it was with a lighter heart that he nudged his way to the station platform to await the 'express' that would carry him home; eventually. His scheduled arrival time was now way past midnight so he'd have to call his operational partner, Detective Sergeant Samantha Milsom to tell her he'd had a few setbacks and might be a little later than usual for the standard briefing at the station in the morning.

The full name 'Samantha" was the only one she ever used. She hated the shortened "Sam" and woe betide anyone who made that mistake twice. Samantha was at that precise moment luxuriating in a deep, hot and very bubbly bath with a glass of white wine and the Times crossword. Life didn't get any better than this she thought as she stretched out and studied 11 across: *"Does he drink fire water around 2 hours before midnight?"*

She scribbled in the margin; two before midnight must be ten, around that another word for fire water, and with a wry smile of respect for the crossword compiler filled in the word 'Hottentot'. She was a little puzzled by the 'fire water' reference – the Hottentots came from Africa, she thought, rather than being fire water guzzling Red Indians. Never mind, she loved this crossword, it was the only one that seemed to challenge her in any way. Even so she very rarely failed to complete the grid in less than the thirty minutes she allowed herself to indulge. Her work as a detective was demanding and she had plenty of hobbies that filled the rest of the day. She went to the gym most days and helped out at a local animal shelter when she could. Thirty minutes were all she could really spare, so she always tried to make the most of them.

Samantha Milsom was black, with skin the colour of rich, dark chocolate and despite her long and wavy, almost jet black hair, her near perfect physique and fresh, attractive looks she was rarely invited out on dates. Her boss and detective partner Neil Dyson claimed this was because men were intimidated by her. She was tall and confident and this, he claimed, put a lot of men off. He also claimed that many white guys find black ladies a little overawing, but she preferred to call it fear and high respect! She didn't really have a type that she was attracted to in men; she was a sapiophile, highly attracted to intelligence. Looks were of course important, if there was no physical attraction then there was little to base a relationship on. At least six foot tall with an air of confidence-even dominance in a man was also attractive to her, but she'd yet to find a guy who ticked all the boxes of height, looks, strength and brains! She'd wait a long time to find a creature like that, as her sister frequently told her and the guys she met on a day-to-day basis were hardly her cup of tea. She definitely didn't want a copper for a hubby; that would lead to a disastrous work/life balance.

She heard her mobile phone beep, alerting her to a new message. That could wait until she was done here. Nothing interrupted her personal bath time if she could help it! When she had rinsed her hair, towelled herself dry and scrubbed her teeth, she took her empty wine glass into her bedroom where her mobile 'phone lay on the bed, its little red light flashing to remind her that a message awaited her attention. She thought about ignoring it, but in the end, thinking it might be important, picked it up.

It was a text message from her boss Neil Dyson telling her that he'd been delayed in Birmingham and would be getting home extremely late. As a result he *might* be a little later than usual into the office in the morning.

Samantha chuckled to herself and shook her head. That guy would do anything for a lay in! She turned the 'phone to "vibrate only" mode, dropped the towel and slid beneath the clean, crisp, cool sheets. She turned on her story CD as she always did - it helped her to forget any stress that had arisen in the course of that day's duties - and then turned out the bedside light. The soft voice of Stephen Fry soothed any remaining tension from her head and she was soon drifting into a deep sleep.

9

Colin's house telephone rang.
'Mr Furness?'

'Speaking.'

'Mr Furness, my name is Abrahams, from Abrahams and Abrahams Financial Services.'

'Don't tell me, your first name; it's Abraham, right?' Colin quipped.

There was a small noise, like a grunt from the caller.

'Er, actually no, it's David!'

'That's still an awful lot of Abrahams!'

'Indeed. My late father was known as Abrahams the Elder. And I was the Younger. When the Elder passed away, er, 17 years ago I was already old, and so the old younger Abrahams became the only surviving one, ergo the Elder; if you see.'

'Yes I see.' said Colin, almost seeing. He already found this man irritating, and he had an unattractive nasal voice, as if he were speaking whilst pinching his nose.

'How can I help you?' he avoided the use of yet another Abraham in any format, young, old or late.

'Well it's more like how I might be able to help you sir. You see, I was your late father's financial advisor and accountant for many years, since he started to turn a profit in fact. In truth I may even be the *reason* he started to turn a profit.'

Colin could almost hear the man beaming with self-satisfaction.

'Well, I'm sure he paid you handsomely for the honour, Mr Abrahams.' he wanted to call him Mr Abrahams "the smugger", but thought he'd keep that one to himself right now.

'Well, I expect you are very familiar with the set up we established?'

'I am actually very *un*familiar with the entire financial arrangements Mr Abrahams, perhaps you might enlighten me?'

'Ah, yes, well. In truth we have, er, that is, we *had* a complex set of circumstances. Your father was one who believed that he, er, he who earned a decent living ought to keep most of that for himself, and anyone who made no significant contribution should receive a pro rata donation. It was in that latter category that he, er, that he placed Her Majesty's Revenue and Customs, or Inland Revenue however you like to think of the tax man.'

Colin was a little perturbed by the man's frequent use of the phrase "*in truth*" when clearly where he was going with this was probably not quite in keeping with the spirit of that saying. He chose to listen a little longer; the man might be able to solve a minor dilemma for Colin.

'Do go on.'

'Yes, er well, in truth we used a system of small companies, invoicing and cross-invoicing and supplying and buying from each other, and ultimately sending monies to accounts registered, er, overseas in the names of companies all belonging to Mr Furness, that is, er, to you now of course. It was all legal and above board, well, at least when viewed in certain, er, certain light.'

Irritating the man certainly was, but he seemed to know what he was doing.

The nasal voice continued.

'Even the two farms are listed as separate entities to maximise revenue and minimise loss potential.'

'Two farms? What do you mean?'

'I mean the old buildings up in the top fields and the newer ones in the lower yard are listed as two separate businesses, all the plant and equipment is registered to the top farm, and the bottom one, the part of the business that actually *uses* the equipment hires it on a day rate.'

Colin was surprised at this; it was true, the two building clusters were quite discreet but he'd had no idea they were treated as separate organisations.

'OK, and what's the advantage of all these transactions?'

'Er well, in truth it means you get to keep the lion's share of what you have earned, and the tax man gets what he, er, what he deserves.'

'Interesting Mr Abrahams. You might find, *in truth* that I am a little different, in an ethical sense, to my father. For instance, I find the whole notion of petty fraud distasteful.'

On the other end of the line he could sense the disagreeable man squirming at the bad news. He softened the blow; not because of any feelings he had for the irritant, but because it served his purpose.

'However; I may have a use for a skilled balance sheet craftsman. If I wanted to make a large sum of money difficult to see for some time, I mean cease to exist in essence, is that something that might be achieved?'

He sensed now a licking of lips at the other end.

'Er, well yes, in truth it's always possible. Complicated and very time consuming, but I'm sure I can do something. How much, er, how much were you thinking?'

'All of it Mr Abrahams. The lot.'

'Oh gosh, that, er, that is a lot. We are talking in excess of thirty million pounds Mr Furness. That would take some, er, very creative accounting and would be very risky. I'd need time and sufficient incentive to bend the rules to that extent.'

Slime bag.

'OK, give me a proposal in the morning and we'll see if I can use your services. I have others who claim they can do this easily enough, but I like to reward loyalty, Mr Abrahams the new Elder.'

Colin was sure the financial drudge on the other end of the line would detect his mockery, but who cares, he thought.

'Er, OK. Tell me Mr Furness; how, er, productive is the farm at the moment? I haven't seen any transactions of any magnitude, other

57

than the refurbishment work you recently undertook? Are you keeping all the receipts in a tin under the bed?' he chuckled.

'The farm has ceased to operate; I disagree with everything, that is *everything* that my father did and had ever done here. There will be no more receipts, just the one task for you to deal with.'
'But you'll need to demonstrate basic financial husbandry Mr Furness. Er, show incomings and outgoings and the like...'
'There will be no immediate need Mr Abrahams. Sort the quote for me and we can talk about this petty shit later.'
'Hardly petty er, stuff, Mr Furness – keeping a clean sheet above decks is always a good sign for our authoritative friends with sharp eyes, strict rules and pedantic ways; we don't want them to, er, to have a reason to start looking into your affairs.'

Colin's short fuse began to smoulder, he recognised the symptoms and consciously tried to relax.
'For now, Mr Abrahams. Let's tell them to ram their rule books and pedantic ways up their authoritative arses and find a way to disappear the funds – OK? In essence I want the money to be untraceable and to be in a situation where I can be anywhere in the world and have ready access to this pot of money that doesn't officially exist. Now if you'd like to call me tomorrow with the solution we'll have a fruitful discussion. If it's a step too far for you, then that discussion will be a very short one. Goodbye Mr Abrahams.'

Smiling, Colin replaced the receiver and did a small skip.

10

When he finally made it through his front door, Neil Dyson was tired, thirsty, hungry, in pain and more than a little pissed off. He scrutinised the reflection of his face and the contents of his bachelor fridge in that order and quickly decided he had a shiner and nothing easy to cook. He briefly contemplated calling Jenny and begging her to produce one of her out-of-nothing magical meals for two but knew the response he might expect at this hour. That would reinforce her argument from the previous evening where she semi-seriously accused him of using her as a surrogate mum, cook, cleaner and sex-toy; a claim he had vehemently denied (although, upon reflection, each of those accusations held merit). It would be one of his stupidest moves to call her now!

There was a 24 hour pizza take away and delivery place he'd used on plenty of occasions when work kept him out until the early hours and he called them now and asked for a 4 cheese special. Opening a bottle of warm beer from a local micro brewery he flicked through the TV channels and found the local late news. A load of pigs had been seen wandering over the countryside north of Brighton. It was unclear exactly how many, or where they had come from but apparently they were largely emaciated. Around fifteen had been caught so far, and due to the poor health of those so far recaptured, around a half would have to be destroyed, said the reporter.
How bizarre the world can be, he thought. Someone must own them.

The doorbell signalled the arrival of the pizza. The delivery guy was paid and Dyson sat down to watch the rest of the late news. His injured eye throbbed and his healthy one was drooping with fatigue so he gave up and went to bed, but couldn't sleep immediately owing to images of the starving, nomadic pigs constantly playing through his mind. Neil Dyson was more into animal welfare than most people he knew. He recalled a minor investigation he'd been part of into an organisation called VOTA. Short for "Voice of the Animal", VOTA was a provincial, largely vegetarian animal welfare group which met every month at one of the members' houses to discuss animal protection, recent RSPCA prosecutions – especially the lessons that might be learned from them - and any ideas for peaceful protest etc. It was described by its members as a "passively determined outfit".

VOTA had successfully campaigned for the temporary closure of a local equestrian stud following reports to the group of cruelty to some of the creatures. At least four of the animals were left in flooded fields throughout the entire winter with no protection from the weather and tethered by short restraining ropes preventing them from even reaching the relative comfort of a hedgerow which would have acted as a windbreak. It was heart breaking to witness the numbed and nervous horses being lead to a warm temporary shelter where two were nurtured back to full health. Sadly the other two were in a very bad way and had had to be destroyed. Such a pointless waste of beautiful, friendly beasts.

VOTA had also been partially successful as catalysts for the authorities to take action against the abuse of animals at a local pig farm. This time VOTA members had been alerted by reports of incessant distressed squeals of the poor creatures as they were maltreated and, according to two ex-employees' statements, habitually beaten for no reason other than "*to get them to move…*". The group had recently put a woman undercover in a cattle slaughterhouse near Pulborough, some twenty miles away, following rumours of killings without first stunning the animals. Such treatment was not only illegal, but also downright unethical and sadistic.

The low level investigation Neil had been involved with had centred on a concern that hard line animal rights activists from London were seeking to infiltrate the group and steer it from its largely investigative and lobbyist stance towards a more action-based organisation. Certainly there had been evidence of a harder line being taken in the local media; full page advertisements had appeared in the local rags accusing a food processing factory of gross cruelty to chickens. The vocabulary had been aggressive and vigilante actions were suggested in the subtext.

This had been the trigger for low-key police involvement and not for the first time Neil's ethics had been challenged in his dealings with the group; the inner conflict between his animal welfare beliefs and the steps the group wanted to take to see justice for domestic animals and wildlife. He had no doubt that the vast majority of members had the best intentions, but it seemed that they were being influenced by the experienced extreme elements. If and when they overstepped the sometimes faint legal line then his duty was first as an upholder of that law. His colleagues ribbed him about his views but he knew that many of them struggled with similar thoughts. In the end it had come to nothing as there was no real evidence of wrongdoing. Intention was not quite the same as deed.

He must have drifted off, because the next thing he was conscious of was the series of piercing beeps from his alarm clock dragging him back to life. With his eye throbbing with every pulse of his heart he struggled out of bed, swallowed a fistful of pain killers and put the kettle on. He was useless in the mornings until he had his first cuppa inside him, and he was a bit of a creature of habit insofar as he would sit with that first brew and read the news on BBC text. Only then could he start to think about breakfast or showering.

The pig story featured again in the local news, along with early commentary about the origins and ownership. Two diametrically opposed so-called experts were debating points of view and opinions. None of this is helping the pigs, Neil thought as he went about his morning routine.

11

'Thank you for coming back to see me Colin. How have you been since we were last together?'

When he usually spoke with Doctor Erikssen, Colin's voice was quiet, almost timid. Today there was an air of pride.

'I have only had three outbursts doctor.'

'Oh that's excellent progress Colin. Tell me about each of those in turn.'

'Well the first was in a hotel er – it's very confidential Doctor.'

'Colin, I think we both know the rules by now; what gets said in therapy stays in therapy.'

'Yes, thank you Doctor, it's just that it's very important this time.'

'Please don't worry, everything is important and it's equally important that we understand what is happening so that we can continue to make such excellent progress. Tell me about the first outburst.'

'It was in a hotel. The cleaners hadn't been following their list - they may not even *use* a list! There was no bath mat and I might have slipped.'

'And did you? Slip I mean.'

'No, I am very careful.'

'But it upset you, the missing bath mat?'

'Yes, of course. It wasn't just the bath mat that was wrong, it was three things; the list wasn't followed-otherwise there would be a mat. The receptionist didn't know the name for bath mat and she was rude when she answered the 'phone.'

'I see. And if it had been just one of these things, or maybe two, you might not have lost your temper?'

'I would have controlled it much better, but they were laughing at me.'

'Who was laughing Colin?'

'The receptionists, Amanda and the other one. I could hear them trying to hide their laughter.'

'And that upset you more than the other things?'

'Well yes of course. It's because of the laughter that I needed to see you again. I am afraid I will explode if I don't manage to control the anger.'

'Are you afraid you might do something bad if you explode Colin?'

'I don't know Doctor. The voices will come and make me think angry things.'

'Have you heard the voices lately Colin?'

'Not really. They just made me kick the door and sweat.'

'Kick the door? Which door?'

Colin realised he'd been close to letting slip a detail he wanted to keep to himself.

'Doesn't matter which door, just a door.'

They talked for another forty minutes along similar lines and at the conclusion Dr Erikssen decided he wanted to prescribe some mood stabilisers for his patient.

'You've been doing so well Colin, but I want you to take some mild medication as clearly there are things going on at the moment which are distressing you and the anger is at risk of re-emerging. '

Colin left with the prescription and the Doctor quickly wrote up his notes from the session. He had a game of golf to get to and he needed to get moving. As a result, the notes were not as comprehensive as they might otherwise have been.

12

As consciousness slowly returned, Babić thought he was laying on an industrial scale Barbecue rack. His head felt as though it had been under a steam hammer and his parched mouth seemed to be caked in dried blood and tasted of vomit. He lay there trying to remember what the hell had happened.

The pig deal…the tall guy – that Furness boy. It slowly came back to him now, the sudden attack, the sickening blow, then vague memories of being dragged across a rough surface, wishing he was dead.

He drifted back into a semi conscious state.

Unseen by Babić, Colin Furness was on his rounds, checking that the cages were all secure.

13

Jenny Marston sat on the edge of her bed painting her toenails a quirky mustard yellow. Neil sometimes joked with her about wasting time on nails that she was only going to cover with thick socks until spring came along. He couldn't seem to grasp her point that she felt naked if her toenails were unpainted. She smiled as she wiped away a rogue drop of varnish with a cotton pad, thinking of her friend Sarah's view;

"Imagine if you have an accident and in the ambulance a hunky medic takes off your socks and sees bare toenails...ugh! I would die of the shame!"

Well, she grinned, Sarah would almost certainly die of shame if she saw nails *this* colour!

Sarah was marrying her fiancé in the summer and Jenny had agreed to meet her and a few friends this afternoon to make plans for venues, music, décor, dresses etc etc etc. Again Neil had scoffed and called it a girly club; god he could be so bloody patronising. But she loved him insanely anyway, his good points were amazing and far outweighed the few stubborn macho bad ones.

She felt a pang of pain for his defeat yesterday; he loved his martial arts and it wasn't often that he lost a tournament, although there had been a few more recently; was he feeling his age at last! He'd definitely be licking his wounds for a day or two and probably be a bit grumpy she expected so she decided to make him his favourite nut roast for dinner when they met later. Jenny was a life-long vegan and had almost converted Neil, although he claimed he'd never be able to relinquish meat all together; "imagine never eating another Full English, and calling that a positive thing!" he would sometimes joke. He did adore her cooking though and she could definitely influence his mood with her nut roast.

As soon as the nail polish had dried she slipped on the aforementioned thick socks and a pair of calf-length boots; she smoothed her knee-length skirt and on her way to the door she checked the mirror. She had never been vain, and Neil said this was one of the things that had attracted him to her; and still did. It never seemed to bother him if she was in worn-out jeans and wellies with her long dark blonde hair tousled and without make-up. But going out with the girls was different. She needed to make an effort. She was petite - Neil called her any number of names, usually the kind found in fairy tales, like "elf", "pixie", "sprite" or worst of all "dwarf" if he really wanted to wind her up. She brushed a rogue hair from her shoulder and although she knew she wasn't the prettiest, was happy enough with how she looked.

She sent Neil a quick text message, saying that she hoped his wounds were not going to stop him coming round tonight, because she was looking forward to rubbing them all better, adding an emoticon of a chuckling devil and a row of kisses.

14

Colin was stood in the huge, purpose-built kitchen in a dreamy and reflective mood. He'd been out riding Vengeance for hours and had then mucked out, groomed and cared for the horse until he realised he needed to push ahead with his other plans. He'd prefer to spend entire days in the company of the huge silent beast, but couldn't afford himself that luxury.

The layout of the kitchen had been one of his key requirements when he'd had the chicken processing plant ripped out and the conversion work done. It had seemed at first to be a huge project, but in reality hadn't been a lot of work, just tearing out most of the existing machinery and some medium-scale interior redesign. The whole job had only taken two months but he'd carefully selected multiple contractors for different phases so that no single company had an idea of the other areas at the facility; they would just know what they needed to in order to complete their specific tasks.

The crowning glory had been the four enormous flat black video screens. It had been a challenge to find the size and scale he wanted but a company which specialised in outdoor events had come up trumps in the end. The result was a modern facility with everything available that he could possibly plan for. And he had planned; night and day for years, fighting his natural urge to get on with the project, knowing that he had to get all his ducks in a row first.

Colin thought about how we use animals in everyday terms like "getting all your ducks in a row" That one was OK, but so often they were offensive, like "flogging a dead horse" or "more than one way to skin a cat". Some people said that not having enough room to "swing a cat" was referring to the Cat-o'-nine-tails but Colin wasn't sure. He thought we should start to use phrases that didn't imply animal cruelty. He had read that some innocent sounding terms were actually based on quite horrid things, such as when people said *"when I kick the bucket"*, referring to when they die, and that sounded OK, except he knew that the "bucket" being referred to was an older English word for a beam or yolk, from which pigs could be strung up and bled or even transported. Slowly dying, they would squeal and kick, and he'd read that the final death throes would be the most desperate and they might kick so high that their legs hit the beam; the "bucket". He resolved to use less offensive terms in future.

He dragged his thoughts back to the present tasks, one of which was food preparation for his disciples. This was the name he's selected for his captives. In his mind they were here to be converted from animal abusers to preachers of the new order; spreaders of the word; disciples.

His long term project to convert society to vegetarianism was reliant on encouraging a significant number of current unbelievers to go out and spread the word. Missionaries, in a sense.
As a child he had been in awe of the great leaders and some of their important quotations, and Lao Tzu's famous *"The journey of a thousand miles starts with one step"* had long been a favourite.
He had heard a song on the radio whilst he had been in the psychiatric clinic and a line from that had become a favourite, it was a singer with the bizarre name of "Sting" and the line *"Men go crazy in congregations, they only get better one by one"* could so neatly be applied to his approach here. He was attempting to convert a crazy congregation, and he'd do it one by one if he had to.

For his plan to succeed his disciples had to become abhorred by the thought of animal abuse and meat eating. During his weeks in the loony bin he'd learned all about the different therapies that can be used and his plan was aversion therapy. He'd build a link in their minds between the maltreatment of a certain animal and its taste. This would be a simple process of showing films of animal cruelty and then serving "that animal" as the day's meal. The meal would consist of his home made pellets and water only. There was no way he was going to use real meat, so he had to produce a vegetarian food which closely resembled each meat group artificially. It had to be good enough to fool them.

Today he was working on pig meat. He needed to make bacon, ham and pork tastes. He hadn't tasted meat for several years, since the last time his father forced him to eat a chicken from his own sheds and Colin had decided that pork was bland, ham was pretty bland too but bacon was very distinctive and was one of the easiest tastes to reproduce, simply because there were commercially available products which he could use, rather than reinventing wheels.

Colin had copied the ingredients list from a pack of vegetarian bacon he'd bought at the local supermarket and for his product he needed eggs, soy bean oil, soy protein, modified corn starch, wheat gluten, glycerine, salt, sodium citrate, sodium phosphate, sugar, torula yeast, caramel and natural smoke flavours, guar gum, malic acid, and a whole lot of vitamin and mineral additives. The latter were not important for taste, but essential to keep his disciples healthy on such a limited diet. He avoided any preservatives and chemical additives normally used by commercial manufacturers of veggie bacon because he didn't need prolonged shelf life and in any case it would be freeze-dried and chilled until used.

He had played around with the ingredients until he found what he considered to be a good resemblance of real bacon and had arranged a steady stream of deliveries of the ingredients, many of which he used in his other meat substitute pellets. It was an expensive way to do things, but for Colin Furness money was no object. He had access now to the entire fortune of his late father, and his bank balance had many digits.

He thought about his father and that fortune and drifted into a daydream.
He was remembering a day when he was around eight years old, his father was alive and they were here on the chicken farm, or rather up in the top part where the farm house now stood empty and the old factory buildings like ghost ships but back then had been a hive of industry where the birds were processed for egg and meat

production. He remembered his father proudly showing him the empire he would one day inherit.

The tall domineering man who was his father was explaining the beginning of the whole process. They were walking around the enormous hatchery where the fertilised eggs were hatched and the chicks roughly sorted into male or female batches. Colin could clearly recall the astonishing cacophony from what seemed like an infinite procession of teeny, pale yellow terrified chicks on an endless conveyor belt feeding them to the greedy machines of the production lines.

"We produce around one hundred and fifty thousand eggs every single day." He was told by the proud and beaming parent waving his arm towards the vast systems of conveyor belts and machines which were essential to make the process efficient.
"You should remember that number; it's the magic number. Anything fewer than 150000 and we won't be able to expand in line with daddy's plan. Any day that we produce more than 150000 is a very very good day. The magic number Colin; one hundred and fifty thousand."

"The chicks here are usually still partly attached to their shells, and travel along this belt into the 'sheller'. This machine gently tumbles the chicks in a drum to separate them from their shells. Once through this they continued to a manual sorting band where these workers sex them. That means they pull out the male chicks and allow the females to continue along the moving belt. The females will mostly become egg producers, the males will almost all be fed into a mincing machine where they are munched into tiny lumps of fluffy meat."

The young boy had some questions
"Why are those ladies being so rough with the tiny chicks Daddy?"
"Well they have to work very quickly my love because daddy wants to make lots of money so he can buy more chickens to feed more people and give more ladies jobs so they can buy nice things for their own children. And I want to buy nice things for you."

Colin thought this seemed very logical and a good thing to do for the people. Applying that logic, he tried to remember a nice thing his father had bought for him, but failed.

"And where are the baby chicks' mummies now?"
The big man laughed and slapped the boy on the shoulder.
"Oh they are all safe in the big sheds my love, making more eggs so we can do the same thing tomorrow and the next day. People wanna eat you know, and if I can make eggs really cheap then they will buy my eggs and not somebody else's!"
The boy seemed satisfied with this explanation.
"And if they buy my eggs we have more chance to hit the magic number...what's the number Colin?"
"One hundred and fifty thousand!"
"Excellent! Excellent!" The big man clapped the boy again on the shoulder. Colin remembered feeling a little proud for the first time in front of his father.

"Why do the boy chicks get thrown into the mincing machine?"
"Well we don't need so many boys son; they can't lay eggs so they are waste in the process."
"Waste?"
"Son; in industry, waste is anything you don't need or can't use or takes up time or effort that you could be spending on useful things. You will learn all these things as you grow up and take on the business from me."
"But why are they minced up when they are alive; doesn't it hurt them?"
The big farmer chuckled.
"Oh gosh no; they don't really have much feeling at that age, they don't understand what pain is so it doesn't affect them-and besides, before they realise what's happening they are squished!"
Colin was suspicious that they might be able to feel pain in the same way he did. He was young too, but it still hurt if he bashed his knee or grabbed a thistle. He dug his fingernails into his arm now to check that pain was still a reality. It was.

71

"Oh look Daddy, there's one on the floor in that machine, it's escaped, is it not feeling the pain from its broken up wings? It looks like it's in pain Daddy."

"Oh the wings are not really important for chickens-they never use them, I always say they were only put there for us to eat something different than breast!" Again the chuckle. As they moved onwards Colin noticed his father hang his leg over the side of the machine and stamp on the tiny ball of fluff.

"Let's look at the beaking line."

They watched as the females went on to be briefly hung by their heads on a rotating rack which fed them past a beak cutter. Under the guidance of a bored-looking employee this cutter removed the tips of their beaks while the pale yellow chicks hung helplessly. Colin observed the bloody stumps that remained on the faces of the tiny birds after this process.

"Why do we cut off their beaks daddy?"

"Well, chickens like to show each other who's boss and because we keep them so close together they would attack each other to get more space and be the boss so we remove the sharp bit."

"But we are cutting off half of their beaks Daddy."

"'Oh it only looks that bad because of the blood and because they are so small. They probably don't feel very much pain in the beak; even though they have a lot of nerves there-it's very quick. It just makes eating a bit uncomfortable for a few days until it heals and the bleeding stops."

"Why don't we just give them more room then Daddy?"

"Well then we are back to what's more important, nice things and food for people, or beaks for baby chickens!" he ushered the boy along a little impatiently.

Colin looked again at the bloody stumps and tried to imagine someone removing half his nose with scissors. He shuddered.

Colin was disturbed and stopped.

"Daddy I don't think I want to see any more animal torture today." His father was clearly cross now:

"What? Torture? My boy, this is standard chicken farming; this happens all over the world. In fact what we have is one of the best farms. You should see some of the American, African and Asian places-now that's torture! But OK, if you want to call it a day for

now let's go and have lunch. Tomorrow we can look at the laying sheds and then the killing lines in detail."

His mind snapped back to the present and he felt relieved to be 'back' in his huge kitchen grinding the frozen veggie bacon product. He mixed it with agar agar, a meat-free gelling agent and some dried, tasteless mineral and vitamin bulk ingredients. He then transferred the lot via conveyor belt into his pelletiser. This was a machine which formed dried bean-sized pellets. When he "cooked" he always made batches of several hundred kilograms; enough for many meals of that particular tasting foodstuff.

Within four hours he had made enough product for his foreseeable needs and set about wrapping it for storage in one of the large drive-in refrigerated cold-rooms. There were six of these in total - legacies of the earlier function of the site. As he closed the last load into the cold-room the house phone rang.

'Mr Furness?'
Yes, hello Mr Abrahams.' Colin had instantly recognised the annoying nasal twang.
'Mr Furness, I have the method to address the matter we spoke about and would like to meet with you to discuss how we might implement that process.'
Abrahams had another annoying habit, Colin realised. He liked to use ten words when two would suffice, and always seemed to choose silly business speak.
'If you mean you know what to do, then please do it. Send me the forms to sign, I am busy.'
'Er, OK. I thought the farm wasn't operating so you'd have time for a meeting. In truth it's a complex series of, er, manipulations which need to take place and you ought to familiarise yourself with the architectural structure so that you have an overview of what's happening to your assets.'
'In truth, Mr Abrahams, the architecture couldn't be more tedious to me if it was yawning and reading me War and Peace in a monotone, I don't want to know *how* it works, just *that* it works. Let me know your fee and send me the forms.'

The silence on the end of the line told Colin that the message had been received.

'Er, OK Mr Furness; will do. I'll have the paperwork in the post this afternoon, recorded delivery, for your signatures. Please return them in a similar vein. Thank you and good luck with, er, War and Peace hahaha.'

Colin replaced the receiver, shaking his head.

15

As predicted, the regular morning briefing was already under way when Detective Inspector Neil Dyson reached the police station at 09.00. He waved an apology to Detective Sergeant Dave "Sicknote" Harrison who had been leading the meeting in his absence. Harrison had earned the nickname during a period of ill health which had begun with a nasty chest infection, followed by an unrelated ear infection and capped off with an operation to expand the constricted airways through his nose and sinuses. In all he had been off work for five weeks, a period viewed as excessive by his police colleagues and the typical humour that exists in many close-knit teams prevailed with a presentation ceremony, (including the playing of a poorly rehearsed and atonal kazoo fanfare), of a framed A3 sized replica of a doctor's note giving the reason of absence as *"Daytime-TV-it is"* and the length of expected time away from his post as *"until all the celebrity chefs have beaten all the motorway cops to all the pointless prizes".* The trophy had pride of place on Harrison's office wall.

Despite this reputation, Sicknote was recognised by the men and women in the room as a highly competent officer who had a talent for getting himself "into the criminal zone" as his colleagues referred to his ability to see the world from the eyes of the crook and he had guided some investigations along paths that might not otherwise have been taken. He was also known for his outspoken humour and incessant practical jokes.

Sicknote Harrison had finished the preliminaries - an update of news and minor incidents throughout the last 24 hours - and was about to get into the meat of the meeting. This was where the team were briefed on any significant matters which would be likely to become the primary focus for the shift and usually beyond that.

'Good contest yesterday then Sir? Asked Carol.
All heads were looking at Dyson's already yellowing and blood-shot eye.
'You should see the other guy Carol' Neil quipped to titters from his colleagues.
'You obviously didn't' grinned Sicknote 'well, not until it was too late' He laughed. More open titters from the room.
'You wanna take over Guv?'
'Oh you go ahead Sicknote, you're doing fine and you're more in the loop than me in any case!'
Sicknote continued.

'Onwards people. We all know it's been surprisingly quiet for a week or so, and so do the top brass, which is why we've been asked to support a missing person case. It relates to a German male by the name of Hans-Werner Fromm. Report was made by his girlfriend, who last saw him at around 06.30 yesterday when he left their shared apartment for work. His colleagues confirm that he attended his IT company office in Brighton as usual and left much earlier than his normal 18.00 as he was heading for an Arsenal match which kicked off at 19.45 at the Emirates Stadium in North London.

This guy is not assessed as high risk, but his disappearance is completely out of character, there's an international angle and most significantly the girlfriend is friendly with the chief's daughter so we need to play the game on this one and help locate the guy quick sharp.'

There were muted coughs around the room.
Neil spoke up; 'Does the girlfriend who reported him missing work in the café on East Street?'

'Yes Guv, how did you know that?'
'Just a wild guess…'
Sicknote stared at Dyson with a puzzled frown but decided to leave any further probing until they were alone later.

'Usual form please guys; details of friends or relatives, places he is known to frequent, health or medical conditions, financial stuff-anything notable happening in his wallet, DNA sample-someone grab his toothbrush. Let's get a couple of recent photographs and find out any events that could be linked with his vanishing act.'

Sicknote looked around at the bored looking faces.

'Hardly Sherlock Holmes stuff I know, but until we get some juicy mass murders let's earn our keep. Need to check records from the stadium ticket office and with his credit card company, but if he paid cash it may prove difficult to verify whether he was in fact there. There is limited CCTV in the ground but we need to check that out please Carol.'
Carol, a tall, blonde 30-something DC nodded her head and jotted a note in her book.

'Check out the footage on the approaches to the gates too, if he was there he might be recognisable; copies of his photo will be rushed through once we have them, let's all have one in our pockets or handbags.'
'That's a big ask Guv' Carol frowned, looking at Neil.
'What? Sticking a pic in your handbag? Feel free to remove mine if you're worried about the old man finding too many strange blokes lurking in your secret depths.'
'No Sarge, I couldn't live without seeing your gorgeous smile every time I go for my tampons! I meant checking all the CCTV.'
Dyson joined the chuckles around the room as Sicknote replied.
'Good to hear it. But you'll be able to eliminate 20% of the faces you need to scrutinise immediately Carol.'
'How so?'
'Cos they'll be the Dortmund fans wearing black and yellow scarves' he chirped with his customary cheeky grin. 'Only leaves you about 35000 faces swathed in red and white to scrutinise - piece of cake!'

'All right, get onto that straight away please Carol' Dyson had respect for Sicknote, but didn't want his penchant for light-hearted banter to get in the way of the job. Without appearing to take the reins, Neil moved to the centre of the room and instantly dominated the space. Within that simple movement he had taken over the meeting. He'd also spotted a flaw in Sicknote's logic.

'Thought you said he's a Dortmund fan Sicknote? In that case he will be wearing yellow and black, so Carol won't need to check any of your 35000 fizzogs bedecked in red and white, she's only interested in that 20% of the faces you quoted surely?'
Sicknote blushed and Carol gave a mock cheer.

'Yay, only ten thousand mugshots to compare. Thanks Guv!'
'That's gratitude for you! OK, Sicknote – can you have a chat with the girlfriend and see what light she can throw on the guy's disappearance-not sure our uniformed friends will have taken her through the details as thoroughly as you might. Use your considerable charm and see if there's anything the plods might have missed.'
'Cool-shall I take her for dinner on expenses; you know, relax her and get her to confess that she did him in because she was desperate to get some face to face time with me?'
A groan went around the room which was quickly hushed by the DI.
'If you can get that out of her Sergeant Harrison then you're even better than your reputation. Either that, or completely delusional.'
The laughter this time was stronger and a light applause accompanied Sicknote's embarrassed chuckle.

DI Dyson was keen to wrap up the meeting and spoke quickly with one of the detective constables.
'We need to open a case file Brian. We'll need a case name too. Come on Sicknote, you're always the genius with these.'

Sicknote spoke up: 'How about "*Verschwunden*"? It means "missing" in German.'
Dyson looked around the room with mock despair on his face.
'I suggest we keep to an English word that we all understand and will cause no offence if things escalate.'

"Project Arsenal's out then' Said Sicknote grinning.
'I sense another moment of genius coming' Groaned Carol 'go on; Sarge, enlighten us'
'Well if it all goes tits up the chief will have your arse and my arse 'n' all'

'Very droll Sicknote. Now, if I can drag this meeting out of the kindergarten please.' The frustration was clear in Dyson's face and the room settled down.

'We'll give it the highly imaginative yet functional title of the Hans-Werner Fromm missing person case for now' said Dyson. 'If and when it changes we'll review that ground breaking decision.'

The meeting wound up with a notice about a high level visit later in the week and the preparation that had to be done to ensure everything was spic and span.

16

Diary entry 3
March 5th

Dear father
A sucksessful day
Just been riding Vengeance, he is so powerful and yet so gentle, very much like me really.

More sucksess in the facility too, even though the people I am getting are not always those I planned to take, they are just right for what I need and my plan is beginning to take shape; feel free to start to feel a measure of pride, however much it hurts.

By the way, I ment to tell you, I dismantled your horror show as my first job and sacked all those evil basterds that did your filthy work. They wanted to take some kind of legal action but it won't happen, they are finished with abusing animals here.
Your son
Colin

PS – your accountant is almost as ethical as you were, as a pair you must have been a match made in heaven.
Oh-and I am worried about the German; he hasn't regained conshousness yet…never mind, one less sausage scoffer on the planet.

17

Babić re-awoke and looked around, wondering again where the hell he was. It was pretty dark but some diffused light from a huge TV screen was spilling across the murkiness and he could make out that he seemed to be in a cage that was stacked on top of two others and surrounded by more to his left and behind him.

The hammering inside his skull was on the edge of being unbearable, and he felt sick from the pain. There was a film running on the giant screen to his left and then he noticed a similar screen behind him. The film was showing pigs in some kind of farm building, not unlike those that might be seen in his native Serbia. Some sows were lying in narrow bays. He knew these conditions well, they were gestation crates where pregnant sows would be confined for the entire four months of their pregnancy and with insufficient room to stand properly or move. They were unable to see their fellow creatures and one was trying to take chunks out of the thick steel tube barriers with her teeth. Babić knew that insanity eventually came to such creatures when kept in this way, but the profits were higher than when animals were allowed to roam freely. It was so much easier to manage them and avoid them injuring each other. He knew that once they had given birth they would be artificially inseminated again and stay in the same tiny pen. Well he seemed to be in a similar situation right now. True, he could just about move and turn around, but the wire bit into his skin uncomfortably and he envied the pigs their solid concrete floor, even if they would prefer mud.

He wondered what time it was. The room was too dark to see much, but the huge screens gave some illumination. He had no idea how long he'd been knocked out but guessed it couldn't have been long, although clearly it was dark now.

He vaguely registered a clanking sound beginning some distance away and he assumed that this was machinery outside the building he was in. He couldn't see if the other cages were occupied but sensed rather than saw a figure in the cage below him. Suddenly the place was awash with bright white light and simultaneously a rattling noise from above him was heard and a small pile of dry grey pellets shot from a chute beside his right arm. He had no idea what these were but assumed they might be food. He heard a scrabbling below and saw that one of the cages contained a woman. She was grabbing fistfuls of the pellets and hoarding them in a small pile. Babić hadn't eaten since France and at first gingerly, then with more gusto he began to nibble at the pellets. They tasted of bacon and he was soon cramming his mouth full of the little grey nodules.

A loud crackling sound cut through the other noises and a booming voice echoed around the place.
'Honoured guests! Disciples! New arrivals! Welcome to your rehabilitation programme. You are the first of many who will grace this facility and if you apply yourselves you could be amongst the first to leave. I am sorry that you cannot see me right now, but rest assured I am watching you from my control centre.'

Indeed Colin was doing just that. From a large control room about twenty feet up the fifty foot high side wall of the main barn he could look through a panoramic window which had originally been installed in the chicken factory to allow supervisors to watch over the entire shop-floor. Alternatively, he could use any number of the fifty two infra-red capable CCTV cameras that covered the farm. In essence, he was voyeur of all he surveyed.

'Each of you has been carefully selected because of the way you have chosen to live your lives. Over the coming weeks we will be examining those choices and you will learn the errors you have been making. I don't *necessarily*....' the word "necessarily" was heavily emphasised '...blame you for some of those choices, but dear people, you have to take the ultimate responsibility.'

'The simple truth of choice is this; you can choose which car you buy, based on the colour, performance of the engine-and hopefully the ethical policies of the manufacturer. You can choose which flavour crisps you eat, or which music CD you will listen to. You can choose an almost infinite number of things, but you cannot simply choose to kill a living creature. That's not about choice, that's primitive - in every sense of the word - and wholly barbaric.'

'I shall leave you now to enjoy your meal of pelletised pig fat. It will probably taste disgusting – indeed I hope it does. Mealtimes will form an essential part of your re-education so learn the lessons well.'

'I have to apologise for any injuries you may have suffered during your capture and your journey here but in time you will come to see that it's for the greater good. Now eat and try to be comfortable in your battery homes. Any comforts you may experience now may be short-lived. Once you begin to act as the brutes you clearly are then you shall learn how unpleasant the life of an animal in our society; *your* society....' again the emphasis '...can be.' Over time I shall break down those behaviours; take you apart and re-align your ethical compasses.'

Babić heard a woman's voice scream from directly beneath him. 'You fucking freak, let me out or I'll make sure you swing for this you bastard.'
Unseen, the tall man did a little dance that seemed as if one foot were glued to the floor and the other was playing hopscotch around it: The PA system crackled again.
'Donna! Lovely to hear you have feelings after all, you sicky sicky girl. Well, shout as loud as you like; no - in fact as loud as you can! There isn't a soul within ten miles and I love the sound of desperation when it comes from murderers. I have heard so much of the other kind of desperation; the sort that comes from the innocent. You will have heard it too, from the little creatures you murder. But you didn't listen to them; not once. So I am going to ignore your pleas just as you did them.'

In his control room Colin began to sweat and spittle formed in the corners of his mouth. He muted the microphone momentarily.
'Fucking shitbitch.' He muttered.
He flicked the switch back to "live".

'But how rude of me, I should introduce you to each other - after all, we will be spending some considerable time in each other's company and you lucky people in the lower levels will probably become quite familiar with the bowel movements of your upper neighbours. In time I may rotate you, so that everyone gets a balanced view. You'll learn to see life from the perspective of the animals you and your type so thoughtlessly confine. I do hope it is purely thoughtlessness that allows you to do these hideous things; although I suspect in your case Donna there is more to it.'

He continued.
'You see; if somebody just doesn't think about the bad things they do, well it's almost excusable; certainly it's understandable. If they maybe don't realise just how badly-kept these living, breathing, *thinking* creatures are, then such behaviour can be corrected; and we shall do that. But for those of us who *knowingly* opt to maltreat other creatures....well the road to salvation shall be an arduous one I guess.'

Colin was becoming more animated and his words spilled quickly through the speakers.
'But it's not just in life; if you have never been to a slaughter house maybe you are just ignorant of the pain and suffering we put these poor creatures through at the end of their short existence. Bred for weight gain, held in intolerable conditions and then butchered brutally and painfully. No my friends, I can understand your ignorance but I will not allow it to continue. As I say, together we can cure you. But Donna; if somebody is sick, I mean sick enough to think that animal skins are her trophies, prizes, fashion articles.....well, that's a different mental position and I think you and I will be spending a lot of time working one to one.'

'For the rest of us, we shall be holding a number of group therapy sessions. Talking to each other about the mistakes we have made, the rotten thoughts we have towards animal welfare and the way that, through our support of the meat industry, we have become part of the problem. When looking at where the blame for this abuse and torture lies, remember this dear people; as soon as we decide to stick our dining fork into that piece of steak we become complicit in all the abuse that has gone before.'

The speaker system fell silent as Colin switched off the amplifiers and made his way quickly from the building. He had a rendezvous planned with an old acquaintance …
Babić hadn't fully understood the depth of this rant, but he certainly got the gist. He tried to quantify the situation he was in, but his simple mind didn't have the wherewithal and instead he collapsed to the wire mesh floor in confusion and head-splitting pain. He tried to think of someone at home who would notice his absence, but there was nobody. He had divorced his wife years ago, had never bothered with his children since; his friends were just vague acquaintances and he realised now that his life was pretty much devoid of meaningful relationships. Probably Zolt, the barman at his local pub, would be the only one to notice that he wasn't at his customary stool tonight. He groaned at the desperation of it. Here he was, in a foreign land, held captive by a crazy, unsure why and nobody knew he was here. On top of that he was battered and bruised and needed a doctor and something for the intolerable pain. It didn't get worse than this. He thought.

The woman below was screaming again and he tried to block out the noise but it cut through his pain.
'Shut up stupid woman.' He shouted, the noise of his own voice causing pain like driving a steel spike through the side of his head. 'I need to sleep. Let me sleep.'
With that he turned onto his side and pulled his coat up around his ears.

18

During his detailed planning sessions, Colin had thought about ways to immobilise his potential disciples at the point of kidnap. The hammer was so brutal and indiscriminate, he wanted to trial the use of his father's old bolt gun as a stunning device in certain situations; there was a delicious irony in that. Cattle were normally rendered unconscious with one or two hits, horses and smaller creatures would usually be killed if the weapon was used accurately and he thought that using it on a human skull would certainly kill; if the bolt didn't penetrate the skull he was sure that swelling of the brain would be fatal eventually.

The gun consisted of a captive bolt, driven out of the end of the barrel by an explosive charge. The beauty was that the bolt was an integral part of the weapon, which made it unlike other firearms, and the small explosive charges he used were fixed in a small rotating circular clip, so there were no discarded bullet casings to be found as evidence. As long as he didn't lose any of those clips he was high and dry. More importantly, there were no discharged rounds to be collected for forensic analysis at scenes of crime. Scenes of crime...he shook his head; he was committing no crimes, he was educating a criminal world, adjusting behaviour and raising the ethical bar. He was distressed that many would see his activities as criminal, when in his mind, and in that of anyone with any intelligence, surely, what he believed put him in the "good camp". The expression "One man's meat is another man's poison" was very apt, and he was sure that in time he would be hailed the hero of modern thinking, the father of animal welfare. Even so, for now he had to follow his plan, and the whole discussion about firearms was a moot one; his aim was to take people alive and convert them; corpses were of no use to his cause. Right now, he had one specific target.

Wilkins the Butcher was doing a roaring trade and was quite relieved to be nearing the end of a hectic day. Ted Wilkins had been cutting up carcasses for over forty years and his father had done so for fifty years before him. They had a reputation for high quality local meat and were favoured by the residents of the bigger houses and by the restaurants and hotels in the surrounding area.

Colin's father had been a regular customer and Colin had Ted Wilkins firmly on his list of people who, having done so much harm to animals in the past, would be devoting a significant element of their future to putting that right.

Colin, sitting in his old Land-rover across the road watched as the last customer of the day vacated the store and Ted Wilkins shuffled around his shop, carrying stainless steel trays which had earlier displayed limbs, bellies, organs, Colin knew not what other remnants of a short and tragic life, for the discerning public monsters to feast their semi-lascivious eyes upon.

The area was quiet now and a final check of its mechanism told Colin that the old bolt gun was ready to fire. Slipping the gun into his big jacket pocket, and keeping his right hand around the pistol grip Colin climbed out of the vehicle, pushed the door softly to and jogged to the shop door just as Ted was about to lock it from the inside.

'Sorry young Mr Furness, Sir; we're just locking up.'
 The butcher called through the closed door.
'Oh I know that Ted, I actually wanted to ask you a quick favour.'
The old man rolled his eyes and reluctantly opened the door and looked up into Colin's face as the tall visitor indicated with a gesture that they should go through to the back of the shop.
'What can I do for you young Colin?'
'Well, we are thinking of holding a small gathering up on the farm and I recall some of those incredible hog roasts you used to arrange for my father'.
'Ah yes. It's been a year or two since we did anything like that for you. How many people are you catering for and when are you thinking of? Come through the cold room to the office.'

They had crossed the shop with its original Victorian tiled floor which always made Colin's heart beat faster since the day his father had explained to him that it was tiled so that the blood could be easily cleaned away when it dripped from the carcasses suspended from the huge meat hooks that were still used to display their macabre wares in the shop window. Colin gripped the bolt gun in his pocket as he moved behind the old man into the chilled storage area. Colin hated this place and wanted to get out. He knew he'd have to be quick to disable the butcher and gripped the gun as they walked through the chilled chamber.

'I keep this little office door locked because I only bank once a week and all the takings are in the safe in here.' The old man explained as they approached the closed door. Jangling a large bunch of keys, the white-coated man stooped to insert one into the keyhole.

Colin stepped quickly forward, removing the weapon from his pocket, finger inside the trigger-guard, ready for action. He wasn't sure how powerful the weapon would be on a human skull and thought that if he held it against the old man's head the bolt would be driven clean through his cranium; that would spell disaster. He leaned forward and held the barrel just a few millimetres away from the base of the old man's skull and pulled the trigger, expecting a loud explosion in the confined space.
Instead he heard the sound of failure; a sharp click, more like a finger snap than the gunshot he was expecting. Reacting to the malfunction, Colin thrust the weapon back into his pocket and stepped quickly away from the stooping figure.

Wilkins looked around stiffly to where Colin now stood, adjusting his jacket.
'Whatever was that?'
Colin raised his eyebrows quizzically.
'What was what?'
'Thought I heard something falling, must be my hearing aid playing up again, really must get it looked at.'

Colin hated the fucking bolt gun. He squeezed his hand tightly around the pistol grip as if trying to inflict pain onto it and tried to think what to do now; reload the charge and try again or abandon the plan? He wouldn't get another opportunity easily so he turned aside to cover his actions and quickly withdrew the gun and examined the charge while the butcher was still pissing around with the bunch of keys.

'It's one of these!' Chuckled the old man

Colin grunted as if he were paying attention, whilst focussing solely on getting the gun ready. He saw a small wad of fabric had become caught between the hammer and the charge capsule; it looked like a piece from his jacket pocket and it must have become caught as he had extracted the gun prior to his attack.

He freed the material and eased back the cocking lever ready for another try.

'Aha!' The old man slowly raised himself upright and half-turned towards Colin as if in triumph, pushing the door open.

A sudden series of knocks from the front of the shop had Colin hurriedly stuffing the bolt gun back into his pocket.

'Ah! My daughter, she is early. Let me open the door for her then we can quickly take down the details for you young Mr Furness'.

Colin tried to hide his anger and disappointment.

'Oh it doesn't matter, it's not for ages, I'll come back another day.'

Colin rushed through the old shop, pushing past the slightly bemused daughter and walked quickly across the road, head down, to the land-rover. Once inside he sat and swore continually for several minutes, his voice rising as the anger and frustration continued to build until spittle formed at the sides of his mouth and he was spraying the inside of the flat windscreen with each expletive.

He took the bolt gun from his pocket and smashed the barrel down hard across the metal rod of the handbrake repeatedly, foul words accompanying each blow. He knew he was damaging the weapon and the handbrake but was unable to control the outburst of violence. For a moment he contemplated bursting back into the butchers and downing both man and girl. He had a sudden, unbidden image of their two cadavers hanging on the meat-hooks for all the world to see, naked, pale and limp.

Gradually the moment passed and Colin began to quieten. He forced himself to breathe deeply and regularly and he slowly unclenched his hands, which had been gripping gun and steering wheel so tight that the circulation to his fingers had been cut. His temper slowly evaporated and his pulse calmed.

He reflected on the failure of his mission and tried to judge how big an impact it might have on his plans. Deciding it wasn't such a disaster, at least he'd got away without arousing suspicion; just. But he hated failure; all his plans had been so well rehearsed except the bit where the firing mechanism snagged on the pocket fabric. That was what angered him the most, the stupidest, most simple mistake had nearly jeopardised the whole project. He'd have to be doubly careful from now on.

Checking his watch, he realised he had time now to go to the VOTA meeting, which he hadn't anticipated making, due to the planned kidnap of Wilkins. He started the engine and slowly drove towards the house of the Smalling family.

19

Sally and Adrian Smalling were hosting the monthly *Voice of the Animal* or VOTA meeting and turnout was good. There were fifteen people crammed into their normally spacious kitchen/diner, including the new couple from London. She didn't like the tone of some of their messages, way too extreme for her, but they seemed popular with the others. The group often invited someone from another organisation to make a small informal presentation to the group, and such events proved popular, indeed turnout was higher than usual today and may have been on account of the visit by the leader of the nearest mosque, Imam Farouk El Hamidiri. Farouk was going to speak on the subject of Halal slaughter and animal welfare.

'Ladies and gentlemen, dear fellow VOTArians; tonight as I am sure you all know we are lucky to be able to bring Dr Farouk El Hamidiri into our fold to explain some of the cultural, religious and ethical issues faced by Muslims who wish to eat meat. Farouk leads prayers at the mosque and is a spokesman for the local Muslim community in many matters. I don't want to pre-empt anything Farouk is going to tell us so without further ado I give you Doctor Farouk El Hamidiri.'

There was a smattering of applause and a slight, light skinned Arab man edged slowly to the front of the group.

'Thank you, Sally. As we all know, in many religions there are very strict rules on meat slaughter and consumption. The Jews forbid consumption of Pork or Shellfish, Hindu Brahmins don't eat *any* meat or eggs, nor do many Buddhists. I think we all know that Muslims have similar restrictions and requirements and I am sure that some of these seem alien to Christians and… (here he paused almost imperceptively) ….non-believers.'

91

But when one takes on the responsibility of religion – and it *is* a responsibility – then one is obliged to live by the codes and ethics laid down in the relevant holy writings and historical practices. In the end, we will all be held to account by our God, and it would be a foolish man who took such a responsibility lightly.'

With a serious look on his face Farouk paused to survey the room. He had been very unsure about this evening; the group had a reputation for unearthing animal welfare malpractice in an objective and balanced way, but he had seen the recent promotional campaigns which had added to his reticence. However, people had legal and moral rights as well as responsibilities and as the leader of the local Islamic community, in his eyes the role of educator and mediator between that community and those around who had other beliefs fell to him. He had to tread carefully here to ensure that these people understood the unconditional demands of his religion and could reconcile those with their own beliefs. He was comforted to see no open hostility; he had anticipated worse.

Smiling a little now, he continued.

'Let's be honest, we are all here this evening to discuss animal welfare; you represent the moral high ground and I am the bad guy!' he made a face like someone trying to balance a pencil on their top lip and raised his shoulders in a shrug amongst mild chortles.

'But seriously, there are many misconceptions about the way animals are slaughtered under Halal and Kosher rules. The most important things are that the flesh is clean and that the animal is treated with respect and suffers no pain. Indeed, it is in our own interests not to distress the animal, because an animal can injure itself if it becomes frightened and an injured animal can no longer be considered pure. Such a beast would be a waste-we could not eat it.'

He paused to sip from a glass of water beside him and one of the group interjected.

'Dr Farouk; my name is Brian Connolly and I have a question about your definition of clean.'

'Well, Brian, the definition is not mine; it comes from the holy words of Allah and really relates to the absence of blood, which is seen as contaminated. I am sure there are parts of an animal that you will never eat' He raised his eyebrows in mock horror. 'It is really little different.' he smiled at Brian.

'Well, there are lots of parts of an animal that I won't eat – I am vegan!'
There was laughter and again Farouk smiled.
'Well then we are well-aligned – neither of us wants to drink an animal's blood nor eat its dirty bits! But seriously, Brian raises an important point and with your permission I will expand a little?'
Farouk took some more water.

'It can be very complicated to try to cover all major religious eating laws, but simply put, when it comes to meat it is the Islam and Judaic faiths which have the stringent rules. Both Jewish and Islamic laws prohibit the consumption of carrion, swine, insects, rodents and blood. Carrion is any animal that has died, other than in the name of Allah, and this is why we prefer to not stun animals before slaughter, because if they should die from the stunning, then they will become Haram, or bad. Also, any food that is poisonous or immediately harmful to the human body is not allowed. Islamists follow the Sharia, which really means Islamic law or ethic; for Jews it is the Halakhah. All solid food items prohibited by the *Sharia* are also prohibited in Jewish law. There are lengthy and ongoing debates about gelatine and also rennet, which is used in cheese production. There is even Kosher wine because the clearing of wine and beer often needs gelatine. Those lucky Jews are thus allowed to take alcohol, but we, the poorer cousins must live a life on Earth unknowing.' He smiled.
'Cheers doc!' Came a shouted toast from the back, followed by at least ten echoes as glasses were raised in the speaker's direction.

'Haha! Yes cheers indeed. But we digress. The important question was raised by our friend here – I am sorry Sir, I forgot your name?'
'Brian.'
'Ah yes – thank you Brian. Brian's important question about what is clean meat and why. Well the two holy laws I mentioned are where the requirements come from. They are similar, and yet have subtle differences. Once we understand the Islamic and Jewish procedures for slaughtering meat we are able to determine its status. Jewish and

Islamic law both require that the animal is alive when it is slaughtered. In particular, Jewish law, my friends, is very definite in that stunning or other procedures to render the animal unconscious should not be used, according to teachings. We Muslims are somewhat divided on that point because a stunned animal might be unconscious for ten seconds - long enough to be killed – and thus be "living at the point of slaughter"'

'Murder you mean!'
Farouk looked up sharply to see who had spoken and saw a tall, hairless man near the back of the room glaring at him.
'Murder is involving humans my friend, not animals. Animals are slaughtered' He responded. He was prone to clenching his jaw at times of nervousness, stress and agitation and he did that now whilst looking into the eyes of the tall man.
'Pray allow me to continue. It is also required that only trained slaughtermen do the job, and they must understand all the religious requirements and must dedicate the kill to Allah. This is most important.'
'Most primitive you mean.' The same voice, this time a little louder and Farouk noted that the tall guy had edged a little closer to him. The voice continued.
'How can anyone think animals don't cry? That they don't feel pain? What moron could believe such shit, even a school child will tell you.'

'Please Colin, let Farouk finish, and then we can ask him questions at the end, I'm sure he won't mind.' This was Adrian Smalling, and he was wringing his hands together as if drying them under some invisible hand dryer.
'Of course I shall be happy to answer all reasonably put questions Adrian.'
The Muslim leader continued for a short time longer explaining the other key points required under Sharia law and finishing with a few words about which internal parts of the animal must be severed and which may not.

'We Muslims are proud of the way we treat our beasts but I must tell you that in parts of the United Kingdom it is not easy to find a proper Halal slaughterhouse; one where the organisation, people and methods meet the strict needs of the Muslim. Even the design is important; in Islamic law a beast should be facing Qiblah when it is killed. This is the direction towards Mecca; it is not essential that the animals look to this place, but I am sure I can taste which ones did.' He finished with a broad smile and placed the palms of his hands together as if in prayer.

'My dear people, I have talked long enough and I am sure you will have some questions for me. We can either take those collectively, or we can talk privately afterwards. Thank you for your respectful attention.'
The Arab sought eye contact with Colin, and in making it Colin was unsure whether he was being challenged in some way.

There was polite applause and Adrian Smalling looked at his wife and spoke out.
'Thank you so much for that interesting insight Farouk. I am sure our members enjoyed your views and, as you say, will have a number of questions. If I might take the opportunity to put a point to you?'
'Please, go ahead Adrian.'
'OK. Well, The Farm Animal Welfare Council in the UK make strong claims that both Halal and Kosher slaughter causes unbearable suffering and pain for the animals. You brushed over the issue of pain; who is right, and why?'
'Ah, well we should be very cautious; sometimes people are really setting out with a very different agenda and want to discredit Muslims wherever they think they can. The truth is that the single deep cut to the throat drains blood instantly from the brain. Starved of this blood the brain shuts down within 2 seconds and there is virtually no pain.' Farouk raised his hands as if he had performed a great conjuring trick and beamed at his audience.

'*Virtually* no pain?' This from Sally
Farouk laughed. 'Well pain is difficult enough to quantify in humans; it would be a nonsense to expect an animal to be able to give us a score out of ten, but if we follow these very strict rules then we are as sure as we can be that suffering is very very short-lived. Who knows, maybe one day scientists will learn that vegetables

95

experience pain when we pull them from the mother plant, then slice and peel them-not to mention boiling them alive!' A look of delight was fixed upon his face and he clapped his hands together in celebration of a point well made.

'Farouk; my name is Colin Furness. I am vegetarian. Firstly let's clarify one thing; vegetables, plants in general have no pain receptors. Nor do they have a central nervous system. It is therefore impossible for a plant to feel pain and a childish trick to try to twist facts in such a way. Secondly, if Kosher and Halal animals are not stunned, no reasonable person can claim that their slaughter causes the animal no pain. That is clearly idiotic and you should not be wasting your time trying to spread your lies to us. Instead you ought to be addressing this unacceptable practice within your own community. Thirdly; I understand that the general population may be eating meat slaughtered in this barbaric manner unwittingly. Is it true that this fruit of torture is sitting on our supermarket shelves alongside meat slaughtered in more acceptable ways?'

'Please please, let us resist the temptation to isolate Muslims from followers of Western ideals and please do not describe the methods of slaughter we have been outlining as barbaric. These methods have been followed for thousands of years in the Arabic and Judaic worlds and are an essential pillar of our respective religious cultures.'

Colin continued to press the speaker.
'You are evading the questions; how can you prove there is no suffering and are the general population of UK carnivores eating meat from tortured animals? Let me put it a different way; Do you have family?'
The Arab looked wary.
'Yes. I have a wife and two sons, but they are currently on an extended holiday in India. What is your point?' The guest was clearly becoming agitated, his jaw visibly clenching and releasing now, giving the impression that he was rapidly chewing gum.

'My point Mr El Hamidiri is this; if they were to die from a slit throat, would you rather they died in an unconscious state, or would fully conscious, hung on a chain upside down by one arm with a deep, vicious cut to the throat be your preference?'

The guest speaker shrugged his shoulders and raised his open palms 'What kind of bizarre point are you trying to make sir? Are you comparing the life and feelings of a dumb creature to those of a high functioning member of the human species?' he looked around the room for tacit support but found only open-mouthed expectation on the gathered faces.

Furness raised his voice and pressed home his initiative.
'Here's my final word doctor. Our discussion takes us away from the core issue. Here we are discussing whether animals can feel pain. You say they cannot, which is frankly ridiculous, and I say they can. The argument is so one-sided that I don't understand how you can even look yourself in the eye. But as I said, the focus is in the wrong place; we should not be discussing whether this way or that way is the right way; we should not be killing animals at all.'

'I shall answer your question in very simple terms; I would prefer that my family were not slaughtered at all.'

'Ah! The penny drops. You have dug yourself into a hole dear Doctor because you are right, the slaughter should not take place at all; there *is* no right way to do the wrong thing'

Colin silently fumed. But the soothing voice of Doctor Erikssen seemed to come from nowhere and was urging calm. With considerable self-control he was able fight through the fog that was his mind in such situations and step back from the brink.

Sally spoke up.
'Goodness me gentlemen. What are you thinking? Tonight was supposed to be a civilised discussion about these things, let us not let it deteriorate into a philosophical verbal boxing match.'

'Well I too am a little disappointed Sally.' Said Farouk. 'It's an emotive subject and I have allowed myself to be drawn into arguments which I have little influence over. If I were honest with you' he addressed Colin 'I would probably prefer to see animals stunned too, but it's decided by a far higher power than I shall ever get close to and I do as my God bids.'

Colin lifted his right hand in a semi-wave; looked towards his feet and shaking his head from side to side spoke up
'No no Doctor El Hamidiri; I should never have put you on the spot in that way and I do apologise. I hope you can accept my act of contrition and not think bad of the group assembled here. We all have our passions but as you say, we are powerless to change the world, even though we might dream of doing that. Let us please forget the whole thing and enjoy the fact that we are all different.'

 A hubbub of multiple conversations sprang up around the room as people began to gravitate towards the drinks and snacks table and to dissect what had just happened. Unnoticed, Colin slipped from the room, left the house and went to sit in his Land-rover. There he waited in the dark, listening to the machine gun rattle of the incessant rain on the roof until the other group members started to emerge. Due to the rain he was invisible to the casual eye, and he had to have the screen ventilation running on the car battery to avoid a complete fog on the windscreen. He sat impassively watching as, one by one, the people left Sally and Adrian's house. The last to leave, with much shaking of hands and hugging was the Muslim. Colin found it all a little theatrical and pretentious. Hatred for the man and all that he stood for burned through his veins.

Finally Farouk took his leave and hurried to his car, head bowed against the driving torrent and waving one hand blindly over his shoulder as he opened the door and climbed in. When he started to roll forward Colin started his own engine and with lights off he tracked the Peugeot along the lane leading towards the main road. Colin knew the roads round here exceptionally well; this was home turf for him and the winding lane soon allowed him to turn on his lights and trail El Hamidiri from a far enough distance without revealing himself. Once on the main road Colin held the rear lights of the Muslim's car in sight and was able to follow him at a distance without arousing suspicion.

He felt desperate for sleep but knew he had work to do. Tonight his facility would become multi-cultural.

20

Despite heavy rain Farouk drove quickly from the house. He was annoyed that he had allowed the rude guy to get under his skin, but he hadn't expected an easy ride and it could have been worse, and at least the moron had apologised publicly, he reflected. As he negotiated the many bends in the narrow lane he felt he needed a reward for the stressful time and once on the main road started looking for a shop that might still be open. After some three miles he spied a small 24 hour store and stopped there to grab some chocolate. Chocolate was his only real frailty, and he would eat it whenever he felt he needed a pick-me-up; it achieved much the same as prayer, and was the only "vice" he knew that could be satisfied anywhere and at pretty much any time of the day or night.

Praying was a little less convenient; he lived in a remote cottage and his own mosque was some distance away so he often had to pray wherever he could. He enjoyed the peace that the countryside isolation gave, but since his appointment as Imam he'd planned to move closer to the mosque. He felt he needed to pray now, although the official night prayer of Isha was long gone and Fajr was hours away.

After a further drive of ten minutes or so he arrived home and grabbed the small bar of chocolate. Once inside he filled the kettle and went to run a bath and whilst the water ran into the tub he made a cup of chamomile tea. As he opened the chocolate bar he was surprised by a knock at the front door; it was well after ten and he expected nobody. This, and the fact that he was so isolated out here made him cautious, so he switched on the outside light and fitted his door chain before releasing the front-door catch. There in the teeming rain, illuminated by the outside lamp stood the tall guy from earlier in the evening. The Muslim was taken aback and immediately more wary.

'Sorry to disturb you.' Said the tall man 'But I was worried that you thought my apology wasn't genuine so wanted to quickly assure you that I am deeply ashamed of my behaviour earlier.'

He carried something in a white plastic bag which he held semi-aloft towards Farouk like some kind of peace offering.

Farouk was relieved and, in the absence of a better plan, invited the man to come in out of the rain.

'Oh thanks-I really won't take a moment.'

'Can I offer you a drink? The kettle has literally just boiled.' Said El Hamidiri, turning towards his kitchen. As he led the way the thought struck him; how had the guy known where he lived....

'A drink won't be necessary' Said the tall man. 'But let me give you this.'

Before he could turn to look at the offering, Farouk felt a heavy blow to his right shoulder and then nothing.

Colin put the white plastic bag containing the 3 pound club hammer back into his deep coat pocket and from the other side removed his customary roll of black adhesive tape. Within a minute he had the Muslim trussed up and unable to move a muscle.

'Right then you evil bastard, a quick journey to the facility and then I think a short, sharp lesson on what it feels like to be hurt. After that we can discuss the necessity of pain management.' Colin smiled deeply, grabbed two big fistfuls of the man's hair and dragged him out through the front door to his waiting Land-rover. The guy was clearly conscious now and trying very hard to wriggle free, but he was small and with his movements so restricted he was soon bundled unceremoniously into the back and Colin shut him in there whilst he went to turn off the lights and lock up.

Within twenty minutes they arrived at the farm and Colin again dragged Farouk along the ground by his hair into the giant barn. Once inside he threw him into an adjoining side room and turned off the lights.

Farouk wasn't sure if Colin had left the room or had remained inside. If so, why the hell had he turned out the lights? A second later he knew the answer to his first question as a thin beam of light flickered on and was played across his face, clearly a small torch.

'Let's do this for a while before I slaughter you "Halal style" or "ala halal" laughed the tall man in his high-pitched, yet strangely calm voice.

'Get that joke? Ala halal, or Allah halal. It's all comic anagrams today – not bad for a severe dyslexic!'

A heavy kick to the stomach as he lay on the floor made Farouk nauseous and he doubled up in agony. He lost his nerve completely as he realised he was probably going to be executed here by this psycho and he tried desperately to find a way to loosen his hands, but the tape was so tight that he couldn't move them more than an inch in any direction. Just as he was beginning to wonder if there would be another blow, it came, smashing into his shoulder blade from out of the darkness. It was the same shoulder that had been struck earlier at the house and the joint seemed to explode in agony and he thought the shoulder must have been broken or at least dislocated. The pain was almost unbearable and he tried to scream through his taped up mouth but, unable to inhale or exhale properly all he achieved was a state of near panic within himself.

In the erratically waving torchlight Colin hadn't seen where his blow had landed but knew he'd hurt the Arab somewhere on his upper arm and decided to exploit that. Colin's head was spinning. This fucking religious worm had all the excuses and bullshit neatly wrapped up in his trite smooth words and Colin had listened to too much of this slime all his life. Time for the Muslim's imagined god to see what Colin thought of all those centuries of abuse, excuses and swill. He had never before felt this level of anger and he unleashed it in a torrent of violence.

A fury was being unleashed upon him and there was no hiding place in the dark, wherever Farouk managed to squirm the monster found him and wave after wave of blows, kicks, punches and even bites smashed, broke and damaged him until he lost all track of time and place.

Consciousness returned slowly and as Farouk lay in agony, hoping the onslaught had stopped, the torch light came on again and his assailant moved forward and stepped onto his damaged shoulder joint.

Colin pushed down with his foot and then stood upon the joint with his entire weight.

He tried again to break free. The pain was like nothing he'd ever felt and again he blacked out. When he came round he felt sick and could actually see little stars before his eyes. These were suddenly replaced by a blinding light as Colin switched on the overhead neons. What Farouk now saw made his blood run cold. The tall guy was stood over him brandishing a long butchering knife.

'Now Mr Halal, let's talk degrees of pain. You are a mammal, correct? Therefore the pain and suffering you experience when I cut through your throat will be similar to the other mammals we were discussing this evening so knowledgeably. We know that they cannot speak, but you can give us a very accurate idea of the pain. If you scream, shake, become unconscious or soil your underwear then I am going to have to conclude that you are terrified and that you *do* experience unimaginable pain at that crucial moment.'
Farouk lay unable to move or speak, but his battered and bloody eyes gave away his terror.

'Wait; let's hear your views on this.' Colin reached down and ripped the adhesive tape from El Hamidiri's mouth and head. Immediately the man began to scream in pain and terror.
'Help me somebody please help me.'

Colin laughed openly and, with the nasty looking knife still in his hand waved his arms around like a conductor demanding more from the orchestra.
'Yes, yes, good! Shout! Shout good and loud and still nobody cares. The only people who can hear you are locked in tiny cages and they won't care two hoots about you. You see, you are a worthless animal to them, a creature to be butchered in the same way as all the butchered beasts in stinking abattoirs the world over. To everyone who can hear you, you are of zero consequence. But not to me Mr Doctor fucking Farouk El fucking Hamidiri; oh no; to me you are

going to be the provider of the evidence that mammals *do* experience pain and stress and terror. Yes, finally after thousands of brutal years we can show the world through filming your slaughter, that you and your Muslim brothers have been barbaric every minute of every day and the Jewish so called fucking scholars have been as bad, if not worse.'

Farouk witnessed the madman doing a little skip wearing an insanely broad grin. He had never seen eyes quite like these; they were almost glowing. Eyes of a psychopath if ever there were, he thought as he bit his teeth together against the agonies in his body. He began to pray subconsciously and through the prayer realised he had to think fast. From somewhere deep within himself he found an inner calmness.
'Sir, I think it is a brave thing you do to try to support your beliefs....' he said through broken teeth.
'...but let me make a suggestion.'
Colin bent down and put his face right up against that of Farouk; their eyes were inches apart and El Hamidiri could smell the insanity oozing from the madman's pores.
'I am listening' said the lunatic.
'If you kill me now, in the way you are saying, then you will never know for certain if the pain I might show is due to your method of slaughter or to the pain I am already suffering because of the injuries you have just inflicted. It would make your experiment worthless.'
Colin thought about this. The guy was right, but he'd never planned to kill him anyway. He wanted to shock him into a confession that his barbaric slaughter method was fundamentally terrifying and caused unnecessary suffering to the animals. He wanted him to confess this on film which Colin would release to all the major TV networks as part of a series of media messages designed to convert the world to his way of thinking.

'OK. If you are right and if I agree with you then we must find another way to show the world. I will set up my camera equipment and then film a confession from you. You will clearly state that you realise the mistakes you, and your religious cohorts, have been making and that Halal slaughter causes unimaginable pain and suffering to the animals. I shall release this to the world and you will

104

become a vehicle for change. You will instruct your fellows that all slaughter is insane and carnivores are lunatics who must be stopped. You will become one of the heroes of the new way, a celebrated cleric. You shall have the opportunity to rewrite history.'

Colin thought briefly about that expression and how absurd it was. There was no way to time-travel and so history was history.

'You can write the future.' He corrected himself.

Farouk knew that what the madman wanted him to do went against everything he had ever learned and that it would enrage his god. He didn't know if he could do this just to save his own skin. He dug deep into his soul and found the same inner strength that had calmed him earlier. He would not do this thing, it was wrong and went against his religion, but he had to play for time.

'Yes. I shall do this thing you ask.' He told the lunatic through clenched teeth. The pain was coming in waves and he was worried he'd pass out and be butchered before he'd had a chance to persuade the lunatic differently. 'On the condition that I do it freely and without my hands tied behind my back. If the world sees me this way it will be clear that the confession was forced from me, and the Muslim world will turn against you. Your message will only serve to reinforce the knowledge that our way is the only true way. Free my bonds and I will work with you.'

'All in good time preacher boy.' Colin said, stepping back from the bound man.

'First I shall set up my gear and you can think of the words to be included in your message.'

With that Colin left the room, turning off the lights to leave the cleric in the darkness again.

Farouk lay in the dark as the waves of incredible hurting continued to wash over him, pushing and pulling him around like an ocean throwing a corpse against a massive, cold, black rock. At times the pain was so intense that it dragged his mind in and out of consciousness.

Some time later he became aware of the lights coming on again, although they seemed less bright now, but maybe that had more to do with his body shutting down its senses in order to combat the pains which threatened to terminate it.

'I have had a change of mind preacher man.' As he spoke, Colin was removing the bonds that had held the Arab's feet and legs.
'You were right about the validity of my pain test; any results would right now be marred by your existing injuries. We shall allow them to heal before a ritual slaughter. For now you may join your fellow disciples in the main facility. Get up!'
Farouk rose to his knees but could get no further; he became dizzy and lay back down.
'I can't, I feel too sick.'
In three strides Colin was at his side and yanking him upright by his relatively good arm.
'Get moving or I'll give you another useless shoulder.'
The threat was enough and Farouk stumbled along beside the crazy guy.

They went through some large sliding doors into a cavernous warehouse-like structure. Farouk could see the two sides but the far end was way off in the distance and partially obscured by some large industrial machinery and a small stack of what looked like wire containers. He was struck by a strong, unpleasant smell which reminded Farouk of a zoo enclosure, maybe Hyenas he thought.
'The disciples are a little soiled and need a clean up, I shall do that later - I do apologise that they greet a new arrival in less than pristine condition, but it's nothing that a quick hose-down can't solve.'

He was being steered towards the containers and as they came closer he saw that they contained animals. They looked like primates, but were partially clothed. Then the realisation hit him; these were people, although they looked to have been medically subdued as they were immobile and paid no attention to the arrivals.
'Welcome to your new home from home!'
A door on the bottom layer of cages was opened and Farouk bundled inside, his injuries causing him to cry out at the rough handling

'I shall leave your hands taped up; in time I am sure you will be able to loosen the bonds, it will occupy your fingers whilst your mind considers broader matters, such as how ludicrous is your argument about pain and suffering and how you are going to get that message across as your last act before your god welcomes you into his kindergarten of fools and assassins.'

'I need the toilet.' Said the Muslim defiantly

'You are sitting in it.' Came his captor's response

'What? You expect me to urinate here, in this cage? I will wait until you take us back to our living quarters.'

A cackle from his neighbouring cage gave Farouk the impression that he had quite clearly misunderstood something about this arrangement and that the cages were not some temporary day-time activity or experiment, but actually the accommodation for the foreseeable future.

'You cannot be serious!' Farouk was enraged.

'Get over it - it gets worse than this!' said another voice from one of the higher cages.

'I shall leave you in the company of your fellow soldiers Mr El Hamidiri. Meanwhile, please enjoy the films; your meal will be served in around half an hour.' Colin looked up at the nearest screen; it showed dogs being rounded up and brutally caged for an annual festival in the town of Yulin, China

'Ah yes; such a state of affairs, such a dog's dinner!' the captor did an almost imperceptible skip as he chuckled at the play on words.

'Pooch pate for your meal today-I trust you enjoy the taste of man's best friend. You will approve though doctor; the hounds of hell are Halal!'

The alliteration caused another little skip .

In truth of course the meal would be as vegetarian as all the others, and whilst he had no idea how dog meat tasted he had found from his online searches that the flavour was like very strong mutton, with unpleasant aftertastes. He'd had fun mocking up the pellets for this one and had almost gagged himself when he tried them and imagined them to be real dog meat.

He went across to the hosepipe, thinking it would do them good to wash their hands before eating.

21

'I hear it kicked off at the VOTA terrorist training camp last night Guv.'
Sicknote was simultaneously smirking and munching a Panini. The effect was to give him an almost alien-like appearance
'Is that so?' It was a statement rather than a question, and an attempt by Neil Dyson to preclude any further discussion. He wasn't in the mood to be the butt of any humour today. However, he was intrigued to learn exactly what had happened, and he asked Hamilton for clarification.

'Some Muslim guy was verbally attacked by the veggie crowd for insisting that slitting a cow's throat hurts the cow less than the pain a spud feels when you skin it alive. Gotta say, I agree with him, but the veggie warriors took umbrage and decided to attack him with verbal potato peelers'
Sicknote laughed and fought a mock duel with an invisible opponent using his finger as a sword.
'Very funny Sicknote, but for once you're confusing me with a guy who gives even half a shit.'
'You should give a shit Guv, they are getting veggies a bad name and your young lady friend won't be happy about that; gotta get your priorities right! And anyway, I heard the Chief wants all vegetarians rounded up, printed, DNA swabbed and forced to confess their sick love of herbiphobic torture.' He grinned his gargoyle-esque grin and went off in search of coffee.

Dyson shook his head and took a seat next to Carol.
'What really happened?' he asked her.
'Not sure boss, you know Sicknote; spies in every camp! I think his wife is pally with the woman who hosted the meeting and some guest speaker whipped up a bit of a storm on Halal slaughter. A

trivial non-event but you know how our friend Mr Hamilton likes to wind people up!'

Dyson opened the briefing.
'OK listen up. Another Missing Persons report, this one, submitted by a certain Abigail Lundy this morning, is the possible disappearance of Donna Southgate from the city. It's not common knowledge, but according to her friend it appears that Donna is a high-end sex worker, specialising in looking after men who want to be made to feel inferior'

Predictably, Sicknote chimed in
"I didn't realise my missus had competition in that field Guv – making men feel inferior I mean; she'll be furious – probably should start with her as number one suspect!'
'Very funny Hamilton. Donna was thought to have travelled to London yesterday by train to do some shopping and her car was indeed found at the station car park in Horsham earlier this morning. Apparently she would drive to Horsham, park there and take the train into town.'

'Let me guess, you want me to check CCTV at the car park Sir?'
'Well volunteered Carol! Alright, let's go through what we know. First there is absolutely nothing to link this disappearance with our German friend, but the chief has asked me to run both investigations. I have been given an offer of some extra help' - he indicated two new faces in the team – 'Brian and Steph will be with us until further notice so let's pool resources and share the load. I want us to keep an open mind and where we can save time kill two birds with one stone.'
Carol spoke up.
'Not sure what you mean Guv-how will running two investigations, looking for different people under differing, un-linked circumstances be effectively run as one operation?'
'Ours is not to question Carol. Let's just do as we are asked to the best of our ability.'

Dyson was as dubious as Carol but the offer of resource was rare and he had to get the most out of the available supply. He took them through the known facts of the Donna case.

After a quick summary of any steps taken in the Hans-Werner case Neil wound up the meeting.

When they were all going their separate ways-most via the coffee machine Neil felt a hand on his shoulder. It was Sicknote.

'Hey Guv, you wanna do something with that eye of yours before it gets an infection.'

'I'm going to get a doctor's appointment soon as I get a second.' replied Dyson

'Ah forget docs, what can they do except give you anti inflammatories and some bullshit about avoiding direct sunlight!'

'Yeah I know, but I want the swelling down quickly, it hurts like hell.'

'What you need is a good raw steak; slap that on it for an hour and the puffiness will be gone before you know it!'

'That's just an old wives' tale Sicknote-nobody really does that.'

'Oh you'd be surprised.' he countered. 'Check this out.'

He turned to the congregated officers at the coffee machine

'Guys; what's the best thing to put on a black and swollen eye?'

'Steak!' They chorused almost as one.

'See Mr sceptic, told you so.'

'Alright alright I'll put a bloody steak on it, but not tonight because Jenny's coming round and she'd go ballistic.'

'Because she's vegetarian?' asked Carol.

'No, because of the cost.' the sarcasm was lost on Carol. 'Of course because she's vegetarian - actually it's worse than that, she's vegan and she'd have a hairy fit if she thought I'd bought meat and then not even eaten it.' Neil declared.

'You can eat it.' Said Sicknote. 'Just run it under the tap when you are done and whack it in the frying pan - better still, get Jenny to cook it for you!'

'I'd end up with two bloody shiners then! OK, I'll try it, but if you buggers are winding me up...'

He left that threat hanging

Dyson dialled his fiancé but got her voice-mail.

"Hi it's Jenny; leave a message".

'Hi Jen. Listen, I know this is a lot to ask, but this eye is not getting any better and Sicknote recommended slapping a steak on it. I know it sounds insane, but a few people at the station agreed with him and I'm willing to try anything. Do me a favour and grab me a steak at the supermarket on your way over tonight...pleeeease.'

The last word was dragged out in an exaggerated way to make it sound like a desperate plea. Buying meat would really be a big deal for Jenny and he'd be amazed if she did.

22

Diary entry 4
March 9ᵗʰ 2014

Dear father

Another sucksessful day mixed with disaster

You see how sucksessful your pathetic son has become, since he lured you into that simpel trap? Simpel is a good word because only a simpelten would have fallen for it. You were so predictable and, dare I say it, simpel.

You called me simpel once. Do you remember? It was the day I pulled your dog away from those chickens. My chickens, the ones I had rescued because they were injured by your demonic machines. It wasn't the dog's fault; otherwise I would have killeb it. No, it was yours. That's why you died, or rather it's one of the reasons. I expect you can think of plenty more. I can.

I have a new disiple by the way. A Muslum gentleman. He's going to be interesting and, I think highly influential. The German still sleeps; I am worried I may have to do something. I have put water in his cage.

Must go, got to make some changes to a bolt gun after the shitty thing mis-fired as I was trying to grab old Wilkins the butcher. Maybe I will go back for him, or maybe he will have to wait. But I will get him….

Your son
Colin

PS did mum ever say anything about me befor she left? You never really told me anything.

23

Colin had just finished his regular round of the cages, checking to ensure that nobody had begun to try an escape attempt. The quality of the enclosures was high, for he had selected the design and materials based on their robust nature, with strength and durability the absolute must-haves. All joints were welded wherever possible, and where fixtures were needed, such as the door hinges, they were riveted rather than screwed or bolted. He didn't want some tricky escapologist using a hair pin to undo all his efforts. He had allowed the inmates to keep the clothes they'd worn when he took them, but anything that might be converted to a tool had been removed. Happy that all was in order he settled himself down at his workbench in an annex to the main barn. It was warm here and the smell of his team wasn't so noticeable. He was getting used to it anyway; becoming acclimatised to the animal stench.

He concentrated on the task, which was to modify the small propellant cartridges from his father's bolt gun. As he had been attempting to grab old Wilkins he had been nervous about the power of the thing and the damage it might do. He didn't want to kill anyone during abduction. This was completely experimental as he had never dismantled a cartridge before, nor had he any clue what impact it would have to halve or quarter the strength of the charge. He had spent a lot of time on the internet last night, researching the effects of bolt gun use on animals but if he was honest he hadn't learned a great deal, certainly not enough to make him feel as if he *really* knew what he was doing, hence his nervous state. There was probably only one way to find out for certain!

Colin set out 12 stubby brass cylinders, each the diameter of a shotgun shell and maybe three quarters of an inch in length. With lightly trembling fingers he gently prised open the crimped teeth of the end cap, eased out the neoprene bung and with infinite care, tipped the speckled grey powder contents onto a sheet of paper. He repeated this until he had twelve small piles of gunpowder and twelve empty cartridges sitting on the bench before him.

That had been the most delicate part for Colin. Now, with equal caution, he refilled each cartridge with roughly a third of the original powder quantity. He hoped that this would be an amount of explosive that would administer a temporarily paralysing shock but not prove fatal. He had planned to also use his father's old cattle prod in his kidnappings; the thing delivered up to a million volts from a single nine volt battery, but it took so long to rearm that he'd given up on it as a useful tool. It was fine inside the facility, but too cumbersome and slow in the field, as he liked to think of his operating arena. Both bolt gun and cattle prod had their uses for controlling animal exploiters, deploying the abusers' own tools against them would be some kind of poetic justice. Ultimately it was down to the right tool in the right circumstance, and if he could get the charge right, the bolt gun was favourite, due to its portability and ease of concealment.

He gently brushed the remaining small heaps of explosive into one pile and contemplated setting a match to it, but thought better of it. Instead he swept it into a small plastic food bag, which he sealed with a short twist of wire. Colin had shopping to do and then he must get some group therapy sessions organised. Today he would be moving into the next phase; the re-education programme. Colin was very excited and a keen observer might have spotted his feet performing an occasional agitated shuffle.

24

Jenny was in the supermarket and she was cross.
She was cross with Neil for the unbelievable insensitivity of asking
her to get him a bloody steak for his eye – she felt that all her values
had been totally swept under the carpet with his short and
thoughtless message. She knew he worked in a stressful job and she
tried to make allowances for the odd slip-up in the way he
communicated with her, but this one had felt pretty tactless and
really seemed to ride roughshod over all she stood for. She knew he
adored her, but bloody hell he could be a detached bastard at times.
Her first reaction had been to call him and tell him where to ram his
steak, but that wouldn't have helped anyone. She was cross with
herself for even being here for the purpose of buying meat, cross that
she'd had to leave early from the bookshop where she worked, and
most pissed-off at the traffic she'd hit coming out of Chichester.

Jenny absolutely adored working at the little fusty bookshop with its
dusty owner, musty old manuscripts, rare first editions and the
opportunities it gave her to indulge her literary and historical
passions. The owner was a wonderful retired Major General who had
lost his wife to cancer and now ran the funny little shop more as a
hobby than anything else – he certainly didn't make enough money
on a day-to-day basis to live from, and by the time he paid Jenny her
hours he can only have been in deficit. But he told her enough times
that he wasn't in it for the money *"...money really can be so coarse
my dear; I am already blessed with bucketfuls of that vulgarity!...."*
– he did it for the love of old things. He and Jenny shared a passion
for the feel of old paper and she recognised in herself the look that
would come into his eyes when he handled a special old volume,
perhaps where a pencil dedication on the flyleaf told part of a story;
she'd tease herself trying to piece together some meaning to the few
words sometimes found there *"To dear Audrey...it was the best time,*

wasn't it...?" Occasionally a real gem would come along and the two of them would get as excited as kids in a sweet shop.

They also sold old maps and prints and she could spend hours looking at the local area as it was in 1650 or 1800. The changes had been astonishing and she was certain that the pace of development would continue until the precious green swathes between the city and the surrounding villages had disappeared entirely. She realised that even London must have started this way. There was no way to stem the population explosion without draconian governmental policies like the single child rule in China, and there was no way she could see that ever being accepted here, nor could she ever agree to such shocking human rights conditions.

At the checkout there was a small queue but the guy in front of her with a fully laden trolley offered to let her go first.

'Please go ahead if you only have that one item.'

'Oh, that's very kind, thanks.' She smiled her best friendly smile and some of the frustrations left her. Funny how a simple smile can make that change inside us, she thought as she dropped the slab of meat on the moving conveyor as if it were still alive and about to bite her.

Behind her, Colin was kicking himself. He'd let this woman go in front and she was buying meat of all things.

'That's an interesting purchase.' He said 'Is that all you needed today, a lump of dead animal?'

'It's for my boyfriend's eye.' Jenny explained 'He got into a fight and wants to treat it with this.'

'For his *eye?'* Colin tried to hide his distaste for the little slut. 'Unbelievable! Now we slaughter beautiful creatures so that people who go round punching each other can pretend to make themselves better! Do you really imagine that the butchered remains of a poor creature are going to make any difference to your friend's flipping eye? That's the craziest, most selfish thing I have heard in a very long time.'

'I know...'

Jenny was about to try to explain that she was against it as much as anyone, when the young man on the till urged her forward. She glanced back at the guy with an apologetic look and then paid and left.

Now she was even more cross at having been berated for something when in reality she was the innocent party. She wished she'd made that call to Neil, telling him to buy his own bloody steak.

As she reached her car she was accosted by an old friend of her mother's and spent a few minutes passing the time. Jenny related the whole sorry tale of the steak and the bloke who'd publicly humiliated her, they laughed about it and when jenny drove out of the car park she was already in a slightly better frame of mind.

Colin loaded his shopping into the trolley, and then he too paid and left. As he walked out of the main automatic doors he saw the steak woman sitting in a car with the door open and chatting to another woman. He loaded his own car with his purchases, watching her all the time and when she closed her car door he decided to see where she was going. He hadn't planned to take her, but she needed to be educated and would make an attractive addition to his small but growing team. Most importantly, it would be sweet revenge on her boyfriend and his clear disregard for life.

Jenny drove left out of the supermarket car park and headed towards Neil's place. She wanted to drop off the meat before it got warm. She had almost no experience of handling meat and was worried it might start to go off if she didn't get it into a refrigerator. Neil lived 2 miles outside the city and she was there within five minutes.

She jumped out and trotted up his path, taking the key she entered and went straight to the kitchen.

She scribbled a note informing Neil that his steak was in the fridge and that she'd be around later. She added that he owed her one, big time, and she'd expect him to be extra nice to her tonight-she'd explain later. Climbing into her car she put on the radio and drove off. She hadn't spotted an old Land-rover pulled up at the roadside twenty-five yards from her car with the engine ticking over.

25

Diary entry 5
March 10th 2014

Dear father
Quite a sucksessful day yesterday
I managed to reduce the charge in the bolt gun cartriges without
blowing my hands off or distroying the place.
Nothing else to add except that I have had no anger issues and am
making good progress with that and with my project. "Your" farm is
looking great and I am using the modified feed distribution system
well – it had to be thoroughly disinfected after you contaminated it
with your innerds.
Must go, got to take someone for a drive.

Your son
Colin

26

Amanda Levy jumped up and down, waving excitedly as her mother stepped down from the train. They hadn't seen each other for over three months and Amanda was burning to tell her all her news. They hugged and walked arm in arm through the exit towards Amanda's parked car. It was a small Peugeot; she couldn't afford anything more extravagant on her hotel assistant wages – and the Swan hotel wasn't the top payer in the industry.

Lost as they were in their catch up conversation, going through the changes in each other's lives and laughing about the antics of some of the hotel guests Amanda had met, they failed to notice the tall man observing them from a faded blue Land-rover parked a few spaces down from Amanda's Peugeot. They further failed to notice the same dusty blue Land-rover tailing them through the heavy lunchtime traffic, nor did they see it pull in fifty metres or so behind them when they arrived at Amanda's address in a small block of 1970s flats.

Had they seen the vehicle, and the driver who emerged once both vehicles had pulled to a halt, they may also have spotted the large holdall he carried, though of course they wouldn't have known what it contained. They would have seen a tall, bald man who stood out in a number of ways; his somewhat odd appearance (this man had a habit of tucking everything he wore on his torso… shirts, pullovers, sweatshirts …into his jeans, making him look geekish), they may have remarked on his height and the way he seemed oblivious of his surroundings, walking at a rapid pace and staring fixedly at something ahead of him with a look of determination on his face. They might have commented that he looked like a man on a mission.

A man on a mission was exactly who the tall, somewhat oddly-dressed, bald man was. He hurried to close the gap between himself and the mother and daughter, catching up with them just as the door to the small block of eight flats was about to close. Amanda's mother saw him just in time and held the door open long enough for him to gain entry to the communal entrance which housed the lift and stairs to the upper level apartments. He muttered his thanks then busied himself with an imaginary call on his mobile 'phone and from the corner of his eye watched as Amanda gathered the day's mail from one of the eight post boxes on the wall. Most of it was junk mail but she took that too. As he spoke with a non-existent person on the other end of a non-connected line he noted that she had removed her post from the bottom right box; number eight.

Flat number eight. Top floor. Perfect.

As Amanda and her mother waited for the lift the man continued his call. Something about the guy's voice triggered a memory in Amanda's brain but she couldn't place the soft, relatively high pitched tone and dismissed the thought from her mind. She chattered further with her mother about some incident that had happened in a lift on a holiday at a time when her father had still been alive. He had succumbed to bowel cancer the previous spring and one of the reasons for her mother's visit today was to try to draw her out of the self-destructive malaise into which see had descended following his death. Amanda had planned day trips and theatre visits along with an outing to the Tate Modern art gallery where a special exhibition was on display for a limited time. Her mother was a great fan of paintings of every genre and Amanda hoped the visit could be combined with the national gallery and would be a catalyst for happier times. Her mother, Barbara, needed to start to live again – she was barely in her fifties and had plenty of life experiences yet to enjoy.

But before those excursions they had a tight time-line because Amanda had booked to see a new film that had just come into the cinemas. It was a surprise for her mum, who had told her that the book, from which the film was an adaptation, was one of her favourites. Amanda hoped that the film would do the book justice; sometimes they didn't. She had arranged to meet her friend Eleanor at the cinema and they would all go on for dinner afterwards.

As they entered the lift Amanda's mother asked the man whether he too was going up.

The man smiled apologetically and without speaking indicated by briefly holding out the 'phone and rolling his eyes that he needed to finish the tedious call first. As the lift doors closed Amanda looked at the guy properly for the first time. His appearance was somehow familiar, but as with the voice she dismissed him; she must have travelled in the lift with him at some point or seen him in the entrance hall to the flats. She turned away and pressed the button for the fourth floor where her small but comfortable apartment was situated.

Unlocking the door to her flat Amanda asked her mum if she'd like a cup of tea. The reply was affirmative and followed immediately by an urgent request to use the loo. Amanda reminded her where to find the bathroom and went into the kitchen to fill the kettle for tea.

She had no sooner turned on the kettle than the doorbell rang. Bloody typical, she thought as she went to open it. She saw that she had neglected to attach the security chain and thought briefly about doing that before she opened the door but felt a little silly; she rarely had visitors and thought it might be a delivery of some shoes she had ordered online, although they were only ordered yesterday, but these days the delivery service was usually pretty quick.

When the door opened she was surprised to see the tall man from the entrance hall standing with an apologetic look on his face.

'Sorry to bother you.' He said in that high-pitched voice.

Amanda was once again niggled by the thought that she ought to recognise the tone. She also noticed that the guy's eyes were unusually widely spaced …. instantly the blood ran cold through her veins....the nut case from the hotel lobby earlier in the week.

Instinctively she went to close the door but his foot was quickly stuck between door and jamb.

'Not so fast you cocky little bitch.' he said in a quiet, menacing voice. Clearly he was trying to avoid the older lady overhearing the exchange, but the powerful kick that forced the door open was loud in the relative quiet of the stairwell.

Barbara flushed the toilet and thought she heard Amanda shout something over the noise the water made. Probably forgotten whether I take sugar she chuckled to herself.

'Can't hear you darling.' she called out as she washed her hands.

As she stepped through the bathroom door she was confronted by the sight of the tall man from downstairs gripping her daughter around her neck and simultaneously kneeing the back of her legs in an effort to force her to the floor.

'Get off her!' she screamed as she watched her daughter's terrified eyes widely staring at her as if pleading for help.

In a surprisingly calm tone the guy said 'Sit down and shut up you stupid old cow or I'll break her fucking snotty bitch neck.'

Barbara Levy did exactly as he had instructed. Although she had been completely surprised by the sudden events she had sufficient awareness that she needed to play it safe with this man; he was clearly unhinged and dangerous.

'We don't have any money worth talking about here, but I can get to the cash point around the corner and withdraw whatever is in my account for you.' She said in what she hoped was a convincing, if trembling voice.

'You think I need your filthy money you evil shitbitch?' The madman's voice had lost its previous calmness. He was almost shouting now and his voice had risen several tones in pitch, sounding as if his throat were constricted.

With alarm Barbara saw Amanda's legs begin to twitch. Oh god, she thought, he's killing her.

With a mother's instinct to protect her young she leapt at the crazy guy, her hands had become talons and she was clawing at his face in an effort to force him to release her daughter. She managed to gouge his left eye and he squealed with pain. She dug her fingernails deep into the eye socket in her desperation to free her child but the monster was seemingly indestructible.

She resorted to another tactic and lashed out at his shins with her 3 inch heels, but this seemed to have little effect on the beast.

Desperate now, she began slapping, punching scratching and kicking and screaming like a fury. Many of the blows missed their targets but she saw some blood appearing on his face and gained some confidence from that. She knew instinctively that the eyes were the most vulnerable points to focus her assault on and aimed again for them.

Seemingly from out of nowhere a fist smashed into her face and she collapsed in agony clutching at her broken and instantly bleeding nose. She was vaguely aware of her daughter being dragged past her and the last thing she saw was a massive boot stamping down onto her already unbearably painful face.

Colin dragged the unconscious Amanda into a bedroom and quickly retrieved his holdall from the landing outside the front door of the flat. He decided that the girl was the lesser risk right now and so attended to the older woman. She too seemed to be out cold and so from his bag he took heavy duty adhesive tape and set to work binding her arms behind her back and securing her legs at the knees and ankles. He used the same tape to gag her by wrapping it several times around her head, passing just under her twisted and bleeding nose.

Not bothering to check whether she could breathe through the smashed nostrils and satisfied that she was going nowhere and incapable of raising the alarm he went quickly to the bedroom and did the same with Amanda's still unconscious body. He pulled her head around to face him and spat over her closed eyes. Pleased by the sensation this caused deep within him, he repeated the action, this time forcing her eyelids open, and spattered both eyes with several mouthfuls of his phlegm. This aroused him in a way he hadn't expected and the temptation to explore the feeling further was almost overpowering, but he knew he had to be quick and that he had to minimise any traces he left. Besides, it wasn't in his plan; and the plan had to be followed. Already he was concerned that the old bag had some of his skin under her fingernails and he'd have to find a way to solve that.

He hadn't realised as he had tracked the girl to the station that she was going there to meet someone, and he'd had no intention of taking the old woman with him, but he realised there was little option now. She had seen his face clearly enough and had his DNA all over her. It complicated matters and he was distressed that none of this was on his list. On top of that his eye was sore and his face stung where the old bitch had scratched him. He checked in the bathroom mirror but quickly saw that the damage was quite superficial.

He'd have to break his golden rule and improvise. The thought worried him; the plan was detailed and comprehensive and should be followed exactly. He was thinking of ways to get her out of the building. The girl would be no major problem; he would drug her, release her bonds and walk her down the stairs. If he did chance to meet anyone on the way it would look as if she was the worst for wear from drink and he would emphasise that by pretending to talk to her as they descended. His car was not so far away that it would cause any issues and he'd be long gone before anyone realised anything had occurred.

He considered sitting it out until it became dark, but thought the complications of women needing to piss and drink and all that malarkey was a buggerance factor he could well live without. He decided instead to proceed with the extraction plan straight away. He left them both trussed and immobile and went to bring his Land-rover a little closer to the front door. It wasn't a big building and was mostly quiet so he'd use the lift as much as possible and trust to good fortune to get them both into the vehicle and out of sight.

In the event he accomplished the task without further hiccup and was soon driving sedately towards his correction facility. He thought back over the last couple of hours and was reminded of the arousal he had felt when spitting into Amanda's eyes. He didn't understand that sensation, and thought it might be fun to explore it a little further when he had her all to himself. She was a very pretty girl, and she had ridiculed him so publicly......

124

124

27

Jenny and Neil strolled arm in arm along the high-water mark of the foreshore. It was a breezy, beautiful day in the tiny picturesque village of Bosham, nestling at the head of one of the arms of Chichester harbour. It was where Neil had spent all his childhood before moving away to university in Brighton. It was still "home" in his heart. He had lectured Jenny far too often on its rich history, and took the opportunity again now.

'You know who drowned in this stream?'

'Oh god Neil, not again, of course I do, and I know she's buried in the church and I know her dad stopped the waves here and that the Crusaders stopped here on their journeys and were made to blunt their swords at the entrance to the Saxon church and I know that Harold came here on the way to negotiate with William of Orange and that the manor house and church are shown as a result in the Bayeux Tapestry and all of that stuff..I KNOW IT!'

They both laughed.
'OK, just wanted to remind you of the critical importance of my little village in English history! Did I ever tell you that the church has the largest Saxon arch in the country? At least, I think it has!'
'No you missed that little gem, and I never realised how many swans there are here.' Jenny said as they reached the little bridge at the Mill.
'Seem to be more every year, bloody queen should have an amnesty and let us catch em for dinner for one day a year!'

'Neil! Honestly, that's horrid. In any case I bet they taste of bread, the amount they get fed here.'

'I expect they're more like turkey.' He smacked his lips together, mockingly,

'Oh stop it! I'll leave you and go and live in a colony with like-minded vegans.' She threatened.

'Off you go then – don't forget your Linda McCartney recipe books.'

'I don't have any and stop teasing, look at the beautiful view instead.'

They wandered across the expanse of thick, resilient grass known as Quay meadow and stood looking at the five small columns of names on the war memorial. A single small wreath of weather-beaten poppies remained from the previous November's ceremony, an enduring reminder of a time less peaceful.

'Let's go and look at the names in the boatyard, they're more fun than dead soldiers.' Neil said and he dragged her off to the right and into the fenced area where boats were kept when not in the water.

'The one to spot the silliest name wins.' he laughed as he pulled her along.

'What's the prize?' She asked, giving him a wicked, sideways glance.

'Dinner.' he said, resisting the bait.

'Here's one.' Jenny shouted. "Mr Bean"! That has to be a winner.'

'Nah, not nearly as silly as some of em I bet. Look here; "Beautiful Briny" that's better than your Beany.

'Never! OK what about this; "Blue Banana Song" are these arranged alphabetically or what?' She mused.

'Here's the winner for definite.' Came Neil's exalted shout. '"Salty Pig Runs Free"! That's definitely the one for you, must belong to one of your animal rights chums.'

They laughed as they made their way to the little pub they liked, where they had a long, noisy dinner amongst the locals and tourists. At six they walked back to the car park and made their way to Jenny's place where a bottle of vegetarian wine and vegan chocolate played the role of entrée to their love making.

28

Hans-Werner's head felt as if it had an axe buried deep within it. He touched the area at the back of his skull and winced at the sudden shock of pain. What the hell had happened? He had no idea where he was and started to feel around in the dark. It felt like some kind of wire mesh beneath him. This wasn't right. He tried to piece together the last things he remembered. He had gone through the door, hung his coat but beyond that nothing.

His mouth seemed to be glued shut and he had a thirst like never before. He continued to explore with his hands and felt a metal bowl of sorts half filled with what had to be water, he lifted it and drank long and deep, hardly caring what the liquid was.

Feeling his way around he found some kind of wire mesh to his right and left. He rose to his knees and smacked his head onto something unyielding. More slowly he eased himself forward and struck something else in the dark, causing yet more discomfort and throbbing. Hans-Werner was a big guy, 6'2" and weighing around a hundred kilos and he was a little prone to claustrophobia. Starting to panic now he swore and reached forward, finding the same wire mesh. He didn't need to turn around; he already knew he'd find the same barrier behind him.
What the hell was this? Was he imprisoned? He thought back again through the events he could remember, travelling back in time from the blackness.

Coat; onions; door; football; mother; No – the freaky guy and the onions – oh shit. He instantly connected the dots; the smell in his flat was the freaky man's coat. The guy had been there when he'd arrived he realised. But how the hell had he known where he lived? Ah! The business card. He'd given him a business card and his address was on his cards. Oh shit; the apology had been a trick for the strange man to find where he lived and get his revenge. And Hans-Werner had fallen for it.

But what did the guy want to do? Lock him up and leave him? Thoughts turned towards escape. He certainly wasn't going to sit here and wait; what if the man had other plans for him? He was clearly imbalanced from the way he had reacted at the game, and who knew what he was capable of. The German was still thirsty and ravenously hungry; he wondered how long he had lain here unconscious

He started to apply pressure to the mesh but it was made of thick wire and very robust. He turned his focus to the corners and the joints, they might be weaker. No encouragement there either. There must be a door, he thought and felt carefully around until he found it. He poked his fingers through the mesh and groped around and discovered it was padlocked top and bottom and he wasn't getting out that way. His headache was unbearable and he sat down to try to ease the pain and to think.

As he sat he heard a door opening and saw a swathe of light cross the floor. In the dim light he could see that he was indeed in a cage. A cage perched upon other, similar cages, all stacked together as if they were bricks in some giant skeletal Lego structure.
He heard footsteps and then saw the elongated shadow of a person walking out of the light. Suddenly there was a bang and the whole place was awash in a glaring white light which caused another shock of pain to bounce around inside Hans-Werner's head. He closed his eyes to ease the discomfort but he had to see who this was and he forced his eyelids open, shielding them as much as he could with his hands. What he then saw made his heart miss a beat.

The tall freaky guy was looking at him with those too-far-apart eyes and his head cocked to one side. His mouth formed a sick grin and in his left hand he carried a long pole with some kind of box attached near where the hand gripped the shaft. The German had seen one of these before. It had been used to force cattle into a pen on a farming programme he had watched and he had a bad feeling.

'The fuckwit awakes. The animal scoffing fuckwit awakes. We were starting to get worried'.
His voice was quiet and menacing.

'Who are you?' Hans-Werner's voice trembled, despite his attempts to appear unafraid.
'I am justice; I am the equaliser of wrongs; I am the revenge; but I am also your saviour and you have come here to be changed from your animal torturing ways.'
'Justice? Revenge? Saved? Vot ze hell are you talking about?' Hans-Werner sensed that this was not just about the spilled onions; he knew he was in the presence of a highly dangerous religious lunatic. He knew he had to play along and await his chance to escape. He spoke more calmly and tried to sound sympathetic; although he knew he wasn't dealing with any reasonable creature here; he had seen that in the football incident.

'I vont to help you.' He continued 'But first I need to know vot I heff done? vy do you call me an animal torturer? I love animals.'

The tall man's face reddened and the menacing grin became a gaping hole.
'Love animals? Love to eat them you mean, that's not love that is pure inhuman greed. You besmear them in filthy sauces and stuff them down your throat like a fucking caveman. I have a good mind to shit on you.'

Shit on me? What the hell kind of nutcase was this guy? The freak was approaching the cage with the pole outstretched towards him and Hans-Werner instinctively shuffled as far away from the threat as possible. This had little effect owing to the size of the compartment and the German started to shout at Colin as he raised the cattle prod level with his chest and fired a bold of high voltage electricity onto the metal mesh. The result was a strong tingle through Hans-Werner's fingers, which were gripping the sides of his prison. Clearly the size of the interlocking metal structure had dissipated the power over a wide area. Hans-Werner knew about electricity; he knew these devices delivered very high voltage but low current and so were extremely painful but not necessarily dangerous. That being said, an electrical engineer friend in Germany had once told him a statistic which he had never forgotten. He had explained that, because the body was essentially governed by electrical signals of the tiniest magnitude, it was highly receptive to electrical stimulus. He had gone on to say that, if delivered at a certain point in the heartbeat to certain parts of the body, then half an Amp for one 500th of a second could be fatal.

Hans-Werner began to sweat and was grateful for the diffusing effect of the large collection of wire cages.

The relief was short lived as Colin produced a large bunch of keys and set to work opening the padlocks; the top first and then the bottom. His intentions were clear and Hans-Werner knew instinctively that this would be his best chance to over-power the tall guy and make a bolt for it. He braced himself, trying not to show that he was preparing to pounce. He had never been a fighter, and had no idea how he was going to tackle the big, powerful looking man, but he knew he had to give it absolutely everything he had in order to avoid the stunning shock of the pole and to knock the guy to the ground hard enough to give himself time to get away.

As the second lock was released the door swung open nine or ten inches and his captor still had the hasp and the keys in his hands. Hans-Werner chose his moment and sprang forward using all the strength of his legs and aiming his open, outstretched hands for the upper chest of the crazy guy with the pole.

As he leapt forward his forehead smashed into the top bar above the cage door and the resulting pain, on top of the already insufferable headache would in any other circumstances be excruciating, but adrenalin fuelled his veins. The collision slowed him but his momentum carried him forward. The lunatic went sprawling and the German sprinted away, or rather, tried to. His legs were refusing to function as they should, clearly he had been confined in the cramped little cage unconscious and unmoving for a long time and his muscles screamed in agony as he forced them into sudden activity.

Colin was taken completely by surprise at the speed and strength of the attack and felt himself flying backwards under the weight of his prisoner. He dropped the cattle prod and it scuttled across the concrete under part of the feed machinery, but he was quick to retrieve it and was soon back on his feet and sprinting in pursuit of the disappearing escapee. Hans-Werner headed straight for the spot where he had seen the first shaft of light when the crazy guy had entered. He saw the open door and, despite his lack of fitness, found the energy to propel himself rapidly towards it. He had no idea where the guy was, and he didn't want to waste a second looking over his shoulder, nor run the risk of stumbling on the uneven surface. He knew the guy was long-legged and that he'd have to put in a super-human effort to get outside and away from him, but he felt that once out of the vast building he'd probably be near some form of dwellings where the pursuit would be in full view of anyone in the vicinity.

As he burst through the open door he was dismayed to see that he was in fact in a totally isolated rural area with nothing but barren fields and a few hedges and trees stretching before him into the distance. He knew in that moment that the game was probably up; he was unfit and his lungs burnt, feeling as though they would burst and his legs were already beginning to become heavy with the numbing fatigue brought on by lactic acid. He threw a glance over his shoulder to see the freak only metres behind him, head down and sprinting like a born athlete. Without thinking the German stopped dead, spun around and launched himself at the big man, driving his fist with everything he could muster into his diaphragm and taking him again completely by surprise. Hans-Werner knew he had mere seconds to try to disable the guy somehow and his aim was to grab the cattle prod and hit him with whatever the device was capable of delivering. He also knew that after firing, the thing would need a few seconds to recharge, and that would be all the time he would have to keep the guy at a distance.

Grabbing for the pole he missed and only caught the crazy's arm at the elbow. He was drained of strength from the sprint and his hand was too weak to maintain a hold and the tall man easily spun away from him and twisted around delivering a crashing blow with his forearm to the side of the German's face. The pain, on top of the earlier assault and the injury to his head caused by his leap from the

131

cage was unbearable and, trying desperately to fight back he fell to his knees and received a final debilitating kick to the head.

For the second time that day he blacked out, albeit briefly and he came to being pulled by his feet over the field with his head dragging and battered on every trough and peak in the roughly ploughed and iron hard ground. The pain was again unbearable and he tried to lift his head from the ground and take the weight on his shoulders but he was weak and his will-power deserted him. He drifted in and out of consciousness until finally he found himself being lifted and thrown bodily back into his wire mesh cell. He had vague thoughts about the strength of the man and that he must superhuman to be able to lift so easily. The door was not immediately closed; instead he heard the high pitch whine of the cattle prod being charged. He lost control of his bowels and fouled his trousers as he realised that the sick bastard was going to attack him with the electrical prod.

He tried to fend off the impending assault but the pole connected with his outstretched hands. A shooting pain ripped through his body and he could feel himself shaking as the energy travelled along his limbs and earthed on the wire beneath him. He tried to scream but his throat seemed paralysed. The madman was shouting something at him but the words were incoherent in his pain.

Instinctively, when the shock stopped he curled into a foetal position and began to whimper in fear, frustration and agony. His head was hurting as if a heavy hammer were striking him every time his racing heart beat and his hands burned from the damage caused by the electricity as it was channelled through them. Still the lunatic was screaming, and now he could understand some of the words. '...slimy shitface, think you can escape the justice that's coming your way eh? Speak up you shit turd...'

He was spraying spittle as he shouted these foul obscenities, but Hans-Werner was beyond caring. He just wanted the freak to end it; kill him quickly and let him rest in an oasis of pain-free drifting for all eternity. Never a religious man, the German began to silently pray for a god that he knew didn't exist to intervene and mercifully take his life.

29

Diary entry 6
March 12th 2014

Dear father
Bad days for anger. I have had to hurt people and it doesn't make me happy.
Last night I dreemed about mummy. In my dreem she didn't run away like you said. In my dreem she was trying to find me and you were stopping her.
I wunder if what you told me happened that day when you argued so much really did happen or if you told me a story. You always tolb me so many lies and I never believed anything you said after that time when you killed my pet chicken. You lied then and you probabley lied many more times.

I also dreemed about your old safe and I wunder what you used to keep in there. I will find the kees later and have a look. You were very seecretiv about the safe so there must be something interesting in there.

Your son

Colin

30

'OK listen up!'
DI Dyson's voice cut through the hubbub that had filled the room
and all eyes turned towards him. All except for Sicknote's; he was
finishing a phone call to a local roofer who had made a bodge of
repairing storm damage to his house and was trying to speak in
hushed tones without losing any of the menace in his voice. The
hushed voice wasn't working and he raised his eyes apologetically in
Neil's direction and left the briefing room to finish the call.
The remainder of the room sat or stood looking with some
anticipation towards the DI.
'OK day three of the investigation into the disappearances of Donna
Southgate and Hans-Werner Fromm. Let's have a quick update on
yesterday's progress before I give you a summary of overnight
developments. Carol; CCTV footage?'

'Still trawling through it Sir; nothing of any use so far, although I've
really only just got all the data sources identified and approved; it
took way too long to get the confidentiality agreements authorised -
can you have a word with our lords and masters about simplifying
that process – seems like ticks in boxes are more critical than crime
prevention and detection at the moment. Maybe we could have a
publicly stated target based on that somehow, and then we'd get
some progress?' She smiled to show that she was half joking.

'Thanks Carol - I'll add it to my Christmas list; meanwhile let's play
the game according to the rules we all understand and see that we get
the results despite those constraints. Having said that, I know how
bloody frustrating it can be and I'll speak with the chief later today
when I update her on the case.'
'Thanks Guv!'
Sicknote re-entered
'Ah, just in time - any update on the girlfriend?'

'Only that my gut instinct was right Sir; she struggled to keep her hands off me at the Ritz restaurant, but I managed to let professional integrity overpower the urge to do a public service.'

'Alright alright - now the version from the real world please – and try to be serious for one minute.'

'Well actually she told me some of his faults – seemed only too pleased to point them out. She did explain about his football addiction and that he wouldn't have missed the Dortmund versus Arsenal game for anything, so it's a safe bet he was at the match. The CCTV footage that Carol gets should be able to tell us if he left in one piece and in which direction.'

'OK-thanks Dave. Any contact with his family? Can they shed any light?'

'Spoke with the brother Guv. Their mother has been ill and he was sure that if Hans-Werner was going to be anywhere other than watching footy it would be at work or with his mother. He says it's completely out of character and is very concerned. I have a contact in the German police who I am speaking with to see if there is any joint work we can do.'

'Great-keep on it. Brian and Steph: anything on our dominatrix lady?' Brian spoke in his thin Geordie voice.

'Got access to her house Sir – it's like a bloody taxidermists! Wall to wall skins and furs and animal handbags and shoes. Grim!'

"Anything of any use?'

'I could use most of the boots Sir!' Laughed Steph.

'I hear some guys like to be walked all over, ain't that right Brian?' Sicknote looked at the addition to their team.

'Steph could stick the boots on and make coming to work a real treat for you!'

'Wouldn't waste good leather on him.' She laughed.

'All very entertaining I'm sure, but what did you glean from the visit?' Dyson was tying to hide his smile; Brian Liddel was a bit of a wet blanket and Steph definitely the one who gave direction to that particular working partnership.

'We took a load of samples for background analysis Sir, speaking to a few friends later and I have her credit card details coming to me shortly, although when I spoke to her friend Abigail, the one who reported her missing, she said she nearly always pays cash, so not holding out for much info there.'

After another ten minutes the meeting wound up with the understanding that there would be a further briefing the following day unless there were significant developments before then.

31

Barbara Levy is struggling.

Struggling to understand where she is, why she is here and what is expected of her.

She is also struggling to get to grips with context. How has her life moved from the perfect entity it was only twelve short months ago to become this nightmare of loss and insanity?

The loss of her husband Andrew had been devastating. For a long time it had been touch and go as to whether he would survive the cancer, and the consultant had seemed to drag out the announcement like some kind of warped TV game-show host declaring who would go through to the next round and whose show would terminate here. She could clearly recall Andrew's look of expectation as he held his breath, gawping at this mighty Master of Ceremonies whilst awaiting the decisions of the panel of judges. Clearly unmoved by his plight and her pleas, her god had deserted them in their hour of desperate need. The experience had left her in a state of numbness; unable to process even the simplest emotions and unable to relate to anyone or anything in a meaningful way.

Her husband Andrew had never been a religious man; he'd scoffed at what he'd seen as a bunch of "absolute nutters" creating some kind of a life form to revere, when it was life itself that they should have dedicated themselves to. He had mellowed in later years from the ardent atheist of his youth. Indeed, towards the very end he had become more of an agnostic, almost philosophical about the afterlife theories and those religions which espoused reincarnation. But in his inimitably dark comedic way he'd said he had wanted to come back as a tape worm and infest his old head master. Although he'd confessed the pleasure would be balanced by the misfortune of being so close to the old bastard's disgusting working parts.

Barbara caught herself smiling wistfully and was wrenched back to reality. Barbara was a very private person, and thankfully, being at the top of the stack of wire cages she was not too easily seen by some of the others. This was especially important to her when she needed to perform the most basic animal functions. For the first week or so she had been unable to move her bowels at all; the ignominy of what it entailed had been simply too great and her body found a temporary solution in constipation. She had urinated of course - but hardly - there was little to pass; she drank so few fluids.

And that was how it had worked until, she guessed, around seven or eight days had passed. Then she had woken with violent stomach cramps, her share of the Serbian Problem, and her shame was forgotten as the bottom fell out of her world, or vice verse.

This god, which she had worshipped since she could speak, had been one of her two bedrocks; the other had been her family. Now, only the second time in her life that she had ever *really* needed him; her god was once again mute and her family dismembered by his cruel insanities.
She curled into a ball, hugging her burning stomach and wept silently, desperately trying to think of a way to end it all.

32

A dog walker passing a remote cottage noticed for the third day running that water was pooling on the road and seemed to be coming from the garden of the dwelling. She didn't want to trespass, but somebody ought to make sure it had been reported, hosepipe bans came along most years and it was crazy to waste water with pointless leaks.

When she reached home she dug out the number for the local water supply company and dialled. She was given a series of options to press 1, 2 or 3 until she heard:
"To report a fault, it's four".

She pressed four and reached a real telephone operator, who asked in an indifferent monotone what the issue was.
'I'd like to report a suspected leak.'
The water company employee asked her for details and she told her where the leak was, and that it had been going on for three days.
'Thank you for the information; I'll send one of our engineers round there as soon as one becomes available.'
The call was ended. She had been made to feel as if she had been offloading a personal problem onto the water company operative, but duty was done.

33

On his way to see Doctor Erikssen in Southampton, Colin had stopped at a service station on the M27 to use the loo. It amused him to stand here on the end of a row of seven or eight other men all staring at a tiled wall twelve inches in front of their noses with their trousers open and draining a balloon of waste fluid through their little dangly hoses. Evolution! Everything in the room was tiled and clean; antiseptic and geared up for efficiency. He chuckled because some genius had printed a tiny red, white and blue circular target inside the urinal for men to aim at. He had seen a documentary once about the amount of urine that spattered all over the place when a man peed at a urinal, and he knew for certain that the guy stood next to him was pissing tiny droplets of his waste onto Colin, and Colin was in turn showering him with his own personal piss-bath; it ought to be enough to start fist fights, but nobody seemed to care. Bizarre! But to treat them all like imbeciles and print a bloody target inside the bowl was, well, taking the piss. Colin actually laughed out loud at his pun, prompting a glance from his neighbour. He had a sudden mental image of rebelling and pointing his penis away from the urinal and quietly pissing all over the wall and floor. That would show them what I think of their patronising targets, he thought as he zipped up his fly and went to the sink.

The guy who had stood next to Colin turned, did up his own zip and headed straight for the door.

Enraged, Colin ran after the guy.

'Aren't you going to wash your hands?' he asked, open-mouthed and incredulous.

'What the fuck's it got to do with you?' Came the aggressive reply.

Every fibre in Colin's body wanted to smash the guy's head against the tiled wall, drag him to the urinals and rub his big nose over the little printed target, but with a herculean show of strength Colin simply turned and walked away.

He was shaking all over with the effort needed to take no action, and the pride welling in his chest for the mental strength he had shown. He would be sure to tell the good Doctor Erikssen *all* about this! He strode, smiling, to the Land-rover, thinking his anarchist peeing-on-the-wall thoughts. He had enjoyed the rebellious distraction and also the fact that he could so easily single-handedly ride roughshod over all their attempts at sterility. The place was tiled and kitted out and cleaned like a hospital and yet there were guys spattering each other in urine and not washing their hands and other guys close to pissing all over the walls. He smiled and thought about human nature and the fallacy that our high standards protected us from illness; he thought it was the opposite; we were becoming ill *because* of the sterility. You were made to feel guilty if you peed in the hedges, yet the hedgerows were overflowing with wild creatures – all of them happily pissing and crapping wherever they wanted to and they don't get ill from it. Not like the sick animals he'd seen in the so-called sterile food-standard factory farms. Some of the animal sicknesses there were wholly unnatural, despite the staggering volumes of antibiotics and macrobiotics pumped into the animals. Or maybe *because* of them!

He thought some more about this. He knew from the TV news that antibiotics were becoming ineffective in the fight against human illnesses, and that people were already dying in vast numbers because of this, in what world health bodies were calling a crisis. He also knew that it probably all stemmed from over-use of antibiotics leading to bacteria becoming resistant. He had read that in the USA around 80% of total national antibiotic consumption was pumped into farm animals, and he guessed the rest of the developed world was similar.
More arguments against the way we have industrialised meat production, he thought! Well that lent even more weight to his cause - as if he needed any more justification.

He started the old diesel engine and within twenty minutes was sat opposite Dr Erikssen, fibbing that he'd had no anger episodes recently and that he felt this was due to the tools the good Doctor had given him, rather than the medication. He related a carefully edited version of the incident at the service station and the doctor seemed genuinely impressed. Colin wanted to be free of medication and he felt that being selective with the truth would be the best way to achieve that.

Erikssen explained that the medicine would only just now be kicking in and it was recommended that the tablets be continued for another month. After that, they could decide the best course of action together. They discussed things in general, but Colin's mind, for once, was not engaged by the psychotherapist and he was happy when he was on his way back to the facility; back where he was needed.

The old Land-rover was roaring back along the eastbound carriageway of the M27 towards Chichester with the driver deep in thought about disposal of the Serbian animal transport truck. He had concealed it on the farm for the moment, but didn't want it there indefinitely. Doctor Erikssen had planted some concerns in his head with his talk of staying on the medication. It had been some time since Colin had weaned himself off of the Lithium mood stabilisers and he had done so because his research showed it to be a treatment for the symptoms of depression rather than anger. The good Doctor however had shown Colin that treating the stress that he thought might be triggering the anger episodes could by default reduce their incidence. But, and it was a big but, the very act of taking chemicals into his body caused Colin discomfort; he liked to be in control.

His concentration was drifting when he was startled by a big wasp or bee smacking into his windscreen. He wondered at the sheer volume of dead flies stuck to the glass already and it was still only spring - imagine how it would be in the warmer months now that the world was heating up so obviously. He idly calculated the global impact;

Average number of dead flies on his windscreen per week in hot months, say a hundred.
Months in UK when flies were active, call it six - or 26 weeks
That's 26 x 100 equals 2600 for his car alone.
How many cars in UK?
He had heard 17 million somewhere.
So if each car had the same flies as his, doing that in his head that was roughly 4.5 billion flies in the UK.

Worldwide....well that was a number too vast to be plausible.

He wondered whether, with all those flies dying, the delicate balance of nature would at some point tip. He knew that the human population was exploding beyond even the wildest predictions and was set to hit 9 billion in around fifteen year's time. The numbers always amazed him; so many people die in the developing world, so many disasters and yet lack of birth control due to ignorance and self-serving church policies coupled with mankind's increasing ability to keep its aged population breathing, despite the bodies often having collapsed through age or lifestyle-related incapacity, meant that the world was fast becoming a small place.

He had seen plenty of films and documentaries about global warming and knew that the temperature rises were directly linked with population growth and the consumption of fossil fuels. It was insanity that governments even now had such short-sighted policies on renewable energy, pandering to the aesthetics of a hillside over the essential, no, *critical* need to power industry and homes. He thought that this was in part due to the limited shelf-life a government had; usually four years in office and all of those trying to show what a cock up had previously been made by the opposition. Unless fundamental matters like energy and the survival of the species – and he saw it in such simple and stark terms – could be taken out of politics, then the world was fucked, and with it the human race. Simple. Colin punched the dashboard of the Land-rover in frustration at the incompetence of world leaders.

But he also knew that the single biggest contributor to global warming was the production of meat. More than all the energy consumption, more than all the emissions from global transport; all the cars, lorries, ships, planes, trains. That was where he could make a difference and that would be his legacy. He might not be the one to save the world, but he'd be one of them.

His thoughts wandered back to the flies and he shook his head at their stupidity, wondering whether at some point in time the flies which constantly seemed to become stuck in houses would have an evolutionary eureka moment and realise that flying repeatedly at full

speed towards a glazed window was futile and that the big opening where the wind was whistling through was the spot they ought to be aiming for. And as his windscreen bore testament, those lemming-like flying insects which chose to exist around roads and railways; they were currently dying in droves, but an evolutionary quirk that could lead to flies avoiding traffic...well it was a small developmental step, surely? But then he compared it to the arrested development of the
evolutionary swamp that mankind seemed to be wallowing in on the subject of animal rights.....

The advancement of species would eventually weed out the persistent head banging flies; only the cautious ones would be left and they would take the open window approach. Once the majority of flies had the modified gene, well, the world would be overrun with insects.
Would that signal the end of the world due to fly infestations? So many questions, so many tiny and yet critical risks which he had no control over. He became agitated and if it's possible to dance at the wheel of a Land-rover, then that's what he was doing. But it wasn't a dance of joy.

Colin pressed the windscreen spray button, but to his dismay all he heard was the noise of the pump pushing air through the nozzles. The vessel was bare and his windscreen would, for now, remain a flies' graveyard. Conscious now of their remains constantly in his field of vision, Colin decided he needed to remove them so he indicated left and pulled off the motorway to find somewhere to stop.

34

Simon Grayson took pride in the way he ran his business. He had worked hard since leaving school with nothing to show for the ten years he'd spent struggling with the labels attached by his earliest teachers. Lazy, stupid, indifferent; seemingly endless negative definitions flung by so-called educators whose inability to spot the symptoms of a complex combination of dyslexia and dyspraxia united them in an exclusive club of incompetents.

He'd endured the seemingly endless frustrations that go with understanding all the stuff but not being able to present it quickly or accurately and had taken any amount of ridicule from other pupils and so-called support staff. Indeed the only true support had come from his divorced mother with her unshakable faith in his inner intelligence. She alone had understood the mental anguish he had suffered as, unable to express himself through written or spoken media he had been driven ever deeper within himself; isolated from schoolmates by the wedge that the education system designed, maintained and nurtured; a statistic, hidden beneath the cloak of glowing OFSTED reports.

He had found relief in food; starting with comfort eating and then bingeing on unhealthy high-calorie treats. His mother seemed to be blind to the damage this gorging was having on her son and even supported it when she stocked up with chocolate, crisps and junk food. With no restraints in place he munched his way into early obesity.

Eventually his local doctor persuaded him – and his mother – that a programme of weight reduction was critical if he wanted to see his twenty-first birthday. Surprisingly, Simon adapted well to the strict regime of portion control and healthy food and began to feel positive about himself as the weight slowly came off. Whilst he was never an

146

active child and was to struggle all his life with the weight issue, he did possess an inner strength. He learned to tackle issues head-on and in time developed a strong determination to succeed against difficult odds. He even went back to college and learned coping mechanisms to help him get through life with his disabilities. He never lost his passion for food and in time qualified as an excellent chef. He opened his own place, slowly earning a reputation locally for his ability to create mouth-watering dishes from the simplest ingredients. Simon's restaurant had begun as a modest café, built on high quality treats and the best beverages at the lowest cost. He did the lion's share of the work himself and so had limited overheads. He reinvested every penny he made to bolster his fledgling business and establish himself as an up and coming name to watch.

Simon believed in the concept that food should be enjoyed visually as well as with the taste buds and as his reputation gathered momentum and he began to attract a more influential and affluent clientèle his in-house displays became increasingly flamboyant to reflect this ethos. The imagination which had lain in the shadow of the mild mental health issues that had gone so long undiagnosed now began to work in Simon's favour and he found he had a flair for creativity that extended beyond his culinary skills into the world of business. He hired a good PR company to promote his ideas and produce ambitious marketing campaigns.

MarkIt was the name of the organisation he chose and they had their offices in Archway, London. He could have chosen from any number of marketing companies but was drawn to MarkIt by their simple logo – the deep red outline of a square box with a big green tick just overlapping the edge. It portrayed a positive 'outside the box' mentality and that sat very comfortably in Simon's organised and creative mind.

Things went from good to great, and within a month of signing up with MarkIt there was talk of a daytime TV show appearance. He was on his way to meet his MarkIt agents to discuss the deal. At the MarkIt offices Simon was met by his agency contact, a tall, curvy Finnish lady called Sammi, with big eyes and even bigger, untamed blond hair. She ushered him into a meeting room where he was introduced to some key players from the television organisation and deluged in coffee and sparkling waters with exotic names, tasting of weak fruit juice. Options were discussed and details thrashed out, culminating in a short but lucrative contract being agreed in principle and a celebratory dinner in the restaurant of a well established master chef in town.

In the taxi home, Simon reflected on the positive turns his life had taken recently and thought about how his personality seemed to be strengthened by overwhelming odds, where others might be weakened. He called his mother to share his great news.

35

The fields were dryer now, and the sun surprisingly warm for early March. Colin wiped the last of the corpses and assorted debris from his windscreen and then ambled across the quiet little lane where he'd come to a halt, towards a worn and leaning Public Footpath sign he had spotted. He stood, leaning against a stile and gazed across the middle distance to where a large flock of sheep grazed peacefully. Here he was less than a mile from the motorway, but the traffic was practically inaudible and no trains or flight paths provoked tension with the tranquillity. The stillness was intoxicating, and the birdsong seemed to harmonise with the bleating animals as if it were a deliberately composed soundtrack to country life; part of some huge symphony for the enjoyment of those who still cared for such natural beauty. He wondered whether there were others like him; people who could still appreciate the stunning richness that his country could offer. He was sure there were very few places in the country where he'd be able to just stand and listen and think and simply just be. A few lines of some almost forgotten poem his mother had once recited came into his mind, something about not being too full of care to find the time to stand and stare. He'd never had a mind for poetry as a child, but as the years progressed he felt occasional desires to take one of his mother's old anthologies down from the bookshelf, blow off the decades of dust and randomly open a page and explore the words he found there. He could never really understand what the poet was saying, not in the way his mother used to be able to explain to him in any case. But the simple beauty of the words with their structure, form and rules, well it was art enough just to behold it. Any deeper meaning he might glean was a bonus.

His mother had had a great skill, he now realised. She had been able to translate the hidden meanings concealed by the fickle poets in the clever rhymes and almost-real words they used so that his childish mind could make some sense of them. She had formed them into stories; adventures on high seas or secrets in peaceful gardens, always there would be a tension, an excitement which he could almost touch. Usually too there would be a sadness; a tale of love gone bad, or yearning.

As he stood looking again at the sheep he resolved to try to write poetry of his own. He could make words rhyme surely? He tried it now.
Sheep; keep
Field, yield. Weald.
He smiled at his wonderful, rich language. How many other countries, he wondered, could make the same sounds with different letter combinations? He was sure that the incidence of dyslexia must be higher in English speaking areas than other languages; it was just such a messy soup of letter combinations. He thought some more on this. Thought about "thought"; the language was amazing and, for a dyslexic, immensely frustrating. His mother had shown him how just the simple letters 'ough' could be expressed in so many ways; fabulous ammunition for an aspiring poet, terrible tripping points for one who struggled with spelling and the complexities of words. Bough, dough, enough, cough, ought, oh he did his little happy dance and clenched his hands into excited fists in delight at his memory. How many others realised the colourful spectrum the English vocabulary gave them. People should appreciate it more.

Lambs. Hams.
No, that one was not so amusing. How anyone could slaughter these bouncy little creatures gambolling around their mothers he could not imagine. He frowned and his face hardened, as did his resolve. He pushed himself away from the fence post and strode towards his Land-rover. Time to stock up on his disciples, and he knew exactly where he needed to recruit the next one.
Lamb, ham, bamm! He sneered. Bamm indeed Mr nearly-famous Restaurateur.

36

Early afternoon the following day, with the restaurant officially closed after the lunchtime session, Simon Grayson had perched his considerable bulk on the edge of a table, completely at ease chatting with an attractive female diner. Danielle was the wife of a local politician who had ambitions in Westminster and consequently spent more time there than he did at home. She was looking at Simon with flirtatious eyes and they both knew where things were heading. They had come close on one or two previous occasions and the conversation so far today had left no room for ambiguity. Simon knew that she resented the way her husband flitted off here and there and left her home alone. Well, what the eye didn't see the mind shouldn't worry about, he thought.

For her part, Danielle had always been attracted to larger, confident men; she liked the comfort of a big, manly physique, liked to be engulfed, wrapped in the bear-like protection. Besides that Simon was dynamic; a go-getter and a leader. She liked to be led, and for all his political ambition, her husband was really just another follower, a doer of other people's wills.

The couple were interrupted by a visitor. Simon called in the direction of the newcomer
'Sorry guvnor, all done for the day.' He was barely paying him any attention, preferring to spend his energy on Danielle,
As he offered her another cognac he was irked to see the tall guy still standing by the door as if he hadn't understood the simple mechanics of opening and closing time.

'I said we are closed' he called again. 'Finito, kaputt' he smiled down at the woman and rolled his eyes conspiratorially as if he and she were part of an exclusive club and the intruder some foolish interloper.

'Open again at eleven tomorrow, but if you really can't survive until then there's a burger van in town tonight from eight – give him my regards and tell him not to give up his day job.' Grayson smirked and blew a silent kiss at his would-be conquest, who winked back; her giggle was a low-pitch growl.

'Have to humour the pond-life' he whispered to her. 'How about you and I take the rest of that fine bottle of Chablis into the house while we wait for the penny to drop for this moron?'

Again the exaggerated wink

'Cool. Let me just call Tony and tell him I am busy, otherwise he'll call me from London later and I guarantee it'll be at *the* least convenient time!'

'I can't imagine he'll be happy when you tell him where you are.' Said Simon in mock horror

'Don't worry darling, I am at a girlfriend's house as far as he is concerned; the benefits of having a few friends who can vouch for your whereabouts occasionally is priceless...not that I ever have need to take advantage of their loyalty.' She bit her lower lip and gave him a sidelong glance

'Haha, I bet! I'll be back in five minutes-just give him the call while I get rid of Mr clever here.'

Simon turned in the direction of where the unwelcome visitor had stood.

'Oh, seems he's got the hint.' He smiled.

'I'll give you a few minutes anyway while I tidy up the last few bits and pieces.'

'Not sure I can wait that long Simon; it's been a while since anyone's paid me any attention, I think if you make me wait another minute I might explode.' She raised her eyebrows.

'But you need to call your old man...'

'Oh I will darling. I can multi-task!'

'You can't be serious...you want to call him whilst we are....well, you know....'

'Absolutely! Oh come on Simon; most men would find that a massive turn-on, shagging another man's wife while she calls him!'

Grayson laughed and admitted to himself that the thought was erotic. She made a mock sad face.

'Unless your morals are really so high and you think we should forget the whole idea…'

He took her left hand and guided it to the front of his trousers

'That's how high my morals are; what do you think?'

'Mmm - you want to know what I think? I am hoping you have a big bed!'

He pulled her against him and their mouths locked, tongues sparring like flashing swords in a duel. Danielle was frantically unbuckling his belt as Simon attacked the buttons of her blouse as if his life depended on getting it off her before she got to him. It was a close contest which she won with one of her buttons stubbornly clinging in place as she grasped him, skin on skin. He grabbed each side of her top and tore them apart and the stubborn button pinged across the room.

Their tongues still entwined Simon lifted her easily and with her thighs clamped around his waist carried her to the big food preparation bench in the middle of the kitchen, her skirt was rucked up around her waist and his rock hard erection pushed against the gusset of her knickers.

No sooner was she resting on the table than she pulled her underwear to the side and he penetrated her in one long push.

Her gasp was one of the most erotic things he'd ever heard and he drove into her brutally and fast until she was screaming with every thrust. Within minutes he felt his climax rising. It seemed to start in his feet and tingle throughout him until he exploded deep inside her. Danielle screamed a final time and dug her fingernails through his thin shirt and deep into the flesh of his back. The pain was simultaneously excruciating and delicious and made his orgasm even more intense.

They remained locked together in the same position whilst they kissed deeply and with less urgency now, taking the time to appreciate the taste of each other.

'Oh my God Simon; I have never ever ever ever *ever* been fucked like *that*!'

'That was a first for me too baby-it felt like the world was ending when I came inside you. You are incredible!'

They kissed some more until she broke away.

'So much for 'phoning Tony!'

They both giggled

'Plenty of time left for that this afternoon.' he winked. 'Now how about we grab that bottle and go and carry on in bed where we left off....'

He quickly fetched the half-finished bottle of Cognac and taking her hand led her through the restaurant and into his living quarters.

In a small room off the kitchen which housed the plate-wash machine Colin stood with his forehead pressed against the wall and seethed. He had heard everything; the whole sordid act and he was disgusted. He punched the wall. The things men and women did when they were alone was repulsive to him. They had behaved like cave men, unable to resist the primeval urges – and in the kitchen of all places where food was prepared for the paying public. He had a good mind to follow them into the bedroom and teach the pair of them a lesson, and it was taking all the anger management tools he had been given by Doctor Erikssen to fight the urge.

After ten minutes of simmering silence he pushed himself away from the wall and forced himself to walk back to his Land-rover, which he had parked some two hundred yards down the road because he had wanted to approach the restaurant on foot.

It was nearly three hours later that Danielle and Simon parted with a final lingering kiss on the doorstep

'Call me.' she said, waving her hand above her head without looking back at him.

Simon Grayson sighed and turned back to the kitchen, realising he still had some cleaning up to finish from the busy lunchtime. He'd do that and then sit back with a drink and think over what had happened with Danielle during the afternoon. She sure was a live wire. With luck and some encouragement from her, that husband of hers would be spending even more time in London. He smiled as he entered the kitchen, it was the perfect set-up, a stunning woman who loved sex as much as he did, and was bloody amazing at it, without all the relationship crap that usually went with it.

He stopped in his tracks as he saw the tall guy from earlier standing in the kitchen, arms hanging loose at his sides, staring at him.

'You again? You don't seem to get it mate, we are closed, there is no more food on offer and I am about to celebrate having done a good service to the local community by shagging the local MPs missus. How about you do a disappearing act and shut the door behind you?'

The tall guy blinked his eyes once and then just stared blankly at Simon. When he spoke his voice was higher than expected and almost without inflexion.
'You served lamb today?'

'What? Yes, lamb was on the menu – what kind of question is that?' Simon became very uneasy in this guy's presence; he was tall, strong looking and had something odd about his face that he couldn't put his finger on. How long had he been prowling around here, he wondered.

'What vegetarian dishes did you offer?'
Simon was not anti-vegetarian as such, but he hated all their questions about "whether the sauce had meat stock" or "if there was gelatine in the ice cream".
'There is just one vegetarian offer on my menus mate; I call it "*Try next door*!" He smiled a smile of false bravado, hoping to be able to quickly get rid of this odd guy.

But the tall intruder pressed on with his questions.
'How do you feel when you see a little lamb running and jumping in the sunshine?'

'What? How do I feel? What is this, play-school kitchens? Well I visualise me rubbing tarragon and mint-butter all over it and checking that the oven is good and hot and has room for one more of god's little delicacies.'
Simon beamed his winning smile straight at the guy, trying to force any nervousness from his voice.

He continued 'And now it's time for us to do that thing where you stand on one side of the door and I stand on the other. I'll have this side - i.e. the one inside the house, and you can have the outside bit. Then you can jump in your car and point it away from here please.'

155

A niggling thought amongst all this light-hearted bluster; Simon hadn't seen, nor heard a car. The guy must have walked, must have been lurking around since lunchtime; maybe he was a sick paparazzi dick taking sneaky photos of MPs' wives....

'I have a better idea...' said the tall man '...we can both stay here a little while longer whilst...'

A lightening fast and immensely powerful punch under the ribs lifted Simon's considerable bulk momentarily from the ground and the wind left his body

'...I immobilise you with a punch just like that!'

'Then I will break your jaw like this.' The tall guy continued.

A ferocious back-fisted blow from the guy's right hand snapped Simon's head sideways and he did indeed hear a loud crack and conceded in a bizarrely detached way that his jaw probably had been broken. But before he could make a sound the guy had clamped his huge hand over Simon's mouth and was twisting his neck at an impossible angle. The pain in his neck and wrecked jaw was enough to make his knees buckle and he collapsed to the floor, feeling like the guy was trying to rip his head off.

'Make one fucking peep and I break your bastard neck, shitcunt.'

The guy was incredibly strong and there was no way Simon could even move.

Shit, who the hell was he? Simon tried to find a way to get some leverage or grip somehow but he was absolutely helpless and just had to lay there in agony, pinned to the floor and await the assailant's next move. At some point the guy would have to shift his weight and then Simon would scream for Danielle, she might still be near enough to hear him. At least the brute wasn't armed so if he could catch him off-guard Simon ought to be able to make a grab for one of his kitchen knives. They were all kept razor sharp and Simon was skilled in their use, he'd disable this guy in seconds by slicing through his tendons-fingers first, then maybe take out his hamstrings and then really hurt the nasty fucker.

'You know what this is?'

Simon was snapped from his reverie by the sight of a squat, fat pistol of some kind. He had no idea where it had come from and how it had got into the nutter's hand, but it looked evil.

'No of course not.' Colin answered his own question, 'you don't do the dirty work you just cook them. It's a bolt gun, a captive bolt gun, used for stunning animals before they are butchered. You should recognise it – your suppliers will use them all the time, unless you use Halal meat? Either way, it's ironic really that I should use one on you.'

Simon was staring at the guy's face-he realised what was so odd about him now, his eyes were way too far apart.

With that realisation came another; he was a psycho and he was going to do damage with this freaky gun. Simon threw all his strength into an attempt to wriggle free, but even with one hand holding the gun the big guy was easily able to restrain him.

The freak was staring at him in a way that proved he was a lunatic but now Simon had eyes only for the pistol, the muzzle of which was pressed painfully against the centre of his forehead.

'Say ouch for Uncle Colin.' He heard the freak say, but didn't hear anything more as the cartridge released the highly compressed air into the bolt chamber.

As he squeezed the trigger Colin wondered in a detached way whether the adjusted amount of explosive powder would be enough, or too much. As he lifted the muzzle away from the fat man's forehead he half expected to see a hole, but there was just a small, livid red patch. The guy was unconscious – perfect. Colin kissed the barrel of the bolt gun and smiled as he wrapped a considerable amount of black tape around the chef's large wrists.

37

Diary entry 7
March 14th 2014

Dear father

The bolt gun worked perfectly and I got the fat man. He will have a head ache I am sure!

Yesterday the electric bill came and it didn't make any sents. There was a breakdown of all the transformers on the farm and a bill for one that doesn't exist, number E1. I checked with the electric company and they said it appeerd on all the bills for the last 3 years at least, they couldn't see earlier records but I can get them sent to me. I don't know what you did with all the old bills, they said they send one every 3 months but they are not filed with the other paperwork. Your record keeping was always so tidy so I wunder if you were hiding something? You were always secrative about many things, like the old barn and the locked sellers and woulb never let me into them. I forgot all about the sellers under the killing lines but when I get time I am going to explor. Other things to focus on first.

Got to go and look after vengeance and ride him out, then I need to feed those other animals.

Your son
Colin

38

The damned hens were on screen again.

Amanda knew all about animal welfare and battery hens of course, which were kept in tiny cages and "encouraged" to produce eggs far in excess of their normal cycle by clever use of light and darkness. Each time the lights came on the hens assumed it was morning, and consequently produced an egg. No wonder the shells were so thin, the yolks so pale and the taste so insipid, despite the additions of who knew what cocktails of substances to counter these flaws. She knew that the vast majority, something like 95%, of all eggs were from hens held in conditions like these until their egg-laying days were prematurely exhausted and they were thrown onto the poultry scrap heap that was almost certainly the route to a soup tin or fast food outlet.

But now she had a far better idea of how the world must seem to such chickens and she swore to herself that if she ever got out of this place alive she'd never touch battery-produced eggs again. Maybe this was what the freak was trying to achieve; revulsion and abstinence. Well, this tactic would work with her and she was certain the others had similar thoughts. Her enclosure was a wire mesh cube approximately 2 feet by 3 feet and maybe 3 feet high. She could not stand nor could she lie down without her legs bent beneath her or her body curled in some other way. Often she would lie in a foetal form, muscle cramps coming and going relentlessly, cuddling herself against the cold and longing for something to wrap herself in other than the old blanket she had been given, which was now so saturated in the filth of the people above and around her that she tried to force it away from her – but there was nowhere for it to go. The cage was simply too small, and she could only keep her head as far from it as was possible.

She feared that she would develop a crooked spine – maybe become a hunchback. She tried every now and then to stretch different parts of her body, but it had become so painful now that any contact with the mesh floor or walls sent shooting pains through her and she knew, even in the dark, that she was bleeding from multiple places where the skin had been broken and the cuts were becoming infected and turning to blistered and weeping sores. But why should she would worry about a crooked spine – she'd trade that for her freedom any day.

The others, how many were there here? Cooped up the same as she was, cramped, cold, hungry, and filthy; slowly losing their minds. The cages were stacked in layers of four, two by two. Each had therefore two sides of the cage exposed to the barn, or warehouse or whatever it was. The two other sides of each coop were then butted up against the other three in the same layer. The external sides were certain to catch the draughts that blew around whenever the huge doors were slid open – usually at night, and, it being March, the temperature fell to a bitter cold, made worse by the lack of dry clothing or clean, dry blankets. Despite the cold she was grateful for the opportunities to breathe fresher air on those occasions and try to imagine it expunging some of the stink from the falling waste that was a constant threat. In turn, her waste fell to the poor people below. She felt pity for them when unbearable stomach cramps forced her to evacuate her bowels violently. In turn, she was subjected to similar outpourings from above.

Although she was rarely given any verbal warning from above, she had quickly learned to spot the signs if she was awake, and usually had enough time now to grab the filthy blanket the freak had given her and drape it, tent-like, over her head and much of her cage. She had tried to attach it to the wire, tearing the corners and tying them around the mesh but it was an odd nylon material and quite slippery; somehow it always fell down again and she was better off with a quick make-shift fly-sheet as and when the need arose. It didn't seem to matter who was defecating above her, as it seemed to distribute itself across all inhabitants. The Eastern European guy was the worst, his diarrhoea was usually accompanied by vomit; a thin, yellow bile from his stomach. There was never an apology from him; only moans and curses in his native Serbian.

Amanda was surprised at how quickly humans had degenerated to such a feral state. She had spoken with the others at first; they had talked about the freaky guy who held them here and what his real long term plans for them were. The German guy was convinced that they would get out, claiming that his government would pressurise the UK and that there would be a major incident team set up to track them down. They spoke about their backgrounds and families and all the things they'd be sure to do when they got out of this hell hole. But some bizarre self-preservation thing seemed to have taken over their minds and they spent most of their time now trying to get each other into the freaky guy's bad books-lord knew that was easy enough to do.

Amanda worried about her mother; they hardly spoke now, and although Amanda constantly called out to her she rarely got a reply from the top layer of cages where she was held. Amanda was thankful that there, at least, nobody could be fouling her with their bowel movements. The Serb spent much of his time moaning incoherently and rocking back and forth on bleeding feet. He had told her he was a Serbian farmer who had been tricked by the freaky captor whilst delivering pigs. She suspected he was a crook of some kind because in his more lucid moments he would shout at the crazy kidnapper and apologise for trying to rip him off.

How many? Eight? Ten? From the layout she assumed there were twelve cages and she could see six other people but some had made their own blanket-tents and as a result her field of vision was minimal. She wondered vaguely how they had all been trapped. Had they fallen foul of the same trick he had played with her? A simple knock at the door? Yet again she rued her failure to attach the security chain before she had opened up. He was a devious sod and clearly planned thoroughly. That didn't bode well for their chances then.

She tried desperately to find some respite from the insanity somewhere deep within her mind but the video was too intrusive.

161

Now showing images of chickens crammed into too-small places, reminding her of lines from a poem she'd heard at a small child's funeral once. The author's name escaped her, but the final lines were seared into her memory; as were images of the dead child's father desperately trying to hold it together as he said his final goodbye to his little princess and come to terms with the infinite scale of the loss:

"...The big words fail to fit....'

He had read, to the achingly quiet congregation

'...Like giant boxes
Round small bodies.
Taking up improper room,
Where so much withering is, and so much bloom...."

Except of course this was the opposite, giant bodies in small boxes. The hens looked like huge sci-fi birds "taking up improper room" in a world as alien to them as this one was to her.

It had been filmed in real-time, unedited, so what the chickens did was directly relatable to what she was experiencing. When the chickens were fed in the film, she was fed. She knew what it would be that came down the chute; when the chickens were on the screen she ate dehydrated pellets of what she assumed to be chicken meat. When the pigs were showing the food was pelletised pork in some form. She was forced through hunger to eat, and was surprised how similar these tasted to the veggie bacon she sometimes bought. But always, the combination of video image and taste made her want to wretch. Part of his plan, she was sure.

There was a terrible film clearly shot by some investigative journalist showing warped farm employees picking up piglets by their hind legs and, their scrawny, tattooed arms wind-milling, killing the tiny creatures by slamming their heads onto the concrete floor where they would lay, trembling and twitching for a while, occasionally kicked, until they became still. She knew this was honest camera work and could see from their casual mannerisms that such acts were clearly ingrained in the behaviours of the twisted workforce. The world was obviously well stocked with sick bastards and defenceless animals were the perfect outlet for their sadism; helpless - in the true sense of the word - and without a voice, these abuses could probably go on for years undetected. She could appreciate the dilemma the person with the camera must be going through; continue to film and capture the violence objectively, or intervene, save one little creature and at the same time blow their cover. She realised that it was only through the dedication of the animal rights people that these disgusting acts were ever brought to light at all. In this film one of the killers was smiling directly at the person with the secret camera and mouthing something she couldn't hear nor lip read, but the sneer indicated pleasure at his own sick behaviour.

There were other animal videos and the consequent accompanying 'meal' would always match the animal on screen. By far the worst was when the animal experiment films were running. Those dogs, mice, rats and monkeys being used for any number of laboratory tests. She couldn't begin to imagine what the food that came down the chute on those days might have been, but she was close to starvation and primeval instinct allowed her to eat the filth.

The only difference between her situation and that of the chickens was that the video had been filmed with some kind of night vision camera so that she could see the birds even when it was dark for them. Maybe the freak was filming her and her fellow sufferers in the same way? Was he compiling a series of sick videos? Who knew what the purpose was. The psycho who held them all here never gave any hint of time-frames or outcomes, other than that they had all wronged the animal world and must all be cleansed; cured. God what would she give to be cleansed in a deep warm soapy bath....she drifted, finally, to a more peaceful place in her mind, but the video ran on.

39

In the police ops room the investigation team were assembled for the morning briefing.

'There has been a further development overnight which *may* be linked to the two disappearances. A mother and daughter have disappeared it seems. Reported as a MisPers last night by a worried friend, Eleanor something, who said they had planned to see a film together and then have dinner. Amanda and Barbara Levy didn't show, and Amanda's mobile is switched off. This Eleanor so-and-so says it's completely out of character – aren't they always – but in light of recent events we need to take it seriously. I've got uniform checking out their home address and speaking with the cinema to see if they have a way to tell who entered the showing and looking at CCTV etc.

Sicknote had his usual flippant comment:
'Eleanor *Something* or Eleanor *Soandso* Guv? Or two Eleanors?'
Dyson bit his lip; he was really getting tired of Sicknote's eternal tomfoolery. He made a mental note to take him to one side after the briefing.
'Thanks for keeping it trivial Sicknote, seems you just volunteered to follow it up!'
'Will do, boss; how old is Eleanor?'
'God sake Dave, you can't stop thinking about sex can you!' This from Samantha.
'It's really getting tedious now, concentrate your mental energy on the cases why don't you!'
'Sorry Miss Serious, I'll come to work miserable in future.'

Neil intervened.
'Let's all of us start to focus on the right stuff please, this thing seems to be getting bigger and I'm worried it's all the same group and what

the next steps might be. To be honest, I'm expecting ransom demands any day now. I'll be drafting in some support from the Met; the Chief is keen to get a handle on it quickly before the press start to join two and two together.'

'And coming up with four.' This from Samantha Milsom, who liked to call a spade a spade.

'That's four MisPers so far Sir, maybe we might want to check with other forces to see if they have any similar events recently?'

'Good idea Samantha, you tackle that angle can you?'

'Sure thing – anyone got a list of contacts in the other areas-all mine seem to have become private security consultants.'

This was a tongue-in-cheek reference to recent resignations from the force due to low morale and perceived under-resourcing.

'I am sure you'll get the people you need if you use the standard contact procedures!'

'Carol; any joy on the CCTV yet?'

'Yes Guv; we have a bit of a result; got two clips of Hans-Werner looking directly at cameras. It's almost as if he's trying to identify their locations. Makes no sense, but it's definitely two positive Ids and he definitely stares straight into the lenses. Both cameras capture him before the game, but nothing afterwards, yet. He seems to be on his own in the shots, i.e. surrounded by different people so doesn't look like he hooked up with anyone.'

'Right, let's assume now that these disappearances are definitely linked. What are the common factors; locations, MO, time of day? What do the victims have in common, if anything, or are these random snatches? Brian, take charge of the pen and white board please and get scribbling. Steph, did you get the mugshots copied I asked for?'

'Just waiting for the two from last night Guv, Amanda and Barbara'.

Sicknote had a thought. 'We ought to capture any obvious differences too sir, sometimes they can reveal something.'

'Sure thing Dave; those too then people. OK, brainstorming time.'

'It's not called brainstorming any more Guv, didn't you see the memo? The ops speak now is "Mind-dumping".'

'Great, thanks for the update Sicknote, I'm sure that will help us moving some grey cells around then.' The sarcasm was self-evident.

Brian stuck a large map of the surrounding area which covered all disappearance locations. Then he wrote:

Hans-Werner Fromm. German, IT specialist, Chichester home, Brighton work.
No affiliations we know about. Then in capitals ARSENAL FAN!!!
Went missing from unknown location at night (or during evening football match-finished around 21:45).

Neil Dyson exploded.
Guys, we seem to be confusing fundamentals here. Fromm was, or rather is, a German and therefore a Dortmund fan. If we can't even grasp the fucking basics we'll be here a long time tonight.
His face flushing bright red, Liddel corrected his work, and then somewhat self-consciously continued to write.

Donna Southgate. English, sex-trade, Chichester home, various work locations!!! Likes animal skins. Went missing somewhere between London and Horsham station. Late afternoon assumed – bank card shows no transactions on day.

Amanda Levy. English, hotel receptionist. Chichester home. No known hobbies. Went missing at unknown location and time, but before 16:00.

Barbara Levy. English, retired, London home. No known hobbies. Went missing at unknown location and time, but before 16:00.

'Hmmn, not much common ground there.' Said Steph; ' looks pretty random right now.'
'Let's assume there is a commonality and we just haven't spotted it yet. Steph and Brian-add this to your tasks. Get around all their friends, families and workplaces and really get into their lives; something is there to give us a hint. No stone unturned. Carol-CCTV at Horsham station. Include the car-park, she might have got that far; talk to the staff.'

'Any door-to-door Guv?'
'Not at this stage Sicknote, let's focus our limited resource on likely hotspots first. OK folks, let's get with it. Dave – a word please.'
'Yes Guv?'.
'Not here; my office.'
Sicknote looked a little taken aback as the team dispersed.

When they were together Neil shut the door and turned towards Sicknote with a serious face, made somewhat menacing by the eye deformities.
'Dave, I know you find everything amusing and I know you think we all need cheering up but it's time to demonstrate why you wear those stripes and others don't. You're making yourself look like a monkey at times and you're in danger of losing the lesser ranks' respect. I don't wanna discuss it or elaborate, just keep it professional and apply that brilliant mind on the serious shit from here on in; OK?'
'Sorry Guv, sure thing.'
'Good. Let's get to it then.'

40

Jenny picked up the 'phone in the bookshop.
'Hello, Chichester Rare Editions, how can I help?'
'Yes, good morning.'
Jenny couldn't tell if this was a man or woman, it had the timbre of a male voice except it was a little high pitched.
'I wonder if you'd be interested in a book I have inherited from my Grandfather. It belonged to his grandfather and is very old?'
Jenny became immediately alert
'Quite possibly, we are always on the lookout for rare editions and interesting works.' She replied. 'I'm Jenny by the way!' She hoped an exchange of names might reveal the caller's gender.
'Oh yes, hello Jenny. My name is, er, Derek.'

Ah; a man then after all! Jenny noticed the slight hesitation but dismissed it as nerves, some people felt very uneasy when they were looking to sell a precious family heirloom or object of value; she found this to be particularly true with books. Old books took on a character of their own, and with age and the acclaim of the author came some kind of reverence. She certainly held many of the tomes which lined the shelves here in awe. She had sold some extremely rare first editions and would sometimes shed a tear afterwards at the mercenary manner of the transaction. This emotion would be less tearing if the purchaser was sympathetic and wanted the book for all that it represented, not just as a trophy to gloat over.

'Hello Derek, what's the book you have?'

'Well, I'd rather you saw it for yourself, it's incredibly rare and I have to be very careful that it doesn't fall into the hands of any unscrupulous traders, my Grandfather would turn in his grave.'

'Oh I know exactly how you feel, beautiful old books are such precious things and we have a duty to preserve their dignity.' This seemingly flippant statement betrayed an ethos which was at the core of Jenny's being. She genuinely thought of herself as a guardian for the editions she watched over. A gatekeeper or chaperone who had to vet all potential suitors.

'OK,' she continued. 'Would you like to bring it into the shop so we can have a look together?'

'I am nervous about taking it anywhere; how about we meet somewhere quiet and neutral where you can take your time evaluating the book's worth. I can meet you this evening if that's convenient – otherwise I am away for a few days.'

Jenny had planned to be with Neil tonight and if she were to meet this Derek it would have to be local and not too late.

'OK-I can meet you this evening, where did you have in mind?'

'Somewhere not too public, you'll understand when you see this book. How about behind the cathedral at around half past seven?'

'Can't you do any earlier?'

'No sorry, I have to prepare for a trip.'

'OK then, where exactly?'

'There's a little access road called Canon Lane; meet me there and prepare to be surprised!'

Jenny was excited, this sounded like it could be one of those books that came along maybe once or twice a decade; these were the moments she dreamed of!

'OK; seven thirty tonight, see you then Derek.' She affirmed.

The phone went dead. She fleetingly registered the point that Derek didn't want to bring the book to the shop, but was prepared to meet somewhere neutral. Only then did she stop to think about the risk she might be exposing herself to; an unknown man calls and offers a too-good-to-be-true opportunity and she jumps at it like a happy child. She'd call Neil, and tell him the arrangement. That way, if anything went wrong he'd know about it quickly. She dialled his mobile and got his voice-mail.

"Neil Dyson, you know what to do"

God how she hated that voice-mail greeting; so impersonal and abrupt; not at all like the real Neil Dyson she knew, but probably part of the façade he put up for the benefit of his work associates. She'd get him to change it tonight!

'Hello hun it's me. Just to let you know I am viewing an old but very exciting book tonight at 7.30 in Canon Lane behind the cathedral I'll be about half hour later than we planned, but feel free to have a glass ready for me-I have a feeling I'm going to need it. Love you.'

It was just gone five pm. She'd need fifteen minutes or so to wrap up here and get to the cathedral and decided she had plenty to occupy her in the shop until the meeting time. Busying herself with some till receipts, she found herself checking the clock every few minutes, her excitement mounting with the crawling sweep of the hands towards seven pm.

At 18.50 Neil picked up Jenny's message. She was an impulsive creature and they'd discussed many times the lack of personal security she exercised, but he was pleased that the safety precautions he'd been drumming in to her finally seemed to be bearing fruit. He decided to surprise her and pick her up at the meeting place. There was a great Italian restaurant around the corner and he'd take her there on an impromptu date. That would be big brownie points! It would take him ten minutes to get to where she was viewing the book and so he had plenty of time to wrap up the last bits of paperwork for the day and prep his meeting for the morning.

At seven o'clock, and unable to wait any longer, Jenny set the shop alarm, locked up and walked through the city streets towards the Cathedral. She'd decided to leave her car in the main car park as it was a very short walk to the meeting place and would be easier than messing around trying to find a parking space when she got there. She went around the eastern side of the cathedral and into the cloisters, thinking that she could reach the meeting place that way, but she found the way barred by a pair of locked wrought iron gates. She had plenty of time and took the opportunity to look at some of the ancient stonework as she unhurriedly retraced her steps.

Still fifteen minutes ahead of schedule she entered South Street and after a short walk turned right into the access road that Derek had mentioned. As she approached the end she saw an old dirty-blue Land-rover with its engine running. She wondered if that might be Derek and strolled towards it. Someone was stood at the rear doors and as she went around to the back of the vehicle was greeted by a tall smiling man.
'Derek?'
'Er, yes, hello you must be Jenny!'
'Hi yes. I'm very excited about this Derek; tell me more about the book before you reveal it to me, it feels like a magical story.'
'Of course.' Derek reached into a large black canvas bag and brought out a bundle of cloth.
'It's wrapped in here.' he said lifting the bundle towards Jenny's curious face.
But what came out of the cloth was a bunch of old rags. Confused, Jenny looked up into the man's face and a flicker of recognition flashed across her eyes just as he grabbed the back of her head and pressed the rags hard across her nose and mouth.

At half past seven exactly Neil drove into Canon Lane and looked for Jenny's car.

It wasn't there, but he realised she may be on foot as it was so close to her shop. He parked up and sat back with radio 5 live sport on in the background. After ten minutes, with still no sign of his fiancé, Neil called her number. The message said that the person he was calling was not available and he should try again later. He tried again immediately and got the same message. After five attempts he knew he had missed her and swung his car round to head home. Shame, the surprise date would have been fun, but he was going to see her in a few minutes anyway.

When he arrived at his place Neil had expected to see the lights on and was surprised to find it completely dark. He opened up and it was clear there was no Jenny. He called her number again. Once more he got the unavailable message. A little concerned, he phoned her friend Sarah.

Sarah hadn't seen or heard from Jenny for a couple of days.

Neil was now genuinely worried and racked his brain trying to think where she might have gone. The thought that something had happened to her wouldn't die, and he convinced himself that the suddenly arranged meeting had something to do with it.

He called his police partner Samantha Milsom for advice

'Hi boss, what's up, she thrown you out because of the steak thing?'

'Samantha, I'm worried.' He quickly told her about the arrangements and his plan for a surprise date. When he'd finished Samantha told him he was probably over-reacting and that she'd turn up any minute with some scatty story about how it had been a Gutenberg Bible and they'd gone off to get it consecrated at the cathedral or similar.
Neil chuckled despite his nerves.
'Yeah of course, you are probably right. All these disappearances are getting to me. I'll chill for a while and see what she comes out with when she turns up! Thanks Samantha.'

'Any time Bossman' she laughed. 'Let me know when she turns up though, right?'

Neil promised he would and ended the call.

41

Grayson was speaking with Amanda in the cage below his. He'd been in the place almost a day and was pumping her for information about the freak who had captured them all so easily and what he aimed to achieve. He quizzed her on things like daily routines, food, exercise and when they might expect to be released. They got to talking about the circumstances of their own capture and a little about their backgrounds. Simon admitted that he struggled with meaningful relationships and had never actually experienced love in its true sense; only lust and infatuation.

She asked about his interests and he explained his troubled education and how he had turned his life around, devoting every waking hour to his ambitions of culinary fame. As a result he had little time for hobbies and apart from watching snooker on TV – he loved the permutations of angles and momentum – he had no real interests in his life. He confessed to her his addiction to sex; especially with a new woman, discovering her body and how her mind worked in a sexual context. He was honest enough to admit that her interests and needs were of little consequence; he wanted to fuck her and through that find out new tricks and techniques. As a result, he said, he was a terrific lover and any time she wanted to sample really incredible sex she need only say the word – once they were out of here of course!

For her part, Amanda was left cold by this bullshit, but the opportunity to talk to someone about relatively mundane day-to-day "normal" things was welcome, even if he was everything she hated in a man and made her cringe. She explained to him that she was studying part time for a degree in English Literature – specifically the early poets. She'd learned to love Shakespeare from her mother's infectious enthusiasm. As a child she would beg to have a bedtime story and invariably her mother would read or quote from memory from the Bard's great and, occasionally lesser-known works.

She worried constantly about her mother, locked away on the top level with only that disgusting anti-feminist Grayson and the loathsome Serb Babić. At first her mother had called to her and they'd had at least a few awkward conversations – her mother never had been one for showing emotion publicly - but she had withdrawn inside herself and hardly uttered a word now. Amanda decided to try to coax her out of her shell.

'Mum, remember some of the poems you used to read to me?' She shouted.
At first there was no answer, and then, in a voice like a lark she heard the simple but oh so beautiful words from her mother, quoting the long-forgotten Shakespeare of her youth.

> *"No, no, no, no! Come, let's away to prison.*
> *We two alone will sing like birds i' the cage".*

Amanda smiled in the dark at the ironic choice. If she could remember such obscure lines, then her mother's mind wasn't beyond saving.

The loud speaker system crackled to life and the voice of their gaoler was heard; a little tinny and with that frustrating booming echo common at railway stations caused by the overlapping of sound caused by time delay between speakers.
'My disciples; welcome to the best day of your lives so far, the day we properly join together to be mended. The day that we learn that it's only when we have fixed ourselves that we can go forth and repair the broken world outside.'
Colin felt like a preacher in his control room pulpit.

The screens now showed a continuous thirty second loop from the disturbing pig farm footage where helpless piglets were being swung over the heads of the clearly sick workers and hammered like slam-dunked basketballs onto the stone floor. The sounds that accompanied the scene were in stark contrast. The poor audio quality of Richard Strauss' *"September"* from his *Four Last Songs* may not have turned heads at a Hi-Fi convention, but in this environment

175

with that visual backdrop it might have been the Berlin Philharmonic. This bizarre juxtaposing of the tranquillity of orchestral Lieder with callous brutality was not lost on Jenny and she sat open-mouthed; temporarily lost in the surreal experience.

'Your starter for ten!' The voice was for once calm and measured, as if carefully delivering an important message to a multi-lingual scientific convention.
'Who can tell me where this film was shot? I shall make it easy for you. It was either

> a) In deepest Africa, where every meal might be your last and killing is a necessity of survival. Or it was
> b) In the sweatshops of the Middle East, where animals have only bartering value – much like plastic chips in some eccentric casino.
> Or
> c) In the developed, welfare-conscious lands of free speech that are Europe or the USA?'

There was a pause of a few seconds during which no suggestions were forthcoming.

'What do you think Babić? Could this have been filmed in your country? Are the people there so retarded that they take pleasure from breaking the skulls of baby animals on the iron-hard ground? How do you see it Farouk with your knowledge of animal pain thresholds? Do you imagine these piglets would give this pain a five out of ten on their scale? Maybe a six? How would you score it? Preferable to receive a sharp slit across the throat I expect would be your view. You know, for once I have to agree with you! Imagine that; *me* saying that these creatures should die from a single cut across their gizzards. But this is clearly not in the Middle East is it? This is hardly Halal, despite the lack of pain management, but even you must see this as overstepping the mark, doctor?'

'Grayson. Simon. I know you support those who take the little baby sheep from their mothers and butcher them like you were all some band of demigods. But where do you think this was filmed? By the way, do you know that after lambs are taken from their mothers to be slaughtered, the ewes walk the field looking for their babies? They search in the corners, they hunt high and low; and all the time they are bleating; calling for their child. They do not understand that their babies have been taken from under their noses so that we, the superior species, can adorn our tables. No, they do not understand that, yet they understand that there is an empty space on the grass where yesterday a happy lamb lay, or jumped and played and ran, and nuzzled for a mother's milk. Their torment has been known to go on for weeks. I wonder if we shall one day be able to measure stress and anxiety in animals. I imagine many of us will hang our heads in shame. Some of us should be hanging them now.'

'No; you are struggling clearly so let me help you, dear friends. This film was shot in the great civilisation that is the U S of A, the United States of America. The Land of the Free. The land of constitutional rights, where the little guy's voice is as important as the big guy's. Well these guys didn't have a voice on this day, nor on any other. And whilst I don't have limitless video evidence, I'd put good money on this not being an isolated incident. These sick morons are clearly acting out a regular pantomime. If the dark play is Cinderella, then the ugly sisters are those monsters with the bright young blood on their aprons.'

The voice was becoming louder and higher in pitch as the speaker became more animated.
'And the great gag here is that these animals were not murdered for dog food or some other low-quality shit; these were heading for one of the biggest supermarket chains in the world, for human consumption – oh but I hate that term. One of those chains that has all the shiny sustainability and ethical trading policies, and holds audits and press conferences about how well they are doing and publishes reports to prove that this stuff doesn't happen. No Sir, not in our shops! Well guess what Mr and Mrs fucking America....'

The voice, louder still, began to crack with emotion and strain

'...it does happen in your shops, on your streets and in your towns and worse than that, it is done by the guys you drink with and pick up your kids from school with and it's still happening-almost

177

certainly right now, as we speak, somewhere in a town near you and in every other fucking town.'

Hans-Werner's head almost exploded from the thundering silence that ensued. Indeed, he thought he had suffered some kind of stroke and lost his senses. The pain slowly returned, refocusing on the front of his skull and the illusion was broken.

Jenny was still staring at the screen nearest to her which had been frozen mid-frame showing a grotesquely distorted piglet's head – captured in the act of shattering against the impassive ground and looking for all the world like a ridiculous caricature of itself. Despite the poor video quality, droplets of blood and mucous were identifiable, caught mid-air in the moment of liberation from the tiny beast that had spawned them. The whole image like some made-up horror film effect. But she knew it was for real, and her heart sickened at the abomination of the act.

She knew this stuff happened in the so-called developed world; knew it would still be happening right now, even as she half sat/half lay in this disgusting mess she knew there were thugs doing this. She had seen the cruelty images many times, seen countless Mercy for Animals and Compassion in World Farming videos, but they never got easier to stomach. These kinds of behaviours were some of her reasons for being vegan.

She wondered, for a single moment, whether what this guy was doing to them was justified in some way.
Colin's voice interrupted her thoughts.
'This was a short sharp lesson in reality my friends. We will be having daily short sharp lessons. I call these single point lessons because we shall cover one single matter each time we come together in this way. You will be feeling discomfort in your temporary homes. You will be cold. You will be dirty; filthy dirty – believe me, collectively you stink like a sewer, but remember; if you learn the lessons and if you can make the simple change that is needed then you will soon be free. Free to breathe the fresh wind, free to run, to play, to feel the grass between your bare toes, if you choose. All those simple pleasures which I have denied you, and

178

which we, people, are denying billions of animals every year. I shall leave you with the last verse of Peter Porter's excellent poem.'

His voice took on a slightly theatrical tone as he recited from memory.

> *'...London is full of chickens on electric spits*
> *Cooking in windows where the public pass.*
> *This, say the chickens, is their Auschwitz,*
> *And all poultry eaters are psychopaths....'*

'People; until tomorrow. Oh-I have a special treat for you tonight; the film I shall share is from a well-known ethical perfume company. You may be surprised!'

With that the place became quiet and the lights were dimmed. The slaughterhouse scenes were replaced by a grainy still shot taken inside a laboratory.

Diary entry 8
March 15th 2014

Dear father
A good day with no anger.

as I was driving today I saw a magpie eating a hedgehog.
I often see them devowering dead animals at the road side and
dispite being amongst the slowest ungainly birds I no, it never seems
to be them that are struck by traffic. This is especially interesting
when we consider the persentage of there lives they seem to spend
hopping arounb in front of speeding cars. Maybe they have a pakt
with the road and the cars, a cleaning up agreement, much like the
tiny birds which live on the backs of alligaters and enter their mouths
to pick the carrion from their teeth?

You'll be disinterested to no that my plans are going well. I have
made my preperations for sending the first message out to the worlb
about what I expect from them. The girl Jenny will help me with
that. She is very pretty and will make a good frontman for my
campaine – well, front person
Mother would have been proud.

Your son

Colin

It was some hours after the "group therapy" as the freak had called it
that Jenny was sat on a hard wooden chair with her hands tied
behind her back in what looked like a large, bare office. The room
was a rectangle, pale cream in colour and approximately 25ft by 16ft
with a door at one end and a window above her head height on either
of the long sides. She'd been marched into here from her cage, but
due to a tight blindfold which had since been removed she had no
idea where she was in relation to the main building; she didn't think
she'd been taken outside, so it must be an annex of some kind. The
freak was there setting up some equipment that might have been
cameras or audio recording gear. He was singing about Babić, who
seemingly was "coshed for money".

'We have to write a note for the TV and papers saying that you are
still alive but won't be very shortly unless the entire population of
England stop eating animals with immediate effect. I cannot read or
write very well at all so your writing will be clearer than mine. I
want something like

"To all disgusting carnivores. You will stop eating animals
immediately or I will be shot"

Jenny was terrified and knew she was going to do whatever the
psycho told her and nodded to try to show him that she would
comply. He smiled and leered at her with that sick look he adopted
whenever he came close to her; she had the feeling that he became
aroused by the dominant role he was playing out, but she couldn't be
sure if it was that or if it was just his insanity. She hoped any arousal
didn't develop into sexual appetite; that would be one horror too far.
For a moment she imagined him forcing himself upon her helpless
body and a violent shudder ran through her. Even after all she had
been through at his hands, the thought of that would be enough to

send her over the edge and she watched him carefully for any sign of physical desire. To her relief he seemed engrossed in his preparations. It was obvious that he wanted to film her holding up the message he had told her to create. She thought about that, and how she might get some hidden clues across to anyone reading it. He wanted her to tell the public to stop eating meat; how could she spin that out in a long enough statement to allow her to build in some secret message? She welcomed the distraction of thinking.

Trying to formulate the words and somehow work in a secret code was hard, her concentration, usually so reliable, was shot to pieces. She thought about anagrams and acronyms, capital letters and sequences but she became too confused to get any meaningful series of words together.

OK, she thought, Maybe I should decide on the words and then try to build in some coded message. What had he said she should work on? Something about carnivores and her being shot if they continued to eat animals. OK OK OK;

"You animal eaters had better stop it right now or this man will kill me"

That gave the message that there was probably one single man. What else could she build into that? What message did she even want to get across anyway? Something about where she was or had been? Something about the guy; his description, his mannerisms? Well he's a freaking oddball that's for sure, she thought. His eyes are so far apart - that is pretty odd, and his voice is high and he has an insanely short temper but not always. Probably bi-polar or something. She wasn't too familiar with that condition but she was quite sure he fitted the mould well enough.
OK then; wide eyes, high voice, bi-polar. What about their location? She didn't know where the hell they were being held, nor what it might look like. She was pretty confident that she had been removed from the barn-type building but had no clue where she was now.

Barn building. Well that didn't narrow it down much, but she knew from her military police training and the frequent conversations she'd had with Neil when he was running through a case and bouncing ideas off her that sometimes the merest snippet of detail can end up as a significant clue. Well the barn was quiet. In the cryptic crosswords she used to do there were many tricks and hints to help solve clues; if she could remember some of them she could use some hints and hope the police had a crossword buff in their ranks.

She was disturbed from her ruminations by Colin's voice.
'Right girlie.' He said in a matter-of fact tone 'Time to get scribing.'
He gave her a flip chart and some coloured marker pens
'Remember; the words "carnivore", "stop" and "kill" are the critical ones. Choose any others you like but make it short, sharp and shocking! It's darker than I thought in here and I have to go and fetch a light from one of the farm buildings or the video will be useless. I will drive so I'll be back in a couple of minutes; have it ready by then.'

He untied her hands
'Oh, and I have to check the cages are all nice and secure, so that will take a couple more minutes.'
'Why are you really doing this? What motivates you so strongly and where did it come from?'
Surprised by the question, Colin sat her down at his feet and spoke very softly.

'When I was thirteen years old I had a Saturday job helping out at a riding stables nearby. It didn't pay well, and it was hard work, cleaning, brushing, feeding and riding the horses. I was there in all weathers, rain, wind, snow, sunshine, it mattered not to me I adored the horses and I never missed a day.
The stable owner, a guy called Mr Gibson, had a reputation for breaking in difficult horses, but I had never seen the master at work. One day I was told that a new mare, Grace, had been brought in for the daughter of some local wealthy couple type and she was to come to ride her for the first time. When she arrived she was the kind of spoiled rich kid that you take an instant dislike to, and her father was an obnoxious git, strutting around as if *he* owned the place. I was treated like an imbecile and made to feel very lowly; fetching this, carrying that…'

183

'Grace was a beautiful horse and after I had saddled her up and made her ready I went about my other chores.'

'There was a terrible shout and a scream and I rushed into the riding hall to see what had happened, to find the daughter lying on the ground and men everywhere fussing and shouting.

Poor Grace was being led away by one of the rougher stable boys'.

'The following week I went to work as usual and heard shouting in the hall. I went to investigate and found Mr Gibson with Grace on a short lunging rein and whipping her with one of those long whips that you see in cowboy films. I don't know how long he'd been doing this, but he was sweating and she was clearly in great distress. I could see blood and swelling all over her face, flanks and shoulders'.

'I screamed at him to stop and ran at him, grabbing a pitch-fork as I ran. He turned in surprise and when he saw my intention turned the whip on me. There followed a brief scuffle which saw me pin him to the wooden wall, the tines of the fork either side of his throat.

Even at that age I was very tall, and all the work at the yard and here on the farm had made me strong and fit. As I held him there I worked my way down the shaft of the fork until I was inches from his red and panting face'.

'What happened next I don't clearly remember, but I became aware that he was lying on the floor with blood over his face and his eyes closed. I managed to corner Grace and led her gently away, talking softly to her all the while and soothing her bleeding flanks with soft strokes. I took her to a stall and began to tend her many lacerations, I am not sure who was shaking the most, her from shock and fear of man, or me from the horror of seeing such a beautiful creature so brutally assaulted. Gibson didn't enter my thoughts for a moment.'

'I do remember her standing listlessly, leaning against the wall and being terrified that she might lie down and simply die; horses can do that, you know, it's a biological weakness. I wanted to call the vet, but I didn't know how. I wasn't very good with telephones and dealing with other people, so I just fetched wet towels and painkillers and stayed there with her until it became dark outside. In the end she was calm and she seemed to accept that I could be trusted.'

'They say you can see the soul of a horse in its eyes. Do you believe that Jenny?'

'Er, I don't really know. They certainly seem to have the deepest eyes of all animals, maybe cows are the same?'

'Hmmn, maybe. When a horse dies you see the soul dying by the light going out in its eyes first. Once that happens, you are too late. Grace still had all her lights on, I definitely could see that and she was a little brighter when it was time for me to leave, my watch told me it was almost seven in the evening, I had been with her for over ten hours and thought she would now be OK so I fed her and went home'.

'Gosh. What happened to Gibson?'

'I don't remember, I received a letter on the Monday informing me that I was not suitable for work with animals and was fired.'

'And Grace?'

'I have no idea. She never would have trusted Gibson again, so she wouldn't be manageable on his terms. I imagine she ended up somewhere less than delightful…'

'What do you mean?'

'I expect she became dog food jenny; Gibson was like that, nasty and vindictive.'

Colin left her then and Jenny heard the door being bolted and locked from the outside.

She had been deeply moved by the story, but now had to think of her own predicament. She moved her arms stiffly. Her first thought was naturally of escape. The door was sturdy and she knew it was firmly secured. She tried it anyway. She wasn't a big girl, but desperation can give strength and she rammed her shoulder against the wood as she had seen done a hundred times on TV. All that happened was that she bounced off and would have a badly bruised shoulder. There was nothing amongst the recording gear that might be used as a tool, and otherwise the room was practically bare.

185

Giving up on the door she began to skirt the room clockwise. The two high windows were covered by a strong wire grill, similar to the material the cages were made from. Behind the mesh the windows were sealed units with no opening mechanisms, and as if to rub salt into her wounds there were sturdy security bars running vertically on the outside of the window frames. No way out through there even if she was tall enough to reach them.

There were no further openings, other than a high level fan unit which was almost buried under cobwebs and dust. She cursed and decided she should work on the ransom note.

She picked up the black marker pen.
He's tall.
High pitched voice.
His eyes; two letter 'I's spaced wide apart.
Stupid, but maybe he was even stupider. She continued, starting to get some ideas now.

"No, Stupid carnivores are to eat Pieces of meat".
The word "carnivore" she thought about the word carnivore, and realised there was scope for a clue.
She used different colours and wrote the C, I, V, O and E in red. No, the colours idea was way too obvious. He'd said he couldn't read well so she had to hide something in the formation of the letters. She continued to play around and doodle until the final message read like this.

To ALL of you reading this, it's HIGH time for stupid CarnIVOrEs to stop eating meat I I will be killed if you don't stop immediately

It wasn't great but the way she had written the message hid four clues. Once again she prayed that anyone reading it would be sharp enough to spot the anomalies and to make some sense of them. Even then, there was little chance the clues would be of much help in any search, but there were at least six or seven people being held captive so there must be a nationwide hunt going on.

With luck this might be the first of several messages – she knew that in some hostage situations demands could be changed over a period of time. If that happened she needed to be ready with more clues – and hopefully better ones!

A vehicle was approaching; rough sounding, but not a tractor. It sounded a bit like the old RMP Jeeps. She knew it must be his and needed to identify it, she might be able to build a future clue. Now that she had some purpose to her time she felt stronger and determined to get through this. A number of lives might depend on her so she needed to be alive to every opportunity. She felt as if she could stomach the disgusting conditions if she could only stay focussed.

The Jeep sound stopped and she heard a door slam and crunching footsteps tensing involuntarily, she checked over her writing. It wasn't good, but she would have to rely on his self-confessed inability to read well. She heard a key in the lock and the door was slowly opened.

'Don't try anything funny because I have a very dangerous electrical stun gun and I will use it if I have any suspicions at all that you might try to overpower me.'
Jenny sat on the chair and said nothing.
Colin entered carrying a four foot pole with two studs protruding from the end nearest Jenny.
'Ah, good girl' he smiled, locking the door.
'Turn around and I will re-tie your hands.'
Jenny did as instructed and fought to resist an escape attempt. She was in no fit state to make a run for it and if she tried and failed, her life would almost certainly be worthless.

'I hope you didn't think anyone could hear you shouting? There is nobody for miles. Actually, the nearest house is two miles away exactly.'
Jenny logged that snippet for a future clue.
'So let's see what message you have composed.'

He went to the flip-chart and cocked his head to one side
'Why have you written it in this fancy style?'
Panicking, she mumbled
'It's just the way I write, do you want me to do it again?'

'Never mind, it looks a bit fancy but the message is clear. You have
done well. Now we have to hope that the idiots follow my
instructions and don't force me to kill you!'
He went over to where he had set up recording equipment and
fiddled for a minute or two.
'OK; now we record. You say nothing, I want you to hold up the
notice and look at the camera.'
He started to record and Jenny did as she had been told, trying
desperately to burn a subliminal message into the lens with her
subconscious "look at the clues, please, please, please look at the
clues and come and rescue us". There was no speaking, no sound at
all, just the ominous silence and the unmoving, intensely staring
image of Jenny and the words she had written.

As soon as he switched off the camera she was hauled to her feet and
pushed towards the door. The guy was incredibly powerful and she
had absolutely no doubt that he could easily carry out his death
threat if he wanted to. She prayed that it would not come to that, but
the whole of the country stop eating meat for the sake of one
woman? That just wasn't going to happen.
He had forgotten to blindfold her; maybe she'd get a glimpse of
something useful.

What she saw was of limited use, but helped her build a slightly
better picture of the location. In essence she had been in a room
coming off the main building. This was what held her attention now;
the building where she and the others were caged was absolutely
huge; football stadium huge. She had had no idea from the limited
view looking out from her cage and now gazed around in awe, trying
to pick up any further clues.

Later that evening from a hilltop some thirty miles from the facility a
pay as you go mobile 'phone sent a message to the major TV
networks and many newspapers. The message contained only a

video clip of a small, pale woman holding a hand-written flip chart page.

44

Colin was doing his security rounds; checking that all was in order with the cages when Donna croaked.
'Hey freak, I need medical treatment'.

'Oh my sweet Donna, the doctors are all gone for the day, sitting at home now with their families, maybe watching some cartoons with their children on comfortable sofas and choosing which animals to cook tonight. Shall they have chicken? Pig? Veal? Oh, so many choices. Maybe filleted salmon or trout? Farm reared, of course, so much cheaper that way. No my dear Donna, no doctors today, or tomorrow. Like the creatures of the cages, the only time any trained medical person will come here will be to certify somebody dead and arrange removal of the corpse….although actually that won't be happening any time soon either, come to think of it.'

'Sick fucking bastard!' was all the response he heard.
He was called over by Hans-Werner.
'What is the matter with you Hans-Werner?'
'You ask me vot is ze matter? You imprison us for days and veeks in zeese too small cages viz food vot is not eatable and very terrible conditions, you injure us wery badly and you are asking me vot is ze matter? I sink you know vee all vant to get out of here; everysing is ze matter.'

Colin noticed that the German's accent had become even more stereotypical since his arrival; he'd hardly heard it outside the football stadium, but now it was so strong as to be almost a parody, a verbal caricature.
'But my German friend, your country has a world-renowned penchant for sausage. It's only fitting that I should have a representative from such a prolific nation of carnivores!'

For his part, the German had already suffered enough at Colin's brutal hands and had no desire to go through anything like that again. Indeed his injuries had yet to properly heal. He knew he must win some favour with the lunatic and wanted to try to make the freak see him as an important ally.

'I voz brought up surrounded by a family vich ate meat at every meal. It never even vent across my mind zat zere is a mistake viz it. Now you heff shown to me a different vay. I never sought it might be a possibility to live vizout ze table piled high viz meats of different kinds. Now I am educated by you and can see zat everysing is possible; ve only heff to look hard enough to see zat. But I sink in Germany zis vill be hard because as you say, it is a nation vich likes wery much to eat meat.'

He had Colin's attention.

'I sink it is a good chance for me to help ze German people to understand vy eating animals is a bad sing. viz your help to design a campaign I sink ve can do zis. My veakness is imagination. Because I never sought about it before, I heff no idea for good rezepte, er how do you call zis, recipes?'

Colin thought about this for a moment. He realised his expectations had been high, but he'd given very little support to his people, just hard facts and bad news. Maybe he had been missing an opportunity for positive influence.

'Hans-Werner, you are absolutely right. I have been selfish. Every day I eat meals of the finest vegetarian quality; delicious and nutritious, whereas you all have to tolerate the disgusting dry meat pellets. I shall give you all the opportunity, once a week, to see how delightful vegetarian food can be.'

Hans-Werner hoped he wouldn't be eating too many of these; he didn't plan on being stuck in here long enough. His reply was a little more diplomatic.
'Zat sounds like a vonderful idea zen. Maybe as ze veeks pass ve could help you viz ideas and preparation? Under close superwision of course, until you sink ve are to be trusted.'

He smiled broadly to show Colin that he ought to be able to trust some of them right now.

Colin was not taken in by this obvious sly attempt to be freed from the cages. He knew the German was highly intelligent-anyone who understood computers had to be. He wondered at the timing of this conversation, clearly the Kraut was hatching a plan. He'd have to watch him carefully and see how he interacted with the others. Were they all making a plan? He determined to be extra vigilant with his cameras and his security checks.

'Yes, that is an excellent idea, Hans-Werner; I shall consider it.' He lied.

45

The major TV channels across the country were showing the short video clip of Jenny holding the sign she had written at Colin's command.

Local and national newspapers were being hastily edited so that the breaking story had front page cover.

People everywhere were puzzling at the bizarre writing, the odd mix of small and capital letters. Theories abounded on their meaning with one individual from Lincolnshire even gaining a "five minutes of fame" local TV slot to publicly air his theories about aliens and how they communicated with him. He claimed they were a peaceful species of herbivores who had a far more advanced system of writing and that the eccentric capitalisations were a deeper hidden message that they wanted to make safe contact with us.
When challenged by a caller as to why these aliens had kidnapped people to achieve this, the studio guest said that the answers were all in the message; we just had to understand what they had written.
The kidnappings were suddenly big news everywhere.

Colin was oblivious to all of this. He had taken a drive down to a little harbour village and towed his new 25' yacht from the boat yard where it had been stored and launched it down the slipway into the spring tide. Now he was slowly motor cruising down to the mouth of the harbour where he would drop an anchor and just sit and think for a few hours. He liked to think in tranquillity like this. He thought again of that poem about having time to stand and stare. Clearly he was one of life's thinkers.

Soon he'd moor her to a buoy and take the little inflatable tender back to the quay. He'd row her, that way the little outboard motor could stay on board the yacht and nobody would steal it. Then he'd take himself back to the facility for the next round of the struggle.

46

Later that same day Neil Dyson called Jenny's mobile for the umpteenth time. He was worried that he'd not yet heard from her and his mind kept diverting itself down alleyways where he was seeking her rather than hunting for these anonymous missing persons. He sat and studied the case notes, his mind on Jenny. He'd pace the floor, scratching his hair with a stubby pencil, Jenny dominated his thoughts. He'd look at the pictures of the missing persons and see only Jenny. This was crazy; why was she not answering his calls.

Samantha too was doing some thinking; having her "me time" relaxing in a deep, hot, bubbly bath with her usual glass of wine and crossword. She wondered why Neil had not called to say that Jenny was safe and sound. She knew he'd simply forgotten to tell her that all was well, but decided she'd call him after her bath just to be certain. She forced her mind back to the crossword.

6 across: *First sheep butts into The Ram and gets up; (6 letters)*
Why was Ram written with a capital and specifically called "The" Ram; has to be a specific ram, she thought.
'Ah!" She blurted out loud. It had to be Aries, the star sign. The rest was easy; she took the first letter from "sheep" and put that into Aries to make "arises", meaning to "get up".

She had only one more clue to solve; 8 down. The answer was two words, six and five letters respectively and now she had four of the letters; interestingly they were all letter "a"s. Second and fourth letters of the first word and third and fifth of the last word. - *a* - *a* - - / - - *a* - *a*
The clue read: *Sounds like president does undertakings for the military (6, 5)*

Ok, she thought; two words, six and five letters respectively.

Sounds like invariably meant exactly that, a word or words which sounded like something else.

President; what sounds like president? Precedent?

Or that might not be the *sounds like* bit of the clue at all. It could be the head of a country.

Or it could be a kind of president of a society, such as a chairman, or CEO of a company.

She looked at the rest of the clue. *does undertakings for the military.* "Does undertakings" was odd. You don't "do" undertakings, you undertake to do things. No, there must be something critical here. For the military....hmmmnn, army? navy? RAF? All of them collectively would be "the military" otherwise the compiler of this one would have specifically stated which arm of the forces. What did all military forces have in common? Weapons, fighters, equipment, structure, orders and discipline.

She wasn't getting anywhere with this one. Back to the president bit. She thought through the list of presidents she could remember, but there were so many. OK start with the most recent.

Barack Obama – hmmnn... 6 and 5 - the words fitted the grid. Convinced this was the right answer she now had to find out why. That was the thing with cryptic clues; one sometimes found the answer through some unplanned route and then had to justify it. It was a little like a suspect in an investigation, get the guy then justify why; burden of proof had to be beyond reasonable doubt. She'd certainly had a few crossword answers which caused her to doubt, and she'd had police cases too where she wasn't 100% certain. But sometimes you had to go with your gut instinct, and Barack Obama was the gut feel.

Then she saw it and laughed out loud. Barracks - the military all had those.

Barack certainly sounded like barrack, but that wasn't why she had laughed; it had been the Obama sound-alike that had done it; in her clue *"undertakings"* was "embalming" so one who did undertakings for the military was a barrack embalmer - sounds like Barack Obama. very good. She laid the newspaper on the floor with a contented sigh and stretched out in the warm water, which had become noticeably cooler but was still fine for a few more minutes.

Her mobile rang. It was Neil Dyson.
'Turn on the BBC news now.'

47

Neil Dyson was sat, head in hands in the ops room. He was beating himself up big-time for letting Jenny down, for not being there when she needed him, for failing to find out where the hell she had got to when she didn't show up at his place the night she disappeared. What had she been through since then? Who were these bastards who had taken her? What did they really want and what were they going to do to her. Were they known to the police? Were they trustworthy? So many questions, but underpinning everything he couldn't shake off the deep guilt that he'd let down the most important person in his universe. He hung his head and silently wept.

Samantha Milsom was at the board looking through the scant material available.
Dyson wiped away his tears with his sleeve and stood looking out of the window. This was doing Jenny no good. He needed to function. He turned to Samantha, conscious that his face was a mess, what with a black eye slowly turning an ugly yellowy-brown and the other red and puffy from crying he must have been a right sight.

'Before we brief the others and get their updates let's see what we have. Five disappearances; we have to assume they are linked and probably abductions by some person or persons unknown'

Samantha was amazed at his robustness. His fiancé was in terrible danger and yet he'd hardly missed a beat. She knew him well, and was aware that he would be happier on the case than off it, and there was no better detective or leader that she had ever come across. Normally she could put the woes of the world to one side and look at a case dispassionately, but this was different; this was more personal and all she could see was poor Jenny in that disturbingly still and silent video with the odd and chilling message. She was distressed to see Neil going through so much pain and tormented by what the couple were going through together, yet so far apart.

So far they had little to go on, the kidnappers were clearly well organised but the clues offered a glimmer of hope. It might be that any breakthrough came from that clever girl giving these tiny yet possibly significant snippets of information. If only time were on their side, she was sure that with Jenny on the inside there was hope. She forced her mind back to the task.
'Let's not assume anything just yet Guv.' She said. 'They might be linked, it might be an organisation or it could be a lone wolf.'
Dyson moved to the white board.
'Let's go through the stuff again.'

He added Jenny's details to the existing list.

Jenny Marston. English, rare manuscript specialist, Chichester home and work.
Went missing between 17:00 and 19.30 between her workplace and Canon Lane. Boyfriend should be shot.

Samantha moved to the video playback equipment.
'Look at the film footage again. Jenny has written this-you recognise her writing. She's a switched on cookie.'
'If she's still alive.' The worry and frustration were clearly visible in Neil's facial expressions.
'She was alive when they shot that video, and that can only have been yesterday.' She added.
He sighed. 'Well they have threatened to kill her unless the whole bloody world dances to their insane tune.' Dyson's look made it clear that the chances of that happening were zero.

Jenny appeared on the screen holding the hand-written sign:

To ALL of you reading this, it's HIGH time for stupid CarnIVOrEs to stop eating meat I I will be killed if you don't stop immediately

'She's done some things with the script that we know is out of character.

ALL and HIGH in capitals. What does it mean?'

Neil wrote it on the board.
'Then the carnivore word; if the capitalised letters mean something what is it?'
Neil wrote C, I, V, O, E and suggested
'Anagram? Acronym? Organisation name? Location? Could be anything-Google it.'
Samantha entered the phrase into her search engine.
'Nothing.'
'Then the letters I and I repeated and separated by an unnecessary space.'
He wrote them on the board.

Dyson looked at the board.
ALL, HIGH, CIVOE, I I
'Makes no sense at all.' He said throwing the pen to the desk
Samantha had a determined look in her eye.'Oh it does, we just need to decipher it.'

Dyson continued.
'OK, ALL in capitals, what other letters are capitalised?'
Samantha interjected.
'Wait, look, if we include the capital T from the first word, and assume it's part of the clue, and add it to ALL – we have TALL'
'Hmnn, long shot, but go on.'

She continued.
'HIGH means what-let's get our crossword heads on.'
She took the pen and wrote:
Tall (building? Person? Story?)
High pitched?
Highly strung?
Hello? (Hi)
Rank?
CIVOE

Civilian something?
Anagrams:
OVICE
EVICO
VOICE – voice!
High voice?
She looked suddenly animated.
'She's describing her captors, or one of them at least - he or she has a
high voice. Women generally have higher voices and that's not
remarkable so why would she point to it, but for a man it could be.'

Neil stood up.
'It's a bit tenuous Samantha, but who knows, maybe you're on to
something.'

'Continuing the theme of describing the guy, the two letter "I"s
separated by a space. What the hell does she mean with that I
wonder?"

Two ""I"s separated..maybe he stutters his vowels? Wait-maybe she
means eye, something wrong with his eyes..blind in one?
'Maybe she means these people are on drugs – spaced out?

Samantha wrote
"Tall, high voice, druggies and/or stutters/ eyes odd?"

'We need more than this.' Neil said in despair. 'Let's grab a quick
coffee before the others get here - see if inspiration strikes.' They
headed for the machine.

On the way to get a drink Neil's attention was caught by his boss
coming out of her office.
'Neil, a word please.' She stood back to allow him through her office
door and closed it behind her.

DCI Sharon Moody delivered the news that, due to the personal
aspect the case had taken on and the potential conflict of interests
she was obliged to remove him from the case. She explained that
he'd be kept fully abreast of all developments as soon as they

happened and that as from now he was to take a short leave of absence. She told him that whatever support, psychological or otherwise, the force might be able to offer was his for the asking. 'Neil, your skills are invaluable and I don't want this to cut you off from the team. Stay in touch through me and call me as soon as you have any thoughts. I'll call you daily in any case.'

Neil had one single thought. It was that if they thought he was going to sit back and leave them to find his Jenny they were dafter than the loonies who had kidnapped her. He'd let her down once too often. He nodded gravely to his boss and left.

48

It was 2am – although none of the disciples could possibly know that – and in the otherwise dark building the screens were showing a bank of thirty or so white rabbits in rows of glass fronted boxes stacked three high. In the centre of the screen a lab-coated woman with safety goggles, white paper face mask of the kind surgical staff might wear and thin, blue rubber gloves, was injecting a substance down the throat of one of the specimen animals with a needle-less syringe that looked as if it might have come from a toy medical kit.

The camera was shaky and the images of poor quality; this was the best that the undercover girl who was working as lab assistant could manage with the tiny recording device secreted in her name badge. But what was clear in the grainy image was the rapidly blinking eyes of the small creature as the yellow liquid entered its oesophagus. Nobody could tell whether this was causing the animal any discomfort, but the hopelessly scrabbling front paws and normally placid deep brown eyes which now seemed over-active were clear distress signals. This was a terrified rabbit.

'Wakey wakey friends!'
The darkness disappeared in a flash of bright lights and the speaker system exploded into life with the clearly excited voice. The prisoners had come to recognise the mood of their captor from the pitch and speed of his words; today he was speaking fast and high, clearly animated.

'Today's group therapy single point lesson will look at little fluffy bunnies and what we do to them in order to make ourselves look even more beautiful than we were when we sprang out of bed. Or, as I prefer to say, to make a mask to cover our hideous visages as we belly-crawl through our unethical lives.'

There was an unmistakable cackle; Colin was clearly in a very good mood.

'First some questions and then some facts – oh but where are my manners-you haven't had a shower …'

A moment later a large pump could be heard; this sound was well-known to the caged people as the machine which drove the high pressure, high-volume water through the powerful fire hose used for "showering" them, as Colin liked to call it.

He appeared now in wellington boots and yellow rain-mac, hosepipe braced under his right arm with his insanely wide eyes gleaming in the bright light beneath his almost comical yellow Sou'wester hat. He pulled back a lever on top of the fat nozzle and was driven momentarily backwards by the pressure of the heavy water jet. He regained his poise and aimed at the top row of cages, playing the jet from left to right, clearly struggling to control the thing.

'Water pressure's high today!' he beamed.

He gradually worked his way down to the middle and then the bottom layers, trying to dislodge the filth from the wire mesh which became thicker lower down. The force of the icy cold water drove the inhabitants gasping against the far sides of their respective cages and as the hose was dragged around the perimeter so the captives would circle within their tiny confines in an attempt to escape the pain and discomfort.

Only Babić didn't seem to be affected by the activity; he had sunk into some kind of deep depression and nothing seemed to matter to him. Babić was numb physically and mentally and there seemed no point in even thinking any more. His body was shoved around by the water like an apple under a waterfall.

The deluge ceased as abruptly as it had begun and Colin laboured with the big reel to coil the huge snake away to its hidden lair. All that could now be heard was the rapid dripping of water onto the concrete floor. Slowly the drips became fewer and the moans began; then the curses.

'You sick mother. One of these days the police are gonna bust that door down and give you what you deserve you freak.' Donna had lost none of her spunk, but her voice was weaker than it had been and husky, due to a raging throat infection. This would soon spread to the other captives and would make their already horrible existence intolerable.

'There! Almost human again!' The sound system seemed to mock. 'How many of us are wearing make-up today?' Unseen, Colin did a little skippy jump; delighted at the confused and conflicting emotions shown on his screens of the cold, drenched faces.
'Oh silly me; none of us! We don't need to pretend to be something we are not in here. Here we can be ourselves; basic human animals. Well hooray for that!'
Unseen skip.

'Well know this my friends: for the cosmetic industry an intolerable number of rabbits, hamsters, rats, mice and other animals suffer and die each year so that we, or some of us, can smear gloop over our skins and pretend we are better for it. How do they die? You will ask. Sometimes in pain; often with deformities and always without dignity. Some in gut-wrenching agony and pregnant mothers are usually killed so that their developing foetus may be extracted and examined. Interestingly, our own government tells us that on average for every animal that is used in tests, 2.2 are destroyed by our laboratories *without being used at all!* That is their own statistic; some of us believe this to be grossly understated.'
The skip this time was accompanied by several seconds of erratic hand and arm movements as if the lanky man were trying to shake water off his hands after a wash.

'My friends, my soon-to-be-believers; every beautiful face you see on TV and in magazines is smeared in the blood of thousands. Every time you meet someone who paints their face as if they were part of some prehistoric cave dwelling ritual is part of the system which supports these abominations. You. Me. We are all wrapped in the culture of beauty, but it's unsustainable and we have to break the mould. The good news is here! The great news is here! We, together my friends, you and I and others who will follow you will dismantle the behaviours that have brought us to our ethical knees. Oh the changes we shall force. The re-shaping of society will be our achievement, our legacy. Your children will sing our praises. We are the agents of change who will give humanity back its soul. It starts here on this farm, in this barn, in these cages.'

A pair of hands were slowly clapped together 3 times somewhere in the bottom layer.
'Great speech, Freak. And what the fuck are you gonna do when we all tell you to swivel and refuse to listen to any more of this lunatic shite?'
'Oh Donna; dearest Donna, I see you are yet to be convinced. Allow me to continue the single point lesson.'
'Forget that crap freak-face and give me a clean blanket, I am freezing cold, wet and starving. My throat is raw and I need a doctor. If you want me to listen to this turd rant then give me some pain killers, otherwise just shut the fuck up.'

In his control room Colin danced a little dance, but this time it was fuelled by frustration and anger. Bitch, she was the problem in this community. He needed to isolate her. But first he would deliver his lesson.

The microphone crackled again.
'I shall deal with Donna after the lesson, unless she wants to interrupt again, in which case she will be hurt like the selfish cow she is. My cattle prod is right here Donna, another word of dissent gets you a million volts to the clitoris'

'Yeah right-if you can even find it loser.' Donna's voice was defiant.

Colin knew he would never be able to locate such a part on the female anatomy, despite having researched it online, that whole area remained a mystery of complicated folds of skin, like some kind of repulsive dermal maze and his voice through the loud speakers now was a scream.
'You stupid woman - now you will be sorry - now you will be hurt properly - now I am coming with my volts and you will so regret your stupid remarks.'

In her cage Donna swallowed without feeling the pain from her inflamed throat; what had been a trembling from the cold became a shaking of terror. In her false bravado she had overstepped the mark and she had seen what the crazy had done to the German guy the other day and the mess it had made of him. Now she was for it. She began to scrabble around in the tiny space as if trying to find a gap that she might previously have missed.

Pausing with his hand on his control room door handle, Colin forced himself to think. What would doctor Erikssen advise right now? He reminded himself that he must do everything in his power to ensure that the people in his facility believed in his dream and that anything he did to alienate them would be a mistake. He turned, and pressing the microphone button again said:
'Donna, good fortune is with you and I have decided that the best way to help you make the necessary change in behaviour is for you to convince yourself. Please don't make me change my mind.'
Donna closed her eyes in relief and knew when to be silent

'I have prepared a few slides for you all as part of my lesson plan. I imagine that these will persuade you more than a few hastily delivered belts of electricity.'
He admired his own inner strength; denying himself the stimulus of administering shocks to that bitch Donna was a good sign. Doctor Erikssen would be pleased, not that he had any plans to tell him.

'Slide one ladies and gentlemen. What kinds of abuse do we subject animals to in the name of cosmetic beauty? Well there are a dozen cruel and painful animal experiments, there's acute toxicity where a substance is administered to animals through a stomach tube, the animals can suffer hours of convulsions, diarrhoea, fever, shivering fits or paralysis.'
The accompanying picture showed a mouse lying in a small pool of brown fluid in a position of rigid agony.

'Then there's Chronic toxicity where a lower dose of the test substance is given over a longer period; usually two weeks.'
There was a pause while Colin changed the slide.

'You will have an exam on these facts so I suggest you pay very close attention; he or she who fails the test, fails the group and will have to be expelled.'

The voice was surprisingly subdued at this point, but became animated again.

'Skin irritant and absorption tests might be applied to the shaven skin of rabbits. If the substance is a skin irritant it causes painful inflammation of the skin. Then we have the Draize test – this is a good one my friends - the substance is dripped into the eyes of restrained rabbits, dogs, monkeys – who cares. The damage is observed and depending on the nature of the substance the eyes will swell, bleed and blister. Usually this test takes 14 days. Wow imagine spending two weeks strapped down in agony; force fed, lying in excrement – that must be some seriously good cosmetic shit to justify that amount of torture. Oh – I should mention Mr Farouk El Hamidiri - there is no provision for pain relief in any of these experiments. Not one. It seems science and religion are united at last; neither believes that animals need pain relief, or as I prefer to think of it, yes they feel the pain but because they can't vocalise that nobody gives a shit; well I give a shit, I give a lot of shits and so will you when we are through here, believe me people.'

The cage dwellers all noticed a significant shift to the pitch of the voice; they believed it.

'Skin allergy test substances are injected beneath the skin of hamsters or guinea-pigs to stimulate the animals' immune system. If the substance causes allergic reactions after repeated contact, painful inflammation will follow – oh and it won't be treated by kindly, caring, trained vets either, just in case you thought there might be a happy end. The monsters who apply these substances are not trained in animal care in any shape or form; they are recruited for their scientific knowledge. Some are even dragged off the dole queue to perform a mundane task such as moving the animals from one prison to another.'

'Don't forget to take notice people, test time will come soon and you don't want to score lowest – believe me! Photo toxicity is where rats or guinea-pigs are injected and then stuffed into a little clear plastic tube for hours while they are exposed to UV light. They get hot and it will be impossible for them to move. You think you are constrained in here? Anyone wants to raise the game just say the word my dear people if you think photo toxicity is a walk in the park; I'm sure we can source some human-sized tubes somewhere.'

The voice rose again in pitch and Colin's breathing became audible as the picture of a rat squeezed into a tiny clear tube was replaced by one of a deformed baby animal; the species was impossible to determine but the large ears indicated rabbit.
'With teratogenicity tests the substance is administered to pregnant mothers and they are killed at various stages of pregnancy to see if the substance has damaged the mother or the foetus. Playing at god? Yes but for a very good reason – so that your friends will compliment your glowing skin and shiny hair, or your shaving foam will spread more easily – now that's gotta be worth fighting for – right?'

Unseen, the presenter did a longer than usual version of his skipping dance.
'And for my final slide I give you ...'
Colin made a trumpeting sound as if playing a short fanfare,

'...the Carcinogens! Hooray, yes hooray. The biggest killer in the human world, and dreaded by any rational person, yet so deliberately and usefully forced upon little animals to see whether they develop tumours. Not because we want to find a cure for cancer; no! Because we want to kid ourselves that we look better. This is cosmetics don't forget, not real medical research. Now here's the thing my friends, and if I were sitting a test at the end of a behavioural change programme like this I might want to pay very close attention to this bit:
Let's forget cosmetics for a minute and talk about *all* animal testing.'
The voice regained some of its earlier calmness.
'First the bad news for Babić and Hans-Werner, sorry gentlemen, but neither of you comes from the champions of the world at this stuff. Surprisingly, perhaps it's the UK that leads the way in sheer numbers. Did you know that recent UK government figures show that 7342 mice are used every day – one every 12 seconds! We use

1545 fish – one every 56 seconds! How about this...one sheep every 14 minutes; a dog every 115 minutes oh and seven monkeys a day and cats and pigs and cows...it's a regular Noah's Ark in those UK labs!'

'Well thank goodness we do - imagine carefully applying your nipple cream before the marathon only to find the bloody stuff didn't work and you were sore for most of the day. That would never do!'

'My friends the great news is here...we can have our cake and scoff all of it. *All* of these tests are possible using in-vitro methods; in other words we can do them in test tubes on animal cells without harming the animal. Oh happy day. So why don't we? You tell me! Perhaps because we are insanely sadistic?'

'But seriously, we have to legally test cosmetics on animals....don't we? The beauty industry's favourite argument to defend animal testing is that there is "some legal requirement" or another. This is bullshit. In most countries, there is no legal requirement for testing, they just have to make harmless products; what they are doing with these test results is protecting themselves, not their consumers. I was hoping to be joined in the facility by a Chinese representative, because they have a role to play in the education of the world. As it stands today the Chinese require all cosmetic and personal care products to be tested on animals. So companies which export these products to sell on the Chinese market all support this barbarism. The Chinese plan to change this, but their track record on human rights is not the best so who knows what they will do for animal welfare. They still guzzle bear bile for fuck sake-and anyone who has seen how they torture the poor beasts for their entire lives to get that would be here with me now, in the control room here, already converted!'

'OK, which of you thinks you don't use any of these products? Come on, hands up. Anyone who doesn't use any animal cruelty products can walk now. Go free, free to spread the word.'

Unsurprisingly, no hands were raised.

'I don't see any of you rushing for the doors...oh I know, it's because you don't even fucking well *know* if you support animal testing or not. People, you are supposed to be the thinking species and yet your ignorance clarifies how little you actually bother to think about what you do.'

'Tomorrow I shall test you all on what we learned today. Remember the consequences of failure. Reminders will play on the slides for the next hour, at the end of the test tomorrow I will know who can add value to the group going forward, and who is to be replaced.'

The loud speakers became silent, yet the building seemed to echo with the spirit of what had been said.

49

The routine was different to the last time. Jenny was allowed to walk without bindings to the media room, as the freak was calling it. She was told what message to write and it didn't take her long to work out what she was going to say; she been anticipating this and had thought through many possible scenarios.

'Tell them the lamb killing must not happen this summer. Usually when the lambs are about five months old they are taken and butchered. If that happens, tell them one of my captives dies every day until I can see that the lambs live. I will replace anyone who dies with a fresh human. I might be anywhere in the country; I will be watching them. Tell them that.'

Jenny had recognised Colin when he had tricked her with the book as the guy in the supermarket queue from when she'd bought the steak for Neil. She had already composed the next message in her head and immediately began to write:

It seems eye might have made a misteak in the last broadcast.
I didn't make the message clear enough. Plans to slaughter this year's lambs must be stopped immediately.
There's CCTV everywhere these days, so Look over the Shoulder, Big brother is there.

She had to somehow get across the sheer vastness of this place. There couldn't be so many warehouse type buildings in the country on this scale. She knew she had only minutes before she would make the video and couldn't think of the right words. He'd let slip last time that they were two miles from the nearest neighbours. That would help too, she was sure.

Sadly she had run out of thinking time. The freak was clearly on a mission.
'That's it. Now let's get the film made and distributed; your public is waiting.'

50

Farouk was watching the Draize test. He thought the other inmates were sleeping and as a result the façade he kept up night and day, when he might be observed fell away and he was no longer a religious leader of his people, but became a "normal" member of the public with strengths, weaknesses emotions and fears.

The laboratory video was running without sound on the giant screens. As he watched, the lab assistant holding a quiet rabbit against her chest was about to administer the test substance via a pipette directly onto the calm creatures eye. He had watched this one before and winced as the substance hit the delicate organ. Immediately the little creature began to wriggle and kick and the woman had a tough job restraining it. He wondered why she didn't use one of the clamps on the work surface behind her as the other employees did. They would clamp the head of the animal firmly, eyes facing the ceiling, and deliver the substance in an emotionally detached way. This particular woman invariably held the animals close as she caused them pain. Either this was an attempt to console it, cuddling it to her maternal bosom, or, and Farouk hoped this was not the case; she took some kind of sadistic pleasure from the act. There was a fleeting image later in the film where she turned her head and the camera caught her smiling. It was as if the very act of being intimately close to the animal, and then breaching its trust, gave her emotional reward.

It disturbed him most to see this woman relentlessly applying drop after drop. Surely one or two would suffice to give the results they needed? When they had completed the dose, the lab staff would record the details on a large chart which was clearly visible on the wall directly in front of the (he assumed) hidden camera. The employees would mark one small stroke, like a number one, on the chart to record (again, he assumed) the dosage given. With one exception they would record a mark for each droplet they had delivered to the subject's eye from the pipette. This woman, however, was that exception. She would deliver ten drops and record four. This action convinced Farouk that she was a twisted individual who enjoyed the act of hurt. Or, perhaps, she was working covertly for a rival company and wanted to sabotage the results? He knew that industrial sabotage and espionage was rifer than was publicly stated in the huge multi-billion pound organisations. The stakes were astronomical and must be tempting.

Privately, Farouk found himself beginning to question some of the things he had so strongly believed were right; the values he had so devoutly and without question lived by. Their kidnapper was clearly evil in many respects, yet Farouk could see he had a heart buried beneath the crazy exterior he presented. Maybe the madman performance was exactly that; an act, designed to manipulate their thoughts? But some of the things he had shown them, some of the points and reasoning he had presented had been thought provoking, and Farouk defied any human to remain unaffected by what they had seen here.

Farouk knew he could never question his God, and he looked to Allah now for guidance.

Sadly, on this occasion, his deity remained silent.

51

Samantha, Neil and Brian Liddel were in the ops room, the rest of the team were out in the field in the hunt for information. Neil turned to them both.

'OK Einsteins, if I get caught with you I'll be grounded, so let's do this quick smart. Let's explore the new info from this press release.' He went to the board where the scribble remained from the last session and attached a screen shot of Jenny's latest message.

It seems eye might have made a misteak in the last broadcast.

I didn't make the message clear enough. Plans to slaughter this year's lambs must be stopped immediately.

There's CCTV everywhere these days, so Look over the Shoulder, Big brother is there.

'She's obviously repeating the message about his eyes. Then misteak spelled that way – definitely a clue. Nothing odd about the next sentence, but then 'Look' with capital "L" and over *the* shoulder - she would normally have written "look over *your* shoulder". Then the word "Shoulder" capitalised.'

He wrote:
eyes
misteak
Look
the
Shoulder

Neil rubbed his sore face; the eye was slowly getting better but still hurt and had started to itch. It suddenly hit him
'Samantha – the eye reference is a new clue. She's writing about my eye-she bought me a steak. There's a link; something important.'
Samantha looked at the floor deep in thought, and then she struck the table with her open hand
'Where did she buy the steak Neil-she's telling us that CCTV footage will show something – maybe one of the guys - probably somewhere behind her; over HER shoulder.'
'It's spurious Samantha, but it's something. She usually goes to Sainsbury's and it's on the way to my place from the shop where she works.'

He went to the door and shouted for Carol.
'Wassup Guv?' She bounced towards him.
'Carol we think we have a lead and I need you to get across to Sainsbury's and check their CCTV footage from 9th March if they still have it. I'm going to tell Sicknote to get on to all the other local supermarkets and butchers to make sure they preserve any CCTV footage before they overwrite it. I left my 'phone on my desk, just going to check the text she sent to see if she mentioned which shop she was going to, don't think she did.'
There was a new spring in his step as he left the room.

'Thank goodness there's a bit of possibly good news for him.'
Whispered Samantha. 'As long as it's not a red herring.'
She explained to Carol how they had arrived at the theory and she agreed it seemed like a good lead.
Neil came back with a nervous look on his face. Samantha could feel her partner's pain.
'No name mentioned in the text message, but it will be one of the two big ones I'm pretty sure.'
'Don't worry Sir, we'll get her.' Carol looked confident.
'Roughly what time would she have bought the steak Guv?'
'Well she left work a little early, but not by much; I'd guess around 16.30 give or take 15 minutes. Start there and if there's nothing go back and forward 15 minutes each way. Remember, we are probably looking for a guy stood at the till behind her-we think. But anything you can spot, well don't disregard it, OK?'

Samantha added:
'Tall guy, we think, with odd eyes!'

Carol did a mock salute 'Got it - don't worry, if it's there to find I'll find it; they don't call me CCTV Carol for nothing!'
Dyson smiled for the first time since Jenny had gone missing.
'Thanks Carol; I know you will. Now get the hell moving!'
He pretended to kick her backside as she passed him.

Samantha spoke: Sir we missed the capital "B" in Big brother. That's a clue too, guarantee it.'
'What do you reckon then?'
'Well, something either big, or starting with a B. If it's the latter it could be anything, and she's been smarter than that so my money is on it meaning something big.'
'OK, so she has told us about the eye and the steak, she's as good as told us that he was at the supermarket; probably behind her. Is she expanding the description of him? Is he a big fat guy? Tall?'
Samantha dialled Carol's number. It went to answer phone.
'Carol; Samantha. Look for a tall or a fat guy-explain later.'

She closed the call and wrote Big on the board.
'Well spotted genius.' Neil had genuine admiration in his eyes; if it weren't for her crossword skills some of these clues might have been missed, or at least not seen until much later. Often these things were only found in hindsight, or when cold cases were re-opened and fresh eyes looked at the evidence and clues. Although it was his girlfriend, amongst others, who was at serious risk here his natural curiosity and problem solving skills had kicked in and he was actually enjoying pitting his wits against this nutter. Especially since he had Jenny on the inside and Samantha helping him on the outside.

'OK Sam.'
She let this abbreviation go as an exception, but wouldn't let it become the norm.
'Now let's get what we know about animal rights and welfare groups out in the open. These guys or guy haven't developed this fascination overnight; somewhere they'll have history, a profile. Maybe even a criminal record. Let's look at anything remotely similar.'

'What about that VOTA group Sir, they had a couple of new faces, bit more militant remember?'
'Good thinking Samantha. Get a list of all their members, and speak with that Arab guy who did the slaughter lecture or whatever it was.'

Neil finished with a warning:
'If my boss asks if I have been hanging around...you haven't seen me!'
They departed to their various tasks.

52

It was a gorgeous spring day outside. Inside the facility it was dark and cool; the loudspeakers crackled to life.

'Good morning campers. You will be very pleased to learn that it's quiz time!'
There was no visible reaction inside the cages, although all except Babić became a little nervous, not knowing what the freak would do if they gave wrong answers.
'Here's how it works; I ask each of you a question until one of you gives me a wrong answer. That person will pay a forfeit. Your first answer will be the one I take, so think before you speak, for some of you that will be a first time experience, but try.'

'Donna. How many mice are destroyed on average per day in the name of human vanity?'
In her cage Donna dug into her memory.
In her cage, Jenny willed her to give the right answer
In his cage Simon Grayson willed her to get it wrong. In his view the more pain the others suffered the less he'd have to endure.
In his cage Bojan Babić didn't give a damn

'Donna; we are all waiting with baited breath!'
Donna was far more subdued than she had ever been.
'I think it was 7340 something...'
'Good Donna! Very very good! Forty two, 7342 to be precise. But you used the words "I think it was"...it very definitely still is my dear, it hasn't stopped yet, although we all know it will if we work together with passion.'

Donna was relieved beyond words. Grayson silently cursed her. He knew he would struggle. He'd always struggled to remember boring statistics. He could remember interesting things, like how many women he had shagged and many of their names but...

His reverie was interrupted.

'We are waiting Simon...'

'Er sorry...what was the question?'

'The question was, what do we call the offensive test where liquids are dripped into an animal's eye?'

'Er that was the Draize test.'

'Very very good Simon-no hesitation at all!'

Furness moved around to stand next to Jenny's cage.

'Jenny, dear Jenny, the star of the media show, the enemy of the carnivorous world, the darling of the anti-burger bunch. How many sheep do we kill in a day in animal experiments?'

Jenny had run through the numbers over and over in her mind and had the facts well and truly embedded.

'Roughly 14. You should be aware that I have been vegetarian all my life and vegan for much of it. I find the maltreatment of animals as disgusting as you do.'

Colin was taken aback

'A nice try Jenny, but remember I caught you buying a fat juicy steak at the shops-hardly the behaviour of a lifelong veggie, wouldn't you agree?'

'Yes but it wasn't for me.'

'I know who it was for my sweet, you told me, it was for your husband's eye.'

'Fiancé.' Jenny corrected him

Colin disliked being corrected.

'Whatever - fact is it was dead animal, killed for carnivores. You should hang your head in eternal shame.'

He moved on to Babić.

'Bojan, my Serbian friend. Which country is the biggest offender?'

Babić was stumped. He didn't understand the question, and had he done, he would have had no clue as to what the answer might be.

'Don't know don't care.' Was his stubborn response.

'Oh goody...not only a peasant, but an arrogant and ignorant peasant. You just won the prize Mr Pigman. I am secretly glad it's you; you were the first to give me nightmares, you and my father and your sick ways. Good good.'

Babić's numbness had not abated and he was as disinterested as ever. Colin disappeared, the lights were doused and the cage dwellers were left in darkness, save for the soft glow of the video screens, which now were showing young male calves cramped into veal crates, where they would spend their entire short but miserable lives.

53

'Hello, could I speak with the manager please?'
Colin Furness was calling the nearest slaughterhouse, some 25 miles
from Chichester.
'You're speaking to him.' Came a gruff voice on the other end of the
line.
'I have three pigs I need to slaughter; do you have any time for me?'
'Sorry mate, we are running at full tilt here.'
'You mean you are still slaughtering, despite the warnings in the
press to stop?'
'What, that nutter who thinks the world will stop because he's too
soft to kill a pig or two? Do me a favour!' there was dismissive
laughter on the end of the line.

Furness was incensed. The slaughter house was running at full
capacity as usual despite his demands. Well that settled it; media
message time, but with a different message. He needed to calm his
anger and thought about Doctor Erikssen and what he would advise
right now. He had once told Colin that everyone reaches a point
when things seem to become too much, when the world seems to
want to overwhelm them with stresses and bad news. On these
occasions the Doctor would take himself off into the countryside
around his home and just "be". He would allow the tranquillity of
nature and the natural life around him to wash over his body and
cleanse his mind. Usually this would reinvigorate him and leave him
in a peaceful state of mind and ready to face up to whatever had been
getting to him so badly.

Colin decided that was sound advice and took himself off find
Vengeance.
He rode him out into the fields and overgrown bridleways around his
farm. He hadn't explored some of these since he was a boy and was
delighted at the timelessness here; they followed the same routes as

they probably had for hundreds of years, since a time when the world was very different, and mankind had not yet caused destruction on the massive industrial scale that was evident everywhere today.

As he negotiated a rickety gate he was caught by the vision of a single magnificent oak in early leaf standing in the centre of a field surrounded by cows. Some were standing, grazing, others laying, chewing the cud in its shade. It looked like some immovable defender of the fields. It seemed to say to him "You men, you can wreak your havoc, and destroy your world, you can mould the planet into your own image; but I shall stand here, as I have for centuries, and be the guardian of these gentle animals and lush grasses until my time comes to go to another place". For some reason, Colin was compelled to nod towards it, as if to say "I see you, tree. I recognise in you the beauty, strength and purity and all the good things you stand for. Vengeance and I salute you".

The moment was shattered by a shot.
It's probably "game" shooting, he thought. We humans are, after all, allowed to shoot most non-human animals legitimately, for sport. It's like some bizarre alien planet where space creatures hunt down and kill other species for trophies and acclaim. My god some of us are retarded.

There are a few limited exceptions, a handful of "protected species"; creatures which we have almost hunted to extinction already and realised far too late that we've messed up. Colin recalled a beautiful short ballet he had seen with his mother in London, one of the few times they'd been allowed out together without the miserable overbearing presence of the old man. It had been called "'Still Life' at the Penguin Café" and was about the extinction of animals, he thought, although his mum had been a bit vague on that. He thought now that her recalcitrance in answering his questions had probably been her way of trying to protect his young mind from the harsh realities of the world. Little point; he'd seen daily the damage his father's kind did; harsh reality was part of his everyday existence.

He turned Vengeance about, and horse and rider walked sombrely back towards the farm.

In the early hours of the next morning Furness entered the barn and went directly to Babić's cage.

'Mr Babić, as loser of the little test and hence the forfeit owner, you have been selected to represent the group in the media this time, young Jenny's messages seem to have fallen on deaf ears so it's time to up the ante.'

In his cage Babić stirred.
'I don't know what you want Mr Furness; I not able to give message in very great English.'
'Save me the sob stories Babić and move to the end of the cage before I zap you.'

Colin, armed with the cattle prod unlocked and opened the cage. He passed a set of handcuffs to the Serb.
'Put these on and show me that they are secure.'
Babić did as he was told.
'OK; out you come pigman.'

Babić crawled slowly to the door and even more slowly climbed down the short ladder to the ground. His legs were almost completely seized through lack of use and he winced with every movement. When he was down Colin marched him towards the big main doors and into the waiting Land-rover.
'Where you take me?' Asked the clearly frightened Serbian pig smuggler.
'We are going to a Barbecue in town.' Replied his keeper.
Babić was confused and untrusting.
'What for? We not eaten proper for weeks, so why now?'
'Oh don't worry Bojan; you won't be eating, although you'll be at the feast all right.'
This confused the Serb even more and he pleaded with his captor to explain. Furness was in no mood to explain anything to a pig murdering swine.

225

Babić was gagged and pushed to the floor in the back of the Land-rover.

'Move a muscle and I will make sure it's the last thing you ever do Babić.'

Unsurprisingly, Babić did as instructed and lay as still as the bumping, swaying vehicle would allow throughout the twenty minute journey.

They arrived in a city that Babić didn't recognise. The city centre was deserted at this hour and the Land-rover seemed to roar in the relative silence.

Luckily for Colin, the people of Chichester were very proud of their low crime rate and the council had recently reduced the level of surveillance in the county. CCTV was seen by some as an intrusion and a nod to the criminal. Others thought it insane to remove one of the few lines of defence. Funds, ultimately, held the casting vote and the number of cameras had been cut from 74 to 50 throughout the local area. This left the centre of the city with very minimal cover, and shortly before midnight a murky figure had entered the city armed with a small telescopic ladder with fold-away prongs which looked for all intents and purposes like a large walking stick. He also carried a can of black spray paint. The three cameras which might have tracked the arrival of a Land-rover and some dodgy activity at the market cross had been quickly disabled.

Now, some two hours later, Colin not only had the place to himself, but also the comfort that nobody had recorded his arrival or would see what he did whilst in the city.

Quickly the Serbian was bundled out of the vehicle and told to lay in the shadows of the Market cross. Such a structure was typical in medieval cities. This one is thought to date from 1477 and is found at the intersection of the four principle streets; each running in the direction of the key compass points.

Colin unloaded a whole range of equipment from the vehicle which included parts of a steel frame he had fabricated, a seven foot long steel pole, sharpened to a point at one end, a scaffold clamp, a small pile of timber and two large jerry cans of petrol. Within minutes he had erected the frame with two vertical struts and diagonal support trusses. He tried to work quickly and silently, but wearing gloves made some of the work fiddly. The gloves were to reduce the personal evidence he might leave at the scene, but Colin realised that in reality he had already left his own DNA all over the place. He should have removed the gloves because his stubborn insistence led to him clumsily picking up the scaffold clamp and promptly dropping it. The clanging sound of it falling onto the ancient stone was unnaturally loud in the otherwise still air and he cursed under his breath. Removing the gloves belatedly he was able to work faster and with a lot less risk of noise.

Once the frame was complete Colin checked that there was still no-one else around and turned his attention back to Babić. Taking his now trademark cloth doused in a substance, similar to dichloromethane, which rendered anyone who inhaled it temporarily but quickly incapacitated, Babić was very soon helpless and Colin moved swiftly to properly secure his feet together. Handcuffed and bound, the Serb would be helpless when he came round. Colin gagged him and placed an old potato sack over his head.

He next picked up the long, thin metal pole and put that in a position nearby; then, taking a small sharp knife he cut away Babić's trousers and shirt, then the rest of his clothes. Naked, the man looked even more repulsive, with rolls of pale flab everywhere and dark hair sprouting at random angles all over his squat back. Colin laid the Serb down on his side with his knees tucked up tight to his chest. His aim now was to shove the pole up through the entire length of the Serb's body, so that the pole could be supported at each end upon the frame he had made, with Babić suspended in the middle much like a human hog-roast.

Roughly, he began to insert the pointed end of the pole into the pig farmer's anus. He worked quickly and forcefully to drive the rod deeper into the body. The work was harder than he had anticipated and he found that the force of his efforts just shoved the Serbian across the ground.

He needed to anchor the guy down, so he stood with all his weight on the fat man's right shin, thus pinning his leg firmly against the flagstones. The loud crack as the tibia or fibular snapped was an annoyance that could be tolerated. Colin then squatted down and drove the pole with all his considerable strength into the body. He struck something hard, which he assumed was the pelvis, and had to withdraw the pole some three or four inches. As the metal rod eased outwards there was a sucking sound which reminded Colin of a time when he was a boy and, with his mother, had gone down to the area where the geese and some of the dairy cows usually gathered. His wellington boot had become stuck in the thick wet mud that sat around the cow's feeding area and as he pulled the boot out there was a loud squelching noise. At the time Colin and his mum had laughed and he'd repeated the sequence, each time seemingly getting funnier until it felt like their sides might split. He had never forgotten that sound and a part of him resented the Serb's mimicry of it.

Angry now, he rammed the pole home with everything he had. This time the sound was like punching a blancmange. Something spattered out onto his arm but he was too engrossed in the grisly task to care. With a final effort the sharpened tip of the pole exited Babić's throat. It caught momentarily beneath the chin but with a small adjustment and a swift kick under the chin to knock the head back Colin had it free and he continued to push until about ten inches of pole was clear of the little man's body.

Colin grabbed the scaffold clamp and attached it to the pole just below the Serb's arse. This would ensure that when Colin lifted the pole at the head-end onto the gantry he'd built, the body didn't slide back down towards the foot-end. With the clamp in place, Colin moved to the head end and grabbed the pole. The thing just slipped between his fingers and Colin had to wipe clean the exposed metal. The clamp did its job as intended and with the head end in position Colin then lifted the pole at the foot-end onto the gantry.

The result was that he now had the Serbian pig farmer suspended on the pole between two gantry supports, looking very much like the hog roast effect Colin had wanted to achieve, and he silently congratulated himself on a job well executed. He giggled at the little pun.

The Serb briefly gained consciousness. He had no idea what had happened but the pain was indescribable. He tried to move but was unable, he tried to scream, but only a muffled noise escaped through the gag and he tried to see but his head was shrouded in blackness. The pain took control of his last moments on earth and unconsciousness mercifully enveloped him.

Colin was in a hurry, despite the hour he knew that at any moment he might be discovered. He knew without checking that the man would still be alive, but he cared little for that. Better that he take a final message with him into hell.

He continued to work quickly, piling the pieces of timber beneath the suspended Serbian and dousing these in petrol. He poured the entire contents of one jerry-can onto the wood and a good half of the second was used to run a short trail to the edge of the market cross. The area was tidied up and the Land-rover engine started. Colin climbed out once more, taking a cigarette lighter from his pocket and igniting the trail of fuel that led to his little pyre.

The entire pile ignited with a whoosh of energy which even at twenty feet singed Colin's eyebrows. He jumped behind the wheel and sped off down South Street towards the A27 town by-pass. As he drove he phoned two local newspapers from one of the cheap pay-as-you-go phones he had bought, the Chichester Observer and the Portsmouth News. To both he had the same message.

'Get a reporter to Chichester city centre immediately. There you will find a pleasant hog-roast. More details will be available for the BBC and ITV main evening news bulletins later. In your news column you should quote the reason as *the failure of the government to halt animal slaughter.* The next lesson will take place in 24 hours unless the murdering of helpless animals stops.'

At the wheel of the Land-rover, Colin had a job to keep his feet from dancing across the pedals. He was whistling Baa Baa Black Sheep.

54

Jenny was becoming accustomed to the routine now and needed no prompting from the crazy. What was different was that she now suspected him of being a killer; Babić had not returned with him last night, so unless he'd moved him to another location he must have killed him. The threats all along had been often vague but very sinister and they all knew how badly unhinged he was.

She took a marker pen and went to the flip chart.

'What's the message?'

'Tell them, in your exquisite style, that they lied and that I found them out. As a result Babić died and if they don't immediately stop killing animals to eat them, then the next death will follow 24 hours after the last one.'

Jenny knew she had to get more critical clues into this message, she had to try to tell the outside world exactly who was in with her because although that seemed obvious to her, the connection might not have been made and there could be any number of forces looking for missing persons, yet not linking them to this. She had limited scope within such a short statement so this was going to be tough.

She wrote

The Serbian, Babić died because you failed to do as instructed. You were warned <u>2</u> times and are <u>MILES</u> away from being <u>ANYWHERE CLOSE</u> to doing as I said.

Donna, me and the other 5 are united behind Colin. Germans and Muslims alike, please do as we ask and stop the butchery.

It was crude and frankly quite pathetic, she thought, but the best she could hope for.

'Read it to me.' Colin commanded.

'It's just what you said really, I just used a few words to let them know we are all united now.'

Jenny held it up for him to read himself and wondered just how bad his dyslexia was; could she get away with just telling the whole story to the outside world, or could he read enough to work that out? She didn't know and it would be stupid to risk discovery. At least this way she could get some clues out, even weak ones. She still clung to the hope that someone was analysing these messages and joining the dots.

To Colin the collections of letters were difficult to transpose quickly into meaningful words, he needed time, but he spotted a sequence which he knew very well.

'Why have you written my name?'

'I am just singing your praises Colin, telling them that you know what you are doing and that they must listen to you. Like I said, we are all supporters now, or I certainly am, and I can't wait to start converting these people.'

Colin smiled; he felt a warm glow, as if this Jenny girl had already been converted. But then he always had realised that she was different. Jenny was videoed holding the script and as usual it was a silent clip. Colin did not want to risk his voice being recognised. Jenny was taken back to her cage and locked in. Colin went to his control room to process the recording and prepare it for distribution via his one remaining mobile to the BBC and ITV networks.

55

The newspapers had a field day with the discovery of Babić.

One tabloid, not known to cater for the big thinkers in society had the banner headline:

"NUT ROAST! Veggie loony Barbecue" with the promise to run a campaign to eat more meat in order to show these loonies that "Britain wouldn't be held to ransom for some far left tree-hugging vigilantes".

Its sister publication focussed on:

"Chi Grilled" (This was in reference to the local abbreviation for Chichester) with the sub-text "the heat is on as veggie terrorists threaten all out war on meat eaters".

Another, known for its blinkered and outspoken generalisations read:

"STAKE & KIDNEY FRY" And followed this up with rhetoric about foreign gangland violence hitting the streets of this once peaceful city. It laid blame at the door of the local council for the removal of surveillance equipment and made it clear that the police were baffled by the "torture and murder of this innocent man, thought to be a German national", despite information to the contrary.

The more conservative approach from the broadsheets focussed on the clear link between recent disappearances and the threats against carnivores.

Most were united in the view that an out-of-control group was roaming the streets and randomly snatching people to torture and kill. Some speculated that it was a lone madman, a serial killer from an animal rights movement, fed up with having an unheard voice.

Following a hastily convened press conference Detective Chief Inspector Sharon Moody, who was leading the investigation, admitted that the police had very few leads and urged vigilance in and around the city.

Workplace and pub conversations and school drop-off chats were almost exclusively about the brutal murder. Everyone had an opinion. None of them was close to the truth and a certain Colin Furness, sat in his control room with most of the newspapers scattered around smiled at the publicity and planned his next move.

56

The twilight was shattered by the bright neons.
'Time for the guessing game my friends' came the familiar voice over the speakers.
'Our friend Babić won't be participating this time, although I think he was dying to be here, he is now busy helping the police with their enquiries.'

Delighted with his wit, the speaker was performing his odd shuffle in the control room.

'We'll start with some hard questions, and then they'll get harder. Remember there's a forfeit for the first wrong answer. Ladies first.'

'Donna; what do we call the confined spaces where calves, usually male, can be confined, chained and unable to move for their entire lives?'
'Cruel and too bloody small!' She answered.
'Haha, oh I like that; it's not the answer I was looking for.'
In her prison Donna swore. Why had she given such a flippant answer?
Colin continued '...but it's a great answer and shows you are starting to get the message.'

The other women were questioned in a similar manner and all answered correctly enough to appease the captor.
'Well that's great progress from our female friends, now it's your turn to prove your prowess men.'
'Simon; you're a real man's man, don't let the side down! What age are lambs typically when they are taken from their mothers?'
'About five months.' The answer was quick and confidently delivered.

'Very good Mr Grayson. Hans-Werner; which country currently insists that all cosmetic products are tested on animals?'
The answer was equally swift.
'The People's Republic of China.'
'Most excellent!'
'Farouk; when will your god send a message that murdering animals is bad?' Colin knew it was an unfair question that the Muslim would be duty bound to answer truthfully.

The answer came reluctantly, but Farouk had to remain true to his faith.
'I can't say for sure, but I think he won't ever do that.'
'Oooooh, how delightfully wrong. Once he sees his flock of blind-faith followers start to question his stance on animal cruelty he will shift into self-preservation mode and suddenly all the scholars will be having visions in the night and rewrites of holy books will be everywhere. That's the way the churches keep their membership numbers artificially high. You and I shall take a drive later.'

With that the microphone was switched off and the lights extinguished. Video of a Halal slaughterhouse soon appeared on the giant screens.
In his cage, Doctor Farouk El Hamidiri began to weep and to pray. He wasn't sure if the direction he faced was accurate, but better to pray incorrectly than not to try at all.

57

'Hello, could I speak with the manager please?'
Colin Furness was calling the same slaughterhouse that he'd contacted earlier.
'Speaking.' Came the same gruff voice on the other end of the line
'I called you last week about three pigs I need to slaughter, do you have any time for me now?'
'No chance, haven't you seen the newspaper campaign to eat more meat and piss these veggie nutters off? Sorry, we're up to our knees in blood and guts here; no spare room at all.'
'So you are still slaughtering?'
'Yep, business as usual, except busier.'

That was all Colin Furness needed to hear. So they'd learned nothing from Babić's death. OK the next would have to be more graphic.

Later, at around midnight, Colin hit the main light switch from his control room and switched on the microphone
'Farouk, I am coming down to take that drive with you. You'll wear the handcuffs and any resistance will be painful for you.'
In his cage on the bottom layer Doctor El Hamidiri felt as if icy talons were gripping his stomach. The last person to go for a drive with the lunatic hadn't been seen since.

The nutter was there almost before these thoughts had formed, standing at the cage entrance, armed with that hideous electric stun gun.
'Farouk, my friend, do animals feel pain?'
'I am sure all animals feel some pain, but not in the way that humans do.'
'Wrong answer; clearly you are not made of the right stuff to become a disciple.'

237

With that he passed a pair of handcuffs through the bars and instructed Farouk to fit them.

The Muslim refused.

'If I put these on then I am at your mercy, and we know what will happen to me.'

When he spoke, Colin's voice was dead calm.

'Let's be clear on one thing; you already *are* at my mercy. Nobody knows what will happen to you Doctor, but put the things on or I shall electrocute your eyeballs first and then your teeth. You'll be blind and unable to chew for the rest of your short and unpleasant life. Now put on the fucking cuffs.'

As if to demonstrate his intent Colin charged the device. Farouk was well familiar with the high pitched sound it made when building up power.

'OK, OK I will put them on.'

He did as he had been instructed and Colin opened the cage door. Watched by silent eyes El Hamidiri was marched through the big main doors as Babić had been before him, and bundled into the back of the Land-rover. Colin checked to ensure that his hands were firmly immobilised and then taped his ankles and knees together. Then he gagged him and drove out of the yard along the small country lanes towards the city.

Once the Land-rover reached Chichester Colin headed for the old market site. As a boy he had been here on market days and seen the cattle and swine bought and sold, and watched his father doing his grizzly business with scary looking men. Now it was a vast car park and due to the hour they had the entire place to themselves. Colin had located the network of cameras and had taken the darkest route to a spot a little off the main thoroughfares. It was a little too risky here to be climbing around on ladders and spraying the lenses but he had blacked out the number plates on the vehicle and had the headlights on high beam in order to dazzle any camera as much as possible without becoming too conspicuous.

He pulled the hood of his coat over his head and removed a large boning knife from his holdall.

'This won't take very long Farouk, I haven't done it myself but I've watched it on enough videos to know how it works. I'll slit your throat; the blood will drain in two seconds, according to you, and you'll feel nothing. Ready? Want to say a silent prayer to your cruel god?'

Farouk fell to the ground and began to wriggle in his bonds like a trapped eel but was getting nowhere.

Colin grabbed a fistful of his hair with his left hand, exposing his throat and with the knife made a small cut.

Farouk screamed into his gag but the sound was inaudible.

'Ooops, not very skilled with this thing.'

He sliced again, deeper this time and a gurgling sound came from the split throat.

'Nearly there Farouk, just remember it doesn't hurt and you'll be fine.'

The Muslim began to fart as his rectum relaxed and released the contents of his colon. This took Colin by surprise, but was an otherwise pleasing sound; to him it was evidence that the victim was indeed feeling mental and physical torment.

He made the third and final slice but it was still not sufficiently deep to kill his victim.

He pulled the head back further and stared into the dying man's eyes, which were wide with terror and pain.

'There we go you shit arse, pain is indeed real. I'd ask you to apologise, but I have probably just slit your vocal cords.'

He laid Farouk's head almost tenderly on the tarmac and left him to bleed to death.

Driving away, Colin was happy that his theory had been proven and that his cause was further justified. The death of one man was vindication enough.

As he drove he took one of the new pay-as-you-go mobiles and called the usual media numbers, explaining the predicament they'd find at the old market place car park.

58

Donna was lying curled on the mesh floor. She had found a way to reduce the pain from the wire which was constantly cutting into her feet and body. She had stripped off all the clothing she could spare without being too cold and laid it like a thin mattress across the floor of the cage. She found that folding over the blanket and laying on top of her jeans and top, she could stem the pain. It left her a little chilly, but at least took the edge off the sharpness.

She reflected constantly on her predicament and spent most of the time building a hatred for this insane bastard who was keeping them like this. She fantasised about a time when she might turn the tables and have him at her mercy. She'd use every trick she had learned over her years of forcing men to bend to her will. Normally she would command a high price for the pleasure, but for this freaky bastard she'd do it gratis, with the greatest of pleasure. She found herself becoming physically aroused as these thoughts built bigger and more rapturous images. This had been the longest period since before puberty that she had lasted without orgasm and she couldn't resist pulling an edge of the blanket over her middle and subtly touching herself. With the visualisation of literally walking all over the creep and cutting his back with her vicious Cat O'Nine Tails she was soon tingling all over. This was the way to spend the interminable days, she thought, squirming under the ministrations of her deft fingers. She brought herself right to the edge of release imagining his inner thighs splitting from a particularly nasty slash and despite her best efforts to be quiet she came noisily, biting her lip hard in a futile effort to subdue the cry that started deep in the centre of her being and erupted through every singing nerve end.

Two levels above Donna, Simon Grayson was alerted to her self-pleasure by the semi-muted cries. He was a serial womaniser, and

240

was, according to his plethora of lovers, damn good at it. As such he was very familiar with these sounds.

Peering through the semi-gloom he could just make out her reclined form partially concealed by some of the blanket, and conversely and erotically partially exposed. Like Donna, his body and mind were used to plenty of good sex and he had been denied this for far too long now. He became instantly aroused and wished he had been in an adjacent cage to her, or even above. He could easily fit his manhood through the squares of mesh and encourage her with promises of reward to pleasure him orally. Wow, if he were next to her he'd even be able to take her. Between him and Donna's deliciously arranged sensuality lay Amanda's sleeping form. Laid on her back, her face had an angelic quality, but right now it was half obscuring the object of his hungry desire.

His willpower was weak after so long without sexual release and he began to stroke himself quite openly. In the confines of his prison cubicle Simon Grayson's highly aroused mind twisted a connection between the exotic Donna, semi exposed to his gaze and flushed from her recent pseudo-public sexual performance, his own total lack of liberty, the reluctant witnesses around him and the insanity of the voyeuristic freak, in whose hands his life currently rested and who might even now be watching him through his secret lenses. Even as he approached orgasm all these elements joined forces and the sum was far greater than the parts. His climax was sublime.

59

Colin sat bolt upright in bed. The alarm clock showed 03:23. He'd been asleep for less than an hour, but whatever had woken him? He couldn't recall any noises and there were no lights showing anywhere. Then it hit him – he'd been dreaming. The dream had taken him through the familiar heartache of a small boy whose mother had run away, but it had changed course from its usual route. It had taken him into new territory – literally; in the dream he had been exploring a strange, new, and yet somehow oddly familiar part of the farm. He was desperately trying to recall the details from the dream but it was too vague. However, something was different and something he dreamed had startled him into immediate wakefulness.

He went down to the kitchen and made a cup of tea. Cradling the cup against the chilly air he quietly walked across the house and took the stairs to his control room. There he sat and watched the camera images of the disciples. He was pleased and proud that all the work he'd put in, all the preparations, the planning and the hours and days and weeks to try to make a successful change programme were slowly coming to fruition. Even the hard-nosed Donna had changed her tune.

He sipped his tea and watched as one of the captives adjusted the blanket around themselves. Had he been too harsh perhaps? Was he expecting too much? As he looked at the cage housing the chef Grayson, Colin saw that the disgusting shit had thrown his blanket to the side and was laid on his back as flat as the small cage would allow, displaying his genitalia.

Colin was jiggling around, wringing his hands together and shaking with fury, but trying to manage the anger. Doctor Erikssen would tell him he needed a distraction. Right now all he could think of was that filthy creature Grayson. Not enough to do sex with that MPs wife, now the disgusting man has to go and exhibit himself. Colin looked around desperately for something to interrupt his thoughts and his eyes fell onto the external CCTV monitors. Desperately trying to divert his thoughts he played the external cameras across their motorised arcs. With just 25 outside cameras he was able to see the entire farm complex. He scrolled through the screens around the perimeter, across the roofs and along to what were called the killing lines up at the old complex. He had hated this, the old part of the farm more than anything in the world, and even now averted his gaze when the cameras swept over some parts of the old house and the sheds. He really should get down there though and have a sort through things. That area had lain pretty much undisturbed since Colin's father had died. He vaguely remembered a whole cellar complex beneath the actual killing lines, as the shop floor there was so tastefully named. His father had shown him once but he couldn't recall much about the area at all. He couldn't sleep in any case so he'd go and have a look around right now.

He was feeling calmer now and with caution took the steps down towards the old cellar doors. They were in shocking condition. Broken bricks and tiles and pieces of wood lay strewn around the tendrils of bramble, but there was a cleared route and he could pick his way carefully through the gloom towards the doors at the bottom. When he reached the doors he was surprised to see that the old wooden things had been replaced by two huge and very solid looking steel fire doors. The collection of dents and scratches, coupled with dense cobwebs told Colin that although these doors were new to him, they'd clearly been in situ for some years. That just served to remind him how long ago he'd been shown down here by his father. After that one occasion he'd stayed well clear, the sounds of a hundred and fifty thousand lives being snuffed out a few feet above his head had been enough to convince the young boy that he never wanted to venture to this part of the farm ever again. 150000; such an unimaginable number!

He ran his hands over the cold metal doors and tentatively tried a handle. Locked; he felt a little shamefully relieved when the door stayed determinedly shut tight. He turned and started to make his way back along the treacherous steps to ground level, wondering why his father had locked the damn doors in any case. Had he kept something of value down there? Colin couldn't imagine what.

As he reached the top of the steps he caught the sound of an electrical fan motor starting up. It was a common sound around the farm, but there should have been nothing in this area that was "live". He ran his fingers across his bald pate and wondered. Too many mysteries. Too many puzzles. Too many surprises. Something was odd and something needed to be explained. At the same moment he made the decision to locate the sound of the motor, the damn thing stopped.

60

Colin shivered with the imaginary ghosts in this older part of the farm and quickly headed back down the hill towards the newer main barn. He decided to give an impromptu group therapy session. He hadn't planned to, but felt the need to educate. Back in his control room he hit the main lights.
'Pay attention and pay it good.'

His voice was too loud so he adjusted the microphone. Despite being two miles from any neighbours he knew how sound can travel in the still air and he didn't want noise complaints being investigated!

'Do you know, that all the pigs and sheep and chickens and cows we can see out in the fields represent only about 5% of the typical farming industry animal population'.
He paused to let the significance of this statement sink in.
'That means that a staggering 95% of all farmed animals are invisible to us. Hidden away in farm factories where the sun don't shine'.
Again the pause.
The voice continued, slightly harder than before.

'Fact. If the consumers in the USA alone - Joe public, as I believe they are collectively known - cut their food waste by 50% they would save in a year more than 500 million broiler chickens. That is to say that currently, in USA alone, excluding the waste in the retail supply chain, one billion – more than one billion chickens are executed for absolutely no reason. Actually the reasons are there, but they are completely selfish. They are things like impulse buying, food allowed to go off, massive portion sizes that even those lard arses can't finish, over-stuffing refrigerators and cupboards for holiday celebrations and a general attitude of treating animals as a low-value and expendable commodity.'

'So, they would spare the lives of 35 million egg laying hens, 3 million cows, 15 million pigs-have you any idea what that looks like? 15 million pigs? And, wait for it, 15 *billion* fish. 15 thousand million fish-it's an ocean full surely? *Just if they reduced waste by 50% and just in USA.'*

The last sentence was practically a shout and an observer in the control room would have seen an almost instant change in character from casual announcer to a fidgeting red-faced fanatic.

'Now if the retailers over there sorted their act out too, the figures would be much higher. I wonder what the figures are worldwide? I can't think in numbers that big, but I have probably cried a tear for each and every one of those poor creatures who are bred and live their entire lives in misery so that they can be eaten, only to find the ultimate indignity of not even getting onto the fork....well if that isn't the definition of a shit life I can't think what is.'

Colin realised his emotions were spoiling the lesson and took a deep, slow breath and a moment to compose himself.

'What it comes down to, dear people, is a fundamental right to a life, and for that life to be free of unnecessary suffering. Breeding animals, holding them captive, murdering them and then not even using their corpses, well, it's the saddest indictment of the human psyche.'

Colin became absolutely calm.
'People, please remember the numbers here are just from wasted food. All those numbers we learned about animal experiments the other day, they were in addition. The numbers are incompatible with a welfare society. Please think about this as you ponder your predicaments here, and remember, you will be freed from these cages. You will go back to your lives, free to run, swim, laugh, eat – yes, free to eat whatever you desire. I am very hopeful that this will be a plant based diet. This is the reason for you being here, kept in

this unpleasant, uncomfortable and completely abnormal environment, in these horrid, dark, cold soulless cages.

We should be searching deep within ourselves during the time we spend here. For this reason I call your prisons the soul cages. Use them to find your souls and save them.
Thank you for your attention. Now I shall leave you to think and sleep.'
The microphone became silent and the lights went out. Unusually, so did the huge screens.

61

The whole team were assembled in the ops room. DCI Sharon Moody was speaking.

'Let's have the CCTV news please Carol.'

'There's good news, bad news and worse news Ma'am, which would you like?'

'Don't piss around with riddles Carol, give it to me straight.'

The stress was clearly starting to affect Moody.

'Sorry! The football stadium hasn't revealed anything more Ma'am, Jenny's credit card records show she bought the steak where we thought but the cameras at the supermarket were down for maintenance.'

'You have got to be bloody kidding me? I bet they have one frigging day a year when they are maintained and that just happens to be the day we need them? Get the security company manager in here, it's too bloody convenient for my liking, the guy needs to explain some things.'

'Ma'am; I checked all that out, it's genuine and is planned for the same day every year on a service contract.'

'But why do it in the middle of the bloody day when there are the most people around?'

'Think about it Ma'am, they are hardly likely to suffer a break-in when the place is full of customers and staff. It's at night when the cameras are most needed.'

'Sorry Carol, you're right. Bad night.'

'Also tried the city centre cameras for the Babić murder, but they've been disabled somehow.'

'Disabled? This is becoming more like a far-fetched film by the minute. Get the technical guys onto it. OK what else have we got; Samantha?'

'I have the lists of all possible animal rights groups active in the area and am getting a full list of the VOTA members later today; all 31 of them!'
'OK-keep on it. We know VOTA had two new members from London who had more extreme tendencies. Get stuck into them first.'

Moody continued.
'Right; two significant developments since we last met. You'll have heard about our body in the car park last night? Local Muslim man by the name of Doctor Farouk El Hamidiri. Throat slit and messages to the media in a similar vein to the previous murder. We can't be certain of course that it's the same group, might be copy-cat, but the brutality of the two events match; let's see what the forensic guys can tell us and work with the facts, but keep the thoughts and ideas flowing. Talking of which, thinking caps on for a brainstorm.'
'Mind dump Ma'am.'
'Ah yes; mind bloody dump. Thank you Brian!'

She indicated the video message from the previous day printed and held by magnets to the white board.
'Here's the new message from yesterday. She read aloud.

The Serbian, Babić died because you failed to do as instructed. You were warned <u>2</u> times and are <u>MILES</u> away from being <u>ANYWHERE CLOSE</u> to doing as I said.
Donna, me and the other 5 are united behind Colin. Germans and Muslims alike, please do as we ask and stop the butchery.

On past evidence there will be several clues in this. Following previous patterns the capitals and underlined words will hold the information. Get talking guys.'
Predictably, Samantha was first off the mark.
'Well obviously the first murder was a Serbian called Babić-first name or surname I have no idea. Then we have "2" underlined and "MILES" and "ANYWHERE CLOSE" capitalised. Knowing

249

Jenny's style, she's telling us they are situated 2 miles from anywhere – i.e. civilisation?'

'Quick thinking Samantha-I am impressed, and that makes a lot of sense to me. Plus we now know that there are 7 victims, including Jenny; one called Donna – has to be Donna Southgate – and we can assume Colin is one of the captors. Anyone disagree?'

The team indicated that they were all on board with those statements. Sicknote spoke up: 'Gotta hand it to DI Dyson's lady, Ma'am, just about everything we have so far has come from her.'

'Thanks Sicknote, let's see to it that we can thank her in person later. On the lists we have, pick out any "Colins". Let's use that juicy piece of info to get us shifting. Carol-please add city centre and market car park CCTV to your list!'

The team split into pairs in some kind of natural affinity instinct and they began to cross- reference the facts they now had against the previously known data.

62

The short visit to the cellars below the Killing Lines had piqued Colin's curiosity. In the midst of all his preparations he'd quite forgotten the old safe that used to sit in what was the old man's office. He knew where the keys would be; his father always hid them beneath a corner of the carpet in his office which wasn't held down with any adhesive. He went there now and found them, and then he turned and looked at the solid, old-fashioned beast with the names Hipkins and Dudley emblazoned across the front. The heavy door had two keyholes, one above the other. These were operated by a pair of very different looking keys. No fancy combination locks, just keys, and Colin had them both!

It was obvious by design which key belonged to which hole and he put both keys into the keyholes and turned the top one a full rotation anti-clockwise. Next he tried the bottom one, but it wouldn't rotate. He removed the lower key and checked it for damage. It looked fine so he inserted it again. Still nothing.
He removed the top key and just inserted the bottom one. This time it easily rotated, but there was no noise of the mechanism turning inside.

Colin was puzzled. Clearly the keys had an effect upon each other but he didn't know what it was. He tried turning both keys at exactly the same time and now the tumblers tripped sweetly around and the door was released. He assumed the safe was designed for the two keys to be held by different people so could only be accessed if both were present.

Holding his breath, Colin tugged the heavy door open. The thing weighed a ton but was soon wide enough for him to see the contents. All that was inside was a folded bundle of sheets of A4 paper and an expensive looking cash box.

He took the cash box first and was surprised at its weight. He was dismayed to see that it had a big combination key-pad as a built-in security system. Damn, he'd never have a clue what the code would be. He shook the heavy box and it clearly held a number of items. It sounded like some more keys were held inside too. It was a tough looking brute and one glance was enough to tell Colin that without the code he was never going to get to see what was inside.

He picked up the papers and realised they were the missing electric bills. Why the hell would his father keep them in the safe? What was so valuable about a few damn bills? He threw them onto the table in disgust and went for a walk around the facility to clear his mind.

After feeding the disciples and washing them down Colin was drawn back to the contents of the old safe. He was tempted to attack the cash box with some heavy cutting gear he had, but he'd heard of safes with special security devices which would destroy the contents if tampered with. He didn't have a clue what those contents were, but didn't want to risk destroying them, at least, not until he'd had a damn good crack at it. What the hell might the combination number be...

He turned instead to the electricity bills. There were dozens, and they were chronologically arranged; going back to March 2003. That date was indelibly etched in his brain. March 2003 was the month when his mother had abandoned them. He was plunged instantly into the pit of sadness that seemed to always envelop him when he thought of her. She had been so beautiful, so gentle and so loving. Even now he couldn't believe that she could have left him. Just got up and left him alone with that beast of a man. He couldn't blame her for leaving his father; they never did see eye to eye on many things, and they had very differing views on parenting and especially on how the farm should be run.

Colin's mum had been an animal lover, and had often argued with the old man, accusing him of gross negligence and cruelty. Colin hadn't understood the meanings of some of her words, but had felt her passion and knew that her heart was good. Whatever it was they argued about, she always lost. No, he didn't hate her for leaving, maybe even admired her for it, but he had lost count of the times he'd cried himself to sleep just wishing she'd at least said a last good bye to him. He wondered for the millionth time if she was still alive, where she might be and if she ever thought of him.

He started to put the papers back into the safe but caught himself wondering again why on earth they would be secreted away. Either the old man wanted them kept safe, which made little sense; none of the other bills or invoices or receipts were ever locked away. Or, and this seemed now more likely, he didn't want them to be seen.

Now why oh why would someone not want electricity bills to be seen? Made no sense at all. Then Colin remembered the query with the electricity supplier about a non-existent transformer. He checked the bills and sure enough, every quarterly statement made reference to a transformer E1. Colin was puzzled and intrigued. Here was something fishy. Something was not right. It was late now and he needed to sleep, but tomorrow he would investigate.

As he walked through the silent house his eyes rested for a moment on his mother's old bookshelf. His father had thrown most of her things out when she left, but had never touched her books. She was a great lover of reading and would enthral Colin with her descriptions of books; their characters, their smells, their patina; she could make even the most ordinary book come alive.

Colin had spent many many hours since she had left him, hunched over one or another of her favourites. He reached out now and took down one of her poetry anthologies. It had been her absolute favourite and Colin had been terrified to touch it after she left. He'd invented some silly thought that touching it would break a magical invisible thread which still held her somehow attached to him, and in breaking it she'd be forever lost. Well that was a silly way to think; she was never coming back. He grasped the book.

As he opened the heavy book a loose piece of paper fell to the floor. Curious, he stooped to pick it up and walked to the lamp to read it. It was covered double-sided with her delicate handwriting, which made him catch his breath; he'd almost forgotten how beautiful she could write, and this was the most exquisite he'd seen.

He struggled to read what she'd written, it would take him an age to decipher the words. He blinked back tears as what she had put down began to take meaning.

My darling. I don't know if you will ever read this, or if it will sit here for all eternity, unread and therefore, in a sense never written.

I have loved my life with you, and dream of a time when I may once again hold you to me, or walk the fields with you, clutching your hand as I explain about the plants, or the trees, or the animals. Or maybe I will read to you. I know what a nonsense the written word is for your muddled brain; but we both know it's a precious brain, and the muddle does not make you any less amazing; it's just a part of your make-up; what makes you unique and special.
Your father is a difficult man; he claims to be god-fearing and fair, and berates me for having no god. Had I chosen one, it would have been a god of leniency and mercy, who taught people to respect their world and their fellow creatures, instead of elevating themselves to some imaginary position of superiority, just because they can.

No; my god is the earth, the moon, the stars. The water and the sky. He calls me a disillusioned hippy for this, but he has his beliefs and I mine. In time you too will develop your own beliefs. I should so much have loved to have been able to shape them with you, given them form; not to drive you in any particular direction, but maybe to hold your hand at those times when you needed a little guidance or an idea.

I am so sorry that you have had to see he and I arguing, but in the end he is the stronger and his will shall prevail. I hope that you will rise above him, and become the man who I see when I look at the boy. Your father is probably going to send mummy away soon, so I write this in case, one day, you miss me and turn to the books that gave us so many hours of pleasure. If I know my son at all, then I am certain you will come here to find me.

I wrote a small poem last night. I have tried to say, in my silly words, what you mean to me. Tried to tell the story of what I see, when I look at you.

254

If you think of me, know this my sweet boy; I loved you without end.
Colin turned the page and read:

Rainbow Boy

He's far more delicate than that
I said. Shielding him from the wind with my hands
But through the biting cold
His intensity seared me

You have to protect his vulnerable edges
I explained. Pointing out the trembling aspects
But despite the shakiness of the peel
Fruit was sweet and nourishing

You'll need to water him often
I warned. Running with my empty bucket to the well
But the abstinence in his voice deceived
He gushed bigger than any fountain
And more colourful
The rainbows that caught the sun in their own hands
And protected colour's existence
He had captured forever with some magic trick.
Or another
Until he became bored and expunged them
As waves wipe sand letters
He'll stifle those rainbows
They said. Marvelling the colours of a sky monster
But he turned to me and showed. He had saved
The most beautiful one
I went away and a tear fell
I'll need to be careful
I told myself
A tear, in the wrong light can deceive
And appear a rainbow

255

To my beautiful little boy; in whose presence rainbows will hide xxx
Physically numbed and mentally broken, Colin fell to his knees. At
first he sat and stared at the carpet. Then, when the mental paralysis
eased, he lowered his head onto the floor and cried deep tearing
eruptions of emotion which had craved release for twenty or more
years. Tears of grief and of relief; she hadn't, after all, forsaken him,
run away without saying goodbye.

63

At some point Colin must have slept, because when he next became conscious of thought he was cold and stiff and filled with a strange juxtaposition of torpidity, and yet a lightness and determination to press onwards with his plans.

It was a little earlier than the usual time for the next test, but he needed a loser so he could send the next clear message tonight. First he needed to tend to Vengeance and make sure he had all he needed for the day, Colin didn't know very predictably when he'd next have time. When he'd exercised, fed and watered the stallion he let him into the field and then went down to the barn.

'Wakey wakey! It's that time again, thinking caps on and eyes down for the third test. Sounds like a cricket tournament, but the loser in this game doesn't lose the ashes, they might well become them!'

Colin was clearly in a much brighter mood since the strange melancholy of his mother's letter and poem. As the bright lights came on the prisoners tried to adjust their eyes to the glare and their bodies to the painful, ever-present mesh.

'Let's start with the gentlemen this time – I like to be fair. Firm but fair, that's me.'

'You first Babić...oh wait, he's not with us. OK Farouk – ah, silly me! We'll have to try Simon then. Gosh, we need to stock up on males – I'll get some more later.'
In his cage Grayson hoped beyond hope that he'd get an easy one and that one of the others would fuck up.

'Simon; what's the square root of ...only kidding. What's the difference between Kosher and Halal meat?'

257

Simon Grayson wasn't really sure, he knew Kosher had to be clean and prepared away from some other products. Trembling a little, he decided to risk a Donna-esque reply.

'Nothing of any consequence, they are both barbaric and must be banned!'

'Oh Simon, Simon, Simon...what a thoroughly excellent answer. You pass the test.'

Grayson was shaking, but a broad smile of relief filled his face.

The questions went around the cages until Colin reached Donna.

'Donna, snake lady, ex-wearer of skins. Have you repented?'

'Oh yes, I shall never be so heartless again!'

Thinking she'd passed the test, Donna relaxed. Only to be brought down to earth with a bang.

'Good, and now for your question. What does the acronym PETA stand for?'

Donna knew immediately that she was doomed. She desperately racked her brain for an idea. Finding no solution there she looked around at the other cages, hoping for some insight. The other prisoners looked away except for the quick thinking Simon Grayson, who whispered down from his lofty perch in the hope that the nutter couldn't hear him: "It's People Exploiting Tortured Animals".

He hoped she'd fall for it.

She did

'I think it stands for People Exploiting Tortured Animals.'

'No no no Donna my sweet, that's absolutely not right, couldn't be wronger in fact. It's People for the Ethical Treatment of Animals.'

'You bastard Grayson; you did that deliberately.' She began to sob. 'He set me up with that the evil shit, take him instead; please take him.'

'Oh but I do wish I could Donna, but you knew the rules, first answer is the one I have to accept. I am sure his day will come. I'll get the handcuffs.'

Donna continued to rant at Grayson and generally plead for mercy. Grayson huddled into the corner of his cage and thanked his stars for his quick imagination. His time would surely come, but not today, and every day that passed gave him hope that they'd be found, after all, they couldn't be holed up here forever.

Colin appeared carrying not one, but two pairs of cuffs. Donna was at least grateful that he was clearly going to take Grayson too, for being such a nasty shit.

To Donna's dismay and Jenny's horror it was Jenny who was told to fit the second pair of cuffs.

'Don't worry Jenny; you're coming along for the ride just so that this message can be more directly communicated to our stupid and stubborn friends on the outside.'

One at a time he escorted the handcuffed women to the waiting Land-rover where they were, as usual gagged and bound and loaded into the back of the vehicle.

64

The team, minus Samantha and Dyson, had been hastily called in to the station.

'Sorry to pull you in at this hour folks, but the VOTA list contains two gentlemen by the name of Colin. It's my opinion that one of them will prove to be a member of our merry band. One lives in London – he's one of the two recent militant additions to the membership and Samantha is right now coordinating his arrest with the Met. The other, according to VOTA member, Sally Smalling – she's the lady who provided the list of other VOTA members is more local, and despite having no history of violence or extreme attitude we do know from Sally that Mr Colin Furness had a pretty strong difference of opinion with a guest speaker at her house on 7th March. Ten points to anyone who can name that guest speaker...'

Sicknote called out the name of Farouk El Hamidiri.

'Bingo! Now we can't find Colin Furness on any local electoral rolls, although his recently deceased father still seems to be, but we do have a load of vehicles registered to Colin Furness along with an address for them so we're getting a search warrant sorted as we speak and expect to move within the hour. I also received a note from uniform saying that, following a report of a leak, Farouk's garden was checked by a water company engineer and upon investigation he found that the water was running beneath the front door from the inside. When he looked through the window he saw the ceiling in one room had completely collapsed and the water was running down from the hole. The local uniform guys investigated and found the hot and cold bath taps fully open. Seems our friend Farouk must have been running a bath when he was taken, so that means he was taken from his house, probably on the same night of the argument at VOTA.' Moody had a determined but pleased look about her as she spoke these words.

'Chill out for a few minutes while we get all the ducks in a row, we'll be joined by a Brighton firearms unit very shortly. For your information, I shall be briefing DI Dyson in a moment.'

Steph spoke from the map attached to the wall.
'Ma'am – the address we have for the vehicles registered to Colin Furness is here. If my maths is correct, it's almost exactly 2 miles from the nearest houses.'
'I don't see your point - why is that significant?'
'One of the clues...' she moved to the white board where the words were written.

"You were warned 2 times and are MILES away from being AYWHERE CLOSE"

'Samantha hit it on the head – 2 miles from anywhere close! It *has* to be him!'
Moody grinned.
'Yep, seems that way. Get me a photo of this Furness guy - and get a description of him from this Sally woman from VOTA – my money says he's tall, got a high voice and has a stutter or something wrong with his eyes!'

65

Colin drove down the lane and onto the main road. He had been driving for about ten minutes when four police cars went screaming past, blue lights blazing, but no sirens.
Colin became thoughtful. He had been living on his nerves and was now worried that the plods had somehow rumbled him. Had he left clues somewhere? Had the car park cameras picked up enough to identify him after all? He decided he needed to know for sure. Spinning the truck around he pursued the police vehicles.

His fears were realised when, before he reached his long driveway he saw the flashing blue lights from the stationary police cars between the trees that surrounded his property.
'Shit!' he shouted and once again span the wheel and raced off the way he'd been going originally.

Colin drove quickly along the winding country roads which were little more than dirt tracks until he hit the A286. Here he headed south, through the village of Singleton until he reached Lavant. There he turned right and drove west through West Stoke, stopping at a small shingle car park on the right. This was a popular place for walkers to leave their vehicles, where they would usually take the footpath north towards Colin's favourite place on the planet.

Kingley Vale was an area of stunning beauty, a National Nature Reserve and home to Bronze Age tumuli. It was elevated and surrounded by woodland and Colin knew it like the back of his hand. The night was almost as black as pitch and the car park deserted at this hour. Colin jumped into the rear of the Land-rover. He freed the legs of both captives and then taped Donna's left arm to Jenny's right, just above the elbows.

'You will walk ahead of me. In the extremely unlikely event that we meet anyone coming down the hill you will stop and kiss each other until they pass. If you fail to do this I will electrocute the other people and kill them. Then I will kill one of you. The other will receive painful blasts from the cattle prod all the way to the top. That's about two miles, uphill.'

Donna was dismissive and knew the end was near for her at least. 'I'm not kissing any woman, mate! God you are a nutter, if you think people are going to change centuries of eating habits and customs just because you can't stomach a bit of blood, well you're crazier than you look, and that's saying something!'

'You are clearly never going to get it Donna, I imagine your dying words will be to beg forgiveness, but in the name of all those poor mistreated creatures whose suffering you have knowingly supported you will not receive any clemency. You will see your own blood spill; that I swear to you. Now walk! Nobody speaks a word until we stop at the top; I want to be able to hear anyone else who might still be around.'

Donna was still defiant but her will was slowly losing the fight. A wave of the cattle prod was enough to gain her compliance.

Before they set off Colin cast a worried look around, half expecting to see more flashing blue lights, but they couldn't possibly know where he was. He grabbed his large holdall from the Land-rover and locked the doors and the odd threesome headed up the chalk path towards the woods ahead. This was an ancient yew forest with some of the gnarled old trees rumoured to be over a thousand years old. Up close in the darkness they could just make out the crooked old forms with huge limbs bowing down to the earth as if attempting a union far from the original trunk and roots. There were many night creatures scurrying and flapping in the near pitch black and the atmosphere was spooky. It was said that witches traditionally gathered here on Halloween to dance naked around fires and carry out their evil work; Jenny thought she could sense the spirits of centuries.

Donna was labouring on the steep slopes and cursed under her breath.

263

'Quiet! If you hadn't spent so long lounging in furs you might find the going somewhat easier; Jenny and I are having no trouble.'
This wasn't strictly true, as despite her relatively active lifestyle, Jenny was short of breath and her thighs were burning a little. This was probably in no small measure due to her recent enforced inactivity.
Eventually the incline eased and the dense woods gave way to open grassland.
After fifteen more minutes they reached Colin's destination; the largest of the three Bronze Age burial mounds.

'Right, get down on the ground and stay down while I set up a few things.'
Colin re-bound their legs and wrapped tape around their heads to cover their mouths. He then went off into the darkness. There was little the prisoners could do but lay on the cold, damp earth in the dip at the top of the largest mound and await their fate.

Before long Colin's head appeared over the ridge of the mound.
'There. All ready; just need to wait a while for the beginning of dawn so we can see a little better, the camera needs a minimum light level. I am going to be benevolent and remove your gags. The first peep I hear and you get taped up again.'

Jenny had seen the flashing blue lights on the way here and had sensed the Land-rover changing direction twice. She knew she had to keep the nutter happy and play for time in the hope that those trying to track them would get to them before it was too late.

'You talk of your vegetarianism Colin, but you miss the point on animal cruelty.'

'What do you mean *I* miss the point? I am the one changing the world, you are only a bit part player, I have the leading role.'
'No; you surprise me with your ignorance. The dairy and so-called free-range industries are almost as sickeningly damaging as the stuff you are so offended by.'
'How can they be?' asked the captor.

'What do you think happens to the animals once they reach the end of their "fruitful" usefulness? You think they are set to pasture in some green and pleasant land? Wake up! They are slaughtered just the same way as those bred for the meat business. Often the cows will suffer terribly with mastitis where the udders have been so over-used or become so used to producing milk daily and then the milking suddenly stops. The udders carry on producing and swell to gigantic proportions. Even walking becomes impossible and the poor creatures are sometimes in so much pain that all they can do is lie down and suffer in silence. Where's your compassion for those creatures?'

How had he missed that? Well the truth was that he hadn't, but he'd somehow allowed himself to dismiss it in pursuit of the bigger prize. Well nobody was perfect, but damn damn damn that it took one of his disciples to point it out.

Jenny continued.
'And what the hell do you think happens to hens when their egg laying days are numbered? Set free to peck and cluck on a peaceful farmyard or on some idyllic English village green? No no, Mr clueless; they are butchered just the same as all the other chickens. I am astonished that you never saw this; you were part of the chicken farm system for so long- were you blind to it?'

Colin bristled.
'I never saw any real evidence of such maltreatment; in fact I was kept away from the egg laying side of the business because of the risk of contaminating the birds with some virus.'
'That's all bullshit Colin; red herrings told to you to keep you in line. Have you never seen the PETA films, or listened to the Podcasts on the stuff that happens in free range and dairy farms? You want to change the world to make it a better place for animals, and that's an admirable thing to do, but being vegetarian and locking up a vegan? Well it's ridiculous! Like a vicar preaching to the Pope. The things people do disgusts you, but you are a hypocrite because what they do to support abuse in the meat industry, you do for dairy and chickens, and you are either unaware or you are ignoring it because it's too difficult.'

Jenny continued, conscious she was wasting potentially valuable minutes.

'Have you ever wondered what happens to the male chicks that hatch? They are not required and are mostly minced up for plant feed. When you next see "bone meal" fertilizer, ask yourself what might be in the box.'

Colin was perplexed; of course he knew these things but he hadn't planned for this. He had seen firsthand the mincing of the tiny newborn chicks and knew she wasn't inventing stories. He had turned a blind eye to certain aspects of animal cruelty and hadn't thought there would be an argument that would put *him* in the bad-boy corner. He began to sweat and he could feel the old anger boiling up inside him. How dare she tell *him* that he was a bad person? He loved animals and would be their saviour. But this girl was tormenting him, trying to throw him off balance.

'I know what you are trying to do; you are winding me up so I make mistakes. Well my list might have had to change, but at least I still have a list, and I am going to pissing well work to it.'
Jenny knew she'd have to try to keep him calm, yet she felt she was beginning to prise open his armour. She took a risk and pressed ahead.
'Colin; I really like you, I think what you are trying to do is amazing. I don't agree with the way you are doing it, but I understand why, and you are fundamentally a good person. But don't you see? Killing all these people won't win you friends or followers. You will be vilified; ridiculed. You will turn people away from the very thing you are trying to engage them with.'

Jenny continued to work on him.
'Did you know that dairy cows are almost continually kept pregnant and lactating and their babies are taken away from them when they are only a few days old? The life of a dairy cow is not as natural as you might think, and most are impregnated artificially'.

Colin looked defiant

'I know all this; do you think I walk around with my fucking eyes shut? That's hardly cruelty though, just manipulation of nature.'
It felt very odd for him to be on the defensive tack.

'But Colin, don't you see, the milk produced by cows is naturally meant for their calves the same as any other mammal. Humans are the only creatures to drink the lactation of another animal-the *only* ones, and the only way for a cow to produce milk is for her to have a calf. But because people want to drink that milk the baby cows are taken away from their mothers when they are only a few days old. That's cruelty because cows are extremely maternal animals and both the mother and tiny calf suffer terribly from being separated at such a tender age. It's common on dairy farms for mother cows to bellow constantly trying to find their babies Some even run after the trucks that take their babies away. Cows are intelligent, you know that more than anyone, and mental anguish is cruelty.'

She saw him doing that odd shuffle that he did when he was happy or agitated.
'You also want to think about the hormones pumped into the cows to keep them lactating; ever heard of rBST? Stands for r*ecombinant bovine somatotropin* and there's a whole lot of evidence showing that rBST usage often results in severe pain and suffering for cows, and is associated with serious udder conditions, lameness and reproductive problems. The future for the baby calves is decided purely by gender. If the calf is male then he is taken away for fattening and slaughtered for veal. These male calves will never see their mothers again. They are taken away and transported from as young as 4 days old. Four days Colin!'

He was wringing his hands. She continued.
'They suffer cold, dehydration and hunger, without food or water for long journeys – and we are talking across continents, while struggling to maintain any footing in the cattle lorry. I beg you to think about this Colin. You and I could work together; you know I am your number one fan. We could be so strong together.'

Donna had heard enough.

'Get real you tree huggers. Cows feeling anguish? Come on, they are just dumb animals. Jenny, you are just trying to get the freak to release you so you can run off and save your own cowardly hide.'

Colin was fuming, he span to face Donna, turning on the cattle prod and staring directly into her eyes as the high pitched whine climbed in frequency until it became inaudible.
'Anguish can take many forms Donna; let's see how long it takes for your anguish to be so strong that you beg shall we? What do you think Jenny, will she beg before she urinates? Or will she have a heart attack first do you think? Let's make a game of it. I reckon she will do it in this order; beg because the pain is too strong, then urinate when she knows the next shock is coming and then suffer a heart attack when the terror and pain of the electricity across her piss-soaked genitalia is no longer bearable. Your turn.'

Jenny shook her head. 'I am not going to play your sick game Colin, it makes you no better than the vile abusers you are trying to stamp out.'

Colin pointed the prod at Donna's face. Where shall we hit you first Mrs fur fan?'

Donna instinctively pulled back her head. With her hands and legs tightly bound she was completely at the mercy of the madman and instantly sweat broke out on her forehead. Colin smiled and did a mini skip as he slowly waved the terminals over her hair. Suddenly he hit the power button and the hair on her head stood high as she screamed, the like of which Jenny had never heard.

Donna collapsed sideways, leaning against Jenny's shoulder.
'If I hit her again now Jenny you will get some of the blast. Do you deserve that?'
'Colin, I don't think any of us deserve what you are doing, but if it makes you feel better and powerful then be my guest.'
The words were the exact antithesis of what she was thinking. Inside she was of course praying that he wouldn't hit the button.

Thankfully Colin moved the prod away from their defenceless bodies. He nudged Donna with his toecap and she opened one eye slowly.

'You've practically blinded me' She shouted. 'Do that again and I will see you hang for it you sick bastard.'

Jenny elbowed her in the side.

'Shut up Donna; you're just making things worse.'

'Indeed!' agreed Colin. But in any case the game is still running, I haven't heard you beg or seen you piss your vile fornicating pants yet. I am looking forward to that, because what you did with those animal skins needs to be punished.'

Donna swallowed and closed her eyes and spoke more calmly.

'Please stop torturing me; if you want me to view things differently you're going the wrong way about it.'

'Are you begging yet?'

'Whatever. Yes alright then, yes, I am begging!'

'Excellent! Urination next if I am to win the bet.'

The high-pitched whine was heard and Donna shuffled backwards, clearly terrified.

'No, no, please, enough's enough, don't hit me again. Hit Jenny, she hasn't been hurt at all yet.' she pleaded.

The tall man smiled widely.

'Good begging Donna; great begging! But how selfish of you to want poor vegan Jenny to suffer in your place. What a cowardly act. Exactly what I expected of you.'

He prodded Donna's chest with the tool and, assuming she was going to be electrocuted, she screamed.

Colin had been watching and waiting for a dampness to appear but Donna defied him. He was annoyed at her screams so quickly gagged her again.

'You didn't pee yourself Donna, that makes Jenny the winner. What do you think Jenny, double or quits, if she has a heart attack next I win. OK?'

Without waiting for a response he waved the prod again, this time towards the groin area, getting closer with each sweep until he was finally pushing it against the prisoner's crotch. Before it got close Jenny screamed.

'You sick man.' She shouted, finally losing her cool. 'Do you want to kill her? You've gone way too far Colin; can't you see the trouble you are getting deeper and deeper into? Is she even breathing?'

'She is fine, look at her; if she were dead then I'd have performed a great service to animals. But as she is still alive I shall have the ultimate star-turn end for her.'

He checked for a pulse, just to be certain and eventually found one. It always amused him in films and TV shows when someone was checking for a pulse and instantly found one-it's rarely possible to pick up a pulse that quickly-especially when all hell is breaking loose and you are yourself trembling from the effects of adrenalin. Even worse was when they *didn't* find a pulse-they grabbed the wrist and said after barely half a second, in a sombre voice: "He's dead!"

'She's alive.' He said, sounding a little disappointed, although in reality it mattered not at all to him.

'Please Colin; can't you see that she has suffered enough? I have always thought of you as an honest and caring man. You are the kind of guy I could really have as a friend, but there are so many sides to you that I don't understand. Can we talk about them?'

Colin looked at her as if seeing her for the first time.
Jenny returned his stare, and as he took in her deep brown eyes he fancied he saw something new there; some form of admiration. Admiration because of his elevated principles and powerful grip on the situation. He smiled down at her.

Inwardly repulsed by what she was doing, Jenny tried to keep an air of sincerity in her voice and body language. She needed to engage in the kind of conversations that can eat up time without risking him wanting any form of physical contact. She knew the situation could go either way. If she played things right he might release her. If things got difficult and she somehow angered him with rejection, then there was only one way this was going to end.

'Of course Jenny; I'd enjoy that, and later we can talk about me and you, and how we might work together. But right now I have the annoying business of a forfeit payment to deal with.
I'm afraid you might be a little disturbed by what happens next Jenny, but please remember it's for the greater good.'
He removed from his bag a short, razor sharp knife and some large tweezers.

'Oh; I should shield you from this.'
He took a sack from his holdall and put it over Jenny's head.
'It'll only be for a short time.'

66

When the squad cars arrived at the facility they found the place in darkness and seemingly deserted. All the external doors were locked and nothing moved.

Detective Chief Inspector Sharon Moody was disappointed; she'd hoped for a neat wrap up to the affair, all the victims safe and all the suspects on the premises, arms stretching forwards ready for the wrists to be cuffed.

The duty firearms unit had been two hours short of end of shift and looking forward to a long-arranged retirement party that had promised lots of free booze and grub. Despite the disappointment of those plans being dashed they thought this would be a quick in, do the business and get out job rather than a lengthy siege situation, although from the briefing they'd just had it was clear there were multiple hostages, and that could lead to a complex waiting game. They were deployed around the site in strategic positions ready for further instructions.

DCI Moody was well versed with normal procedure for entry to premises, which would be the so called 'knock and announce' process. Here the police would behave as any ordinary visitor would, i.e. knock and wait "a reasonable amount of time" for the resident's response. She was more in favour of the "exigent circumstances" clause, which allows for forced entry where police think evidence might be destroyed or a life might be in danger, but policing had become a game of politics and political correctness; it was vital that she follow procedures unless given no choice.

The farmhouse was totally silent and clearly unoccupied and Moody had no reason to believe that lives were in imminent danger.

She opted for 'knock and announce' and when there was no change at all stepped back from the old front door.

Sicknote came over to where Moody was standing.
'It's dead quiet all round the place; your call Ma'am, sit it out and wait for their return?'

For the first time Moody showed signs of uncertainty
'Yes, but let's use the time wisely. Get a team into each of the outbuildings; start with that old barn, that looks the most likely place for a lock-up.'
After some manipulation and a lot of swearing the old doors were forced open and the team rushed into the black void within.

The air was fetid and still and none of the light switches worked. Two huge battery powered lamps were quickly set up to illuminate the place and it was just as quickly confirmed that the cupboard was bare.

Sicknote cursed and began to herd the team back out and into a smaller neighbouring barn.
The result was much the same, as it was for the remaining outbuildings.

Sharon Moody couldn't hide her disappointment.
'OK, I'm not prepared to wait any longer and put people at risk; let's take the house right now, that's the only place they can be and we've made enough noise here to wake the dead so if there *is* anyone in there, they won't be sitting around playing Cluedo.

She strode ahead of the team, who were left scrabbling around for the tools and equipment they'd need to force entry. This included the 'Enforcer' battering ram; 30 inches of steel-encased concrete, which could lead to a surface pressure of around 30,000 lbs when the flat end struck an immovable object, such as the front door of the old farm house.

The team was quickly reassembled at the front door, with armed officers posted to the rear and at other possible exit points, such as the large conservatory on one side of the property.
Following a confirmation nod from Moody, a shrill whistle blast signalled action and all hell seemed to break loose. In a matter of

seconds the door was hanging from one bottom hinge and accompanied by screams of "armed police" ten or more armed dark-clad bodies were bursting through the opening into the dark hallway, dividing into twos at each door they encountered on the way through the house.

Shouts of "Clear" could be heard periodically, as rooms were opened, searched and verified as empty of occupants. The thump of heavy boots was heard upstairs as the procedure was repeated on the first, and then the smaller second floor .

All reports came back negative and Sharon Moody sat on an old wooden kitchen chair with her elbows on the table, her head in her hands and a dumbfounded look on her ruddy face.

'Makes no sense Ma'am; all the clues seemed to point here. I was convinced this would be a wrap-up job'.

'Yes, I was too Harrison, like you say, it makes very little sense. But we have done this place to death and drawn a blank; we clearly missed something so let's get back to the station and see if we can find it.'

The team was given the instruction to return to their various bases and dispersed; some with downcast looks, others, notably the firearms team, with a somewhat cheerier step.

67

Colin was becoming more nervous by the minute. He hadn't made a plan for failure. Evasive action didn't appear as a line on his list. He had no bolt-hole which he could run to or equipment that would help him avoid capture.

He had no Plan B.

He realised instantly that his plans had been inadequate; he'd been so blasé about his mission and had felt untouchable. He had failed to plan for failure and had failed to cover his tracks. Failed. Well maybe the police were a little slyer than he'd thought and had found a way to pinpoint his farm and now they were out to get him, but they hadn't got him yet.

The thing to do right now though was to execute the plan that he *did* have. Casting all the doubts from his mind he dragged Donna across to the slightly smaller tumulus.

'You'll have to excuse me Donna, but I've never done this before.'

Donna made some muffled sounds through her gag.

'You'll need to speak up my love if you want me to understand you; it just sounds like a load of silly noises!'

He loved his ability to make fun of bitches like this. Making gags at their expense. He laughed aloud – gag gags! He really could be just too funny sometimes!

68

The team were studying the evidence boards, desperately seeking whatever it was they had missed, or misinterpreted.

Moody was staring at the old map of the area pinned up there.

'Can we get a bigger map please Sergeant Harrison?'

'Sure Ma'am, I'm just logging onto Google now to see what's on their maps pages-sometimes you can get really good images in the satellite mode. Any particular area you wanna concentrate on?'

The DCI massaged her chin.

'Yes, the area where the farm is. It's too odd that all the clues point there and yet there was clearly nothing. Whatever we missed must either be right under our noses or the clues are wrong.'

'Well this is interesting.'

Carol was looking over Sicknote's shoulder.

'What is?' moody was there like a shot, desperate for any lifeline.

Carol moved a little closer and indicated a spot on the computer monitor.

'Zoom in here Dave.'

He did as requested and a large grey rectangle filled the screen.

'What's that?' Moody's voice had more than an edge of excitement.

'Looks like a massive barn Ma'am' Sicknote's voice was also animated.

'And look where it is, 200 bloody metres from where we did the raid-it must have been built after the shitty old maps we were given were produced.'

'That wouldn't surprise me, the document control standards have slipped into the cellar recently. Can you print that?'

Sicknote laughed:

'No wonder document control is bollocksed Ma'am…yeah, printing now!'

Moody was incredulous:

'How the hell did we miss that?'

'It's along this track, hidden down behind all these trees and hedges look.' Harrison was indicating the mass of greenery between the two building clusters.

'There's no way we could have spotted that in the pitch dark.'

Moody was less forgiving:

'We bloody well should have done, we must be blind, it's the size of a fucking planet.'

Nobody in the ops room had heard her swear before and it did something to lighten the tension.

Sicknote coughed.

'Er, shall I get the armed response guys back Ma'am?'

'Yes please DS Harrison, only this time let's make damned sure we go to the right location. Silent approach definitely required this time I feel.'

Calls were made and teams reassembled into the same vehicles that they'd only recently refuelled and shortly the small convoy of marked and unmarked vehicles rolled out of the city station in a manner that betrayed the racing pulses of the occupants.

The armed response unit were supremely pissed off that just when the retirement party had seemed a racing certainty they'd had the carpet pulled from beneath them for the second time in as many hours.

69

Donna's legs were beating a crazed tattoo on the ground in a
desperate attempt to get his attention. Colin ignored her completely
and continued his preparations.
'Just make allowances for my poor technique, there's a sport!'
He turned towards her, his face now an inch from her right ear.

'You wouldn't realise, Donna, but for some weeks, months even, I
have been following you and watching you buying your luxury items
in the corrupt stores of West London. I observed you choosing
handbags, belts and gloves. I saw you select furs and other precious
items. I have followed you home and looked through your windows.
Dear Donna; I have seen the trophy kills that adorn your walls and
floors.'

'I also know what a huge fan you are of big cat skins, and that you
prefer them with the head intact and the rest of the pelt arranged
below that. I guess that's quite standard. I won't say it's normal,
nothing as grim as that can ever be classed as "normal". I call it the
"squashed in the road" look. Knowing now how much you adore that
look, I shall replicate it when I skin you in a moment.'

70

DCI Moody had just finished an update call to Samantha when a shout from the huge warehouse doors had her full and immediate attention.

'You'd better get in here Ma'am; bring a gas mask.'

Moody jogged across the sixty feet of farmyard from where she stood and entered the building.

Two things hit her simultaneously. The absolute vastness of the place and the strong animal stench inside.

'Oh God! What has died in here?' she coughed, reeling from the immovable wall of odour.

'Over here Ma'am!' It was Sicknote calling from half way down the enormous building.

Moody slowed to a fast walk and the smell became stronger.

What she saw then took her breath away.

A stack of ten or so cages, each little bigger than a large dog kennel, stood next to a huge industrial machine in an otherwise cleared area.

Inside the cages were creatures of some kind; judging by their postures, she guessed apes.

It was only when one of the creatures began to laugh and shout that she realised these were actually humans. That was when the penny dropped and she knew she was looking at the kidnap victims.

Sicknote was calling Jenny's name, hoping all the victims were kept in this one location.

The DCI tried to see how many people were imprisoned here. There were three layers of cages with what looked like four units per layer. Twelve in total; but the majority were empty. She could see one person on the lowest level, one in the middle and what looked like two on the highest.

Steph was stood at a cage talking to the only inhabitant on the bottom layer; a male who she thought looked to be between thirty and forty years old. It was difficult to be more precise as they were all dishevelled and completely wild-looking. She thought they looked almost feral, and there was some evidence that they had been using this prison area as a communal toilet. She wondered why they didn't use their proper accommodation area for that; they must have proper toilets there surely? Then it dawned on her; this *was* their accommodation.

The prisoner was talking to her saying something in Dutch or German.
'Do you speak English?' She asked him.
'Sorry; yes of course. My name is Hans-Werner Fromm and I vos kidnapped by a lunatic freak and held here for several veeks I sink.'

'Ma'am, This is Hans-Werner.' She called to Moody, who came across to her.
'Hi Hans-Werner; we have been looking for you. we are the police and we are going to get you out of here. Where are the terrorists?'
'Terrorists? This guy is just a vegetarian lunatic. He has taken Jenny and Donna to kill zem ve sink.'
Sharon Moody felt the panic rise inside.
'Where has he taken them? How long ago did they leave? Is he working alone?' She was incredulous. Although they had always kept an open mind, the true assumption had always been that there were a number of protagonists.

'Bevare his hot stick, it burns like hell and vill make you scream.'
Steph looked at her boss, puzzled. The German was hallucinating it seemed.
'Hans-Werner, listen, this is most important. We need to catch this man before he kills any more. What does he drive? Is he armed? What's this "hot stick" you mentioned?'

The German kept drifting between English and his native language. Sharon thought this was hardly surprising, judging by the things he must have been through.

280

'He is driving einen Land-rover und is carrying sometimes einen langen Stock viz electricity in it and a gun; eine Pistole.'

The DCI snapped into action.
'Right everyone, here are the immediate priorities. Get these people out of here and to hospital. Steph; call St Richards in town. Tell them what we have and that they will need mental health specialists as well as medical staff. Tell them to get those people in; I don't want to hear any crap about it being the middle of the night. No idea where the keys to these padlocks are so let's use a less conventional way. Help those two down from the top.'

She paused for a moment, trying to think straight, fighting the panic that was bubbling just below the surface.
'We know he has taken Jenny and the Donna woman in his Land-rover – Steph, get the details on that vehicle and make sure the whole world and his dog are looking for it. I am going to get some resources mobilised. Hans-Werner tells me he is armed with a pistol at least.'

She paused for breath and realised she should update Neil Dyson; she'd given her word that he'd know the instant there was news. She dialled his number and gave him the situation status.
'How are you holding up Neil?'

'Not too bad Ma'am, what's the score?'

Moody gave him the facts as she had them, including what they had found and what they suspected was happening now.

'Listen, we have more force personnel on their way and alerts have gone out for the vehicle. It's a lone perpetrator, which will make recovery of the victims easier. Have faith Neil; I'll keep you posted. If you want to go and wait in the station that's fine with me, maybe you can sift through your board and see if any clues as to his possible destination stick out?'

Neil Dyson was reeling under this latest hammer blow.

'I won't allow anything to get in the way Neil.'
He thanked her and she went to advise the team which had arrived to set up an incident centre.

71

The hammering of Donna's feet became more frantic, and the noises behind the gag took on a demented sound.

'Oh dear, Donna; bash away with those pigskin-clad feet of yours and scream away merrily behind the gag. We are nicely isolated here and nobody will hear you. Nobody will hear you ever again as a matter of fact. But you will be seen by many.'

With that, Colin grabbed the terrified woman and forced her onto her back on the ground.

'Not used to this girl are you? The *man* on top? Whatever next. I'll be asking *you* for payment at this rate.'

He took the small, razor sharp knife and easily slit her expensive, but filthy pullover from the bottom to the top. Then he did the same with her jeans, slitting them up the inside of each leg and then from the back of the crotch to the front. He had nicked her a few times with the blade and a little blood appeared in places. When he had cut through all her garments he tore them from her body, leaving her completely naked. He tried to see what it was that attracted men to women, sexually, and failed. All he saw was the person he knew, the evildoer. He shuddered.

Colin knew that there were two main layers of human skin and that he needed to get them both off together if possible, otherwise the thin top layer could be too fragile and might well tear.

He threw her onto her front and forced her legs apart. Despite Colin's strength, it was a struggle to hold her still enough to make a good job of it and when he tried to make the first cut just above her anus her bucking and rolling made him lose his rag. He cursed her and told her to lay still or he'd get the fucking cattle prod. This had absolutely no effect and so he yanked her head sharply backwards by her hair and began to punch her face. His aim was to beat her into unconsciousness, but after just two powerful blows he realised he was bruising her face. The last thing he wanted was a blemished skin for the newspapers. He changed tactic, pushing her face down into the dirt and aiming blows at the back of her head. It was taking some time to subdue her and his fist was becoming bruised and sore so he resorted to striking her with the palm of his hand in an open hand punch. He actually achieved more power this way and within five hard blows she became still.

Colin was sweating from the exertion and from the thrill of taking some kind of revenge on such an evil and twisted bitch. He was a little miffed to see a small trickle of blood run from beneath her nose. He could clean that off for the photo, he was quite sure.

He started afresh with the incision above her anus, the plan was to run the blade up the centre of her back, pulling the skin away from her torso as he went. At first he cut a little too deep and drew a lot of blood and because her heart was still beating this was flowing quite readily all over her body and all over his hands and clothes. The knife became slippery and the task was that much harder to complete accurately. He was getting everything very messy and was annoyed at how slimy blood made everything.

In the end he resorted to roughly hacking away at the skin as he had seen slaughtermen do in abattoir films. He was occasionally hampered by her regaining consciousness - triggering several more blows to the back of her skull – but was soon at the nape of her neck. He wasn't quite sure how to proceed from here, but decided that he wasn't going to produce the best piece of flaying that had ever been done so he might was well just hack his way straight up the back of her skull and over the top.

He made a decision to leave her lower body as it was and just use the top half; that was all he needed in any case. He was intrigued by the appearance of her flesh where he had removed the skin. It reminded him of serious burns victims he'd seen in a film about the Vietnam war. There was a rawness about it, a vulnerability. An image came to mind from when he was very young, watching his mother skinning a rabbit. He remembered his father telling her to pull harder and stop whining; she'd had to tug really hard to pull away the fur and the flesh beneath looked just like Donna did here. He wondered why people generally found it OK to eat animals, but not humans.

Out of interest he checked Donna for a pulse, and was a little surprised to find a rapid, weak heartbeat. Amazing what the human mind could tolerate, he thought, but he knew shock would soon finish her off. He didn't care either way, one less person encouraging poachers in Africa.

Finally the wet, messy skin was off and laid out, face up on the grass, looking remarkably like the top half of a big cat's hide. Colin inwardly smiled at the thought of taking it back to Donna's place and hanging it on a wall. But time was ticking, the police were on his tail and he had much to do. He grabbed handfuls of wet grass and tried to wipe the worst of the blood off the face, with limited success, then carried the skin across to the larger tumulus where Jenny was waiting patiently.

'It's only me Jenny. Well, me and a friend.'

He told her to sit still and she wouldn't be harmed and draped the skin over her hooded head and shoulders, like a cloak put on backwards.
'Perfect! Well, sufficient at least.' He commented.

Within a couple of minutes he could be ready to film, but he was concerned with the passage of time and chose, instead of setting up the camera, to use one of the cheap mobile 'phones. He was sceptical about the limited light because it was still quite dark, and although the first birds were awake and dawn was just starting to emerge in the East from the blackness and despite the gathering urgency he thought he'd wait a few minutes yet. It wouldn't hurt Jenny to have her friend's arms around her for a while longer. He smiled, despite the tension mounting within him. All he could do was to wait for a little more light.

Now that the immediate actions were done he had time to think, and the thoughts that burst into his head were all bad ones. They were scrabbling around in there trying to find their rightful place in the queue where he could analyse them. He needed them to prioritise themselves, there were too many thoughts for him to sort through; he needed their help.

Without a list Colin couldn't make a plan. Instead he walked around the tumuli wringing his hands and doing his strange skip every seventh step or so.

72

Neil Dyson had no intention of sitting in an empty police station with a desk clerk and custody sergeant. He wanted at least the illusion of doing something useful so he drove around the area randomly, half his mind looking for the Land-rover Moody had described and the other half trying to imagine where the sicko would be taking his next victims. He'd killed at the Market Cross and in the old market car-park. Market market market...there was a building in North Street known as the Butter Market – it was a long shot, but the only one he could see in an otherwise empty shooting range.

73

The waiting was interminable and Colin ceased his pacing. To pass the time he removed Jenny's "temporary" skin, hood, gag etc and whilst awaiting dawn he chatted with her.

'What made you decide to live a vegan life? What is it that you see in animals Jenny?'
Despite her nervousness jenny continued to try to play for time and so took a moment to think.

'It's their lack of guilt more than anything, I think. I like that they can live their lives free of those guilty thoughts which can plague us in moments of reflection. Never has an animal had to justify its actions, or convince that he or she did the "right" or "just" thing. Their acts are all intentional, for a reason of survival, not done in order to elevate them above other species or make a luxurious lifestyle. But if I am honest, for me the greatest thing about animals is that they don't invent a god and then murder each other in its name.'

'I agree that we could learn a lot from animals, but our arrogance obstructs the learning path. Do you know what Gandhi said about animals?'
Jenny shook her head.

'He said something like *"The greatness of a country and its moral progress can be judged by the way it treats its animals."* Or something on those lines. But you know, I do think the fox is an exception, Jenny. My evil father used to curse them and donate funds to all the local hunts. He said if a fox got into a chicken coop it would kill everything in there and only take one bird.'

'Right and wrong Colin. Foxes, in nature, will kill all easily available prey and if they have the time and it's safe to do so, they will then bury what they don't immediately need and keep it for lean times. Unfortunately, through our greed and drive for profit it's us humans who have messed up the system as usual. When we breed a large number of the fox's natural prey in a confined area the fox will do what it has evolved to do. It can't distinguish between "corralled" food and "naturally occurring" food. It just sees food and does what it has always done, takes what it needs now and keeps the rest for those days and weeks when there is nothing to eat. It's like us going to the supermarket and buying a packet of sausages. If they are on special offer we'll grab two packs – whether we need them or not. What we do know for certain is that we will only need one or two single sausages today. The remaining four or ten or whatever, we store for another day. We have evolved like the foxes. The only reason we don't kill all the cattle in a field as soon as we see them is because we have developed a safe way to have them nice and fresh whenever we want them. And there's nobody with dogs and guns to interrupt us. We have no natural predators; we eliminated them all.'

Colin looked thoughtful.
'I guess we are worse; as soon as somebody mentions a shortage of some kind of food, even non-essentials, we rush out and buy as much of it as we can. Humans are the real monsters!'
She interjected:
'Don't be so harsh on monsters Colin; Frankenstein's monster was vegetarian!'

The light was slowly improving and colours becoming distinguishable. With the improving light Jenny suddenly realised that Colin was absolutely covered in blood and chose that moment to look around and saw, for the first time, the horror that had occurred on the hilltop.
When her eyes fell upon the skin laying just behind where she sat she was about to scream, but fell into a faint.

Colin was concerned that the shock might be too much for her; she'd been through a lot, they all had. He checked that she was OK and knew that if she recovered and saw the skin again she'd make a scene so he reapplied the gag, hood etc and revived her with gentle slaps on the arm. Eventually she resurfaced. She was shaking violently and giving real cause for concern. Colin hoped the gag wasn't interfering with her accelerated breathing.

He decided the light would have to be sufficient now; to wait any longer would be to court disaster. He gently draped the skin around Jenny's shaky body, telling her not to move and squatted a few feet from her, taking four pictures from slightly different angles with his mobile. He viewed them and decided they were good enough. It was a little difficult to make out exactly what the image was, but a few accompanying words when he sent the message would clarify things. Important was that it was recognisable as a human skin and that it was graphic. In fact it was absolutely shocking. The partially visible hood peeping out from behind Donna's semi-collapsed, but just about recognisable as blood-stained human face, had the most macabre effect, and the limited light gave it an eerie quality. Perfect.

He removed the skin for the final time from around Jenny and took it quickly back to its previous owner, casually flinging it across her torso. On a whim he felt the temperature of her legs but found only a coldness that seemed to say "Yes, I am now dead. Please use my skin wisely; I paid a lot of money to keep it looking so young and fresh."

Colin hurried back to where Jenny sat and removed the hood. He left the bindings and gag in place. His next planned task was to send the image to the usual suspects. Until now, he had always done this from close to the scene of the crime. After all, he wanted the bodies to be easily found. He was fairly sure that the cheap 'phones he used had no GPS capability and so couldn't be "pinged"; a process whereby a signal was sent to a 'phone and its location could then be pinned down through triangulating between signal transmitters and receivers. He had read that this was a simple process where the time taken for the signal to be returned to the transmitter showed the distance between the two. It was then a very simple computer task to calculate the location to the nearest five meters or so.

Colin had also read that, with a mobile telephone with GPS capability, the same thing was possible digitally. He didn't understand the subtleties; it was enough for him to know that as soon as he'd sent the message he needed to get himself somewhere else. Had he been able to think straight and been better prepared, it would have made sense to be near his Land-rover when he sent the message. That would have given him maximum time to put distance between himself and this location.

74

When the message came through to the TV and other media offices the mood was buoyant; so much news and so juicy. So many tales to be told and so little air time or page space to do it. Journalists, reporters, editors, they were all running around with concerned looks; their faces sending the message to their colleagues that said "Oh! Isn't it shocking, all this violence and such a disturbed mind. Wherever will it all end?" Mostly, though, their inner faces, the ones that were invisible to the world screamed joyous things. Great stories and wonderful sales figures. The punters will be hanging on our every word; clamouring for more and clambering to get to it. It will be like a feeding frenzy at the news-stands. There was a determination to be the first on the scene when this gang were tracked down

At the police station in Chichester and at the farm the mood was different.
Here the expressions of dread and fear really were genuine. The only determination here was to get to this guy before he killed his one remaining abducted captive. It hadn't been clear from the recorded image which of the two women was featured, and DCI Moody held off with any updates to Dyson until she knew more.

The prisoners who had been left in the huge barn had been taken to hospital where they had been fed and cleaned up. They were now being assessed for physical and psychological damage.

Over the telephone, Neil Dyson was discussing the limited developments he was aware of with Samantha. She told him again how sorry the whole team was that he was no longer actively on the case; his sharp detective brain would be missed. She took some comfort from the fact that he had been given the Chief's word that she'd keep him abreast; at least that way he would have immediate information and the opportunity to offer up his thoughts at any time. The down side was that, should things not go well, he'd hear it pretty bluntly and with plenty of graphic detail she thought.

As soon as the messages hit the media, "requests" were passed to mobile phone companies to do whatever they could to track the call. The problem was that the cheap equipment Colin had used didn't make this easy, and the fact that he'd used the option to withhold his number by dialling "141" before making the calls gave an almost impossible task. Certainly there would be no speedy answer to that particular question.

75

In the press, Colin had become known as the "Cereal Killer", and this was great fodder for the wordsmithing editors who were hurriedly re-working the papers:

"Semi-Skinned; Cereal Killer strikes again"

"Fully Exposed! Cereal Killer skins latest victim alive"

"Cereal Killer Gets Under Police Skin

And

"Hide and Seek; Police Clueless on Psycho Skinner"

The broadsheets were as usual a little less sensationalist:

"Tumuli Tumult; killer strikes at Sussex beauty spot"

And

"Victim Laid Bare at Bronze-age Bank"

76

After their dialogue Colin felt much more comfortable about Jenny; she really did have animal welfare at heart and shows empathy for him and his beliefs, he thought.

'Jenny, I know you feel as strongly about things as I do, and hate having you trussed up like this and treating you with so little trust. If you give me your word, I shall remove some of the constraints and give you back some dignity.'

Jenny was still numb with shock. He had done the most sickening things, and yet inside he had a transparent honesty. He might be a monster, but he was a monster with a cause, and that was something she'd never come across. He repulsed and shocked her with the way he had kept them, what kind of mind could devise such a scheme? And although she had not seen how he had disposed of Babić or Farouk, what he had done to Donna was beyond comprehension. He was a murderer; a sick, mass murderer, volatile and completely insane, and weren't murderers by definition untrustworthy? She didn't really know what to do, how to get through this. She needed help now; it was too much to go through alone.

What she *did* know was that she needed to somehow stay alive; she felt she had it in her power to prevent any more tragedies at the hands of this man. It was her words and actions over the coming minutes and hours that would determine how this finished, by and large.

She desperately needed to see Neil again. During her time in captivity she had come to truly understand the significance of their relationship. Speaking with the other captives, it was clear that none of them had what she and Neil had; an honest, trusting relationship that had all the elements of a "happy ever after" story. She was buggered if she was going to let a mere mass murderer get in the way of that, and if making promises to a beast like this and then breaking them at the first opportunity was what she needed to do, then the answer to his question was simple. With fresh resolve she answered.

'If you give me your word not to hurt me, or anybody else, then you can trust me completely Colin. I will do whatever you ask and I will do it willingly. But nobody else is to be harmed; do you understand? Otherwise please just kill me here and now.'

Colin thought about this. It was fair enough. He'd treated her, all of them, abominably. But he'd had pure intentions. He'd known all along that the task was a difficult one, and through all the detailed planning he had maybe become obsessed with the "what" and disregarded the effects on others of the "how". He had known that he was in a minority, a relatively small group of free-thinkers who could see what was to them glaringly obvious. The problem came with convincing those who saw it differently, or worse, who had decided not to see it. Sometimes it's more convenient not to know things. It reminded him of a quote he'd read. He couldn't remember who had said it, but it rang true to him.

There are two ways to be fooled. One is to believe what isn't true; the other is to refuse to believe what is true.

At the end of the day, a person is responsible for their own ignorance. Those who choose to ignore the facts live in some kind of convenient preferred oblivion.

'Yes Jenny, OK. You will not be harmed, and neither will anyone else, as long as you behave as you have said. I will leave just your hands tied behind you.'

And so, with just her hands now secured behind her back, they began to make their way back down the loose chalk path towards the little gravel car park where the land-rover stood.

'As soon as we have done the next little film message we will take a drive to my boat and sit tight there for a while. Maybe sail out of Bosham for a bit. Are you good on boats Jenny?'
She shook her head.
'Don't really know, I hope so, or I'll be sick everywhere. Mind you, the way I must smell right now it won't make a lot of difference I'm sure.'
'You smell just fine, but on the boat is a nice shower and you can have a relaxing time in a real bed. It's tight but you are used to that.'
His smile, she felt was almost apologetic.

 Jenny needed a reason to dally on the way down, so that she could find a way to leave clues.
'Colin, I have hardly eaten anything for days, I need something. Do you mind if we try to find some berries on the way down?'
'Berries? At this time of year? It's way too early, but let's see if there are some mushrooms you can eat. I am good at finding them.'

They paused at a small clearing and Colin told her to wait while he had a quick look around.
'If you try to run you will have broken your word, and I will catch you easily Jenny. Don't even think of it.'

He moved off a few yards away from her and as he stooped to look at the ground she squatted and with her hands behind her back picked up one of the small pieces of chalk that were strewn around everywhere . Leaning back against a rough-hewn fence post she scribbled a figure at about waist height on to the flattest part of it as best she could with her hands tied behind her.

Colin turned, empty handed and they walked on. As they passed the next post she distracted him with comments about flowers on the verge or snails she pretended to see and hastily scribbled another letter. This she managed to repeat on four of the next six posts. She knew the place would be crawling with police and media soon and hoped desperately that someone would see the markings and make a connection.

When they reached the Land-rover Colin made her write a quick media message on the flip chart which he had brought for this purpose.
'You know the score Jenny; Donna is now dead; their fault; when will they stop etc.'

Jenny was desperate to get something about the boat into her message.
'What is your boat called Colin? Does it have a nice name?'
'It's got a funny name; she's called *"Salty Pig Runs Free"*.
Jenny's jaw fell open. Quickly she tried to conceal her surprise.
'Really; what an interesting name!'
'OK let's get on with the message then we need to leave.'

As he was untying her hands she thought quickly and then wrote:

"you CAN'T Ever get the message can you. Stop eating animals and Set the Pig Free."

Colin had a quick glance and thought it was a little light on content but the key point was to get some kind of message across as usual so they all knew it was him and that he was still operating.
'OK, that will have to do. Hold it up.'

He shot a ten second video of her silently holding the written message. It was as creepy as the others, she had Donna's blood on her face and hands which showed up now in the gathering light. He told her to get in the front seat next to him and then retied her hands only. As he drove left out of the car park he hit the send button and after a few minutes the mobile phone, minus its battery, went out of the window into an overgrown ditch.

They drove in silence and Jenny thought about how it must feel to be Colin Furness, believing completely that his way was *the* way. She realised that if someone believed something to be true, really believed it, then it became the truth for them, such was the case with religions she thought. She wondered what had been the trigger for

298

this in his mind; what moment had he realised that he had to take on this ridiculous task of converting the entire planet to abandon meat. He was clearly insane on a number of levels. She was no expert on sanity but the things the guy had done were unfathomable to a rational person.

And yet, still a part of her held a spark of admiration, a flicker of empathy. To go into this so uncompromisingly, to risk everything, knowing – surely – that he was doomed to fail. Or was he just an absolute basket case with no concept of reality? She had no way of knowing.

77

Neil Dyson's 'phone rang.
'Hi, it's Samantha. Just sending you the latest video message. Good news is that Jenny is clearly still alive. She looks in a bad way, but she's strong so you need to be too. When you get it call me and we can go through it together.'

Neil's 'phone beeped and he opened the clip.
The image was horrible, and the flip chart message made no sense. He called Samantha.

'What do you make of it?' He asked her when she answered the call.

'It's odd, as always, but she's left clues for definite. First thing, sentence starts with a small letter "y", but she uses capitals in the second and third words.'

'Yes I saw that, so what is she saying Samantha?'
'Clearly the word "CAN'T" and the following "E" from Ever are important. Must be an anagram, thoughts?'

'Not an anagram as far as I can make out, at least not a useful one. What about the bit about setting pigs free?'
'She actually writes "set the Pig Free" - i.e. singular. It's odd and because it's odd it's critical. Listen Guv, I have to get back to the team but I'll call you if I find anything.'
'Sure thing Samantha - same here.'

Something was niggling at Neil's memory. There was something in that message that he knew he should be picking up on. What the hell was it?

78

The Land-rover was parked in a small lane where Colin knew it would attract no immediate attention. He took Jenny down a small pathway through the churchyard and down to where he'd left the dinghy tied up. The tide was almost high so they had to carry the little inflatable only a little way across the stones and mud until they reached water, which was slowly filling any available spaces - breathing the life-blood into the amphibious saltings; areas of mud and reeds which spent half their lives as "land" and the rest under water.

They climbed aboard and Colin took the oars.
'Colin, if we fall in the water I can't swim with my hands tied.'
Jenny's concern was genuine.
'Sorry, sure, I'll untie you once we get moving.'
True to his word he took the same little knife that had so recently been removing Donna's outer layers and slit through the thin rope.

Rowing against the current wasn't difficult due to practically zero wind and before long they were coming up alongside his boat. He tied the inflatable to the side and climbed the short stainless steel ladder onto the low deck, offering his hand to assist Jenny, which she refused, preferring to climb under her own steam.

Undeterred, Colin showed her where the little bathroom or "Heads" as he called it, was located.

'You can take a shower here, the water will be hot in a few minutes, I will give you a towel and some of my clean clothes. They will be too big but you can fold them and make some kind of sense of them I am sure. I will make us something to eat. I don't need to remind you of our deal Jenny; if I feel I cannot trust you we can go back to tying up routines - your choice. And by the way, I am an excellent swimmer so don't try going overboard. As soon as I am sorted out I shall close the hatch in any case.'

She nodded her thanks, a shower would be amazing!

79

Neil's 'phone rang again.

'It's me again. On the route to the crime scene at Kingley Vale one of the uniform guys spotted six characters written in chalk on the fence posts. They were fresh; otherwise the recent rain would have washed them partly away.'

'What did they say Samantha?'

'In ascending order the word "MAH" followed by the number "508". Neil literally scratched his head.

'Means nothing to me.' He said.

'They may have been scribed on the way *down*, of course, in which case we'd have "805" followed by "HAM" she added.

'Also, Steph's eyesight is better than mine and at her insistence I froze the latest video and enlarged the text, the apostrophe in the word "can't" is not an apostrophe at all; it's a tiny letter "u". Taken with the capitals around it, it spells "CANuTE". I assume the king, but does it mean anything to you?'

Bingo! A light bulb flashed bright in Dyson's brain. He started to run as he continued.

'Yes, and I know exactly what she is telling us. The number on the fence post wasn't 805 at all, it was the letters "BOS" add that to the "HAM" and we have BOSHAM. We need to get down to Bosham- that's where they will be heading. Get all available bodies down there Samantha - but do it quietly. Get to the boat yard to the north of Quay Meadow. I will meet you there. They are heading for a boat called "Let Salty The Pig Free" or similar. Check with the coastguard or harbour master or who bloody ever to see who owns that boat - my money is on our friend Mr Furness.'

Neil was immediately moving. He was only three miles away and if he was quick, and he would be, he'd be there long before them. He leapt into his car and with blatant disregard for any traffic rules hammered his foot to the floor. For all intents and purposes he spent most of the next ten minutes on two wheels.

When he reached the shore Neil pulled up on the quay itself, and jogged silently over to where he and Jenny had stood only a few days ago to find the boat. When he got to that spot it was vacant. He let out a series of quiet expletives and started to look around. Broad tyre tracks showed where the trailer had been pulled out and he was pretty sure the thing was in the water. Shit! Jenny could be half way to France by now.

He made an instant decision. Running back towards the quay in the dark he fumbled to dial Samantha. He got only her voice mail - she was probably on her way here right now at similar speeds to those he'd just been hitting.
'Samantha it's me. The boat is in the water. Get coastguards and everybody with an official boat to locate her – they'll be sailing south towards Chichester harbour or beyond, they won't have got too far yet. I am going to have a mooch around here for a bit.'

On the quay was a row of seven or eight upturned rowing dinghies. He grabbed the nearest one to the water and flipped the fibreglass hull over. On reflection he thought she was a little small, Jenny might be in any number of conditions and he might have to lay her down. The third in the row was a bigger, wooden craft. This one weighed a ton but Dyson had temporary super-human strength and he dragged her unceremoniously to the steps leading down to the water.
The tide had just turned and he allowed himself to drift on the slow outgoing current to midstream where most of the bigger boats were moored in line astern formation.

The outgoing tide and lack of any wind meant that the boats were all pointing towards him; i.e. the stern sections – where the names were mostly displayed – were furthest from him. This arrangement meant that Neil had to travel the length of the boat before he could see her name, but also allowed Neil to drift noiselessly from one to the next with ease. He had soon checked the names of seven boats, all of which were sat in complete darkness and none of them were his target, although he felt the pang of a fond memory when he spotted *"Blue Banana Song"*.

Boat number eight was illuminated by very subdued lighting. But it meant that someone was at home. His heart thumped hard in his chest when he read the name. "Salty Pig Runs Free".
Silently Neil looped the short rope on his dinghy around the line of the inflatable that was already tied to the yacht. He stepped carefully from his boat into the inflatable and then put a foot onto the yacht's ladder.

He felt the all-too-familiar fighter emerging within him and the adrenalin coursing through his body. He was itching, actually itching, to get into the same space as the freak Furness. His mind seemed to be dominated by an uncontainable rage and a desire to cause harm to this sick individual. From somewhere a warning flashed, urging him to consider the last physical contest he'd been involved in. Then he had lost a contest, a sports match, a nothing event. Now the life of at least one other person was at stake; and that person was the most precious thing in his life.

Pausing a moment to gather his wits, he realised he ought to formulate some kind of plan, rather than simply go blundering into who-knew-what. He gingerly stepped back from the ladder onto the inflatable and craned his neck to see if anything was visible through the nearest porthole. A curtain was drawn across it, blocking 95% of the view, but from the remaining fraction he could see that beyond the glass was a galley, and in the galley stood a microwave oven, and reflected in the door of that microwave was the figure of a man. He seemed to be preparing food. There was no sign of anyone else and Neil assumed that Jenny was being held prisoner elsewhere on the boat. It wasn't a huge vessel, maybe two or three berths, so the places he'd need to check were limited. He might be able to get to Jenny unnoticed by the lunatic.

First he had to gain entry and then either sneak around and live on his nerves, or neutralise the nutcase. He decided to first see whether he could even get inside. If the door or hatch was locked he was buggered either way, and he'd have to try some kind of diversion. Placing his foot back on the ladder he began to ease his way up towards the deck. He was quickly aboard and looking around for the main entry hatch or doorway that would take him inside the cabin. He saw it immediately towards the stern and tiptoed across the few feet of deck, taking extreme care to slide his feet slowly so that he wouldn't dislodge any obstacles and, importantly, wouldn't trip and fall arse over elbow.

He made the door without mishap and slowly reached out his right hand. He had no way of knowing where the psycho was, or what he was doing, so he just had to keep his eyes and ears alert and hope. He eased the awkward handle anti-clockwise and was relieved to feel it turn easily and to feel the door open slightly outwards. This was the most critical moment. The guy could be busy making pot noodles, or he could be standing just behind the door with a fire axe.

Dyson had never been timid, nor overly cautious and so he did what came naturally. He opened the door, praying that it had been recently lubricated. Salt water was notoriously bad for mechanical fittings and he half expected a screeching shriek of ill-maintained hinges. To his relief the door opened easily and silently. He realised he'd been holding his breath and took a second to recharge his lungs.

Now or never, he thought and stepped inside.
He found himself in an open plan area which clearly served as galley and living space. There were two other people in the room. About three feet in front of him, with his back towards him was Colin Furness. Tall and bald and looking out of proportion in the small space. Beyond him, and looking directly at Neil sat Jenny. In an instant Neil saw she was wearing oversized pyjamas, clearly belonging to the nutcase. Her eyes locked onto his and she made the first mistake since she had been kidnapped; she acknowledged his presence for a millisecond as her eyes widened and her mouth dropped open.

Colin was handing Jenny a sandwich when he sensed a change. There was an almost imperceptible breath of air across the hairs of his neck. At the same time, Jenny's eyes lit up and she gasped almost inaudibly. Her eyes then flitted to him and he knew intuitively that they had company. He did two things simultaneously; the first was to mentally kick himself for not securing the hatch, the second was to spin round, releasing the dinner plate he held like an inverted Frisbee.

Too late Neil reacted to avoid the missile, and it hit him squarely across the bridge of his nose. The pain was instant and numbing and he instinctively clutched at his face. As he was blinking away the tears that automatically filled his eyes he caught the movement of a large body hurtling at him. He flung his arms up in a defensive gesture and felt himself being cannoned into the wall, where he struck his head on a brass window fitting. As he tried to blink away the pain from that he saw a huge fist coming down onto the bridge of his already damaged nose. His martial arts muscle memory tried to block it but he was dazed and slow. The punch landed full on his nose and he felt it break under the power of the onslaught. Blood seemed to explode from all over his face and he was vaguely aware of more blows raining down on him but his pain receptors seemed incapable of registering them as hits, although almost every one of them landed on his face and head, causing increasing damage.

Colin had the intruder on the floor now and started to kick him in the face and head with his size 13 boots. If he angled his right foot in a certain way, the guy's head would be smashed backwards against the door frame. He probably succeeded in that manoeuvre five or six times. He decided he'd continue until the guy was dead.

The time between seeing Neil enter the cabin and Colin having him pinned down and beating the life out of him was probably as little as twenty seconds. Jenny had never been in such a violent situation and sat stunned and immobile for the first 15 seconds of the attack. The next four seconds were spent desperately looking around for a weapon.

Neil's brain had shut itself down. He was beaten and incapable of defending himself. He lay there unknowingly taking kick after kick to the head.

Colin had no sooner made the decision to kill the man when he caught the reflection of a sudden movement in the door of the microwave. The next moment he felt a terrific pain as something heavy smashed into the side of his face.

Jenny lifted the solid old frying pan high for a second strike and brought it down with everything she had left. It hit his upturned face across the jaw and it jumped from her hands with the shock of the collision. Jenny threw a glance at Neil. She was sure he was dead, but strangely the emotions which would normally root her to the spot in floods of tears were absent and instead she found herself crashing towards the door. She was vaguely aware of Colin lunging for her and kicked out blindly. Her foot struck something semi-soft, she knew not what. She had only one thing on her mind, to get out of the boat, get away and summon help for the seemingly lifeless love of her life.

Sobbing, she scrambled across the deck and plunged into the water, flailing her arms in wide arcs as she ploughed towards the few lights she could see on the shore, some eighty yards distant. She was not a bad swimmer, but not particularly fast and she knew Furness would be strong. She was weak from the recent days of inaction and poor diet, and so much smaller than the giant freak, and the ridiculous pyjamas were a real handicap but with fear came strength and she made good headway against the sluggish tide.

Jenny heard a splash behind her and knew that he was in the water too; she had no idea if she could stay ahead or even what she would do if she reached the shore before him. She would scream, certainly, but that would only drain her of oxygen, and she'd need as much of that as she could possibly get. She reckoned she had a twenty yard head start, which was nothing like enough. She put her head down and went for it.

80

As Jenny was making her desperate escape attempt, six police cars were heading for the village; blue lights flashing and sirens wailing. DCI Moody had considered a silent approach, but then decided that they might have a better chance of flushing their quarry out if they made some noise and panicked him.

81

Jenny threw a quick look over her shoulder as she pulled herself exhausted from the sea. He was further behind that she had hoped, and this gave her renewed strength. She set off at a sprint, cursing the over-sized clothing and instinctively calculating the pros and cons of stopping to remove the trousers. Fear got the better of her and stopping, even for a few seconds seemed counter-intuitive. She ran along the quay, desperately trying to think of a place of safety or where she might hide. She shouted for help as she ran, letting out the cries as she exhaled so as to try to build a steady rhythm. There were very few houses near the quay, and the chances of being heard were not high.

It is said that a dying person sees their life flash before their eyes and that this might be the brain trawling in extreme fast-forward mode through all its life experiences trying to find a solution to the dilemma. This was what her mind was doing now; as she ran her brain raced through her knowledge of the immediate area, recalling the walks she'd had here with Neil and pausing for microseconds on any potential place of safety.

When she had almost reached the end of the quay she remembered the Millstream which empties into the sea. Neil had shown her the old mill building which was now the yacht club and the attached ancient water wheel. Beneath that, he had said, was a kind of cellar-cum-store room where they used to hide as kids. It was a bit awkward to get to, because to reach it she'd have to climb down a slippery vertical wall into the stream itself and wade through maybe twenty feet of knee-high, fast-flowing fresh water, but she was at the end of her limited endurance and she knew Colin was in far better shape so it had to be worth trying for.

She risked a glance backwards but could see no trace of her pursuer. She wasn't sure whether this was good news or bad. Either way she could do nothing to change it. She came to the point of no return now, if she reached the little store room she would be well hidden, but if he saw her climbing down into it she'd be trapped with the sea on one side and the water mill itself blocking her retreat in the other direction.

She scrambled down the wall into the freezing freshwater and along to the opening of the little hidey hole. Throwing herself through it she collapsed to the concrete floor, her chest burning and pulling in huge gulps of salty air. She tried to breathe as quietly as she could and desperately wanted to risk a peep through the opening to see if she'd been followed. If he was on to her the last place she wanted to be cornered was down here; out of sight of anyone and completely at his mercy. Looking out was too risky; instead she tried to listen for any tell-tale footfalls or splashes. She heard neither and began to find a little hope.

Jenny looked around in the gloom and could just make out the four walls. She guessed the space she was hiding in must be around twenty feet square and six feet high. After maybe three or four minutes of crouching there, wet and shivering now from the cold, she thought she heard a scraping sound just outside the entrance. A moment later a huge shadow filled the opening and a figure ducked its head and burst into the small space.

Jenny screamed and threw herself at him will every ounce of her remaining strength.

82

Colin hit the water in a shallow dive and came up some fifteen feet from the yacht. As he surfaced he was already swimming fast towards the shore. He could see the splashes made by the girl and knew he'd catch her easily. He decided to let her exhaust herself in the water with her frantic, energy-sapping strokes while he eased off and conserved his strength. He'd get to the shore almost at the same time as her and within a few strides would have caught her.

As they both neared the quay he changed his mind and decided to grab her in the water and pull her under. She would go into a complete panic and be so much easier to subdue with her lungs full of sea water. He was actually enjoying this and thought it would be fun to hit her from underneath. The mind can play tricks swimming in the sea in the dark, and the silly girl would probably think he was a giant sea creature.

Colin took a huge breath of air and torpedoed his powerful body beneath the surface a mere two feet behind the flailing Jenny. As he reached out his arms to grab her, his world went black. He had struck his head on something large and totally unyielding. Unbeknown to Colin, where the quay ended a concrete ledge continued out into the harbour. The ledge was designed for launching smaller craft at lower tides, when it was perfectly visible. However, when the tide was anything above halfway in, the ledge was invisible beneath the water. When Colin struck it with his head it was submerged by about 18 inches.

He remained conscious but was heavily stunned and, unable to stand without falling he had to sit, waist deep in the sea whilst he tried to clear his concussed head. He saw Jenny some fifteen feet ahead clambering over the same ledge and up some wide steps onto the quay proper. After a few moments he stood, fell, rose again and stumbled shakily after her. By the time he'd mounted the steps she was nowhere to be seen.

83

Neil lay in the bottom of the hull, battered, bruised and bleeding. That, combined with his failure to rescue Jenny put him in a mood of abject failure. He had no idea how long he'd been knocked out, nor where the lunatic had taken Jenny, but he knew he had to find them. He staggered to his feet and promptly fell back to the deck. His head span and he felt nauseous.

'Pull yourself together for fuck sake.' he said aloud and, grabbing the leg of a fold-away table hauled himself groggily to his feet. The room span again and he had to steady himself with two hands. He breathed deeply for a moment or two until his vision cleared a little and then staggered towards the door to the outside world and fresh air. He literally crawled up the five steps to the deck and went on all fours to the rail, where he peered towards the little harbour.

For a moment he thought he saw bodies in the water, then dismissed this as a symptom of the double vision which was coming and going. His first thought was to dive into the sea and get to shore as quickly as he could, but he knew that in his current state he'd be more likely to drown. He climbed down into the little inflatable dinghy and paddled as fast as he could towards the shore. His progress was agonisingly slow, as his coordination was useless and he seemed unable to make his arms work in unison. He realised the heavy wooden dinghy he had used earlier was still tied to the inflatable and causing unnecessary drag so he unhitched that, gritted his teeth and pressed ahead.

From the low-lying dinghy Neil had very limited visibility of the events unfolding, but he thought he saw a small figure, presumably

Jenny, drag herself out of the water and scramble her way up onto the quay. Once there the figure ran. Neil looked for signs of pursuit but at first could see nothing. Then a taller figure crawled slowly from the sea, clearly the Furness nutter, floundering around in knee deep water. Despite Neil's limited ability to focus it was clear that Furness was unsteady on his feet. Had he, Neil, managed to hurt him in the fight? He didn't think so; it had been pretty much a demolition job from the little he remembered. Frankly he was amazed the guy hadn't killed him; maybe he'd been interrupted....maybe Jenny had distracted him? Good girl Jenny; the thought that she still had some fight in her spurred him on.

84

Colin was bleeding heavily from the deep gash on the top of his head where he had struck the submerged ledge. The blood was pouring down his face and causing him visibility issues. He paused, removed his soaking shirt, which seemed to want to cling to his skin like a limpet, and held it firmly against his scalp. With one hand holding the cloth in place he slowly stood and lurched across the quay. He could see no sign of the girl and couldn't imagine she'd been in any fit state to run beyond his sight in such a short time. He spied the row of upturned dinghies he'd seen earlier and convinced himself that Jenny would be found cowering beneath one of those. The first was made from lightweight carbon fibre and he lifted it easily. There was nothing underneath it.

The second was solid timber, clinker built and weighed a ton. He couldn't raise it one-handed so dropped the shirt to the ground and grabbed the gunwale with two hands. Two small crabs scuttled away in fear and blood trickled back into his eyes. He dropped the boat with a loud crash, narrowly missing his feet and went to the next.

'I know you are there Jenny dear.' He shouted through clenched teeth.

'Uncle Colin is getting closer and when he has his fucking hands on you he is going to be pissed off with you and tear your fucking head off.'

His voice was rising as he moved to the next boat. Again there was nothing beneath. He threw this one away in disgust and moved to the next. Again this one yielded nothing and he began to think he might be wrong.

With a vision of the girl laying helplessly beneath the last boat awaiting him to uncover her he skipped the intervening two and went straight for it. It was another heavy one but his anger gave him strength and he threw it aside with one hand. He howled in frustration to find yet another zero and went back to the two he'd bypassed.

Neither of these was Jenny's hiding place and he screeched at the top of his voice:
'You bitch! I am coming for you. I can see you. I will fucking bite you.'
He lolloped across the quay to an ancient wooden structure which stood in the gloom. He knew the building as the "Raptackle" and that it had been used for centuries to store fishing equipment when Bosham was one of the largest fishing and oyster harbours in England. Now it was more likely to hold sailing gear. All the old doors were padlocked and he quickly saw that there was no way she could have got inside. The structure stood on brick and oak "stilts" which raised it above the standard high water mark and Colin suspected she might be lurking beneath the building. He had to head back to where he had climbed out of the sea to check this and after crawling around beneath the building he could confirm that she wasn't there either.

Increasingly desperate now he made his way along the quay to the eastern end, it was the only area he hadn't checked and if she'd got that far she could have fled by now along the shore road and be well away. As he looked east he saw a figure cross that end of the quay and head towards the old mill. Relieved, he set off in pursuit.

85

Neil had an idea where Jenny might be heading. When they had last
been together in Bosham he had told her stories about hiding under
the old mill in his youth with his small gang of mates. They'd sit
there and smoke stolen cigarettes and tell stories and dream teenage
boys' dreams. If she had listened she would know what a great
hiding place it was. He was in no fit state to take on the big man and
decided his best option was to continue to paddle quickly and quietly
in the water parallel to the edge of the old quay towards the end
where the mill sat.

As he moved along the water's edge he could hear Colin above him
on the quay throwing something around. It went on for a while and
Neil assumed he was flipping up the overturned rowing boats that
were kept there. Good, the longer he spent doing that the more
chance Neil had of finding Jenny before him. He reached the little
bridge of the channel that led to the mill and abandoned his
inflatable. He splashed as quietly as he could through the last few
yards of stream and climbed the wall that led to the hiding place.

He wanted to call Jenny's name but was unsure where Colin had got
to and so didn't want to risk it. He stumbled through the low entrance
and blinked to try to adjust his eyes to the gloom. Suddenly he was
hit by a steam train and bundled backwards against the wall. The
beast that was attacking him had claws and spikes and teeth and a
vicious sting of some description. He was about to execute an
effective Taekwon-do block and counterstrike when the mad assault
stopped as suddenly as it had started.

'Neil? Neil! Oh thank god it's you!'
'Jenny! My god you almost killed me, where did you learn to scrap like that!'
They threw their arms around each other and Neil thought his ribs were going to be crushed under the pressure of her embrace.

'Jenny we don't have much time. He may have seen me come in here, let's get the hell out while we can.'

No sooner had he uttered the words than a shape filled the small entrance hole. Enlarged by the lights behind him, Colin's shadow appeared monstrous as he squeezed through the four foot high opening.
Neil didn't give the guy the chance to get in and stand upright. He launched himself forward in an attack known as a spinning side kick. Neil's foot smashed into Colin's chest and the force of the strike propelled the big man back into the wall behind him. He was momentarily stunned and in the blink of an eye Neil followed up the attack with a jumping snap kick to the chin. Colin collapsed in a heap.

Ordinarily this combination would have put a man out of action for some time, but Neil knew the guy was strong; he'd seen what he had done to his victims and so took no chances. Grabbing Colin by both ears, Neil lifted the psycho's head and drove his knee into his face, aiming for his nose but actually striking a little high. He repeated the blow, this time hearing the satisfying noise of smashing cartilage and bone. He went to hit him again but the man was completely limp. He threw him to the ground and grabbed Jenny by the hand.

The fleet of police vehicles announced their arrival with wailing sirens and screeches of tyres.

'Come on you, let's leave him to the cavalry and get you to safety.'
Sicknote was the first to spot the couple emerging from the store.
'Over here guys.' he shouted and ran towards them.
'Jeez Guv! You've got a *pair* of mutilated eyes now – been scrapping again? Did you meet the last bloke's big brother!'

319

'Thanks Sicknote, I feel great. Get this young lady a blanket, a hot drink and a lot of sympathy while I brief the DCI on what's been happening - or as much of it as I can piece together at least. You'll find the bad guy in the cellar there-go easy on him, I think Jenny bashed him around a bit to soften him up for me.'

He glanced at the little lady by his side and raised an eyebrow in question.

She smiled.

'I did introduce his head to the heavy bit of his frying pan.' She confessed. 'A couple of times!'

Neil gave her arm a gentle squeeze and handed her over to Steph, who stood ready with a blanket and relieved smile.

'Take it easy with this one Steph, she's tougher than she looks!'

As he walked across to report to the DCI on the way events had unfolded a flushed and clearly mightily relieved Samantha leaped from apparently nowhere into his arms and gave him the biggest, most inappropriate hug.

The DCI said something about professional etiquette, but neither of them seemed to be listening.

Epilogue

'And what's in it for me my pretty young thing?
Why should I whistle, when the caged bird sings?
If you lose a wager with the king of the sea
You'll spend the rest of forever in the cage with me'

Sting; *The Soul Cages*

In the woods around a Bronze age burial ground on the top of the South Downs a sow teaches her eight piglets to sniff out truffles. She is a long way from her native Serbia, but truffles are similar the world over and they look like a happy, healthy little family.

In a cell at the police station a man suddenly sits upright on the cold, hard bench. The cash box in the safe, the combination lock...the magic number....150000

In a cellar somewhere an old woman shuffles faded photographs of a young boy across a table and raises the stakes with the rats she knows so intimately.

As always, she keeps the ace up her sleeve; the shot of the young woman and the boy together, smiling, eating ice cream outside the Royal Opera House. It's the most faded of all, but regardless of the game they have chosen to play, is always the ace of trumps. She calls it the "Truth Card".

She hasn't seen her husband for a while; still, she has enough food and drink to last a week or two if she's prudent, so she isn't overly concerned.

Above her head somewhere a fan kicks into action
